Sally Armstrong was born in Ipswich, Suffolk, but now lives in Hampshire, with her husband and four-year-old son. Having qualified as a teacher she then joined the airlines and flew for several years on long-haul routes and Concorde. *Racers* is her first novel and she is currently working on her second, based on life in the airlines.

# RACERS

Sally Armstrong

PAN BOOKS

First published in Great Britain 1994 by Corgi

This edition published 1999 by Pan Books
an imprint of Macmillan Publishers Ltd
25 Eccleston Place, London SW1W 9NF
Basingstoke and Oxford
Associated companies throughout the world
www.macmillan.co.uk

ISBN 0 330 39336 7



1 3 5 7 9 8 6 4 2

A CIP catalogue record for this book is available
from the British Library.

Printed and bound in Great Britain by
Mackays of Chatham plc, Chatham, Kent

*To Barrie*

# *Acknowledgements*

I would like to give special thanks to the following people for their kind assistance in helping me during the preparation of this book: Creighton Brown, Lynda Baston, Rita Bonus, John Blunsden, Jilly Cooper, Desmond Elliott, Gerald Donaldson, Ken Fegrado, Murray Pollinger, Nigel Roebuck, Charlie Creighton Stuart, Frank Williams, the Silverstone press office and Nigel from Brabham.

# Timetable for the Grand Prix Year in *Racers*

## Last race of the season:

23 October Canadian Grand Prix (Gilles Villeneuve circuit)

## New season:

6 March Brazil (Jacarepagua circuit)
23 March Long Beach, California (street circuit)
10 April San Marino (Imola)
1 May Belgium (Spa Francorchamps)
16 May Monaco (street circuit)
21 June Detroit (street circuit)
5 July France (Paul Ricard circuit)
12 July Great Britain (Silverstone)
26 July Germany (Hockenheim)
9 August Hungary (Haungaroring)
16 August Austria (Osterreichring)
6 September Italy (Monza)
20 September Portugal (Estoril)
18 October Mexico (Autodromo Hermanos Rodriguez
1 November Japan (Suzuka)
15 November Adelaide, Australia (street circuit)

# I

Max Gregson strolled down the crowded pit lane followed by a horde of photographers anxious to get a final shot of the racing driver before the big race. If Max won this, the Canadian Grand Prix and the finale of the race season, he would be the new World Champion, a prize that he had striven for in his demanding five years in Formula One. The racing calendar for the current season had taken him all over the world and now the final cliffhanger was to be played out at Canada's prestigious Gilles Villeneuve circuit located on an island a short distance from Montreal.

Above the dark rippling water of the Saint Lawrence Seaway, heavy clouds gathered and despite the thickness of his fireproof undergarments and red racing overalls, Max shivered in the chill October wind.

'Max, how do you feel about the race? Do you think you can beat Jean Claude Duprès in the Renault?' asked one of the clutch of journalists fighting for his attention.

Max gave one of his slow, rueful smiles as the barrage of cameras clicked around him. His face, which by anyone's standards was handsome, creased up into tiny lines around his eyes and lips, which were broad enough to make them sensuous and appealing. His nose was strong, but it was the alert yet playful deep mahogany eyes that held one's attention. He smoothed back his brown hair that fell in soft waves to just above the collar of his race suit and his tanned expressive face turned serious for a moment. Jean Claude had been his mentor the whole season. Now only a couple of points separated them and

Max had to win the race if the coveted crown was to be his.

'Let's see what happens, shall we? I'm pretty confident – so is the whole of the Delta team – but to win, first you have to finish . . . '

'G–R–E–G–S–O–N' shouted a group of Union Jack waving fans from the heart of the cheering crowds in the grandstand. But Max did not hear his loyal supporters as more TV cameras and press surged in on him. He was aware, however, of the mass of yellow Renault flags and the French tricolour in the stands, the majority of fans being French Canadians and loyal to their French hero, Jean Claude.

Max was grateful to reach the sanctuary of the Delta garage which, like those of all the other sixteen teams, opened on to the pit lane. Inside the clean business workplace were the two Formula One race cars, smart and pristine in their colours of pale yellow and blue. The mechanics, also dressed in the Delta team colours, were bending over them making last-minute adjustments. In close discussion with his mechanic was his team mate, Helmut Krüge who, Max had learnt yesterday, was to be replaced next season. The humourless German had tried his best for the team, but as Max knew only too well in this cut and thrust game, trying was not enough. The owner and sponsors who financed the top teams at vast amounts of money needed results. To succeed, one had to be blessed with a God-given talent, burning ambition and, sometimes, an almost suicidal desire to win.

As Max finally slipped on his blue and yellow helmet over his balaclava, the sound of the three and a half litre engines roared into ear-splitting life up and down the pit lane. Then the familiar high-revved whine as the first car made its way out on to the track. Max was soon one of their number as he made a slow circuit around the track to his line in the front row of the start line. Max Gregson, Formula One veteran, aged thirty-three, was on pole position and about to start the drive of his life. Everything that had gone before now hinged on this race. It was the culmination of a tough career, and the ultimate dream of every driver – to be the best in the world – to win the Formula One championship. It would also guarantee a millionaire's bank balance. But Max knew that however superbly he drove, however fast he made a lap time, there was always an element of luck. That was the part he and his team had no control over. He remembered the words of his first team owner in Formula One: 'To be a good driver you have to have guts, talent, determination and to stay lucky.'

The words 'stay lucky' echoed in his head as his gloves clutched the small racing wheel. Despite the chill of the day, his face behind his balaclava was clammy, his fingers restless on the tiny gear stick alongside his leg. He felt nervous and wished he'd made time for another pee. His eyes flicked from the dials in his cramped cockpit to the empty track ahead of him, then to the start lights above the track. Behind him was a vast cacophony of noise as the twenty-six cars revved up, waiting for the red light to appear. The crowd of a hundred thousand was silent. The atmosphere was electric, mesmeric. The cars strained to be unleashed, like a pack of dogs lunging forward at the scent of a hare.

Two cars back in a yellow Renault was the man who was going to try his damnedest to beat Max Gregson. The wily Jean Claude Duprès would not easily relinquish the quest for the Championship. He was a tough fighter and Max knew he would have to give the race everything he'd got to stay out in front.

Then the red light appeared. Every pair of eyes in the cockpits of the cars on the grid focused on it, waiting for green. Max's adrenalin was flowing and his heartbeat pounding at three times its normal rate. 'Where's the green light?' he cursed to himself. 'Why is it taking so long?'

It was a time lapse of a mere four seconds. With lightning reaction Max let the clutch go and accelerated the car away from the rest of the pack. To a man, the crowd craned forward to watch the cars turn into the first bend.

Up in the commentary box, commentators from all over the world were relaying the race live on television and radio. Leaning urgently into the microphones they prepared to unfold the chapters of the race, at the same time feeding in the statistics of both teams and drivers to the race fans. It is a job that needs a cool head. Michael Richardson, a worn-out-looking fifty year old, was rooting for Max to win.

'His driving has been superb this year.' His eyes leave the TV monitor in front of him to flash down on Max's results of the season. 'A first in Monaco, first in Belgium, Italy, Rio and winner of the British Grand Prix, he has shown us that he has the consistency and talent to be World Champion. He has the aggression and determination to win today. But he also has a hungry Frenchman on his heels. Max must increase his lead if he is to rest easy. Jean Claude Duprès will be fighting every inch of the way and yes, he's doing it now.'

Michael Richardson, hanging on to his headphones, peered out on to the track as the cars below roared past the commentary box. At the next bend he watched with undisguised disappointment as the yellow Renault overtook the second placed Ferrari with a swift, precise manoeuvre. 'Now the Renault is hard on the heels of Gregson,' he continued. 'But the Delta driver must keep a cool head now. Everything depends on it. He must not allow himself to make a single mistake.'

Michael Richardson had seen many a driver forced into mistakes by the pressure of a driver close behind him. Sometimes there was a heavy price to pay for an infinitesimal lapse in concentration. Last season he had witnessed the death of a promising French driver, Pierre Bulot. He had been in the lead for the first time ever in his Formula One career. He had been hounded by an aggressive Italian. At the moment of overtaking, the Italian had come very close to his car and the young Frenchman had panicked and left the track. He died the next day with appalling back and leg injuries. Michael Richardson hoped that he would not live to see another accident like that.

Then before his eyes Max made a slight error of judgement. It was enough to let the Frenchman through. Max had braked too early going into the sharp chicane. Seizing the opportunity, the yellow Renault was past him as they exited the corner. The commentator's voice, hoarse with tension, relayed the account second by second of Jean Claude's carefully timed overtaking manoeuvre. 'You have to admire the brilliance of the Frenchman's driving,' he conceded. 'It's early days yet though,' he reassured the millions of fans who he knew would be watching the race live at home. 'Max still has thirty of the sixty-four laps to go. There is two seconds between the cars and Gregson is not allowing Duprès to increase his lead. He's sticking firmly on his tail.'

Colin Pritchard, owner of the Delta team, stood by the pit wall, flanked by his engineers watching the Longines clock monitor the lap times of the cars. He swallowed hard to relieve the dryness at the back of his throat. His face, saturnine and steely, betrayed no emotion. Only his narrow eyes blinking rapidly gave any indication of the tension he was feeling. This race meant as much to him as it did to his number one driver. It too had been his blinding ambition to win the World Championship. After years of dedicated work his dream was nearing realization. It hadn't been an easy road to success. But his determination and hard work had paid off – almost . . . Max must win, he told himself. They were too close to victory now . . . too close to lose the Championship through one place. Dick Chance, his team manager, stood alongside him. A frown passed over his young face, as he fiddled with his headphones. His eyes, like Colin Pritchard's, switched from the TV monitor relaying the race to the lap times, then to the race track in front of him. He knew Max was driving a hundred and ten per cent, as he always did. He had made a crucial error on the chicane, but Dick Chance knew Max well enough to know that that would only fire him up even further. He had no doubts in his mind that Max would regain his lead. Max was not the sort of driver to give up. The only unsure quotient was if the car broke down; so many things could break on these highly sophisticated pieces of machinery. They were so finely tuned that a possible failure of such precision engineering could not be ruled out.

No such thought clouded Max's mind as he hounded Jean Claude. With barely a second between them they were overtaking backmarkers – the cars now a lap behind the leaders – and Max had increased his lead sufficiently on the Ferrari in third place not to have to worry about pressure from behind. Twenty seconds separated him from the Italian, Terri Dacco.

By lap fifty, the tension of the race was tangible. The crowd held its breath as Max closed right up on Jean Claude once again. The TV cameras were focused exclusively on the two leading cars battling for victory. Michael Richardson, his voice now several octaves higher, leaned forward in his chair. 'Never have I seen such a close race as this and what a gripping end to the race season. Max Gregson and Jean Claude Duprès really have given us a race to enjoy today. Their driving is superlative as they fight for the Championship.'

The crowds gasped as Max made a daring move to overtake on the next bend. The wheels of the yellow Renault and the Delta car came to within a centimetre of touching. At the last moment Max eased off the accelerator and Jean Claude pulled ahead once more. The crowds broke into a roar of approval as yet again their French hero retained the lead. As Max passed the pit lane he glanced at the board hung out by his race mechanic: FOUR LAPS TO GO. Blinded by concentration, Max was oblivious to the sweat soaking his balaclava, the pain behind his eyes caused by the tension and his aching arm and neck muscles.

But on the next lap, luck played into Max's hands. He saw his chance. Duprès had slowed down, his path blocked by one of the backmarkers. Duprès tried first one way, then the other to overtake. Then he made an unforgivable mistake. Busy watching the car in front, he momentarily forgot about Max and was unaware of his rival's manoeuvre until Max was alongside him and it was too late. It was a courageous move on Max's part as at any time the two cars could have driven into his path. As Max looked fleetingly into his rear-view mirrors he saw it was the young Argentinian driver, Mario Rodriguez, who had caused the problem for Duprès. He smiled as he headed down the straight and into the last three laps, now certain of his place in the history books of Formula One.

As Max crossed the finish line and passed the marshal vigorously waving the chequered flag, he felt peculiarly light-headed. He waved to the crowds on his victory lap, punching the air with his fist. Even if their hero had lost they still could acknowledge the skill and share in the joy of the winner now before them.

In the pits the Delta crew were ecstatic, hugging each other and jumping up and down. Even Colin Pritchard, the team owner, who was shaking hands with the gathering group of well wishers, swallowed back the lump in his throat. He had waited fifteen years for this moment.

Max turned the car slowly into the pit lane and, witnessing the jubilation of his pit crew, the full force of the victory hit him. He climbed out of the car and was mobbed by his mechanics and fans who had appeared from nowhere. Removing his helmet, balaclava and ear plugs, he smoothed down his hair, wet with perspiration, and took large gulps from a bottle of mineral water. Then, pouring the rest over his head, he broke into a large grin as he saw his old friend Julian Lascelles-Hunt approaching him wearing an oversize baseball cap with the words MAX IS CHAMP emblazoned on it.

The next hour passed in a euphoric haze. People were congratulating the new World Champion from all sides. Up on the rostrum, Max held the gleaming cup aloft, his face radiating the pride and happiness that suffused his being.

Back home in England, two women were avidly watching the live television pictures of the scene, separately sharing his joy and triumph – Vicky Gregson, Max's wife, at home in Oxfordshire, and Kelly O'Brien, his mistress, in London.

# 2

It was dusk by the time Max returned from the track to his penthouse suite in the Hyatt Hotel. The sun had made a last brief appearance behind the office blocks of the Montreal skyline, reflecting dazzling colours of orange and flame red in their windows, and the small island that had played host to such a magnificent and thrilling spectacle was now emptying of its satisfied spectators.

As he closed the door of his room Max was hit by a wave of tiredness. The post-race media interviews and television coverage had been hectic. Then there had been the sponsors to meet in the hospitality tents. Already there was a pile of faxes and messages from friends and colleagues all over the world congratulating him. He smiled to himself as he hurriedly sifted through them.

Wearily, he threw off his jeans and trainers as he prepared for a bath. His body was like that of a trained athlete. Broad shoulders and chest, characteristic of all racing drivers because of the strength required to drive the cars, narrowed to a trim waist and muscular legs. At five foot ten, Max was one of the taller drivers and with his captivating charm, was a firm favourite with women. But since his arrival in Montreal, he had purposely dismissed the bountiful and beautiful distractions that had come his way. His mind had been totally concentrated on the Championship. Now he recalled the emptiness he had felt on waking that morning, the loneliness of being unable to share his anxiety. But it had been the only way. Having anyone else to share his bed would have been unwelcome. Suddenly his thoughts were interrupted by the harsh ring of the telephone.

'Max?' He recognized the excited, vibrant voice of Kelly O'Brien at the end of the phone. Max had known Kelly for over a year now. She was beautiful, alluring, and one of the few women he had met with that rare combination of wit, personality and obvious sex appeal. Although her job as a fashion model made for frequent absences, when they did meet, she and Max enjoyed a tantalizing and voracious sex life. Max had to admit that she possessed the unique talent of holding his interest both in and out of bed. She had made no attempt to hide her disappointment when he had told her she could not come to the race with him. Now hearing her at the other end of the phone, Max half regretted that she was not there with him. 'Kelly? How are you?' he asked her, his voice softening.

'Darling, I'm stuck here in miserable old London and missing you terribly. I'm so proud you won! It's fantastic. Well done. You must be over the moon.'

'I am – and I'm sorry you're not here to share it all with me.'

Kelly knew Max well enough by now to realize that he was turning on the charm. She also knew that tonight he would be busy celebrating and with the many women available to him, he would hardly have time to give her a second thought. She had pleaded with him to come to Montreal, as she was his frequent companion at the races. This one, however, Max had been totally adamant about. He was to go alone. To make matters worse for Kelly, he had left without even phoning to say goodbye.

'Have a wonderful time tonight and send my congratulations to all the team. I miss you.' The last word hung in the air. Kelly was at a loss as to what else to say. She realized how desperately she wanted to be with Max. If there had been a flight leaving that evening she would have been on it, but she knew the idea was out of the question. It was already well after midnight in London.

'Kelly, I'll make it up to you when I get back home. I promise. Let's have breakfast together next week – and lunch and dinner.'

'Don't worry, I won't let you out of my bedroom.' Kelly laughed spuriously. As she said goodbye to Max and put the phone down she sank back on to the pillows of her silk-covered king-sized bed and wept tears of disappointment that she was not there to share Max's moment of glory. Her only consolation was that Vicky, his wife, was not there either. She wondered what sort of wife would choose to stay at home and not be with her husband on the most momentous day of his career. Had she chosen not to go, or had Max decided she should remain at home too? Whatever the reason, as she listened to the hum of London traffic outside her flat, Kelly hoped that Max would not succumb to one of the glamorous 'groupies' who would no doubt be clamouring for his attention that evening.

By eight o'clock the celebrations were well under way in a private suite of rooms in the hotel. Max arrived alone, casually dressed in a white Boss shirt open at the neck and grey wool trousers. A cheer went up as he entered the crowded room and guests approached, eager to congratulate him. He returned their goodwill with smiles and handshakes. A waiter offered him a glass of champagne which he took and joined in the toasting. Suddenly Max found himself the most sought after weekend and dinner party guest. His celebrity status in the course of a few hours had leapt to that of a Hollywood movie star. Yet he found himself surprised by his lack of response to it. He was now feeling totally drained, mentally and physically, and try as he might he found it difficult to share the enthusiasm of the partygoers. His only genuine emotion was relief that the whole shooting match was over. Much later he would admit to his friends that winning the Championship had been an anticlimax. Even the fulfilment of a life's ambition did not stop the wheels of life from turning. Already there was next season's racing to think about. It was also on his mind that Colin Pritchard, Delta's team owner, had been particularly reticent about discussing the signing of a new driver. Everyone knew that Helmut Krüge was leaving, but there was still a lot of speculation about who was to replace him. Max had hoped that Colin would discuss it with him before the last race, but 'nothing definite had emerged' had been Colin's vague reply when questioned.

With these thoughts in his mind, Max spotted Julian Lascelles-Hunt talking to one of the team personnel. Julian broke off his conversation and they talked alone for a few minutes. 'Max, it's a great party. Cheers, and well done! But something's bugging you, I can see that.' Julian raised his glass to his old friend and gave him a warm pat on the shoulder.

Julian was often described as Max's playmate and their friendship had continued over many years in motor racing. Julian had first met Max in the early days of their career when both had been aspiring Formula Three drivers. In Formula Three, the training ground for young drivers to enter the hallowed sanctuary of Formula One, together they had earned themselves the reputation of being the two wildest hell raisers on the circuit, having a lively appetite for both life and women. But although young and keen and having the financial backing from an extremely wealthy family, Julian was not gifted with the natural driving ability that Max had been born with. After two seasons and a major shunt, his father had come to the conclusion that supplying money for his only son and heir to risk his life was foolish. Julian, therefore, had resigned himself to a more conventional career as a city broker, while enjoying frequent weekends at the race track as a spectator. Together he and Max made a dashing pair. Julian, taller and leaner than Max, had a head of distinctive curly red hair, and with his fine aristocratic bearing he, too, had a charisma that won him many female hearts.

Max took another sip from his glass of champagne and grinned. 'Nothing serious – nothing a gorgeous woman couldn't put right.' Max felt the champagne lift his jaded spirits.

'I would have thought you'd have been too tired or too busy. I can see you're neither,' said Julian, smiling back and following Max's eyes around the room to where a tall, elegant blonde in a short, backless dress was showing off a deep suntan.

'Did I tell you I had a telegram from the PM?' asked Max casually as they both admired the girl from a distance.

'England has a new hero. Will it be Sir Max next year?'

'No way,' smiled Max. 'I wouldn't qualify for that on the grounds of bad behaviour.'

They were interrupted by a message from the organizers of the evening to say that the Prime Minister of Canada would be arriving shortly and would Max be introduced to him?

'Looks like you're on duty again,' said Julian.

'Too much work and no play makes Max a very frustrated boy.' Max had no doubts that his very strong sexual needs were all inextricably linked to his job. The fix of adrenalin that he got from that spilled over into his personal life. Sex was all part of the energy that he needed to expend and like his racing it was also pretty addictive. He glanced once more at the pretty female and felt a surge of arousal.

But once the Canadian Prime Minister had made his appearance and left, along with a barrage of photographers, it was the girl herself who made the first move. She had taken particular care over her appearance and had been gratified by the response from the men at the party who craned their necks to admire her curvaceous figure sheathed in a tight-fitting black dress and her long hair, the colour of ripening corn. After a few drinks she felt confident enough to target the man of the evening.

'Max? I'm Marie-Louise,' she said in a breathy voice with a heavy Canadian accent and held out a delicate hand. 'I'm thrilled to meet you. I was watching the race from the grandstands. It was my first time.' She took a deep breath. 'And now I'm completely hooked on Grand Prix racing. I can't believe you guys drive so fast . . .' Her eyes widened in admiration.

Max gave her one of his warm smiles. Despite the fact he had heard the same thing all evening, he returned her interest warmly. 'Thank you, Marie-Louise,' he said in a way that sent shivers up and down her spine. She hoped her goose pimples weren't showing. Max's eyes never left hers for a minute. 'You must have been one of the few Canadian fans out there today rooting for me. Most of them were for Duprès.'

'Oh, those French Canadians . . . they go crazy about him – but I've always been a fan of yours.'

'It's good to know that my fans here are the most beautiful if not the most numerous,' he replied as he watched her intently, his eyes never leaving hers for a minute. From the moment Marie-Louise had met Max, she felt as if she were the only person in the room with him. His undivided attention gave her the impression that he was one of the nicest, kindest men she had ever met and that she was as much a celebrity as he was. After another glass of champagne, Max, suddenly weary of all the noise, suggested they try somewhere quieter for a drink. Marie-Louise, now totally at ease with her companion, slipped her arm through his.

'Oh, yes,' she trilled in an excited voice. 'I know a great little bar not far from here where they serve the most wonderful Irish coffee.'

'Sounds perfect. What are we waiting for?'

As they headed for the door, Julian gave Max a knowing wink. 'He's as fast with his women as he is with his driving,' he murmured aloud to his companion.

Two minutes after Max had left the room, Julian bumped into an old journalist friend of Max's called Reg Watkins. Reg, a craggy Australian with a face florid from observing the inside of too many beer glasses, appeared slightly uneasy.

'Hi, Julian. Is Max around?'

'No, he's just left to do some celebrating of his own.'

Reg looked relieved.

'What's the problem, Reg?'

'I don't want his evening spoiled, that's all. There's a group of journalists just come from a press meeting with Colin Pritchard. He's announced the replacement for Helmut.'

'Who is it?' asked Julian cautiously.

'Mario Rodriguez, the young Argentinian.'

'What?' Julian's face grimaced in the way that Reg had expected.

'I know. It came as a thunderbolt to the rest of us, I can tell you. I just wanted to warn Max that the rest of the news hounds were after a comment from him – tonight of all nights.'

Julian nodded. The news that Colin Pritchard had signed the crazy Rodriguez would come as an unwelcome surprise to Max. After all, Delta was now unquestionably the best team and Colin could have afforded to sign up any of the new rising stars. Young Rodriguez had the reputation of being unpredictable and tempestuous on the track. It would not make for an easy partnership between him and the new World Champion.

# 3

The café was small and unpretentious. Candles burned in bottles on the red and white check tablecloths and the soothing tones of a saxophone drifted along with the cigarette smoke in lazy spirals around the room. A crowd of locals were gathered at the bar, but seated in an intimate corner, Max felt himself switching off from all the hype and pressure of the last few days.

'Well, how does it feel to be the World Champion?' asked Marie-Louise, noticing the dark shadows under his eyes which were accentuated by the glow of the candles.

'Much better after a breather from all the craziness going on out there. I must have signed more autographs today than I ever have – and that was before the race.'

'I guess your life is going to stay pretty crazy from now on.' Marie-Louise knew so little about this man and his life. She sighed, regretting that she probably never would have the chance to do so.

'That was why it was so nice to get away from it all tonight – especially with such a beautiful companion.' Max paused and they exchanged a look of mutual longing. 'Would you like another Irish coffee?'

Marie-Louise shook her head. It was getting late and Max felt himself fighting off waves of tiredness. Marie-Louise leaned across the table and gave him a mischievous smile. She had enjoyed every minute of their evening so far and she willed him not to cut it short.

'Where to now?' she asked.

'Where would you like to go?' he asked, taking hold of her hand and squeezing it gently.

'Somewhere warm, quiet, not too far from here,' she whispered conspiratorially.

Max smiled. 'I think I know a place.'

Max poured two glasses of champagne from a magnum sitting in an ice bucket, while Marie-Louise glanced around the elegant hotel room furnished with antiques. Max's helmet and kit bag lay underneath one of the silk tapestry chairs, his driving boots next to a vast bed with an ornate carved headboard and a heavily embossed quilt. On a mahogany inlay table there was a colourful arrangement of flowers. Otherwise the room was neat and impersonal.

They each took a sip of champagne and slowly embraced. Placing his glass aside, Max took Marie-Louise in his arms, kissing her with an intensity that set alight every nerve in her body. She drew back from him, examining every inch of his face. Then, very gently, she brushed her lips across his forehead, his dark eyes, and then, meeting his soft, warm mouth, she kissed him with renewed passion as she ran her fingers through his hair.

They shed their clothes, letting them drop to the floor. Standing naked beside each other, they paused in the dim light, savouring the moment. As Max pulled her closer, Marie-Louise felt the strength of his broad, muscular arms around her and the pulsating of his hardness pressing against her. She was no longer fighting back the longing that had suffused her all evening.

'Max, take me,' she murmured. 'Every part of me.'

They fell back on to the bed and as Max entered her, Marie-Louise gasped with delight at the sheer size of him. Breathing heavily, their bodies locked together in mutual desire, Max made love to her tenderly and passionately.

Then, with a final burst of energy, they climaxed and Max collapsed exhausted on to the pillows.

'Thank you, Marie-Louise,' he whispered. 'That was a perfect end to the most wonderful day of my life.'

A moment later, the new World Champion had fallen fast asleep and as Marie-Louise looked into the serene and handsome face, she marvelled at the talent she had witnessed from this man earlier today. She stroked the arms that had driven the fast, dangerous car at such high speeds. She remembered how he had diced with death as he drove alongside his rival, Duprès. He was a ruthless fighter with reactions so precise and infinitesimal that Marie-Louise recognized there were few men alive with this ability. She knew that after tonight, she would probably never see him again but she savoured the moment of being alone with him, watching him sleep. As she reluctantly gave way to sleep herself, she hoped that this caring and sensitive lover would never fall victim to a race accident. He was the most wonderfully exciting man she had ever met and she wondered what fortunate woman was waiting at home for him. She consoled herself that whoever she was, she had not shared with him those first hours following his triumph. That had been her prize. Tonight Max had been hers and nobody could take that away from her.

Max awoke the next morning aware of a tight band of pain across his forehead and a pair of soft hands at his waist. Despite his headache, he smiled to himself as he recalled his victory. A whole new life was beginning. He watched Marie-Louise stir beside him as he recalled their lovemaking a few hours before. He hadn't exactly broken any records on that score. It had been short and sweet, but then he was amazed that he had managed at all, considering the energy he had expended in the car that day. His thoughts raced to the day ahead. Tonight, thankfully, he would be away from the superficial world of hotels and motor racing. He would be home with his family. He pushed away the niggling feeling of guilt as he thought of Vicky. Marie-Louise, he reasoned, had been a small indulgence after a long hard race.

The telephone stirred him from his reverie and he sat up to take the call. It was the NBC network – an invitation to appear on *Good Morning America* the following day. He politely declined. Time did not permit him to stay over in New York. As he made to get out of bed, the phone rang again.

'Hello Max,' came the cheerful voice of his wife Vicky. 'At last I've got hold of you. I was trying to call you all last night.'

Max remembered guiltily that the phone had rung during his lovemaking with Marie-Louise, but he had been in no mood or position to answer it. 'Sorry, darling. We had a pretty hectic night – there was a lot of partying. I tried to call you too,' he lied, 'but couldn't get through. It's been non-stop here since we won.'

'I'm so happy for you. We had a pretty good party here too . . . ' It was at that moment that Marie-Louise inadvertently gave a small sneeze. Max shot her a look of alarm.

'Max?'

'Yes, darling?'

There was silence at the end of the phone and then Vicky's voice took on an icy coolness. Max could feel she was on her guard. 'When are you coming home?' was her next question.

'I'm leaving for New York this morning and catching the Concorde out of there at one thirty. It lands in London about ten this evening. Can you pick me up at the airport?'

'Yes, of course.'

'Are you all right?' Max lowered his voice, aware that Marie-Louise was listening.

'I'm fine. I'll see you later. Oh, and Sophie sends her love. She can't wait to see you again. 'Bye.'

Max had missed his daughter, too. He realized at that moment how much. 'Send her my love,' he added quickly. "Bye Vicky.'

Damn, he thought as he put down the phone. Vicky must have heard Marie-Louise. That would gain him no favours with his wife, although he suspected that Vicky, being the cool and silent type, would never question him about it. Emotionally as well as physically they seemed to lead more and more separate lives these days. Vicky was no longer the adoring, doting wife she had been when they were married. She was loyal, he was sure of that, but there was a distance between them now and to Max's disappointment even more so in bed.

Max had met Vicky at the race track through a mutual friend, Rachel, the wife of Colin Pritchard who was already making a name for himself as a successful team owner in Formula Three. Max was still trying to make a break with one of the lesser-known teams. At twenty-four he was impulsive and irresponsible, yet was captivated by Vicky's calmness and easy-going manner. He had wined her and dined her in the most expensive restaurants he could afford, sent her flowers and showered her with presents. To his friends, the insouciant bachelor and roué was acting totally out of character. Max, however, quickly realized that Vicky's presence, particularly at the race track, had a calming, reassuring effect on him. Ravishingly attractive, she was also sensible and undemanding on his time, yet shared all his enthusiasm for his career. She was to Max the perfect companion as well as an irresistible lover in bed. They lived together for a short while before Max proposed and they were married within a year of meeting each other.

Three years later, their daughter, Sophie, had come along. Now five years old, she held together the fragile relationship between Vicky and himself. Although Max had secretly longed for a boy, he adored Sophie. Vicky had developed complications after Sophie's birth and despite seeking every medical opinion, none gave her hope of conceiving again. Both he and Vicky resigned themselves to the fact that they could never have another child. Apart from winning the World Championship, it was Max's dearest wish to have a son, but now such yearnings were rarely voiced.

His thoughts were brought back to the present by Marie-Louise kissing the back of his neck. Max turned to her and gave her a casual kiss before getting up to go to the bathroom. Marie-Louise lay in bed admiring his strong physique as she watched him go, at the same time having a sneaking suspicion that she was being dismissed. The passion of last night had evaporated like a morning mist and she felt cheated. 'I suppose that was your wife checking up on you,' she called to him.

Max gripped his toothbrush, brushing his teeth vigorously, and pretended not to hear. He appeared out of the bathroom wiping his face with a towel. Marie-Louise repeated the question, her face showing her disappointment.

'Yes, that was my wife on the phone,' he answered absently.

He had an hour to pack and check out before his breakfast meeting with a new sponsor. He also wanted to see Julian and Colin before he left. He picked up the phone and ordered a large pot of coffee and orange juice. Marie-Louise stirred, arranging herself seductively on the bed, so that one leg and her smooth bottom were exposed. Max just managed to resist the urge to go and sink his teeth into its delightful roundness. 'Excuse me while I have a shower,' he said, hoping this would spur her into action.

The warm water played over his aching body. The race had taken a heavy toll on his arm and neck muscles. Suddenly he heard a movement behind him and felt Marie-Louise's soft hands taking charge of a much lower part of his anatomy. 'Mind if I join you?' she murmured, squeezing in beside him.

Her hands slipped up to his shoulders, expertly massaging the soreness out of them. Max turned and taking her firm dripping breasts in his hands, moved against her. The confined, steamy space of the shower and the sensual gushing of water heightened their intimacy. Then, with one swift movement, he lifted her legs around his waist and entered her slowly, as Marie-Louise wrapped her arms around his neck and buried her face in the wet strands of his hair.

Their cries as they climaxed had blocked out the sound of the breakfast waiter knocking at the door and later, when Max had retrieved the tray from the corridor, he went straight to the newspaper, turning quickly to the sports' page. The story of his dramatic win over Duprès dominated. But it was the last paragraph that held his attention. Max paled as he read the last sentence. 'Colin Pritchard announced yesterday that he has signed the young Argentinian, Mario Rodriguez, as Max Gregson's number two driver for next year.'

Mario Rodriguez! The very name of the inexperienced young Latin incensed Max. Was Colin out of his mind? What the hell was he up to signing that hotblood when there was so much other talent around and why the hell hadn't he had the decency to discuss it with him first?

Max picked up the phone and dialled Colin's room. There was no reply. Even paging the lobby and coffee shop still produced no result. Hurriedly, he collected his things together, leaving Marie-Louise adding the final touches to her make-up, and as the lift door opened on to a crowded lobby, he spotted Colin entering the revolving hotel doors with Rodriguez at his side. Striding purposely towards them, Max noticed that his boss's face was lit up with one of its rare smiles.

Of average height and slim build, Colin Pritchard struck an ordinary figure in his brown loafers, loose-hanging trousers and waxed jacket. His hair, brown and slightly thinning on top, had been ruffled by the wind. He was making a futile attempt to straighten it with his hand when he saw Max coming towards him.

'Good morning, Max,' he said affably.

Then the radiant, handsome figure of Mario Rodriguez nodded to him.

'Max, you've been introduced to Mario Rodriguez?' said Colin.

Max's glowering expression didn't change.

'We know each other on the race track, but not off it,' volunteered Mario, his broad smile showing a set of perfect white teeth that contrasted strongly with a deep suntan and a mop of chestnut hair, a lock of which fell boyishly over one eye.

'Is it true?' demanded Max. 'Is it true you've signed Mario as number two driver for next year?'

'Max,' replied Colin smoothly. 'Let's take some coffee in my suite and we can talk about this in more detail.' He lifted his hands out of his pockets and made a gesture forward. A couple of journalists who had been loitering in the lobby couldn't believe their luck at finding the

Champion, his new team mate and their boss all at the same time.

'Colin do you have time for an interview with Mario?' asked one.

'Max, what is your response to Mario being signed to the team?' asked the other eagerly.

'Bloody dismal,' Max snapped back, while with a bewildered Mario and a furious Colin he made his way to the lift, ignoring the smiles and greetings from fellow race personnel who were in the process of checking out of the hotel.

Colin, realizing Max was in no mood to exchange pleasantries with his new team mate, suggested to Mario that they meet as prearranged at ten o'clock for another press conference. As the lift door opened on Mario's floor, Mario bade the two men a cheerful goodbye. Max remained stony faced and silent until they were inside Colin's room.

'What the hell has been going on? Have I been too busy busting my ass to win the Championship that you haven't had time to inform me of your plans for next year?'

Colin blinked nervously and slipping off his jacket, he rummaged in the pocket for a handkerchief. It was an ordinary gesture but it served to lighten his reaction to Max's fury. Then he sat down on one of the sofas next to a large picture window that showed a blustery sky and a spectacular view of the skyscrapers of Montreal. Max remained standing.

'Sit down, Max. I expect you're exhausted after your day yesterday. I'll order some coffee.'

'Thank you, but no. I have a meeting in ten minutes with a personal sponsor for next season.'

As well as the team sponsors who were responsible for funding the teams for a major portion of their budget – upwards of thirty million dollars – Max was also being fêted by personal sponsors eager to have their logo on his helmet and race suit. Like the advertising on the cars, it was a prestigious form of publicity that reached a worldwide audience. For Max, the financial rewards boosted his already considerable salary.

'Yes, of course,' replied Colin and having blown his nose was now replacing the handkerchief in his pocket. Max noticed, to his annoyance, that typically Colin's body seemed to be in a state of permanent motion. 'You want to know about Mario?' he went on. 'Yes, it is true. I have signed him.' He put a hand up to interrupt a further outburst from Max. 'I apologize for not informing . . . discussing the matter with you before, but I figured that it was best for you to concentrate totally on the job in hand without any worries about who your new partner would be.'

Max's voice tightened in exasperation. 'Any of the top drivers out there would give their right arm to join Delta – you know that. Yet you chose a guy still wet behind the ears and with no real talent.'

Colin's eyes widened in anger. 'How can you presume such a thing? Listen to me, Max. That young man has talent, I'm absolutely sure of it. How can he prove anything in the rattle box he's been driving all season? He'll come right, believe me.'

'You're crazy.'

'No, *you* wait and see,' retorted Colin emphatically.

'OK. I hope you prove me wrong, but if you play any more of your secretive games with me, you can find yourself another driver to partner your young Rodriguez.'

Angry with Colin at having mishandled the situation, Max was even further annoyed that the day should have started so badly. The elation and euphoria of yesterday already seemed a lifetime away. Already he was embroiled in next season's politics. He was the World Champion and yet Colin had given him no consideration in his plans. Max stormed out of the room, hoping that there were no other reporters hovering around for quotes on the inexplicable antics of his underhand boss.

Despite his flight being ten minutes late into New York, Max still made the connection for the Concorde to London. Once on board, and sitting in the comfortable grey leather seat of the aircraft, he closed his eyes, enjoying a moment of relaxation after his hectic few days. He hardly noticed the stewardess place a glass of champagne in front of him.

'Congratulations, Mr Gregson, on winning yesterday.' The stewardess's smile was full of admiration and Max felt his humour returning.

'Thank you,' he said, returning her smile and giving her one of his sensual, lingering looks.

The stewardess fussed over him attentively in the three and a half hours it took to fly to London, and as the argument with Colin receded from his mind, Max couldn't suppress a broad smile as he read the front pages of the London newspapers: MAX GREGSON WINS F1 CHAMPIONSHIP.

# 4

It was past midnight when Max arrived home at the large rambling farmhouse nestled in the wintry Oxfordshire countryside. As Vicky pulled the car up outside the oak-studded front door, Max looked up past the timber-framed walls and leaded windows to the Elizabethan chimneys silhouetted against the moon. He loved the house almost as much as Vicky did. They had bought it in a sad state of repair just before Sophie was born. With Vicky's flair for homemaking, the drab, neglected interior had been transformed into light, spacious rooms tastefully furnished with rare antiques.

Max could hear the labradors barking noisily from somewhere inside and, as he entered the hall, they gave him a wet and boisterous welcome. He climbed the wide oak staircase and tip-toed into Sophie's bedroom, where he watched her for several minutes, listening to her light, shallow breathing. More and more she was beginning to look like Vicky with her pale, translucent skin, her ash blonde hair and petite nose. But her dark magnetic eyes matched his own. She had also inherited his strength of character. He bent down and kissed her, half willing her to wake up. Each time he returned from the danger and tension of a race, he thanked God for moments like this.

Later, Max and Vicky sat in the lounge enjoying coffee and brandy. Vicky stretched out on the pink and cream sofa watching the flames in the large inglenook fireplace play hide and seek amongst the logs. The heavily beamed walls and ceiling glowed in the firelight and a faint smell of wood smoke scented the room. A Beethoven symphony played quietly in the background.

'You've no idea how good it feels to be back home,' Max said contentedly.

'And the World Champion to boot,' laughed Vicky. 'I always wonder how you feel coming home after all those months of jet-setting . . . whether you might find it dull after a while.' Her pale grey eyes questioned him. Max waited and wondered if she would mention her phone call the morning after the race.

'No way,' he said, trying to hide his unease. 'After all, it's part of the job, all the travelling, but by the end of the season I've had enough. I don't want to see another hotel room for months.' But Max was only too aware that although the new season didn't start until early March, there was still a busy schedule of testing at home and abroad between times.

'Well, let's hope you'll be around for a while now. Sophie is beginning to wonder who her father really is.'

'She really misses me when I'm away, doesn't she?'

'Of course she does. I'm surprised she went to sleep tonight, she was so excited at the thought of you coming home. She pleaded to come to the airport and tried to bribe the au pair to go out tonight, so that she would have to come. She certainly has got a will of her own. And we know where she gets that from.'

'Well, it's no bad thing. As long as we can handle her.'

'Sometimes I find it difficult on my own. I do miss you, Max, when you're away.'

'Do you? I don't think you've told me that for a very long time,' said Max, surprised.

Vicky got up and went to kneel by Max's chair. He

caught her silhouette in the firelight and thought how attractive she was, her soft grey mohair sweater complementing her eyes and blonde hair perfectly. It seemed as though he was almost looking at a stranger. Having spent so much time apart, this year had been another great test of their marriage. Their lovemaking had become less frequent. Max often came home exhausted from the races, and with all his other business matters to attend to, little time was left for themselves. He took her hand and pulled her gently towards him. She sat on his knee and he wrapped his arms around her. 'I know it hasn't been easy,' he said. 'We must try and make up for lost time in the next few weeks.'

'Good. How about a weekend away in a hotel – somewhere by the sea?'

Max gave her a horrified expression.

'Don't worry, it was only a joke.' But as Vicky said it, she realized that sadly they probably wouldn't take a holiday. There would be new demands on Max as World Champion and as always he would be selfish and want to stay at home.

'Then how about coming to bed?' she said quietly.

Max yawned. 'Now that sounds like a very good idea.'

He pulled her gently up and kissed her on the mouth. Their arms around one another, they made their way upstairs and into the warm, welcoming bedroom which Vicky had decorated with small bowls of freesias. She disappeared into the bathroom, carefully undressing and putting on a new cream silk nightdress. Climbing into bed next to Max, she heard faint snores coming from his lifeless form. He had fallen asleep in minutes. Exasperated and disappointed, Vicky could only hope she would do the same.

* * *

The month of November passed in a hectic schedule of press and television interviews and receptions in London. The phone never seemed to stop ringing as potential sponsors and publicity agents all clamoured to have the name of Max Gregson on their books. It was an exciting time and Max enjoyed all the media interest. His part-time secretary was now putting in a five-day week as his diary filled up with appointments.

Time had been so short that even the forbearance of Kelly had been severely tested, and it wasn't until the end of the month that he finally managed to see her. Max had promised to spend two nights with her when he was in London for meetings and their first evening together had been a passionate reunion at her flat, followed by a romantic dinner at an Italian restaurant, Luigi's in Knightsbridge. On the second evening he had arrived past midnight a little drunk after a dinner with one of his sponsors. Kelly, however, was reassured that the sexual chemistry between them was as strong as ever. Max was in fine form and they had made love until the early hours of the morning.

As Max joined the traffic out of London on the following day, he should have felt on top of the world. He had just taken delivery of a red Ferrari Testarossa at a favourable discount from a friendly Ferrari dealer, and now dived in and out of the traffic, trying out the performance of the superb, sleek machine. Pedestrians and other motorists looked on in admiration as the car passed by.

Max should also have felt elated because he was on his way to the Delta factory to preview the new race car for next season, something which normally made him as excited as a child before Christmas. The development of the car would continue until the first race of the new season.

During the test sessions, it would be put through its paces. Last year's car had been outstanding, but everyone at Delta felt confident that this new design was something extra special.

Max, however, was far from being in a good mood. He was on his way to see Colin and, after the secretive signing of Rodriguez, he had good reason to distrust his boss. It was well known among Formula One folk that Colin could be devious and ruthless, but it was the first time that Max had had cause to question his methods of business. Had he for one moment believed he was involved in a sport whose members were scrupulous and principled, he would have been a fool. Money and power were an integral part of it and he had seen it all in his time – the cynical manipulation, the pawns and the losers. But he had expected better of Colin. Had he discussed the choice of driver, or even forewarned him, Max wouldn't have minded so much, but he did not like the way he had found out. Once he was on the M40, however, he put his foot down and within seconds the Ferrari was cruising at a hundred miles an hour, its engine throbbing with the mesmeric sound that comes with having twelve cylinders under the bonnet. It had a calming, reassuring effect on him and by the time he arrived in Oxford his spirits were restored.

The Delta factory, set inconspicuously in a leafy lane just outside Oxford, had the clinical appearance of a private hospital and was run with the secrecy of a space laboratory. Max made his way through the smartly painted reception and into a corridor which led to the factory floor. This was a large airy room, where only an impressive array of machine tools gave a hint that this was a car workshop of the most sophisticated kind. It was spacious and immaculate. In the centre of the room two new cars stood in various stages of assembly. The mechanics working on them with the precision of surgeons looked up as Max walked in. He took one look at the new design and whistled in approval, as if examining a rare masterpiece.

'We reckon this could make you World Champion all over again next season, Max,' said Tom O'Leary, the chief mechanic. 'You wait till we start testing it. It'll scream off like a bat out of hell, mark my words. We'll have the opposition scurrying back to their drawing boards.'

'I'm looking forward to the tests, that's for sure,' said Max, smiling proudly as he walked round the car to admire it further.

The cars stood gleaming in their distinctive colours of Miami blue and yellow. A new, longer nosepod gave a sleek appearance to the five hundred and forty kilograms of precision engineering. At the tip of its gently tapering V, the front aerofoil wing extended horizontally. Further back, where the nosepod thickened, its fat front tyres were connected by several rods or 'wishbones'. The cockpit, small by anybody's standards, was dominated by the roll bar directly behind it. The highest point of the car, it is designed to support the car's full weight in the event of it turning over. Behind was a fuel tank capable of holding a hundred and ninety litres of fuel. Around the cockpit, the car bellied out into wide sidepods and air intakes. More wishbones connected the chassis to two even fatter rear tyres and the two large venetian blind style rear wings.

Max could feel confident that this potentially lethal projectile had a greater margin of safety than cars in the past. The materials used – carbon fibre, Kevlar and honeycomb – although lightweight, were extremely robust and capable of withstanding an impact of a hundred and fifty miles an hour. Twenty-four layers had been built up to make the mould and then baked in long sinister ovens or enclaves that reach temperatures of six hundred degrees centigrade.

Each component was crafted with extreme care and Max always had the utmost confidence in the rigorous quality-control tests that Delta put each of their cars through. Formula One had taken too many young and daring lives in former years, especially in the early seventies when many drivers had burnt to death. Now the danger of fire had been considerably reduced with the introduction of single fuel cells built of rubber and fitted into bullet-proof containers. But there was still the unforeseeable to be reckoned with – a tyre bursting, or a vital piece of equipment breaking whilst driving at maximum speed. Max would as always push these possibilities from his mind.

After more discussion with the mechanics, Max tore himself away from the new cars to sprint up the stairs to Colin's office. Colin was deep in conversation on the telephone when Max put his head round the door. Raising his hand, he beckoned him in and continued to scribble figures on a pad. Max sat down glancing at the two latest editions of the motoring press on the coffee table. His photograph was on both covers. Around the walls hung the original drawings of earlier Delta car designs and photographs of the drivers who had competed in them. It was a poignant reminder of the risks involved in the job. Several of the drivers in the photographs had lost their lives in terrible crashes. But things had changed dramatically at Delta since the arrival, four years ago, of Jean Mercier, the chief designer. In his time with the team there had been no fatalities and his work, particularly on the strengthening of the chassis, was an inspiration to many of the other racing-car designers. At thirty, Mercier was one of the youngest in his field and his talents were much sought after by other teams.

Colin replaced the telephone. His face creased into a colourless smile. His eyes were as keen and piercing as an eagle's and their rapid blinking gave him an agitated appearance. 'Hi, Max, how are you?' he asked in his usual reserved manner. He could see by the look on Max's face all was not well.

'Fine. I see the new car is almost finished.'

'At least a week ahead of schedule.' There was a glimmer of pride in Colin's eyes. 'So we've managed to bring forward the test date to next week.'

'Where's it to be?'

'At Silverstone.'

'With Mario?'

'No.' Colin's left eye gave a slight twitch. 'He's staying in Argentina until the launch of the new car. We've a few things we'd like you to try out first.'

It was apparent to Colin that Max was still upset over the Rodriguez affair. Colin cleared his throat as if to add emphasis to what he was about to say. 'Look, Max, I know we've talked about this in Montreal but . . . OK, I handled the situation with Mario badly. I knew you wouldn't approve of him and I didn't want you getting uptight before that last race. But he is your team mate and it's not going to help matters if you bear the guy a grudge.'

'But *why* Mario?' snapped Max, still incredulous at Colin's choice of driver.

'Because I believe he's going to be good. He's young and a little immature at present. But he's got talent. Trust me, he's going to be all right.'

Max thought of the irony of the words. Trust was the one thing he seemed to have lost with Colin.

'Besides,' Colin went on, 'he comes with a few million dollars of sponsorship money from an engineering company . . . '

'Can an Argentinian company afford to pay out a few million dollars on a racing driver?'

'It's the usual deal. Strictly hush hush, of course. The company gives us so much money and we give them an amount of sterling to keep them happy.'

More fiddling with foreign banks, thought Max. He had heard of it before. The poorer countries would try anything to get hold of hard currency. Still, it put Mario up a point in his estimation. Coming to the team with a few million bucks was no bad deal.

'When's the launch of the new car?' asked Max.

'The eleventh of next month, which is why we have to keep this test session secret. I don't want the press getting any sneak previews.'

Max recalled all the wet, gruelling days he had spent testing at Silverstone and did not relish the idea of being there in November. Often during a two-day test session he would drive over six hundred miles, which at flat-out speed was tiring enough. Then he had to hang around while the mechanics improved the fine tuning of the car. They were long and often frustrating days. If, however, Jean Mercier had produced the car as near perfect as possible, the chances were it could be exhilarating.

The phone rang again and Max hurried off for a meeting with Mercier and his race engineers. Before he left, Max led all of them outside to inspect his new Ferrari. Like religious converts at a Bible Convention they followed and stood engaged in reverent discussion at the wizardry of Italian engineering.

Colin glanced at his watch and cursed silently. It was already gone seven. He had promised his wife, Rachel, to be home by then as guests were expected for dinner. Rachel had lately been complaining about the number of hours he spent at work. Usually at the end of the season he allowed himself a short holiday away with the family. This year Rachel was having to make excuses to their two daughters as to why they were seeing so little of their father. It was just as well they were at boarding school, Rachel had told him.

As Colin closed his office door the phone rang. Reluctantly he went back to answer it. It was the producer of sports documentaries for the BBC. He was anxious to arrange a meeting with Colin to discuss the making of a film on Colin's life and achievements. 'Can we make Thursday definite then?' The man's clipped patronizing voice irritated Colin. He hoped the film wasn't going to be an ordeal. They had already hinted that they wanted to include his family and home life. Rachel had thought the idea exciting. But Colin was adamant. He wanted his personal life kept out of the film.

# 5

Driving home in his Jaguar, the stereo playing quietly in the background, Colin thought about the aspects of his life the programme might cover. His early career as a racing driver had looked very promising. After leaving school with a disappointing academic record he had worked as a garage mechanic in between jobs and had scraped enough money together to begin Kart racing. It was a slow journey up the ladder of success. Graduating from Formula Three, Colin continued his success in Formula Two, with enough money from sponsors who believed in backing this fresh young talent.

Then at twenty-two he was hot favourite to win the Formula Two championship. His dream, however, was to drive in Formula One and everything was a stepping stone to that end.

When at last one of the teams had signed him on as a test driver for the following season, he was ecstatic. His only taste of driving a Formula One car had been at Silverstone before one of the last races in the Formula Two season. He had never forgotten that first drive. Sitting in the cockpit shaking like a frightened terrier as the car exploded into life, he had watched hypnotized as the rev counter needle flickered backwards and forwards like a viper's tongue. But he had resolutely selected first gear and let out the clutch. The power of the acceleration was like nothing he had ever experienced before. His head was snapped back as the beast took off. Ten seconds from starting off, he had hit a hundred and forty miles an hour. After a few laps he had lost the feeling of blind panic. The clamminess that had swept over his whole body had disappeared and he settled down to enjoy the supreme experience. His mind became crystal clear, his concentration focused on improving his time for every lap. Everything seemed to come to him in slow motion, his mind always one step ahead of his next move. He had proved to himself and the team that he had the talent of a true racer. His lap times had clearly illustrated the point and he was more determined than ever to break into Formula One.

Then came the last race of the Formula Two season and the decider for the championship. Colin had had a premonition that something might happen. The accident was described as massive. Colin was cut out of the car with two shattered legs and a fractured spine. The other driver involved, a close friend of his, was killed instantly. After six months and three operations, Colin was forced to accept the awful truth that his racing career was over. The doctors gave him little hope of ever regaining the full strength of his legs. However, a few years later his career unexpectedly took off in a different direction. He leapt at the opportunity to manage a small Formula Three team and worked fervently to make it a success.

His first big break was meeting Claude Dupont, the French designer. With Colin's organizational ability and Claude's design flair, they had the perfect combination to create a winning team. Then Colin appointed a young Italian, Alberto Scapini, to help with sponsorship and a year later the two of them had bought the team and set up in partnership. That was when Colin's troubles began. The Italian had cheated him out of every penny and he had learnt first hand the harsh lesson of trusting business associates too easily.

Two years later, Colin was managing a Formula One

team. It was sufficient for him, for a time. But his ultimate ambition to be a team owner never deserted him. Money was his biggest problem. Given that single prerequisite, he believed he was capable of creating a strong and competitive team. Fortunately for Colin it was around that time that Rachel came into his life.

Rachel was the fun-loving daughter of a multi-millionaire property developer and she fell desperately in love with this introspective, serious young man. She admired his single-mindedness and determination. A few months after their first meeting, they were married and Rachel was financing his business interests. Delta, their Formula One team, was set up on a shoestring and Colin was on his way.

Colin remembered the day of the launch of their controversial new car. The press had assembled at the Silverstone circuit, expecting only to write a small piece about the new team. Few thought there would be anything worthwhile to report. At the last minute Delta's driver had fallen sick. It looked as if it would be a disaster of a day. Finally the car was wheeled out of the garage and a substitute driver emerged, unrecognizable in helmet and overalls. The journalists were certainly impressed with the innovative design of the car, but they wanted to see it perform. The car accelerated out of the pits. It completed several laps before its speed was timed. Claude Dupont, the car's designer, who had stuck loyally by Colin, nervously held the stopwatch. It was only two seconds short of Silverstone's lap record. Suddenly, everyone was watching with keen interest and after ten more laps, the car returned to the pits to cheers of acclaim, which turned to astonishment when the driver stepped out and took off his helmet, to reveal the proud face of Colin.

The press made a big story out of it. That was history

now and the team had come a long way since then. Colin had lost a few friends and made a few enemies, his ruthless determination and ambition always coming before personal loyalties. Now that he had reached the pinnacle of his career, he was even more determined to protect his private life.

As he turned into the long drive that led to his manor house, he could see the bedroom light was on. Rachel was probably taking extra care over her appearance. Colin guessed that the young Italian driver coming to dinner tonight was going to be the target of her attentions. He had seen it several times before with the young drivers he had introduced her to. She was fascinated by them. Colin preferred to turn a blind eye to these short-lived dalliances and, only if she threatened to be indiscreet, would he interfere.

The sad fact was that he felt no jealousy of his wife's wandering attentions. He knew that he was unable to satisfy her physical demands. Colin wished he could desire Rachel, but beautiful as she was, he could not, nor any other woman. There was a side of himself that he tried to ignore, but more and more he was coming to recognize the direction of his sexual desires. Even more disturbingly, he was forced to admit it was Mario who was responsible for the change. Yet he cared deeply for Rachel. At thirty-two, she was eight years his junior and the antithesis of his reserved nature. She was extrovert, happy and warm-hearted, with an infectious energy for life. She always managed to find out the little secrets of other people's lives, and those who knew her own indiscretions marvelled at Colin's tolerance of it all.

As Colin made his way up the stairs to their large bedroom overlooking the small lake and the expanse of the front lawns, he wondered how Rachel would react to his lateness this time. Opening the bedroom door, he heard her favourite classical guitar music. She was sitting at her ornate mahogany dressing table, so that Colin could see her reflection in the mirror. At that moment, she reminded him of one of the pre-Raphaelite women – tall, graceful, with gleaming copper hair that fell in heavy tendrils about her shoulders – making Colin feel like an intruder into some scene from a bygone era. Rachel's ivory skin glowed warmly in the firelight. A coral blouse of heavy lace contrasted with her dark, honey-coloured eyes. She was adjusting a pair of long crystal earrings and turned as she heard Colin's footsteps.

'Colin . . . at last. Do you know what time it is? Our guests will be here shortly.'

'Sorry I'm late. I broke all the speed limits to get here as quickly as I could. The producer from the BBC rang me as I was leaving.'

'Well, I should know by now that there is always someone, somewhere who is going to make you late home.'

Rachel stood up and kissed Colin lightly on the cheek. His expression softened. It was one of those rare tender moments they shared together. His piercing, anxious eyes seemed almost compassionate for a moment. 'Have I time for a quick bath?'

'Yes, I should think so. I left out a clean shirt for you over there,' she said pointing to the chest of drawers. 'Mother' Brooks, as Rachel called the housekeeper, had finished pressing his shirts that afternoon. 'Could you help me with the button at the back of my neck?'

Colin gave his attention to the small mother of pearl stud on her collar. 'You look lovely tonight,' he said fondly.

Sadly they both accepted that however beautiful Rachel looked, she never succeeded in exciting him.

Leaving Colin to bath and change, Rachel skipped downstairs to supervise 'Mother' Brooks' cooking. She felt light hearted as she poured them both a sherry. She had planned an elegant dinner party with good company and she could hardly contain her anticipation at meeting the young Italian driver whom she had heard so much about.

Rachel had never divulged her reasons for staying with Colin. She loved and respected him deeply for the success he had made of his life. He was almost a father figure to her, who spoilt and pampered her like a young child. He would buy her jewellery, cars and clothes, anything to compensate for what he could not give of himself.

It was only a few months after their marriage that Rachel realized that her husband's sexual desires in no way matched her own. After the children had come along, which in itself was a miracle in her eyes, the fights and arguments grew worse as she struggled to contain her frustration. Incensed at Colin's indifference, she ran off briefly with a young French racing driver. It had shaken Colin to the core and exposed a vulnerability Rachel had never known existed. In an emotional, tearful reunion he had threatened to kill himself if she left him again. He needed her desperately, although he admitted the physical side of their marriage held no interest for him. After that they had an unspoken arrangement. Rachel could indulge in the occasional discreet affair as long as their marriage, however superficial it was, continued.

# 6

Vicky rose early after a fitful sleep. She had lain awake listening to the wind howling down the valley and stirring the heavy branches of the oaks outside her window. It had been a lonely and seemingly endless night, her thoughts tormented by Max. He was up to his old tricks again and had stayed out without calling her. She had wanted to ring the flat in London, but she knew she would get no reply.

As Vicky entered the kitchen, Sophie and Phil Adams, their groom, were sharing a joke. Sophie, her mouth full of milk and cereal, was giggling hysterically, much to the disapproval of the long-faced and still half-asleep au pair, Maria. She was in no mood for any of Phil's jokes. She felt he was already far too familiar with Mrs Gregson and spent far too much time in the kitchen.

'Morning everybody,' said Vicky with a forced cheerfulness, smelling the rich aroma of Italian coffee that Maria brewed every morning.

'And how is my little angel?' she asked, kissing Sophie's cheek. That Vicky was looking very drawn and had dark circles under her eyes did not go unnoticed by either Phil or Maria. That Max's car was not in the driveway had also not escaped their notice.

'Can I come riding with you today?' asked Sophie, wiping the remains of cereal from her lips with her sleeve.

'No, darling, not today. Phil and I are exercising the horses,' she replied, pouring herself a cup of the supercharged coffee. When was Maria ever going to remember to make it less strong? She diluted it with hot milk.

'How about when you get back then?' Sophie's apple-round eyes looked appealingly first at her, then at Phil.

Phil leaned against the large kitchen table, his hands in his pockets. His lean, lithe body was as taut and supple as the leather bridles he had just finished polishing. The chill wind had whipped colour into his cheeks and ruffled his light brown curls into a dishevelment that Vicky found curiously becoming. She found herself warming to his straight, uncomplicated character, which only reminded her all the more of her own suppressed anxiety.

'OK,' he said before Vicky could think of her plans for the day. 'Let's take Fortune for a ride round the paddock when we get back. It's a perfect morning for it.'

Sophie's eyes lit up in gratitude. Vicky realized how much Sophie had come to depend on Phil. He made up for the frequent absences of her father and gave her encouragement and advice on schooling her pony. Vicky had also come to value Phil's friendship. Although he had been with them for only three months, he was already one of the family.

'Mind if I take Brigadier for a change?' asked Vicky as she and Phil, in their riding gear, strolled to the stable block that flanked the rear of the farmhouse. The smartly painted building was always a pleasing sight to her and even more so as her two horses whinnied their noisy welcomes.

'Are you sure you're up to him this morning?' ventured Phil, knowing what a handful the horse could be.

'I can handle him.' Vicky's voice was listless. 'I need a lively horse to wake me up – even Maria's coffee failed me this morning.'

They saddled up the horses together and Phil held Brigadier as Vicky mounted. She looked an elegant picture as she sat, tall and erect, her hair tucked into a bun beneath her riding hat. Her black jacket and fawn breeches fitted her slender figure perfectly and the gleaming boots completed the immaculate dress of a well-groomed horsewoman. Phil admired Vicky for her neat appearance, but often wondered if she ever looked any other way. He found himself wondering how she would be when she woke up in the morning. Would her hair still be smooth and shiny as it always was, or tousled? Whichever way it was, he was becoming more and more attracted to her. She represented a challenge to him, for he was sure that beneath her *froideur* was a woman of passion and warmth.

At twenty-five, Phil had already seen enough of life to be mature for his years. He had spent three years in Jamaica as head stable lad to a wealthy horse owner. His good looks and charm had opened many doors in the horse-racing fraternity. A welcome guest at all the expatriate parties, he had quickly grown accustomed to the extravagant lifestyle. Things could not have been sweeter until that fateful day he was caught with his manager's wife. She had tormented him and teased him for months. Bored with her comfortable, cossetted existence, she had looked on him as an interesting diversion. Rumour had been circulating the ladies' lunch parties of his prowess as a lover. After an intimate champagne lunch together and a smoke of hashish, she and Phil had slipped naked into the pool. Later that afternoon her husband had caught them making love under the shower.

The next day, a flight ticket to London was delivered to Phil's house. In a dazed state he boarded the plane to London and within forty-eight hours he had applied for the job at Max and Vicky's farm.

* * *

As Vicky and Phil made their way on horseback down the long straight driveway, the elms broke the rays of the early morning sun. They turned into a country lane, Vicky breathing in the invigorating air and enjoying the fresh, earthy smell which always follows a shower at dawn. In the hedgerows, heavy dew-laden cobwebs glistened like a thousand pieces of glass. In the trees, some shrivelled leaves still clinging persistently to the branches trembled in the slight breeze. A blackbird could be heard in full song until, startled by the sound of the horses, it abruptly finished and with a sudden cry took off across the fields.

Vicky's thoughts soon became preoccupied with Max again. She remembered the last time she had found out about an affair. It had wounded her deeply. They had gone through all manner of dramas, arguments and questions, and Max had sworn never again to get involved with another woman. He had made a hundred excuses why it had happened and sworn he still loved her deeply. When all the heat of the accusations and tears had died down, she still suspected Max had gone back to his philandering.

Now something had died in Vicky. She had lost her deep love and trust of him. They had tried to build bridges many times, to rekindle their devotion for each other. Outwardly, she was still the model of a caring wife, but deep inside there was a growing frustration that was not helped by Max spending so much time away from home. Vicky found herself turning more and more to her horses. Riding was her only bid for independence in a world where Max and his career always came first. Somewhere inside her a voice was crying for attention and love, but she had no idea how near the surface it really was.

It wasn't as if she hadn't known what Max was like before their wedding. Her parents had not approved of the wild character she had been introduced to at a motor race and there were forced smiles when they announced their engagement. Max, in her parents' eyes, was an incorrigible playboy and marriage would never reform him. Her mother had wept tears of pity, not joy, as she watched her daughter walk up the aisle to start a life of certain disillusionment. Vicky had listened to her mother's recriminations many times since that day, and now grudgingly admitted that she had not found the idyllic happiness she had hoped for.

The first few years had been hard with very little money. Max had been fired and hired so many times by different teams that Vicky had believed they would never enjoy the comfortable existence he had promised her. But Max had never for one minute given up hope that he would be successful. His determination drew them along like a current in a stream, then further into deeper waters until they merged into a wide fast-flowing river, never to look back. Once borne on the tide of success, it was inevitable that Max's work should keep them apart. After Sophie was born, Vicky had stayed at home, where she missed the travelling and sharing in her husband's success.

But as the material benefits came to them, and she and Max began to drift apart, she found consolation in owning thoroughbred horses and she channelled all her energies into showjumping. Later she encouraged a willing Sophie to share her interest.

With Phil leading the way, they left the bright sunlight and entered the eerie stillness of a sprawling pine forest. Taking comfort in the knowledge that she was sharing her pleasure in riding with a like-minded companion, Vicky felt her tensions evaporate. The track stretched out in front of them, and the horses needed little encouragement to head off at full gallop with Phil giving great whoops of delight. Vicky also felt exhilarated and spurred Brigadier on to catch Phil, who was disappearing round a slight bend between the trees. It was familiar ground to them both and they rode with abandon.

Two days previously, however, foresters had felled some of the larger trees in the area and they had left some of the trunks piled across the track. As Phil came round the corner he saw them at the last minute, and with an almighty push he and the mare cleared the obstacle safely. Then he reined in urgently, turning to give warning to Vicky. But it was too late. Brigadier, startled at seeing the obstruction, jerked to a violent halt. Vicky, off balance, was catapulted through the air over her horse's head, landing heavily on the other side of the timber in the pine-scented mud.

# 7

Kelly O'Brien drifted in and out of sleep, floating on a cloud of contentment. Her body glowed with the satisfaction that had come from a night of intense lovemaking. She and Max had expended every last ounce of energy until finally they had fallen asleep in each other's arms. She squinted through one eye as she saw a cheery Max standing before her with a tray laden with breakfast.

'You're dressed,' she said, both surprised and disappointed.

'Fancy some breakfast?' Max sat down on the bed looking on appreciatively as Kelly stirred gently on the rose print sheets, her petite form the colour of alabaster.

'Oh, lord,' Kelly groaned. 'I ache all over. I feel like I've just run a marathon.' She leaned back on the pillows.

'You have, in effect. Ten minutes of hectic lovemaking is the equivalent to running a mile. We must have done twenty-six at least last night.' Max gave her a wicked grin.

'Well, at least one of us came out of it all right. Not that I'm complaining, darling.' Kelly sighed, studying the breakfast of orange juice, tea and buttered brown toast cut into neat triangles. 'You are such a lovable hunk and where *did* you learn to please a woman like that in bed?' She gave him one of her alluring smiles that told Max he had totally satisfied her.

'You look like the cat that got the cream,' he said smugly, stretching over to kiss her.

'Mmm. Last night I could have died and gone to heaven.' Then, taking a sip at her glass of orange juice, she asked, 'Are you going somewhere?'

'I'm afraid so – I have a meeting at nine in Knightsbridge.' Max checked his watch. He was already thinking ahead to the day's busy schedule.

'After the amount you had to drink last night, I'm surprised you know what day it is.'

'I feel wonderful, thanks,' he said, tenderly stroking her hair. Lying naked before him, her breasts standing out like beacons of temptation, Kelly was irresistible.

'Shall I see you later?' she asked.

'I have to go home and make my peace.'

'Oh, come on, Max darling, you at least owe me lunch after taking you in off the streets last night,' she implored.

Max had phoned her at midnight after an expensive evening's gambling in the Sporting Club with Julian.

'OK, but it will have to be a quick one. I'm testing the new car at Silverstone tomorrow and I've a lot to do before I leave.'

The night before, Max had arrived to find her dressed in a silk kimono and sleepy-eyed from being woken up so suddenly. He had carried her into the bedroom and slipped off his clothes, covering her naked body in warm kisses and whispering tenderly how much he had missed her, how much he wanted her. Kelly, now wide awake, responded to his caresses and revelled in the tender, caring lovemaking of her insatiable lover. Their absences only served to heighten the frisson of meeting again. It was like a new discovery each time. And yet Max was always like an old and trusted friend to her and she was aware how much she depended on him.

Then there was always the surprise and fun element to Max. Kelly shrewdly recognized that the less demanding she was of his time, the more he would find the excuse to call by or take her out for a lavish meal in London. Or he would unexpectedly phone up on his way out of a meeting and arrange a rendezvous later that evening.

Kelly ran her fingers through her tousled blonde hair. Her face was pale and fragile yet still stunning without make-up. Their lovemaking last night had exceeded everything that had gone before . . . but one thing had remained in her mind. Despite their closeness and the pleasure they gave to each other, Max had never once mentioned that he loved her. She wondered as he kissed her goodbye how he really felt. Sometime soon she would ask him.

Kelly had a leisurely breakfast. A steady drizzle feathered the windows of the flat, distorting the view of the bare trees outside. She didn't envy Max testing at Silverstone at this time of year. Their first meeting had been on just such a day at the same race track the previous December. An icy northerly wind had been blowing viciously across the circuit and there seemed no respite from the cold. She had been on a modelling assignment for sportswear and Max had spotted her while the mechanics worked on his car. She had aroused his curiosity as she posed calmly in flimsy outfits with a camera crew fussing around her. He had invited her to share some coffee with him. Then it was back to work for both of them.

Max had completed ten more laps of the circuit before his engine had finally died. Kelly had been watching him from the pit wall, marvelling at the speed with which he flew past her down the long straight before braking sharply for the corner. It was a breathtaking spectacle.

'I guess your job gets as frustrating as mine,' she had said as they watched the mechanics remove the monocoque and stare at the engine in puzzlement.

'You can say that again. It's the hanging around that gets to us all.'

Despite having changed into trousers and a jacket, Kelly had shivered as the wind whistled down the pit lane and Max had removed his large padded Delta jacket and draped it over her shoulders. In the shelter of the pit garage Max had learnt to his surprise that Kelly's interest in motor racing was more than casual. He had explained to her about the engine problems they were having and answered her questions patiently. Then after Colin had finished debriefing the team he had asked if she wanted a lift anywhere.

'I live in London,' she had replied. 'Don't worry, one of the photographic crew is giving me a lift.'

But something about Kelly had made Max want to worry. There was a feeling growing inside him; some small sensation urging him not to let her disappear from his life. He wanted to know more about this beautiful woman. Her eyes, as lambent as an Irish mist streaked with sunshine, commanded his attention. They were playful, expressive and wildly exciting. 'I'll get you there in half the time – if you don't mind the fast driving,' he had said at last.

'Sounds great – I'm ready when you are.'

Kelly had found Max very attractive and easy to talk to. His charm and dry sense of humour were not quite what she had expected. She had read in the press of him being arrogant, aggressive and uncooperative, but she found him quite the opposite. In fact, he reminded her of the sweet-natured cocker spaniel she had once had. She had loved that drive back to London and had watched intently as he negotiated the traffic at breath-taking speeds. He had dropped her outside her flat and a week later they had dinner together.

From the beginning there was the most wonderful sexual chemistry between them. Of course she had known he was married, but that had not stopped her falling hopelessly in love. Even now she didn't expect anything and he promised nothing. She just lived for the time they spent together – sometimes only a few hours a week. But sometimes he would fly her to a Grand Prix meeting for the weekend. She adored the atmosphere of the racing scene and although the team had treated her sceptically at first, she soon became popular with everyone. There was only one cloud on the horizon. She knew one day he would walk out of her life and there was not a thing she could do about it.

# 8

Vicky dared not move, fearing the tearing pain of a broken limb. Like a trained polo pony after a fall, she lay there catching her breath.

'How do you feel?' Phil looked at her white face anxiously. He bent over her and, removing his jacket, lifted her head out of the wet leaves.

'I think I'm just winded,' she murmured breathlessly. Slowly she moved her legs, then her arms. 'No pain, no broken bones,' she said with relief.

'Lie there a minute until you get your breath back.'

'I feel as if I've just finished five rounds of mud wrestling.' She managed a smile as she felt the mud seep through her riding breeches.

'Here, let me carry you over to the trees. The ground is drier there.' Picking her up gently, Phil moved her on to some dry leaves. She leaned against one of the towering pines and pulled off her riding hat. Her hair tumbled about her shoulders and, as she moved her neck, she gave a slight wince of pain.

'Does it hurt?'

'Mm, just a little.'

'Let me see to it for you.' Phil lifted her hair away from her shoulders and gently massaged her neck.

'Thanks. That feels tons better. I don't think I've had a fall like that in years,' said Vicky, enjoying the feel of Phil's strong hands. 'Dear old Brigadier, he couldn't quite make it.'

Phil watched as the two horses grazed quietly a few

yards away. Just then a shaft of sunlight broke through the trees and somewhere above a solitary bird started its tuneful call. Smelling the pine needles beneath her, Vicky suddenly felt a heightened awareness of the beauty all around.

'I would never have forgiven myself if you'd been hurt,' Phil said gently.

'It wasn't your fault. I could quite easily have come down here on my own and the same thing would have happened.'

Their eyes met briefly. Vicky's hand trembled as she brushed away a strand of hair. At that moment she looked so fragile. Phil felt an overwhelming desire to protect her and care for her. He studied her determined yet delicate face, her pale blonde hair usually swept back fell carelessly about her. She looked younger than her thirty years. Gone was the assured and aloof woman he had first met. Instead, he saw a vulnerability he had never seen before.

'How did you meet Max?' Phil said at last.

Vicky raised her eyebrows in surprise and gave a short laugh. 'That's a strange thing to ask.' But now being alone with him, away from the house, she felt comfortably relaxed – she saw him as a friend not as an employee. 'If you must know, we met at a race track.'

Phil thought for a while. Vicky shot him an enquiring glance.

'Why do you ask?'

'It's just . . . if you don't mind me saying so, I don't see you as a couple, that's all.'

'Yes, I know,' said Vicky slowly. 'We seem to lead totally different lives now. It's been lonely these past few years. Max is in demand more than ever. I suppose that's the penalty for having a successful husband.' And one with a wandering eye, she thought, as she painfully remembered the previous night. 'But I have my horses and . . . ' she stopped abruptly as she realized she was about to say the word 'you' ' . . . and Sophie.'

She had been pushing dangerous thoughts away from her mind for some weeks now: how attractive she had found Phil's rugged looks and how much she had enjoyed his company; how she looked forward to their rides together. She had thought up some excuse for him to come shopping with her and Sophie the other day. Could he help them choose a new bridle? she wondered. They had shopped in Wallingford and enjoyed lunch at a small restaurant close to the river. Vicky had laughed and relaxed more than she could remember.

'But that doesn't compensate for having someone to share your life,' Phil continued.

'I know.' Vicky was suddenly desperately miserable. She had hidden her loneliness for so long. And now she was going to have to face the awful truth that Max was probably having an affair with one of his 'pit groupies' – one of the many attractive women who followed the Formula One circus. Well, she needed the physical caring touch of a man as much as Max needed that of a woman. Her world was becoming a cold, isolated one and being here alone with Phil reminded her how much she longed for the touch and reassurance of someone. She stared intently at the ground in front of her.

'Vicky?' She heard the tenderness in Phil's voice, but dared not look at him. 'Vicky?' he repeated. He leant over and took her face in his hands, brushing his lips against hers in the merest hint of a kiss. Vicky almost jumped out of her skin at this sudden and unexpected display of affection. Phil's body was suffocatingly close to hers. 'Relax, Vicky,' he said and kissed her more urgently.

For a brief moment Vicky hesitated, turning her face away from his.

'Phil, I don't think we should . . . ' her voice trailed away as she was powerless to finish. She gave herself up to his embrace, weak and trembling with desire. It was as if he was reawakening her dormant senses after a long hibernation and Vicky revelled in the strong, vibrant urges that swept through her. Now Phil's body pressed closer to her own. She could feel his hardness pressing against her and as he buried his head in her chest, she stroked the curls she had wanted to touch for so long. She felt their silkiness and breathed in the familiar, musky smell of his leather jacket.

'Vicky, I want you so much,' he whispered. 'Please don't say no.'

'Phil . . . I want you, too,' she replied breathlessly, and as she uttered the words, her need for him hit her with such force that her eyes blazed with desire.

Sensing the change, Phil lifted himself and straddled her legs so that she was unable to move. With one deft movement he released the button of her breeches and easing himself up, pulled them over her hips. Then he was tearing off his own trousers and and as Vicky caught sight of his nakedness, her heart pounded with excitement and she felt herself moisten in anticipation of what was to come.

Vicky drew breath as he slowly entered her and she revelled in every sensation until the hard pulsating shaft had penetrated her very core. They coupled like two animals in the wild, their rhythm mounting until it reached a fierce crescendo, and as Phil shuddered and exploded inside her, Vicky cried out, dispelling all the frustration, sadness and loneliness that had been a part of her for so long.

* * *

They rode back to the farmhouse in silence, the sight of the Elizabethan chimneys and timber-framed walls already putting distance between them. Phil helped her down from her horse, holding her waist longer than necessary, but aware that Maria's prying eyes might be watching them from somewhere inside the house.

'You may stiffen up after your heavy fall. I would go and soak in a hot bath if I were you.' The message in his eyes told her that he would like to be sharing it with her.

'Yes, that's a good idea. Perhaps we better leave Sophie's ride until tomorrow.' She felt embarrassed that they should part so formally after the enjoyment they had just shared. She wanted him to kiss her just once more. Instead, he stood apart from her holding the horses. Vicky felt Phil's eyes on her as she made her way back to the house. There was already a nagging guilt in the back of her mind. She would have the rest of the day, the rest of her life to figure out what it was that had made her be unfaithful to her husband for the first time. If it hadn't been for the pine needles she found clinging to her when she undressed for her bath, she might have thought it had all been a strange dream.

# 9

The launch of the new Delta car in December was staged at one of London's top hotels. It was a lavish affair. Press and sponsors were present as the car was lowered into the centre of the large hall in an orgy of blue and yellow laser lighting and a fanfare of music. After the show everybody rose to their feet in spontaneous applause.

Max and Mario presented a united front to the assembled journalists, many of whom were surprised to see the two getting along so well. Reg Watkins, the Australian, was in full flow. After his umpteenth glass of Laurent Perrier, he had already forgotten the six o'clock deadline for his column and was deeply engrossed in animated conversation with another journalist, Martin Moffat.

'How long will it be before it all turns sour?' Reg remarked.

'It only needs that young Argentinian to get within half a length of Max's car and Colin will have to send in the Peace Corps,' the other man replied.

'Well, that's hardly likely, now is it? Not on the same lap anyway.' Reg took a salmon cornet from a tray of appetizing canapés and swallowed it with the eagerness of a hungry cormorant.

Moffat, however, was still unconvinced. 'I wouldn't take bets on it,' he said. 'Anyway, if that Mario's worth his salt, he'll be lying low for a while and not going too crazy.'

They drained their glasses simultaneously as a young waitress tottered over to them with a fresh tray of drinks. Reg gave her one of his leering smiles and hoped that she couldn't read his lewd thoughts. 'Max is none too pleased with the choice of driver, or the shabby way Pritchard treated him over the whole affair,' he said returning to the issue in hand. 'It was pretty abysmal, if you ask me.'

Moffat nodded in agreement. 'And I shouldn't be at all surprised if Max quits at the end of next season.'

'And goes where?' Reg wondered if there was something on the grapevine he hadn't heard about.

'Mm, not so sure. Ferrari? Well, they don't approve of his wild living. He would have to change his ways before he went there. Max certainly wouldn't go with a French team. That only leaves the Scapini team who would be able to pay his salary and give him a competitive car.'

Reg wondered how Max would fit in with Alberto Scapini. The man was an unknown quantity and so was his team. No-one knew exactly where his funds came from, although there was a strong rumour that he had connections with the Mafia. 'I can't see Max with that outfit. Besides, he would have to speak fluent Italian.'

'Why?'

'To understand what the bloody mechanics are saying, that's why. They don't speak a word of English. It's all arm waving and foreign lingo in their garage. He would do well to steer clear of Scapini anyway. He's not the sort of guy you'd want to work for.'

'I don't really know about the mechanics,' said Martin, rather piqued, 'but maybe you're right. Didn't Scapini have a running battle with Colin Pritchard some years ago?'

'Yes, he did, now you come to mention it. Those two are a good match for each other.'

'Yeah, you're not kidding. They're both as wily as foxes, but Pritchard's all right underneath it all.'

'Then I guess Max best stay where he is. That new car

looks bloody good. Mercier is still the best designer in Formula One.' Then Reg gave a large smirk. 'And look at the talent that hangs round the team.'

Reg was admiring a stunning South American girl who had wandered into the room to join Mario. After draining his champagne glass he left his friend and wandered over to Max. 'Who's the female?' he asked casually. The dark-eyed girl seemed totally unaware that so many eyes were focused on her.

'No idea,' replied Max nonchalantly. 'Probably flown in from Buenos Aires to enhance Mario's new image.'

'New image?'

'For sure,' said Max, mimicking the Argentinian's favourite phrase. 'You want to hear the latest? Colin's just landed Mario a nice fat contract modelling sportswear. He's behaving like a mother to him. Wouldn't be surprised if he washes his damn socks into the bargain.'

Reg laughed. So all was not as sweet as it appeared between the two drivers. He had a good idea that life in the Delta pit lane would be worth a close watch this coming season. Although he was duty bound to cover the facts and figures of the sport, his main interest lay in the individual characters of the drivers and teams. Max's direct manner and flamboyant roistering set him apart from the pack. He was always good copy for the Formula One scribes. Reg counted himself lucky to be one of the few who had Max's confidence.

'Listen, mate,' said Reg in an attempt to cheer the Champion up, 'don't let your nose get put out of joint too soon over this. When your new team mate starts doing his party piece round the track, old Pritchard'll soon have that smug smile wiped off his face.'

'Don't be too sure of that. He already treats him like the son he never had.' Max gave a wry smile and drained his glass. 'Got to give Mario one thing though – he's got good taste in women.'

'Got to agree with you there, mate. She'll certainly make the pit lane look pretty this year. She'd knock a toucan off its perch and no mistake.'

It wasn't just because the press were giving Mario most of the attention that Max was put out. His plans for the afternoon had also been spoiled by Kelly. He had invited her to the launch and she had declined.

'What do you mean, you can't come?' he had asked her over the phone the night before.

'Look Max, I can't drop everything. You might have given me more notice.'

'Who mentioned taking your clothes off? It's only for a couple of hours, then we can sneak off and have a late lunch at the Claremont.' It had the makings of a pleasant afternoon.

'I have a modelling assignment tomorrow. I don't know what time I'll be finished.'

'OK.' His voice dropped. 'I'll call you on Friday.'

As Kelly put the phone down it occurred to her that since Max had won the Championship he was becoming even more self centred than usual. She hoped for his own sake that all the attention he was now receiving wasn't going to make him insufferable.

A week later Max took Kelly in the Ferrari to another test session at Silverstone. It was now mid-December and in the unseasonably bright sunshine, Kelly was enjoying the relaxed ambience. There was none of the high tension of race day and the team had been pleased with the performance of the new car. After the test they all tucked into a hot meal at the trackside café.

'Isn't it time you took Kelly round the circuit and

showed her what it's all about?' one of the mechanics suddenly asked.

Max looked faintly surprised. 'Did someone put you up to this?' he asked, grinning at Kelly's innocent smile.

'No, but it's a great idea. How about it?'

'There's only one problem. Two can't fit in a Formula One car.'

'What about your Ferrari?'

Max considered for half a second. 'OK then, I'll have to have a word with the guys at the track.'

Ten minutes later Kelly was strapped tightly into the sleek Ferrari, watched by an eager crowd of mechanics. Max, still in his driving overalls, revved up the car. In sharp contrast to the high-pitched scream of the Formula One engine, the Ferrari accelerated away almost purring. Kelly felt herself being pushed back into her seat. The first bend took her completely by surprise. She was certain they would never make it at such high speed and she sat riveted to her seat, her hands tightly clenched. Then they were through and with a sudden squeal of braking tyres, they were into the next corner. Kelly closed her eyes and prayed. At a hundred and sixty-five miles an hour, the crash barriers seemed only inches away. She glanced over at Max who appeared totally relaxed as he gave a casual wave to the group huddled over the pit wall. They flew by and after two more laps, Kelly felt she had enough adrenalin in her system to keep her charged for a year. Her relief was undisguised as they cruised back to the pits.

'That was something else, Max,' she gasped. 'Driving will never be the same again.'

'It's good to have a spin in the machine – to really let it go. Mind you, I might be needing a new set of tyres next week.'

'I'm glad you don't drive like that all the time. It must

be frustrating having a beautiful car like this and not being able to . . . '

'Like having you around, Kelly, and not being able to make love to you when I want to. How about we go home and make up for the last few days?'

Kelly could think of no better way of ending the day.

Back at the flat, Kelly was preparing a light supper while Max poured two glasses of champagne.

'You're spoiling me today,' she murmured happily and curled her arms around his neck. Taking the glass he offered, she gave him a lingering seductive look. 'Here's to the world's fastest driver and most wonderful lover.'

They drank from their glasses holding each other closely.

'I hope I didn't scare you too much.'

'You know something, you scare me more off the roads than you do on them.' Kelly tried to sound casual as she went back to preparing the salad. 'If you want to know the truth, I'm shit scared of falling in love with you.'

She cursed the fact that she had chosen this moment to plunge her knife into an onion. Her eyes welled up with tears.

'Hey, now that is scary,' said Max. 'Give me a Grand Prix down the side of Everest. I could handle that better.'

Kelly sniffed loudly, rubbed her smarting eyes and turned towards him. 'Max, do you ever let anyone know what is going on in that head of yours?'

'You think I should be more open about my feelings, is that it?' he asked, casually pushing his hands into his trouser pockets.

'I think you'd make a good politician. You have the most annoying habit of answering a question with a question.'

'I guess I'm better at handling cars than relationships.'

'Do you love Vicky?' Kelly asked tentatively.

There was a long pause. 'Love? I'm very fond of her. But *in* love? I don't think I've ever been in love.'

Even at the age of thirty-three, Max had never stopped to consider there might be something lacking in his life. He enjoyed women's company and had adored many in his time, but he had always stopped short of becoming too close. Kelly had suspected this about him, but his words hit her like shattering glass.

'A lot of people say I don't take life seriously enough,' Max continued. 'It's the same with my relationships, I suppose.'

'Live for today. That's your motto.' Kelly almost spat out the words, assaulting the onions with a vengeance.

'Is that so terribly wrong?' said Max guardedly.

'Not if you don't go round hurting people.'

'Have I hurt you?'

'No, not yet.'

'Well then, what's all the serious discussion about?'

'I just wonder if the word "love" ever features in your vocabulary. You've never once told me you love me. In bed, you tell me you want me, need me, but never that you *love* me. Is it so terribly wrong that I want to be loved by you?'

'No.' He paused. 'Kelly, we're lovers, we are friends, mates even. We have a good time together, but there can't be anything more . . . '

'Because you're married? Bullshit. You cut yourself off from your feelings. Why?' Kelly's voice was high pitched with emotion. For some reason she had been terribly wound up lately. She wondered if the uncertainty of the relationship was getting to her, never knowing when she would see Max or for how long. Something had changed in her over the last few weeks. She found herself getting possessive and she knew that was a sure way of losing him. Max, more than anyone, revelled in being a free spirit. 'Why?' Kelly repeated when her question had met with a wall of silence.

'Involvement scares me. It's as simple as that.'

Max refilled their glasses and he drank thirstily.

'So, you're the one who's scared. You're scared of being hurt.' Kelly felt relief. At last she was getting through to Max. He was at least talking openly of his feelings: something she would never have imagined before now.

'Maybe.' His voice was quiet and he slumped down on the kitchen stool. 'Perhaps you would understand better if I told you something of my past. It's not usually something I care to talk about . . . ' Max paused and Kelly pulled up a stool next to him.

'Go on, Max,' she urged.

'When I was twelve I came home unexpectedly from school one day. It was lunchtime. I didn't normally come home for lunch, but I had forgotten my football boots or something and had dashed home for them. I remember I was looking forward to seeing my mother. It would be a surprise for her. She'd often said how long the days were when I was at school. I adored her more than anything . . . ' Max took another drink from his glass. 'I went through the back door and heard music and laughter coming from the lounge. It was a strange high-pitched laugh I'd never heard from her before. I stopped and put my head round the door. My mother was half naked and they were making love on the sofa.'

'Who was?'

'My mother and a stranger . . . I'd never seen him before.'

'What did you do?' asked Kelly, shocked.

'I ran out of the house. I can't remember where to. I

just kept on running, hoping that the awful image would disappear.'

'Did your father find out?'

'Eventually, although I never spoke of it.'

'And your mother?'

'She cried a lot and begged my forgiveness. She was distraught, saying she had never wanted to hurt me.'

'What happened?'

'She left after a few weeks. Ran off with her young lover. She begged me to go with her, explaining that she couldn't live with my father any more.'

'Did you?'

'Go with her? No. She had let me down. I no longer felt I could trust her. I guess at that age what I wanted most was security. I saw her infrequently, during the holidays mostly, but I felt I'd lost the mother I had adored so much. She left my father a broken man.'

Kelly sighed. 'That's pretty heavy stuff, Max. I'm so sorry. It was a terrible thing to happen.'

Max gave a wry laugh. 'Well, I've never thought about life too deeply, but that left its mark on me. It made me wary of getting too involved . . . '

And afraid of being hurt again, I shouldn't wonder, thought Kelly. She wrapped her arms around his waist. 'You miss out on an awful lot in life by not allowing yourself to love.' She leaned her head against his shoulder. 'I just hope you will tear down that tough exterior of yours and love me . . . one day.'

Max put his glass down and embraced her gently. He was feeling mellow from the champagne and swept her up in his arms.

'Let's make a start, shall we?' he said gently.

# 10

Vicky could hardly wait for the morning to come. She lay beside Max watching him sleep. A glance at the clock told her it was seven o'clock. Max had come in at midnight the night before and Vicky, already in a deep sleep, had only managed to mumble 'good night' to him.

Max stirred as he felt Vicky's arms wrap around his shoulders.

'Max?' she whispered.

'What time is it? It's not even daylight. What's the problem?' Even half awake, Max could sense Vicky's restlessness.

'I saw the most beautiful colt yesterday. It's a one-year-old dark chestnut. Max, I want to buy it, then in a couple of years break it in.'

'Then what's the problem? Buy it . . . ' said Max, not sharing the enthusiasm Vicky had fought to contain since she had set eyes on the animal.

'Thanks, darling,' she said. 'You will love him. He's got a white star on his forehead and the most beautiful eyes. His legs are strong, his back is well developed – he's going to be a superb horse. Sophie's so excited.'

'Sounds terrific,' replied Max, fighting back a yawn.

'Do you want to come and see him today?'

'I'd love to,' he lied, 'but I'm having lunch with Colin at the factory and I've got a seat fitting at eleven thirty.'

'Well, don't worry, Phil can come along,' Vicky said quickly. 'Honestly, darling, it will be two thousand pounds well spent.'

Max winced. 'That's a lot of money, isn't it? What are you buying – a Derby winner, or something?'

Vicky smiled, but not at Max's closing remark. She had a new project, and not only that but she had Phil to share it with.

There seemed little point in staying in bed. Max had drifted off to sleep again and Vicky could tell by the light filtering through the curtains that it was going to be a bright day. Even Maria hadn't stirred as she crept past her door and into the kitchen to make herself some coffee, the way she liked it. Through the kitchen window, the dawn was nudging through a sky streaked with patches of rose pink and pale blue. She wondered if Phil was up and about. The foolhardy side of her wanted to dash over to his cottage and jump into bed with him. If she had known how difficult it would be to restrain herself from wanting to spend more time with him, she might have given more thought before allowing him to become her lover. But there had been no choice, she decided. Fate had interceded. It had happened so naturally and he had given her a new zest for life. She felt complete again.

She and Phil had managed to make love only once since that first time three weeks ago. They had ridden out into the forest and Phil had packed a wool rug and a flask of coffee and brandy in his saddle bag. The day had been warm for the time of year and they had laughed at the thrill of it all. The forest was the only place they felt safe. Vicky, whose most daring exploit in the past had been to make love on a beach at night on her honeymoon, now found the prospect of being taken on the soft, damp earth, amongst the stillness of the trees, wildly exciting. And now as well as Phil, there was that new horse to look forward to. For once,

Vicky didn't seem to mind that Max was showing little interest.

As she sat daydreaming in the kitchen, she saw a movement by the stables and her heart thumped as Phil, hunched up in his leather jacket, opened the half-door. She switched on the outdoor light a couple of times and even in the half light, the spotlights gave out a bright glare, enough to catch Phil's attention. He made his way over to the house.

'What's this, a new signalling device to tell me the coast is clear?'

'No, silly, I just wanted to attract your attention. Fancy a coffee?'

'Yes, please.' Phil brushed his hair from his face, feeling slightly ill at ease, knowing that at any moment Max or Maria might appear.

'Max has agreed to buy the horse,' said Vicky, her eyes bright and keen. 'Shall I call the owner and see if we can pick him up in a couple of days?' She poured a mug of coffee and handed it to Phil.

'Yes, that'll be fine. I should have the other stable ready by then. Another coat of paint and it should be as good as new.'

'Phil, I can hardly wait. He's such a beautiful foal . . . '

He moved close to her. 'Where's Max now?'

'Still asleep.'

Phil bent over and kissed her slowly on the lips. 'Sorry, I couldn't resist it. You look so pretty today.'

Vicky smiled at his compliment. 'We better be careful, Phil.'

'I know.' He coughed and assumed a heavy local accent, 'Well, Mrs Gregson, I'm just awaitin' your orders, like I do every day . . . ' He winked at her. His eyes promised untold joy. Vicky wanted to kiss every long lash.

'How about a ride this morning, then?'

'Fine, m'ladee. I'll have everything ready by eleven.' And planting another quick kiss on her lips, he disappeared out the door taking his coffee with him.

# 11

Kelly had spent a lonely Christmas and New Year. She had shunned the many invitations from admiring escorts – the London parties and nightlife. Suddenly she had tired of it all. She preferred to spend time on her own rather than throw herself into what had become a superficial, empty world without Max. Her close friends had noticed a dramatic change in the normally vibrant, fun-loving girl. However, Kelly was now fearing the worst. Her body and moods were undergoing subtle changes. Finally, unable to ignore the signs any longer, she made an appointment to see her doctor.

It was now the sixteenth of February. She would never forget that dark, dismal day, the gloom that encircled her as she left the doctor's surgery. One careless, reckless night with Max and the unthinkable had happened. She was pregnant. She remembered the night. He had come to her flat late and woken her up. It had slipped her mind completely to take her usual precautions.

It took her an hour to walk home. She made her way through the busy streets and when she recovered her thoughts she realized she had been wandering aimlessly. By the time she found herself back in the familiar surroundings of her mews, she had decided to call Max. Later that afternoon she dialled his home number. She let it ring three times before replacing the receiver. Suddenly she felt frightened, afraid of his reaction. Instead, she decided the easy option was to discuss it with Julian.

* * *

Julian leaned back in his chair. His normally smiling face was etched with worry lines. Kelly sat opposite him, her hair swept back and tied with a black bow, not unlike the way Vicky wore her hair, Julian thought ironically. Her face was pale and drawn against the upturned collar of her jacket and the only sparkle about her was her large silver earrings. People bustled back and forth across the Grosvenor House foyer and the sombre couple in the corner attracted little attention. Julian poured tea from the large china pot.

'Do you want Max's baby?' he asked after he had taken in the bombshell Kelly had dropped on him.

'Very much, but I don't want to lose him.'

Julian's concern was indeed over Max's reaction. He couldn't see him welcoming the news like an unexpected present.

'I felt I had to talk to you about it. You probably know him better than anyone.'

Julian sighed. 'Max is a law unto himself. He has a genuine heart of gold and yet . . . '

Kelly nodded. 'Sometimes I feel so close to him, then at other times he distances himself from me like a stranger.'

Julian reached over and took her trembling hand.

'Kelly, I'm sure you know Max as well as I do. What you must have realized by now is that he rarely lets anyone get close to him. He's afraid of relationships and only gives so much of himself.'

Kelly remembered the conversation she had had with Max about his mother. She knew why it was now, but it didn't make it any easier for her. She fiddled nervously with her collar and pressed her lips tightly together, hoping to quell the tears that were escaping from her eyes. She had been so emotional recently, having to cancel modelling assignments as she fought against the storm that wracked her mind and body. 'I have a terrible feeling he will turn his back on the whole thing, which is why I can't bring myself to tell him . . . '

'I don't understand the way he thinks sometimes and I wish I could give you some advice . . . Now if you were having my baby, we'd be celebrating with champagne.'

Kelly managed a wry smile. Dear Julian. He really was her anchor man. She needed his strength at this traumatic time. He was a dying breed of gentleman, always so considerate and sincere. He was truly concerned for her and she valued his friendship deeply. If only Max was as sensitive and caring.

They finished their tea then made their way out into the bustle of London traffic. As Julian kissed Kelly goodbye he gave her a warm hug. 'Kelly, whatever happens I hope it's for the best. And don't forget to call me, I'm always around. You won't find a broader shoulder to cry on.' He stood back and looked into her doleful eyes. 'Who knows?' he added, 'Max might enjoy being a father again.'

Plucking up courage, Kelly had called Max's secretary and been put through to Max. She had asked if they could meet the following day. She wanted to talk to him urgently. Max had not asked any questions but suggested they lunch at Luigi's.

Kelly spent a troubled night, sleeping little, unable to make up her mind what to do. It was only in the last hour before her lunch date while she was showering and changing that she finally decided she was going to have the baby, whatever Max's reaction. Choosing a pair of immaculately tailored black trousers, a white Chanel blouse and black jacket, she suddenly felt cheerful. By the time she left in a taxi, she had dismissed all her fears and almost convinced herself that Max would stand by her and support her financially, if nothing else.

Max was already seated at their usual corner table when she arrived. In his hand was a large Scotch and soda, beside him a file of papers. He caught a whiff of Kelly's perfume as she bent over and gently kissed his cheek. He stood up and returned her kiss as a waiter glided over to pull out her chair. Max noticed that Kelly looked pale and tired but declined to comment.

'You look busy,' Kelly said, indicating the file. 'How did the meeting with the sponsors go?'

'Fine, they've agreed to pay my price – £50,000 for the logo on the overalls, which is £20,000 more than last year.' Max felt smug that there had been no objections to his rather exorbitant increase in the fee. 'This however,' he said patting the file next to him, 'is a proof of my biography. We finally finished it. The publishers will have it out by spring.' Max beamed proudly. He was in a particularly good mood today. Money and fame – all seemed to be falling into his lap.

The waiter brought Kelly a Buck's Fizz and another Scotch for Max. 'Let's drink to the book,' said Max raising his glass. Kelly raised hers. Max's high spirits were infectious. He almost made Kelly forget the reason she had wanted to see him so desperately. But she knew she had to break the mood before they both got carried away and the moment passed.

'There's one detail you might have to amend in the book,' she said at last, not daring to return his gaze.

'What's that?' asked Max casually.

'There's a baby on the way.'

Max took a large drink from his glass and brushed the

palm of his hand across his face as if suddenly tired. 'Holy shit.'

'Is that all you can say?' Kelly watched Max's expression instantly change like a sudden cloud blotting out the sun. The room turned cold. Kelly suppressed a small shiver.

'Well?' she whispered fiercely.

'Well, I must say it's a bit of a surprise. What happened?'

'The night you came round to the flat, very late. I was still half asleep when you made love to me. I forgot to do anything about it.'

'You've had it confirmed?' asked Max, hoping that there might be a chance Kelly had got her dates wrong.

'Yes, I saw the doctor yesterday.'

Max toyed with his glass, watching the ice moving in the golden liquid. His mind was working rapidly. This was a slight hiccup but nothing that couldn't be resolved. He was trying to stay calm. 'Have you thought about an abortion?'

'Yes. But I've dismissed the idea. I've decided to have the baby . . . our baby,' she corrected herself.

'Kelly, you're only twenty-five. You've got your whole life ahead of you. What about your career? It's not really . . . '

'Convenient?' Kelly's eyes turned from mellow to icy sharp and Max got the message they conveyed. 'Life is not like that, Max,' she continued. 'Not everything runs to order. Not in the world of us ordinary mortals, at any rate.'

'Kelly, calm down. Let's discuss this rationally.'

Kelly threw her head back, took in a deep breath as if to gather strength and folded her hands on the table. 'OK, Max. Let's do that.' She lowered her voice and leaned forward. 'The facts are that I love you and I'm having your baby. The question is, are you going to stand by me?'

Max felt acutely uncomfortable at Kelly's sudden directness. He was being pushed into a corner. 'It's not as simple as that. There's Vicky to think of . . . and Sophie. *If*, however, you decide that you really want it then I could support you financially but . . . '

Max winced at the words. His mind was suddenly full of the possible repercussions – the scandal, grossly exaggerated newspaper stories. He might even end up in the divorce courts. It would be like opening a flood gate. And what damage might it do to his public image? He must persuade Kelly to have an abortion and not encourage her to go ahead with this absurd idea. 'Kelly, I really think you should reconsider. Have you thought of the problems of bringing up a child on your own?'

'Of course I have. I'd cope because it's your baby and I'd love it more than anything in the world.'

'Are you sure it's mine?' Max asked quickly.

'Max, that's the most despicable thing to say. How could you think there was anyone else?' Kelly exploded.

'I'm sorry, I . . . '

Kelly stood up and pushed her chair back. 'I've heard enough. I'm leaving,' and as she turned, she almost bumped into the waiter who was about to hand her a menu.

Max leapt up, scooped up his file and hastily pulled out a twenty pound note from his pocket. 'Here, this is for the drinks,' he said, pushing past the speechless waiter.

'Old Bill Rogers? He's a decent sort of chap.'

That was how many of Bill's friends described him. After twenty-five years of devoted labour at the local electronics factory he was enjoying his retirement. He had spent the last few years looking forward to this time and had put money by to enjoy a few of the luxuries in life. His wife, Amy, had passed away three years before and he had long since adjusted to living on his own.

Stephen, his seventeen-year-old grandson, was a frequent visitor to his small London flat. Together they paid regular visits to Stamford Bridge to watch Chelsea. But his grandson's greatest love was motor racing. He followed Formula One regularly and would be glued to the television even on hot summer Sunday afternoons.

Last year he had persuaded Bill to make the trip to Brand's Hatch to watch the British Grand Prix. Despite setting off at six thirty in the morning they had still met miles of traffic queues as the fans made their annual pilgrimage to the race. Bill's old Morris Marina had overheated and they had walked two miles to the nearest village to get some water. By the time they got going again most of the traffic was already at the circuit and they made good time to reach it for a hamburger and beer before finding a good spot to watch the race. Bill was feeling quite exhausted by the time the twenty-six cars were assembled on the grid. The long journey had taken its toll and he would have much preferred to be watching it in the comfort of his small flat. For a while the noise of the cars screaming down the straight startled and distracted him from his tiredness. He studied the youthful faces of the drivers in the programme and wondered what drove these men to risk their lives and seek danger so avidly.

The race was won by the Englishman, Max Gregson, and the crowds let out deafening cheers as he drove his victory lap, waving in recognition of their applause. Stephen waved his Union Jack hysterically and Bill looked on in amusement as he saw the pleasure on the young lad's face. 'He did it in the end,' said Stephen excitedly, whacking his hand with his programme in emphasis. 'Did you see the way he overtook the two French cars on that last lap? And right in front of us?'

He had wanted to go to the podium to see the winner presented with the trophy and champagne, but Bill had thought it best they begin their long journey home. And that, he thought ironically as they started on their way, was motor racing – five and a half hours of traffic jams and two hours of deafening noise and brief glimpses of the world's most highly paid drivers pushing themselves to the limits.

A copy of the latest racing magazine lay on the kitchen table of his flat. Max Gregson's face stared out from the front cover. The magazine had caught Bill's eye in the newsagent's and he'd bought it for his grandson. He would be seeing him tomorrow. Bill gathered up his pension book and string shopping bag to make his weekly visit to the Post Office. Normally he made the trip in the morning, but today he had decided to spring clean his flat. He was becoming quite houseproud these days now that he spent so much time at home. At three o'clock he closed the door on his flat and set out to collect his carefully budgeted pension.

Max pursued Kelly out of the restaurant, hastily explaining to the maitre d' that his companion wasn't feeling too well.

The maitre d' shook his head after he had gone. 'Poor Meester Gregson,' he said, shrugging his shoulders dramatically at the doorman. ''E's not 'aving a good day. First 'is Ferrari 'as developed problems and he 'as to hire a car and now 'e is in big trouble wiz 'is mistress.' He smiled sympathetically.

Max quickly caught up with Kelly and grabbed her arm.

'Kelly, wait. What do you think you're doing?'

'Let go of me. I'll find my own way home,' Kelly said icily as she tried to shake off Max's hand.

'I'm taking you back to the flat.'

'Max, you've made it perfectly clear you're not interested in this baby. It's made me realize just how selfish you really are.'

Kelly struggled to control the hysteria she felt. She was crying openly now as Max guided her firmly towards the car. He didn't want a scene. He unlocked the door of the white Granada hire car and urged her in. Max felt himself becoming irritated and frustrated. His frustration turned to anger as he got behind the wheel.

How could an easy-going, uncomplicated relationship be thrown into such confusion by one forgetful moment? He revved up the car and accelerated quickly away, driving as if he were back on the track. He shifted gear rapidly, overtaking a nose to tail line of cars. Traffic coming towards him flashed their lights in annoyance. If he had stopped to consider the fact that he was over the limit of alcohol, he would have taken a taxi. Instead, he drove heedlessly on, as if speed alone would dispel his anger. A car hooted at him as he swerved off the main road down a narrow street that was a shortcut to Kelly's flat. Max accelerated sharply. He caught a glimpse of a man at the side of the road. Suddenly, he saw him step off the pavement, saw it all in slow motion. Just as he calculated decisions on the race track with split second timing, so he stamped on the brakes. Even under the influence of alcohol his reaction was three times faster than the average driver's would have been.

* * *

Bill Rogers had been staring absently at some pigeons chattering noisily on the guttering above him. He hadn't seen or heard the fast white car approaching as he started to cross the road. It hit Bill a glancing blow before screeching to a halt.

Max was out of the car in a second. The impact of the car had sent the old man reeling back on to the pavement. Max knelt beside him.

'Stay where you are,' he said as the old man moved awkwardly to get up, 'I'll call an ambulance.'

Bill felt a sudden pain in his chest, but apart from that he was just winded. 'You were in a bit of a hurry, weren't you?' he asked, catching his breath. He looked up into the face of the concerned man who was supporting his shoulders.

'Yes, I'm sorry. How do you feel?'

'I'm a bit shaken, but I don't think I've broken anything.'

The old man stared hard at Max as he tried to recollect his thoughts. Something about him was familiar. Pleasantly so. It was something connected with his grandson. Something they had shared together, not too long ago . . . ''Ere, you're not that racing driver chap, are you? Max Gregson?'

'Yes, that's me, and I'm afraid I was driving as if I were back on the race track.'

As Max bent over him, Bill could smell the alcohol on his breath. He would be in a right mess if the law was to come along. What would his grandson say if he got his hero into trouble? Fancy stepping off the pavement like that, Stephen would say.

''Ere, young man, you better be on your way a bit smartish. We don't want the police getting curious. It could be the end of your driving for a while.' His kindly face broke into a smile.

'Come on,' urged Max, helping him to his feet. 'I'll take you to the hospital where they can check you over.'

'I'm all right, Mr Gregson.' Bill said the name proudly. 'I just need to get my breath back.' A driver hooted impatiently as he came up behind Max's car parked in the middle of the road. 'Now you be on your way, only not so fast this time.'

Bill was already thinking about how he would ring Stephen and tell him how he met his hero; bumped into him more like. If only he could catch his breath a bit more.

'You'll be all right?' asked Max.

'Fine. I think the lady in the car needs more attention than I do.'

Max turned to see Kelly sobbing hysterically, her eyes wide and frightened. He had forgotten all about her.

Bill watched as the Ford Granada drew away. It's all rush and hurry these days, no time to enjoy life, he thought to himself. Without warning, a piercing spasm tore down his side. Bill gulped desperately for air, unaware that his main artery was being blocked by a large blood clot. The clot had been in his body for a few weeks now, but the sudden shock of the car hitting him had dislodged it and sent it racing towards his heart. As Bill collapsed on to the pavement, his life was already ebbing away.

# 12

Vicky was preparing breakfast the next morning when Max came into the kitchen. She noticed his eyes were heavy and ringed with dark circles. He had come back late again the night before. It was gone three when she heard his car pull up outside the garage.

'I'm sorry about last night. I met up with Julian and a couple of mates at the Club,' he said by way of an apology.

'Save your excuses for later,' she replied, quietly angry and not wanting any argument to be heard by Sophie or Maria, who were both in the kitchen.

Max was already in a bad humour and chose to ignore her remark. He had spent most of last evening trying to console Kelly and talk some sense into her. He had had enough aggravation from the women in his life for a while. 'How about some of that brew of yours, Maria? I could do with a strong injection of coffee this morning.'

Only Sophie seemed pleased to see him. He gave her a hug and sat down next to her at the scrubbed pine refectory table.

'Have you made any plans for today?' asked Vicky tartly. She placed slices of melon and a rack of toast on the table.

'I thought we could take Sophie into Oxford to buy her those new riding boots,' said Max, hoping it might help to assuage Vicky's coolness.

Sophie's eyes lit up at the mention of her boots.

'Maria, I'm going to have bright shiny black ones just like Mummy's,' she announced proudly.

As Max browsed through the morning papers there was a light tap at the door and a fresh-faced Phil popped his head round.

'Morning, any chance of some coffee?' His voice was bright and cheerful.

'Phil, good morning. Come on in,' Vicky called out. She noticed his smile fade when he caught sight of Max.

'Morning, Mr Gregson,' he said politely.

'Morning,' Max looked up briefly from the newspaper.

'I can't come riding with you this morning, Phil,' Sophie beamed a satisfied smile at him. 'We're going to Oxford to buy some new riding boots.'

'Not if you don't eat your breakfast,' Vicky warned, watching Sophie play with her cereal. She got up and poured Phil some coffee, handing it to him with a smile. 'How are the horses this morning?' she asked.

'Fine. I'll put the colt out in the paddock with the other two if the weather warms up.'

Vicky flashed him an appreciative glance. 'Thanks. I'll be over to see him later.'

But Phil had caught a disapproving glower on Max's face and, clutching his mug of coffee, was already heading for the door.

'I've got some cleaning to do in the tack room. Better be making a start.'

When he had gone, Max, who had noticed how Vicky's mood had lifted as soon as Phil appeared, said, 'He's getting a bit familiar round here, isn't he?'

'How do you mean?' she asked nonchalantly.

'Coming in here at eight thirty in the morning for coffee, that's what I mean.'

'For goodness sake, Max, don't be so pompous. The poor boy's frozen out there. He just came in to get something to warm him up.'

'As long as he does a proper job with the horses, that's all,' said Max, piqued.

'Phil happens to be a very nice guy and works extremely hard. I can't see the harm in him joining us for coffee in the morning.'

Irritated, Max went back to reading the *Daily Telegraph*. The events of yesterday were still uppermost in his mind. He had slept badly. He was in turmoil over Kelly's news and the accident. But, it could have been a lot worse, he reassured himself. He could have badly injured the old man and be sitting in some police cell facing a whole list of charges.

'When is the Ferrari going to be ready?' asked Vicky.

'Today. They've sorted out the problem with the ignition and the garage has promised to deliver it before ten this morning.'

'Good. Then we can leave for Oxford straight after?'

'Yes, we'll take the Ferrari. I don't really want to be driving a hire car for the rest of the day,' said Max absently.

He was glancing through the newspaper and, by chance, his eye caught a small headline at the bottom of page three. Had he passed over it, he might never have known the consequences of his erratic behaviour the day before. As it was, a stunned numbness flooded through him as he read and re-read the small inclusion.

'HIT AND RUN DRIVER LEAVES PENSIONER DYING IN STREET.' It gave brief details of the accident, the time, the name of the street. The police were looking for the driver of a white Granada. The shockwaves ran through him as he dropped the paper and the blood drained from his face. The old man had died in the street.

'Max, are you all right? You look as if you've seen a ghost,' asked Vicky.

Max was up and out of the room before she had time to say anything more. She picked up the page Max had been reading and looked for the article that had upset him so. She found nothing. Maria returned Vicky's blank gaze and shrugged her shoulders.

'Per'aps my coffee has bad effect on his bowels.'

'He's probably gone to collect the car,' said Vicky lightly for Sophie's benefit.

Max was staring at the finger of brandy left in the bottle. It had taken him from late afternoon until late evening to realize there was little comfort to be had in the fiery stuff. But it had numbed his mind to the pain for a few hours and he was grateful for that. He had known fear before. The first time he had sat in a Formula One car it had roared into life with such power it had frightened him. But it had been a fear tinged with excitement. It had given him a euphoric feeling and he had been hooked on it ever since.

He had brushed with death many times. He had witnessed the deaths of fellow drivers, but they had known what the odds were. Now he had been responsible for someone else's death, through his own carelessness, and he was afraid.

Max had made an excuse to Vicky about some urgent business in London and driven to their flat in Fulham, where he had spent the time in a confused and muddled haze, not helped by heavy drinking. The only person he felt he could confide in was Julian, but he had left for a skiing holiday. He had tried to call Kelly, but got no reply. Later that evening the phone rang.

'Hi, Max. It's Julian, I'm back.'

At the sound of his friend's voice, waves of relief flooded through Max. 'Julian, it's good to hear from you. I thought you were away for a few days, skiing.'

'I was. Had to rush back from Verbier just as I started enjoying myself because some business deal hit trouble. Sod's law, isn't it?' Julian's voice dropped and sounded unusually flat. 'I've just come from seeing Kelly. She's in hospital.'

Max groaned. 'What the hell has happened now?' His life was rapidly going to pieces.

'She's lost her baby, Max.'

'Is she all right?'

'She's pretty devastated right now. What the hell's been going on?'

'Can you come over right away.'

'Give me ten minutes.'

Max was on his second cup of black coffee when Julian arrived. Julian was shocked to see his friend looking so haggard. He was unshaven and his eyes were bloodshot. The small but elegant living room was in a state of disarray. An almost finished bottle of brandy, dirty glasses and coffee mugs were scattered on the table. Max cleared a space for the freshly brewed jug of coffee.

The usual banter between the two men was clearly inappropriate and Julian sensed Max was in trouble. 'You look as if you've hit a few problems,' he said soberly.

Max brushed a wave of hair off his forehead in a heavy, bewildered gesture. 'You could say that. You knew about Kelly's pregnancy then?'

'Yes, she was desperate to talk to someone about it.' Julian sat down on the sofa while Max poured him some coffee and a brandy.

'What's been happening, Max? Kelly was in a bad state when she arrived in hospital. The doctors believe it was shock which brought on the miscarriage.'

'Where is she?'

'The Central Middlesex.'

Making a mental note to send her some flowers, Max told Julian the whole story. 'A couple of days ago we met for lunch. Kelly told me she was pregnant. I guess we were both pretty fraught. I had had a couple of drinks and was driving too fast. I came down a side street and knocked down this old guy. He seemed all right at the time and told me to disappear, as he could smell the alcohol on my breath . . . so I drove off.' Max paused, waiting for some reaction from Julian. There was none. 'I offered to take him to the hospital, but he insisted he was all right. The odd thing was he recognized me. He said his grandson was a fan of mine.'

'Have you heard how he is?' Julian asked slowly.

'He's dead.'

Julian sat silent for a minute, staring into his glass of brandy as the words sank in. 'How do you know?'

'It was in the *Telegraph*. Pensioner killed by hit and run driver. Same time, same street.' Max felt a sickening shiver run up his spine. 'I can't believe he died . . . I just can't believe it.'

'So where does that leave you with the police, Max?'

'As luck would have it, I was driving a hire car from the local garage. I doubt if they could trace it. There were no witnesses – not that I know of.'

'Does anyone else know?'

'No, not even Vicky. I couldn't bring myself to tell her. What's the point? It would only upset her. Of course, there's Kelly . . . she saw the whole thing. I expect that's why she's in hospital now. She was pretty shaken up.'

'She still is, but she never mentioned the accident.'

'What the hell to do now . . . ?' Max voiced his thoughts aloud, despairingly. 'I just wish I had taken his address. At least I could have got something to his family.'

'Max, go to the police. There's no way they can prove you'd been drinking and, as you said, the poor guy admitted he wasn't hurt. If you come forward and tell them your story, it would clear your conscience of the guilt . . . '

'Julian, are you crazy? The bastards would probably throw the book at me – I would lose my racing licence and end up in jail for God knows how long. No, I can't even consider that – it's too risky. Besides, there would be all the adverse publicity. That would really throw my future in the balance.' Max shook his head wearily.

Julian, who was now wearing the same melancholic expression as his friend, realized it was pointless to try and persuade Max to change his mind. 'When are you leaving for the test session in Rio? It must be soon?'

'The day after tomorrow.'

'Looking at you now, I would say it's time you got your act together, sobered up and started focusing on that.'

Max looked up from his brandy glass. Julian had never seen him so shattered. The lines etched on his face in the glow of the lamp aged him beyond his years. Gone was the gregarious friend he had known for so long. Instead, he saw before him a man broken in spirit. He wondered how this awful tragedy would affect him. The first race which followed shortly after the test session in Rio was only a couple of weeks away. It was a vitally important time for Max and the Delta team. Everyone was expecting the World Champion and the team to repeat their performance of last season.

Julian and Max talked long into the night. The stillness of the early hours passed and by the time Julian left, the first commuter train could be heard in the darkness of the bleak February morning.

# 13

Twenty-four hours later, Max was on his way to Rio de Janeiro, still nursing a giant hangover. On another flight, a DC10 freighter, were the tools of his trade – the cars, tyres and a hundred and twenty boxes for each team packed with tools and spares for the testing.

In the next few days another six flights would transport more cars, equipment and personnel to Rio's Galileo airport. It was a massive airlift that would eventually bring together the twenty-six cars for the race scheduled two weeks after the test session.

The backdrop to the Jacarepagua circuit, forty minutes outside Rio, was beautiful enough, the mountains changing colour from pale mauve at dawn to delicate blue at midday and deep purple at sunset. But the track itself was in poor condition and uncomfortable from the drivers' point of view. This, together with the searing temperatures and humidity, made it a tough circuit.

The afternoon sun beat down relentlessly, causing the track and flat grassy areas to shimmer delicately. Now and again a faint breeze drifted in, but nothing could dispel the almost choking humidity. Inside the cockpit of the cars the temperature was reaching a hundred and twenty degrees.

Mario Rodriguez stepped from his car feeling rivulets of sweat making a determined path down to the small of his back and soaking the layers of fireproof clothing he was wearing. Seeking the comparative cool of the garage, he sank down on to an old chair, resting his neatly booted feet on the steel rim of a wheel. Apart from the usual inquisitive journalists and the occasional scantily clad bimbo, there was little at the Jacarepagua circuit to distract the drivers. Removing his balaclava, he wiped his forehead and welcomed the bottle of mineral water one of the mechanics handed him. He took long swallows, relishing the cool liquid on his parched throat.

'It's a tough one today,' commented one of the mechanics as four of them wheeled his car into the space behind him.

'For sure,' Mario laughed, 'and I'm one of the locals. It's good to get out of that sweat box.' He took another long drink of water to combat the dehydration caused by the exhausting heat.

Mario was enjoying his new team. He had eagerly anticipated the time when he would wear the blue and yellow Delta team colours and drive the much acclaimed Delta car. Now it had come and, despite his exhaustion, he felt charged with an exhilaration which would grow and grow until race day arrived.

Here at the Jacarepagua circuit, the testing of tyres took a very high priority. The right choice of tyre for the race could make or break a winner. From the many different compounds to choose from, it was important the team tried every variant to select the one most suited to the very high temperatures and rough surface of the track. A tyre that exceeds its maximum working temperature quickly loses its grip and the car starts to handle badly. With cornering speeds of up to a hundred and fifty miles an hour, having the right tyres is vital. So tyre selection is a key part of the test programme. It is always an exacting process. Each time the car returns to the pits, tyre temperatures are recorded at three different points. Infra-red sensors also record any changes of temperature on the circuit.

Then there are further adjustments to find the right 'set

up' for the car – the fine tuning of many facets such as wing angles, suspension settings, fuel consumption and gear-box ratios. The test session is also a good opportunity to see how fit the drivers are after a few weeks out of the car.

Max returned to the pits just as Mario was finishing his debrief with the race engineers. He sat for a while in the cockpit of the car discussing its performance before climbing out – not without some with difficulty. He went to the ice box, opened a bottle of mineral water and poured most of it over his head.

'It's a good way to sweat off those extra pounds, Max, don't you think?' Mario called over to him, raising his bottle of Evian.

Max noted the smug smile on his face. Mario's body showed no sign of the excess flesh that Max had accumulated over the winter break.

'Do I hear our new team mate already throwing in the wise cracks?' Max commented aside to Tom O'Leary, the chief mechanic, who was removing the monocoque from the car with two other mechanics. The men grinned at each other. So the fireworks were about to start between the two drivers. They had guessed as much and on the flight over had taken bets on how long it would take.

'Well, well now he might have a point, Max,' said Tom in his soft southern Irish accent. 'It would seem to me that the cockpit is causing a little difficulty?'

Tom had been Max's chief mechanic for three years. He was always frank with Max. If he thought that Max had put on weight, he would tell him.

Dick, dressed in bermuda shorts and open-necked shirt, appeared looking cool and relaxed, in stark contrast to Max who was sweating uncomfortably.

Max gave him an envious look.

'Are you OK, Max?' asked Dick. Max wiped his flushed face with his balaclava.

'Just acclimatizing to this heat. It's a bugger today.'

'Here comes the master and Mario with the lap times,' said Dick as Colin approached with Mario in tow.

Even after three days in the sun, Colin's skin still had the dull pallor of an English winter. He had been watching Mario's car from the pit wall. His times were improving. If this was going to be a sample of what was to come, Mario would be a credit to the Delta team. He certainly had no regrets about signing him.

There was something else, too. As he watched Mario laughing and smiling, dressed in the Delta team overalls, he was overcome with possessiveness, and the knowledge of his feelings shook him.

'How does the fact sheet read, Colin?' asked Max.

'Take a look. We're still down on the times of the other cars. How's the understeer?'

'If you want my opinion, she's like a sore tart on a Monday. Still far too much understeer. I'm losing her on the corners and the gear change is sticky.' Max gave a low whistle as he read the times. 'Those Ferraris are putting in some fast laps.'

'Don't worry, we'll have the car competitive with those times come race day,' Colin assured him. 'Mario, how about you take a break for ten minutes while they adjust the wings?'

'For sure,' said Mario brightly, 'I will go and get something to eat in the motor home.'

Colin's eyes followed him closely as he wandered off. 'He seems to be settling in well, don't you think?'

Max noted the glint of pride in Colin's voice. There was little chance of him doing other than settling in well, thought Max, as he again observed the way Colin fussed around Mario. What is it with this guy? he found himself wondering.

'He's handling the car well,' Max conceded at last.

'Well, his times aren't that far off yours.'

Max ignored the sardonic tone he detected in Colin's voice. Colin had hit a raw nerve. While driving, Max had found his concentration slipping on occasions, and once out of the car his thoughts would drift back to the death of the old man. It hung over him like the billowing cloud on the mountain behind him.

After the last of the cars had finished testing, Colin closed the lid on his timing computer and watched as Max drove into the pit lane. 'Are you thinking what I'm thinking?' he said, turning to Dick. 'Either our number one is out of condition or he has something on his mind. I've never seen him look so wiped out after a few laps.'

'I must say, he does look a little under the weather,' agreed Dick, not wishing to express his concern too strongly. Max was definitely not his normal self. In fact, Dick had never seen his friend so low in spirits.

On the last day of testing, Colin arrived at the track in a heavy mood, his face as dark as the skies that threatened to open the heavens over Rio. Eventually they lifted; Colin's mood did not. Having ranted at the mechanics for a slow tyre change, he bawled out an Italian journalist trying to arrange an interview with Mario in the garage. The mechanics had been politely working around this intrusion into their space. 'Leave the guy alone and get the hell out of here until we've finished,' he yelled.

Max was in discussion with Tom, the chief mechanic, when they heard Colin's outburst. 'What the hell's eating Colin?' he asked, as he watched the journalist beat a hasty retreat.

'He's touchy, all right. Better be ready for it today,' Tom said, scratching his thick head of hair.

'Time I got in the car and disappeared off for a quiet life,' said Max, as he twisted his ear plugs in his ears. 'Sure you don't want a set of these?'

'I can handle Colin and his tantrums, don't worry,' replied the ever placid Tom.

It was a long and hard day's driving for Max; seventy-three laps, the equivalent of driving a full Grand Prix. Both Delta cars performed well and improved their lap times of the previous day. Despite the success of the day, Colin still seemed to be preoccupied as he entered the motor home, where Max and Dick were hurriedly collecting their things together. They would just have time to return to the hotel for a shower and a meal before catching the flight back to London.

'Do you want a lift to the airport, Colin?' enquired Dick.

'No, I've had a change of plan,' said Colin briskly. 'I'm flying to New York tomorrow to see Harvey Leewood, Vice-President of Western Oil. I'll be back at the office Thursday morning.'

He reached for a handkerchief from the pockets of his loose-fitting trousers and wiped the perspiration from his head. 'Max, a word before you go. I think it might be an idea for you to increase your exercise programme. We need you a hundred per cent fit for this season. We don't want extra pounds slowing the car down any more than necessary.'

Without waiting for an answer, he dived out of the motor home to speak with a Goodyear tyre specialist who was passing.

'Well, I'll be . . . ' Max exploded. 'We haven't even started racing yet and he's already started his turns. What's he so bloody edgy for?'

'No idea, Max,' said Dick, watching the deepening look of incredulity and anger on Max's face. But it was typical of Colin's blunt approach to delicate matters, he thought. He had a hundred other problems buzzing through his mind. The fitness of his driver was just one of them.

Max and Dick made good time for their flight to London and despite an hour's delay in departure, they were in good spirits when they boarded the plane. Max made his way to the first class cabin, while Dick joined the overcrowded 'steerage section', as he called it.

Max sat alone with his thoughts. By submerging himself in the last few days of testing, he had managed to maintain control of his fears and the nightmare of the previous week's events. Now the reality of it all was clouding his mind again like a black dye spilling into clear water. A number of doubts persisted. Had the police traced the car? Would they be waiting to question him when he got back? How was Kelly after all their problems? They had spoken briefly on the phone, Max making the excuse that time was so short before his departure to Brazil, he couldn't visit her in hospital. He had tried to joke, saying how much he loathed hospitals. He had heard Kelly's muffled crying and she had finished the call abruptly, but not before Max had told her he still cared for her deeply and he would come and see her just as soon as he got home.

Then there was Vicky. There was something different he had noticed about her lately. He couldn't quite put his finger on it, except that she didn't seem to mind him going away now. And there was the matter of their sex life. What had once been a raging torrent of physical desire was now reduced to a trickle. They had both grown indifferent to each other.

At least he had fulfilling and adventurous sex with

Kelly. Or did he now? After her miscarriage perhaps she wouldn't want to see him again. He brooded on the incongruity of it all. At the very time his life should be running smoothly, there seemed to be some malevolent quirk of fate intruding. Circumstances were occurring over which he had no control. The idea was disquieting. He just hoped it wouldn't overspill into his racing.

The weary stewardess hid her annoyance as she returned again to the passenger in 3A with the bottle of Remy Martin.

'Another one?' she asked. Max could detect the boredom in her voice.

'How could I resist your charming and persuasive ways?' Max remarked as he held out his glass.

If she had possessed hackles they would have surely risen at the sarcasm in his voice. She refilled the glass, giving him a good measure. If he wanted to drink himself into a stupor, that was up to him.

Eventually, Max drifted into an alcoholic sleep, unaware that a journalist, upgraded to first class, had been witnessing his excesses. To the discreet observer, it served only to confirm his suspicions that the World Champion was not himself. The normally easy-going character appeared strained and aloof. Whatever was weighing heavily on his mind, obviously needed the distraction of alcohol.

Max Gregson was playing a dangerous game.

# 14

Colin had said goodbye to the rest of the team in the hotel lobby and returned to his room. It looked a mess. Having spent so little time in it over the last few days, he had left clothes lying on the floor and the writing table resembled a cluttered office desk. Papers were strewn everywhere. Had he allowed himself a few minutes to review the situation, he would have realized this was completely out of character. He took pride in his methodical, organized way of life. His office reflected his systematic, clear-headed approach to his job. Colin sat on the bed feeling jaded and tired. A stomach upset plus the gruelling humidity had left him out of sorts. He knew he should start packing his clothes for the early departure next morning to New York. Instead, he fell back on the bed hoping a short rest might restore his spirits.

An hour later he was woken by a knock at the door. He forced himself out of a heavy sleep and, still feeling confused, answered the door. Mario stood there, dressed only in the smallest pair of silk swimming trunks, his body gleaming in the half light of the corridor. Colin could smell the sweet perfume of coconut oil. Over the young driver's shoulder was a large white bath sheet which further emphasized his deep sun tan.

'Hi, Colin. I was on my way to the pool for a swim. Can you join me?'

Colin, struggling against his drowsiness, looked

astonished. 'Sure. Sounds like a great idea,' he muttered. 'Give me five minutes to get myself together.'

Mario gave him a lingering glance and made as if to say something more. Instead he turned and with a smile sauntered off down the corridor.

Colin sat down on the bed feeling wildly tormented. From the first moment he had spoken with Mario he had wrestled with a strong attraction for the younger man. Now the nagging and dangerous desire had returned. It had been the same many years ago with a young Frenchman. Then Colin had finally been forced to recognize his homosexuality. Now here it was staring him in the face again. Was his mind playing tricks or did Mario share the same feelings?

The poolside was abundantly decorated with large palm ferns and tall, shapely women. As Mario executed perfect swallow dives, one after the other, there was not a woman present who did not admire his beautifully proportioned and supple body. His jet black hair, now sleeked back and glistening in the sun, accentuated his handsome profile and sensuous lips. His male friends envied his good looks and talent. To be a racing driver in Argentina and to reach the heights of Formula One was almost akin to having presidential status. His female fans would wait for hours outside his house to catch a glimpse of him in his Ferrari before the electronic gates swallowed him up into the privacy of his estate.

Never short of female company, the press were always keen to photograph Mario with his latest beauty. And he always made sure they did. He had realized at the age of twenty-two that he did not particularly enjoy making love to women. He loved to have them around and had done his share of laying the young and beautiful. He had tried every colour and nationality. Yet something was missing. It was like eating tasteless food. Whatever he tried it was always the same; bland and unexciting. No female he had met, however sensual, could take him to the heights of passion he sought. He just hadn't met the right woman, he assured himself, but one day he would.

Colin lay on a sunbed, all interest in his newspaper forgotten. He watched as Mario repeatedly dived into the pool, swooping as gracefully into the water as a kingfisher, leaving barely a ripple behind him. He realized how much he enjoyed the company of his latest team member. Mario was as dedicated and single-minded as Colin had been at the same stage in his driving career. But was there something stronger than professional interest between them? As they chatted about cars and Mario's home country, soaking up the last of the afternoon sun, Colin was even more convinced that there was. These first moments of relaxation were there to be savoured and the tensions of the motor-racing world seemed a million miles away.

Later that evening they dined together in a small and intimate restaurant outside the city, totally absorbed in each other's company. Afterwards, as Mario drove them back along the coast road, a rumble of thunder signalled an approaching storm. A few spots of rain hit the windscreen of the car. Lightning streaked across an ink-black sky, lighting up the shanty towns behind the city. Colin watched in awe as the sea glistened in the sudden luminosity of another flash. The thunder grew louder, echoing around the mountains.

'I believe the storms here are always spectacular,' remarked Colin.

'When the lightning strikes near the Corcovada,' said Mario, 'then the locals always fear something is going to happen to their city. God is telling them to turn back to Christ.'

They could both now see the Corcovada's magnificent illuminated statue of Christ overlooking the city. It was awesome on such a night. Colin shivered.

'Tonight, it will be a very big storm,' Mario said, as they drew up outside the hotel. 'Come, let us watch it from my room. It will be very beautiful.'

Colin had never seen a storm like it. Lightning lit up the city again and again. The noise of the thunder was lost as the rain cascaded down, hammering on the window-panes in a threatening fury. Mario and Colin looked at each other in the half light. Neither spoke.

Their emotions were as tumultuous as the elements outside. Mario's body trembled. Before him stood the man who had secured him a brilliant future in the racing world. The man he had always admired and revered. Yet there was more. He knew he was about to begin an irrevocable journey of self-discovery with Colin and it started with physical desire.

Colin embraced the young boy before him, tentatively at first. Mario stood passively, then gently responded. Neither knew nor cared to know what had gone before. The moment was now, as they both realized their deep need for one another.

# 15

Vicky sat alone in the drawing room looking out through the French windows at the large oaks which bordered the sweeping lawns. The house was unusually silent. Maria had taken Sophie to a ballet lesson and Max was in London for another of his meetings. It was three in the afternoon and she was drinking alone, something she rarely did. But on this occasion she relished being alone with her thoughts. As the grandfather clock chimed, her thoughts drifted back to Phil. It was over a week now since he had disappeared. They had received a brief call which Maria had taken to say that he was with his brother who was in hospital in London. Vicky had been dismayed that he had not rung again and Max had reacted angrily, saying that he would fire him when, or if, he returned.

She was not in love with Phil, of that she was sure, but she was very much attracted to him. She missed his open, smiling face which seemed to light up every time he saw her, and she missed his energetic, optimistic approach to life. As each day passed she had grown ever more anxious about him.

She helped herself to another glass of wine . . . and another, surprised at her own recklessness. Only the sound of a car making its way up the drive broke her from her train of thought. She was feeling the tiniest bit squiffy, and she hoped to God it wasn't the vicar's wife on her weekly uninvited call to deliver the church magazine. Her heart leapt as she saw Phil's battered Land Rover making its way to the stable block. Hurriedly she threw on her jacket and raced to the stable, where she found him stroking Brigadier's ear.

'Phil,' she called excitedly. 'Where have you been?' Concern showed on her face.

He turned round slowly and Vicky was taken aback at his changed appearance. His normally bright face was haggard and unshaven. There were dark shadows under his eyes and his hair was uncombed. A flood of pity swept over her.

'What's happened? You look awful,' she stammered quietly.

'Hi Vicky.' His voice was unexpectedly casual, as if he had only been gone for an hour. He went back to stroking Brigadier, avoiding any eye contact with her. 'My brother had a car accident in France. They flew him back to London six days ago, but not before they had amputated both his legs.'

Vicky's mouth dropped open in horror. 'I'm so sorry.'

'He was one of Suffolk's best horsemen. He's been competing for as long as I can remember. Riding is his life. He's taking it pretty hard . . . ' His voice faded and he turned to her, his eyes hollow and expressionless.

'Why didn't you call me? There might have been something we could have done.'

'What could you have done? What could anyone have done?' he said wretchedly. 'It's too late now.'

Vicky moved closer. 'You mustn't distress yourself like this.' She touched him lightly on the arm and he reached for her spontaneously, holding her tightly for what seemed like a lifetime.

'It's been one hell of a week. I'm sorry I didn't call.'

'Don't worry, you're back now – that's all that matters.'

Even in his dishevelled and distraught state, there was something very sensual about him. Perhaps it was his vulnerability. How different from Max, she thought.

He stroked her hair and his strong hands caressed her shoulders as they had the first time he had touched her. He kissed her gently at first, then more strongly. She felt the roughness of his stubble on her chin as it pressed into her smooth skin, but that only served to strengthen her arousal. His tongue teased her mouth.

A hundred objections stampeded through her mind; she should stop and pull away, Sophie would be home soon, Max might return from London early. There could be so many complications . . . but like a drowning man battling for his life against mighty seas, the result was inevitable.

Phil led her gently to the bales of straw piled high in the corner of the tack room. 'I can't tell you how much I've missed you,' he murmured.

Vicky stroked his hair, smoothing his curls gently into place. 'Don't ever go away like that again – don't ever go without saying goodbye.'

Suddenly from the next-door stable they heard Brigadier give a small whinny. Something had disturbed him. Phil lifted himself up and turned towards the door. It swung on its hinges and they both shot each other a look of alarm.

'It's only the wind,' he whispered as a gust rattled the tiles on the roof above.

Oblivious to the cold and roughness of the straw, Vicky responded to his passion. She had missed him terribly. The last week had seemed like a lifetime. Her body had a gnawing hunger that only he could satisfy. This time she would feel no guilt. She moved quickly to help Phil's urgent fingers, struggling to undo the fastening at the waistband of her jeans. She lifted herself up so that he could more easily peel them from her and throw them to one side. The touch of his hand on her naked skin, and the feel of his mouth on her engorged nipples, was wild and exhilarating. She felt weak with anticipation, wanting him inside her at once. When at last he entered her, she responded by pushing against each deepening thrust. Then as his pace quickened, her back arched towards him and, with a cry of pure joy and pleasure, a searing orgasm scorched through her body and she fell back on to the straw. Phil lay next to her panting heavily.

'Phil, that was wonderful,' she sighed. 'I feel I've come alive.'

Phil lay next to her, laughing and fighting to catch his breath. 'That's funny,' he managed to say at last. 'I feel I've just died. You've taken the very last ounce of my strength,' he whispered.

'Do you think we'll ever get to make love in a bed?' Vicky asked with a short giggle as she stroked his curls now drenched with sweat.

'I promise you the next time there will be no damp stables, no wet pine forest, but a warm comfortable bed where we can make love without hurrying – *and* without me freezing my balls off.'

Vicky laughed. 'My poor darling. I really think you should go home and have a hot bath and a good night's rest.'

'That's just what I intend to do,' Phil said, bending over Vicky and plucking some straw out of her hair. 'Perhaps we better straighten you up first. You look as if you've just had a good romp in a farmyard.'

'Oh, but oi 'ave and with a lusty young farmer,' trilled Vicky. Laughing, she pulled on her clothes, brushing away the straw. Then she caught hold of Phil and kissed him gently on the lips.

'Phil, it's good to have you home again.'

He wrapped his strong arms around her. 'It's good to be back, Vicky.'

But as he made his way back to his cottage Phil wondered where it was all going to end. They would have to be very careful. He had already experienced the wrath of a jealous husband in his last job. He would be foolish if he let it happen again. And Max Gregson was not a man to cross.

# 16

The first day of March brought an unexpected snow fall and as Max drove up to London to lunch with Julian he mused on the irony that in two days' time he would be in Rio for the first race of the season. Negotiating the snow-covered roads of Oxfordshire was probably the easier option to battling against the humidity of the tropics in his race car, he concluded as the fat tyres of his Ferrari firmly gripped the icy surface of the roads.

Julian was already seated at their table in Luigi's when Max arrived. He noticed his friend looked out of sorts, and as lunch progressed, that he was drinking heavily. Max loudly ordered another bottle of Barolo, and in the crowded Italian restaurant heads turned discreetly as customers recognized the familiar face. After all the publicity on television and in the press over the last two months, he had become a household name. A small boy of nine approached the table. 'Excuse me, Mr Gregson, my father says, please may we have your autograph?'

Max took the menu and scribbled across the top. The boy beamed back in admiration and disappeared as quickly as he had come. Max was subdued. Normally he would have chatted to his young fan.

'You don't seem yourself, Max,' said Julian. 'What's up?'

'I'm knocking back too much of this, for one thing.'

'You do seem to be having a few more than usual.'

'Not what is expected of a Formula One driver, is it? Moderation in all things is the rule. Well, fuck the rules.'

Max took another drink.

'If it's the problem with Kelly and the accident . . . ' Julian said carefully, avoiding the word death.

'No, it's not that – although, God knows, I can't forget it. I've had another bloody shock this week.'

Max was interrupted by the maitre d'. 'Excuse me, Signor Greegson. There is someone on the table be'ind who would like to meet you.'

'Who is it?' asked Max, with barely concealed indifference.

'Ees name is Signor Fleurie. He say he meet you at Monaco last year and would like to talk you – about business.'

'Tell Monsieur Fleurie I'm having a private lunch and I'm not in the mood for interruptions. Take his card and tell him I'll call him – if it's that important, which I doubt it is,' Max replied curtly.

'That was a bit to the point,' remarked Julian, visibly surprised at Max's response.

Max grinned. 'I know. I saw him when I came in – he's one of the PR goffers for a French cigarette company. They've tried to sponsor us before.'

'And no good?'

'They offered us pennies. I'm not interested, especially during lunch.'

The waiter came over with the main course and served two large lobsters dripping in butter. They ate silently for a few moments.

'So Max, what's your problem?' asked Julian, dabbing the butter from his lips with the heavily starched napkin.

'The first problem is the au pair girl, she's leaving tomorrow.'

'What did she do?'

'*She* did nothing. She came to me yesterday morning. "Mr Gregson. I 'ave something to tell you, you will not like. I see Mrs Gregson kissing with your groom in the stable. I don't want to stay 'ere with such things going on." '

'What?' asked Julian, astounded. He could never imagine Vicky – the sweet pure Vicky – misbehaving.

'The truth is that this groom is screwing the ass off my wife. I got it out of Maria in the end. I should have guessed it myself.'

'Have you confronted Vicky?'

'No. After all, my track record is hardly impeccable.'

'It's a bitter pill to swallow, 'specially on your own doorstep.'

'In my own stable,' corrected Max.

'I would never have imagined it of Vicky.'

'Nor me. They say trouble never comes singly.' Max sighed heavily. 'If I'm going to concentrate on my driving this year, I don't want to go away worrying if that young stud is getting his leg over.'

'Why don't you take Vicky to Rio with you?' suggested Julian.

'No, I shall resolve the problem at home before I go.'

'Get rid of the groom?'

'Yes and I shall make sure he never sets foot near my wife again.' Max gave an artful smile as he snapped his lobster claw sharply in half.

The following morning, Phil woke early in his small cottage bedroom. Judging by the darkness of the room, it was another sunless morning. He thought how different it was when the sun streamed through the curtains beckoning him out of bed. He rose sleepily, the chill of the morning stiffening his body. Reluctantly, he dressed, remembering there were a few things to do in the tack room before exercising the horses.

He descended the stairs to the kitchen, still buttoning his shirt and yawning loudly. As he filled the kettle, instinct told him he was not alone. He heard something moving on the worktop. He couldn't recall having mice in the cottage but it sounded like he had some now. He reached for a steak mallet and moved the clutter of pots to one side. What he saw made him step backwards, transfixed with fear. A long brown snake was staring at him with evil, glinting eyes. His heart thumped wildly and his legs turned to jelly as the reptile lifted itself towards him and hissed menacingly.

Phil backed away slowly, his eyes never leaving the loathsome creature. When it uncurled itself towards him, he took fright and made a dash for the door, slamming it behind him without pausing to consider how the snake had got there. At the front door his eye caught a piece of paper pushed through the letter-box. Still in a state of panic, he hurriedly unfolded it and read its contents. He made an instant decision to leave, to get out of the place. Who knew how many more snakes might be in the house?

Five minutes later, he had packed most of his things and was out of the house. His Land Rover spluttered into life. His head was spinning, his throat dry as the words written on the note reverberated in his head: 'LEAVE MY WIFE ALONE.'

Vicky, still half asleep, stirred as she heard Phil's Land Rover accelerate sharply away. She wondered where he was going so early in the morning. After breakfast, she went out to the stables for her morning ride. There was no sign of Phil and the stable doors, which were normally open, remained closed. As she came back into the kitchen Max was reading the newspaper.

'Phil hasn't fed the horses this morning. I hope he hasn't taken a trip to London again,' she said anxiously, picking up the phone. 'I'll try the cottage.'

Max looked up casually from the sports page he had been scanning. 'I wouldn't bother ringing him if I were you.'

Vicky caught his eye. Curiosity was instantly replaced by fear as she read his eyes. They bored through her like icicle tips and she shivered in response.

'Phil no longer works for us,' said Max in a steely voice. 'And he won't be coming back.'

'Why?' challenged Vicky, but inside she already knew why.

The awful truth was dawning as Max replied, 'You mean you don't know why?'

Vicky stood frozen to the spot.

Max threw the paper down and strode aggressively towards her. 'Why him, Vicky, why *him*?'

Vicky turned away. The tears coursed down her flushed cheeks. The guilt, anger and bitterness that had been hidden away for months rose up like bile in her throat.

'Why? Because I wanted to hurt you.' She turned and saw the pain in Max's shocked face. But she couldn't stop now. The floodgates had opened. 'All your womanizing, your affairs. It was my way of getting back at you. What do you think I am? Some sort of insensitive robot that only comes alive when you press the right button? I *need* love too, in case you'd forgotten!'

'We could have *talked* about it. There was no need to go and screw the bloody groom.'

'And what was so different between him and all your bimbos?' Vicky shrieked.

'Don't point the finger of accusation at me. You're the one who's been having it away in my house!'

'That's a lie.' Vicky spat out the words. She sobbed and wiped away her tears. 'Where is he?' she asked quietly.

'He's gone. He's gone for good and don't ever think about seeing him again.' As he spoke, Max noted with a glimmer of satisfaction the hopelessness that swept over Vicky's face.

'You're a bastard, Max.' As Vicky ran out of the room, her remorse gave way to self-pity as she realized that not only had she lost Phil, she had also been found out by her husband, and that was not an easy thing to live with.

# 17

By nine-thirty in the morning, the beaches of Copacabana and Ipanema were already crowded with beautiful women, eager to begin another day of sun worship. It was Thursday, three days before the Brazilian Grand Prix, and out at the Jacarepagua circuit the stands were almost as full, even at that hour, with disciples of another cult – motor racing. For the fifty thousand-strong crowd which had flocked to the circuit to watch the practice sessions, it was an annual pilgrimage that only death or something close to it could prevent. In South America, Formula One was the next best thing to a religion and although Mario was an Argentinian, he was, nevertheless, the crowd's new hero and they had come to pay him homage.

In the garage that housed the two Delta cars, mechanics were busy fastening on the chassis and the huddle of activity around the rear of the car signified last-minute preparations were being made. The walls of the garage were white-washed and the concrete floor was spotlessly clean. A work bench down one wall was clear except for a fire extinguisher, a spray can of polish for the chassis and Mario's helmet. Underneath the bench were rows of narrow drawers holding a multitude of tools as clean and neatly arranged as a surgeon's instruments. Several pairs of ear defenders, a necessary part of a mechanic's equipment when the engines were revving high, hung on the wall above. At the rear stood large drums of fuel, stainless steel boxes holding spares, a tall gas bottle for the air-pressure starter and a set of exhaust systems. Along the other wall, resembling the desks of an airport control tower were banked an array of computer screens, their green print indecipherable to anyone save the specialists, whose job it was to translate the facts and figures that the machines would shortly be relaying from both cars. Motor racing was now about as dependent on technology as the average space mission. The effluvium of oil and fuel hung in the air, even though one side of the garage was open to the pit lane. Here photographers, journalists and notables of the sport had gathered to watch the team at work. Dick Chance stood chatting to one of Delta's race engineers.

'Any driver who gets in the way of Mario is going to get lynched,' he remarked, watching the sea of faces in the packed grandstand opposite.

At that moment, Mario appeared in the pits. His car was ready to be wheeled out for its first excursion of the day. The crowd erupted. A deafening cheer, along with frantic waving of the Argentinian and Brazilian flags, signalled that the waiting masses had finally glimpsed their idol.

Meanwhile Colin, business-like with clipboard and headphones round his neck, materialized.

'Where the hell is Max?' he snapped. 'We're off in two minutes and he still hasn't shown up.'

Already in a high state of anxiety, Colin would remain so until the end of the race on Sunday evening. Until then, there was the usual two days of practice, enabling the mechanics and engineers to make final adjustments to the cars, and the drivers to qualify for their grid positions.

Colin spotted Max surrounded by photographers and accompanied by a stunning Brazilian girl. She was wearing skin-tight silk shorts of bright purple, cut high above her thighs and leaving the two perfectly formed cheeks of her backside protruding below. A cutaway T-shirt barely covering her full breasts left exposed an expanse of tanned midriff, and her long bronzed legs were shapely and as finely muscled as those of a dancer.

Max strolled into the garage. The mechanics, temporarily mesmerized by the vision of beauty that had entered their sterile work place, stared unabashed. She gave them a brazenly seductive smile and flashed a pair of sultry eyes that only further entranced the male onlookers. All, that is, except Colin. Hiding his annoyance, he glanced anxiously at his watch.

'OK, we're ready to go.' As if on cue, a Ferrari engine in the garage next door screamed into life, then another, indicating that the serious business of the day was about to commence. The quiet was shattered as the engines competed with the excited cheers of the crowd in a cacophony which would remain constant for the next hour and a half. The mechanics, now oblivious to the temporary distraction of the girl, wore solemn, intent expressions, as they concentrated on the job at hand.

Max, unrecognizable in helmet and overalls, slid into the tightly fitting seat of his car and was strapped into his harness. Raising the index finger of his gloved right hand, he gave the signal for the mechanics to start the car and as the engine roared into life, the old familiar urge returned to him. His body tingled with a thrill of expectancy as he waited to go. He wanted to drive the perfect lap, to learn every braking point, to find the fastest line round every corner. Despite the heat and the discomfort of the cramped cockpit, he concentrated his mind on the task ahead.

Mario, too, was more than ready for his first initiation in qualifying with his new team. He was intent on performing as well as any of his ambitious and ruthless competitors.

As the chequered flag signalled the end of the morning practice session, an air of almost tangible peace settled over the pit lane as the cars cruised in and were pushed silently back into their garages. The mechanics took a short sandwich break before recommencing work in the blasting, sultry heat.

The Delta race engineers, together with Jean, Colin and both drivers, conducted the usual debriefing session in the air-conditioned motor home. Colin was well satisfied and confident that the cars would set a good time that afternoon. It was these times that would count towards the grid positions and it was vital that the cars were running smoothly.

At the other end of the motor home, Dick was entertaining two of their newest American sponsors. Casually sipping cans of Michelob, they appeared overwhelmed at the sophisticated techniques used in the racing. 'And ya mean to say that these computers can read off oil pressure, fuel consumption and all that kinda stuff?' asked the heavily built New Yorker.

'Yes, the information is relayed from the car to the pits and then back to the driver via a radio transmitter,' replied Dick.

'That's real neat,' commented the other equally thick-set American. 'And what goes on tomorrow? The same as today?'

Dick nodded. 'An untimed session in the morning and then the final timed session in the afternoon. Their times are worked out to one thousandth of a second, so you can understand how crucial it is.'

Dick was surprised to see he had a captive audience. In America, Formula One racing does not have the kudos it does in other parts of the world. He looked across and saw Max getting up. The debrief had finished. He could see by the faces of the two Americans that they were eager to meet the World Champion.

'Let me introduce you to Max Gregson.'

Max, hearing his name mentioned, looked across and came over.

'Max, meet two of our sponsors from Western Oil. Chuck Goldstein and Dan King . . . this is our number one driver.'

'Hi, nice to meet you, Mr Gregson,' they replied, standing up and towering over him. They shook his hand effusively.

'Is this your first time at a grand prix?'

'Sure is, Max, and we're finding it pretty exciting stuff. Isn't that right, Chuck?'

Chuck nodded. It was the first time he had met a racing driver in the Formula One class. The fact he was the World Champion made it even more of an honour.

'I haven't been so excited since I went to my first baseball game,' he chuckled, hitching up his leather belt on to an expanse of waistline in proportion with the rest of his gargantuan frame.

'The exciting part is still to come,' Max said. 'Wait till Sunday. You're staying for the race, aren't you?'

They wouldn't miss it for anything, they assured him. Max excused himself to go and get something more to drink. Driving in such sweltering heat always made the risk of dehydration acute. The temperature in the cockpit often reached a hundred and thirty degrees Fahrenheit.

At one o'clock precisely the first car roared out of the pits followed by another, then another. The pit lane wall saw huddles of personnel sheltering from the exhausting afternoon sun under wide parasols – their various uniforms, like the cars, reflecting the colours of the team's main sponsor. There was the cool blue of Osella, the canary yellow of Renault, the familiar red of Ferrari, the emerald green of the Gordon team. And so on. It made a dazzling display of iridescent colour under the sharp luminosity of blue sky.

The Delta team was distinctive in Miami blue trousers and cool crisp shirts of pale yellow cotton. The dozen or so mechanics waiting attentively in the pit lane were more practically dressed, wearing shorts of the same blue and matching trainers. On the pit wall clusters of portable computers and the Longines timing monitors were ready to blip out their facts and figures. Headphones were donned to cut off the high-pitched scream of the cars as they flew by just a few feet away.

Dick, along with the two race engineers, raised a congratulatory smile as Mario and Max finished the session barely half a second behind the Ferraris. If they could maintain these times tomorrow, they would be sitting on the second row of the grid for the race. It was an encouraging start to the season, or so Dick thought. Colin obviously disagreed.

As the hooter sounded the return of the cars to the pits, his face was set in a grim frown, reflecting disappointment. His astute eyes, barely visible from squinting in the bright sunshine, scowled at the tall Brazilian beauty waiting in the pit lane, as if she were responsible for Max not setting the fastest time. He expected the best from his drivers and only the best would do. All Max needed was to squeeze the last half second from the car and he would be on pole position. He conjectured how much of Max's concentration was on his driving and how much on other distractions close at hand.

Mario, however, had driven remarkably well, bearing in mind the wide gap in experience between the two drivers. Colin caught Mario's satisfied smile as he removed his helmet. He smiled back. Mario had been thrilled at the performance of the car, and his lap times, so close to Max's, showed that he was now establishing himself as a worthy competitor to his rival. The support of the fifty thousand crowd had given him a new wave of confidence and he threw his arms in the air in a gesture of pure joy as the mechanics and fans congratulated him.

# 18

That night, the music in the crowded restaurant temporarily excluded any conversation as the three guitarists playing a samba hit a crescendo. The locals were indulging in two of their greatest loves: music and food. The waiters bustled around, heavily aproned, carrying platters of steaks and lamb kebabs, which they presented on long swords with a great flourish.

Colin was in no mood for merriment. He had gone there on Max's recommendation and then Max had failed to turn up. Colin would have much preferred a restaurant without loud background music. To his further annoyance, Mario had entered into the spirit of the Brazilians' roistering and had burst into full song, much to the delight of the other diners who stood up and clapped along with him.

Colin's eyes narrowed. Why did Mario have to draw attention to himself like that? Jealousy flooded through him as he became more and more tormented at the thought of having to share Mario's company. Then, a Brazilian girl as fresh and as pretty as apple blossom appeared at their table dressed in a simple white dress that offset her long black hair swept back in a ribbon. Even Colin was stunned by her beauty. Grabbing Mario by both hands, the girl pulled him out of his chair and began writhing her hips in time to the beat of the music, never taking her eyes off her partner. Colin felt a sting of pure hatred for this intrusive female who had so blatantly captured Mario's attention.

The musicians played louder, and Mario found himself enjoying the impromptu party. After the tensions of the day's driving, it was a relief to be laughing and singing with this happy group of people. Lifting his companion on to an empty chair he joined in the chorus of the song, his eyes sparkling with merriment. It was only when he sat down at the table, laughing and joking with his pretty companion, that he realized the empty chair she had taken was Colin's.

Up on the twenty-third floor of the Intercontinental Hotel a cocktail party was in full swing, as the wealthy and influential of Rio mingled with the élite of the motor-racing world. Max, dressed in a loosely cut, pale grey suit, looked every inch the famous and successful racing driver. He had been caught by the wife of a government minister and was yet again extricating himself from more Brazilian hospitality. 'I would love to have dinner with you and your husband,' he replied smoothly, 'but unfortunately I leave for London the evening of the race.'

Max was not sure when he was leaving Rio but he never believed in committing himself during a race weekend.

'It is such a shame. We are entertaining a group on our yacht. We would love to have you join us,' Ana Torrens was enthusing in her heavy Brazilian accent.

Max was trying to put an age on the attractive and well-preserved woman standing elegantly beside him. Her neck showed the tell-tale signs that she was over forty, but her figure was that of a much younger person. As if reading his thoughts, she smiled knowingly at him. 'You like what you see? We have the best cosmetic surgeons in the world here. After thirty-five it is *de rigueur* to have the eyes and bosoms done.'

Max smiled, admiring her honesty and embarrassed that his thoughts must have appeared so transparent.

'One of them is over there, Dr Antonio Negri,' she cooed, nodding her perfectly upswept chignon in the direction of a tall, distinguished man. 'Most women in this room owe their figures to him. It must be wonderful to have such talent. Rather like your own, Mr Gregson.' Her eyes flashed an appreciative smile.

Max looked out through the large windows to the dazzling panoramic view of the coastline lit up in a swathe of fairy lights. It was then he caught the reflection of an exquisite face. As he turned he saw that the face belonged to a shapely body and long legs that even the famous Dr Negri could not have improved on. Max made his excuses and went in search of another drink. As he spotted a waiter, he felt a hand gently touch his arm and he turned to find the tantalizing beauty standing beside him.

'Max Gregson? My name is Sylvia Bochira,' she purred. She was tall, elegant and in her late twenties. Wearing a short dress of cream silk which accentuated her long thighs and mane of dark hair, she held out a long and carefully manicured hand and Max caught a seductive whiff of her perfume.

He returned the handshake, and taken aback at the suddenness of the introduction asked, 'Are you with someone connected with motor racing?'

She threw back her head and laughed. Her eyes shone like fireflies caught in the moonlight. Max felt a ripple of excitement run through him. 'I am sorry to laugh. It is rude of me. I am here purely as part of my job.'

'And what is that?' asked Max, eager to know more about her.

'Tonight I represent my country. I am Miss Brazil.'

'If you know nothing about motor racing, then how come you recognize me?'

Sylvia hesitated for a moment and then with a smile that made Max think of a large bed and cool silk sheets, she replied in halting English, 'I have read about this English driver and I see for myself you are as good looking as your photographs. It is nice to meet you.'

'Thank you,' said Max, touched at her directness. If the custom in Brazil was for the women to chat up the men, she wasn't making a bad job of it.

The room was now emptying as groups sauntered off to go to various dinner parties. Max was due to join the rest of the team at the restaurant, but he had other ideas.

'Shall we go and have dinner somewhere?'

'What about your drive tomorrow? I have heard the drivers go to sleep early.' Her eyes were wide with curiosity, at the same time her voice held a hint of mock seriousness.

'Brazilian drivers might need all the sleep they can get, I also like to relax. Let's go and find somewhere to eat.'

'That's fine. I have my driver outside.'

An hour later, they were enjoying dinner in the elegant restaurant of one of Rio's top hotels. Max listened as Sylvia explained how she had been chosen to represent her country. Her eyes danced in the half light and her full, red lips moved sensuously. Max found himself concentrating on her far more than on the tempting dishes placed before him. In fact, he hardly noticed what he was eating. As the waiters cleared away their main course, Max made a discreet point of looking at his watch. 'How about some dessert?' he asked.

Sylvia shook her head and Max noticed the way her curls shimmered about her face.

'Coffee?'

'I think it is getting late for you?' She tilted her head provocatively. Her large flirtatious eyes were testing him. He could either go along with her suggestion and retire early or . . . the temptation was too great. He knew that if he went back to his hotel he would never settle down. Sylvia had given him a sex urge that was far too strong to sleep on.

'Yes, you're right. It is getting late. Do you mind if we skip the coffee?' he suggested.

'Sure. You know, it is a great pity you have to work tomorrow. At midnight, Rio becomes alive. We could have so much fun.'

Max could well believe that. As they drove back to the hotel in Sylvia's limo, the streets were teeming with chic young couples and Brazilian girls.

'You see, at night the girls look for fun. They go out dancing, partying and meet young men. Maybe they sleep with them.'

'So, it's true the Brazilian girls enjoy sex like the sunshine?'

'It is part of having fun in life, don't you think?'

She turned to him and her silky hair brushed against Max's face. She drew close and her warm lips touched his, then she locked Max in an embrace that sent uncontrollable urges through him. Her hand slipped between his legs feeling the hardness through his trousers. Her fingers lingered there lightly before moving up his body. They kissed slowly, each enjoying the other's response. Max reached for her breasts, slipping them easily out of her dress, kissing the firm sun-darkened nipples. The driver of the limo kept his eyes ahead, concentrating on his driving. He had seen it all before.

As they pulled up outside the hotel they slipped out of the car, Max straightening his tie and Sylvia smoothing her hands down her tight dress. Max took her arm and led her quickly across the lobby. He was in no mood to meet anyone.

Once inside the lift, they embraced again; Sylvia's thighs pressed against his, as his hands explored her body. In the bedroom, they undressed each other slowly. Max marvelled at her glistening skin, the colour of burnished chestnut, at her full breasts and narrow hips and her supple, long thighs and slim ankles, each adorned with a gold chain. Even her feet, which Max had never reckoned to be the sexiest part of a woman's anatomy, were beautifully shaped with long painted toe nails. She had a litheness and grace about her that Max, seeing her naked for the first time, was almost afraid to touch.

Max sat and watched, mesmerized, as she moved slowly and provocatively towards him like a panther totally aware of its physical perfection. Fixing his eyes with a look that forbade him to move, she knelt down, exploring his body with her tongue, as Max shuddered and ran his fingers through the wild profusion of her hair. Then it was his turn.

He reached for her, gently pulling her by the arms until she was on top of him on the bed. He penetrated her quickly and as she straddled him and moved above him, her head thrown back in primitive abandon, he could feel her long sharp nails running up and down his body and scoring the sides of his buttocks. His senses were alive and electric. For a moment he thought of Vicky and how little pleasure they had brought to each other over the past year. Was it not possible to rekindle this kind of joy with someone familiar? Then his mind shut off and he gave himself totally to Sylvia. They made love slowly, erotically. Max was in a blinding ecstasy that was a coming together of Sylvia's beauty, the freedom with which she gave herself to him and his own blissful arousal. Her perfume hung in the air, her hair and fingers tantalized his skin, now wet with perspiration as they moved rhythmically together. Finally, Max felt his tormented body succumb to a release which seemed to drain the very deepest part of his soul.

# 19

Saturday, the last practice day before the race, passed uneventfully. Max gave no hint as to his previous night's exploits. Colin, however, was left with his suspicions when Max fell asleep after lunch and had to be woken for final practice.

After a tough battle with Ferrari, Max and Mario secured third and fourth positions on the grid. The new Ferrari design was going to prove difficult to beat. Nevertheless, Colin's dissatisfaction with his number one driver was even more apparent than on the previous day.

Max left the circuit as soon as debriefing had finished and hotfooted it back to the hotel to shower and change for Sylvia's arrival. He was enjoying a cold beer when her knock came at the door. He answered it to find her dressed in a white bandeau, skin-tight black pants and not much else.

'Good evening,' he said smiling. He kissed her immaculately painted lips and as he did so, removed the beautiful orange orchid from her hair.

Most of the teams were attending a pre-dinner cocktail party that evening laid on by the Brazilian sponsors. Mario was standing quietly with a group of people.

'What's up with you tonight?' asked Colin as soon as they were on their own.

'I'm OK,' Mario answered abruptly.

'It certainly doesn't appear that way. You've hardly said a word all evening.'

'I'm all right, I tell you.'

'Would you rather skip dinner tonight with the others? We could go and have a quiet meal somewhere else.'

'Colin, will you stop making a big fuss like this. You worry too much. People will begin to notice.'

At that moment Dick breezed over. 'Colin, there's a guy downstairs from *Race* magazine who wants to interview Max. I can't find him. The guy's been here since six. Could we use Mario instead? It looks like it's going to be major coverage.'

'Where the hell is Max?' Colin demanded sharply. 'Mario. Would you do the interview?'

'For sure.' Mario would gladly step in for Max and have the publicity. He was also glad to get away from Colin's questions. They went down to reception where a weary-looking journalist was paying the waiter for his third coke. Colin apologized for Max's absence and then walked over to one of the house phones. He dialled Max's number.

Max and Sylvia were locked in passionate lovemaking on the edge of the bath when the phone rang. Better answer it this time, Max thought. Christ, it's eight already. Two hours of frolicking with Sylvia had passed far too quickly.

'Where the hell are you?' snapped Colin.

'In room 1315.' Max couldn't help irritating Colin further.

'I know that, for Chrissakes. Why aren't you down here for your interview with Dan Hanson, from *Race* magazine.'

Damn. Max had forgotten all about it. He was getting good money for this. 'Tell the guy I'll be down in five minutes.'

'Too late. Mario's agreed to do it instead.' Colin hung up.

Max put the phone down and watched as Sylvia massaged oil into her naked body. He was angry with himself for missing the appointment. He could easily make up some excuse for Colin's benefit, but he realized it was time to sort his life out. He couldn't allow this slackness to spill over into his driving. Otherwise he could be a dead man.

The next morning, Max began his usual ritual to concentrate his mind on the race ahead. He threw a towel on the floor and went through his routine of press-ups and stretching exercises to loosen his muscles. Then he pulled on the same red underwear he had worn when he won his first Formula One race. Although frayed around the edges now, he would never have dreamt of wearing anything else. Then came a pair of red socks. He would leave the fireproof clothing until the final change at the track. Dressed in jeans, T-shirt and trainers, Max emerged from the hotel after breakfast to drive to the circuit with Dick. Tactful as ever, Dick had not mentioned the problems of the night before.

The bright sunshine that had shone without interruption for the last few days was missing. Instead sultry, grey skies hung over the mountains, adding to the stickiness and humidity. At the Jacarepagua track it was hot and uncomfortable. The race was going to be gruelling, and both Delta drivers stayed in the comfort of the air-conditioned motor home for as long as possible.

The vast crowd was in a carnival spirit as the cars paraded on their warm-up laps, cheering and screaming in a frenzy of excitement.

Dan Hanson, still bitter over Max's failure to show up the previous night, strolled down the pit lane, admiring the scantily clad Brazilian girls. He consoled himself that he'd got a good interview with the young Argentinian, but it wasn't the same as the World Champion. He decided to visit the Ferrari camp and see what was new there. He bumped into Alex Cordoni, their team manager, on his way to the motor home after the warm-up laps.

'Hi, Dan. Heard any good stories lately?' Alex asked briskly.

Dan stepped in with Alex's fast walking pace. 'Not really, but congratulations on yesterday's timings.'

'First and second on the grid? It's great, isn't it? Just what we want.'

They made their way through the bustle of people, past the expensive and luxurious motor homes lined up behind the garages, until they came to the one painted in the eye-catching red of the Ferrari team. Under the colourful awning where only the selected few were allowed to sit and relax, a buffet lunch was being served. Terri Dacco, one of the drivers, was sitting deep in conversation with the team's designer.

'I guess it's an interview with Terri you really want. Come and have a drink. We'll grab him when he's finished with Mauro.'

They each helped themselves to a can of Coca Cola and sat down at one of the tables gaily decorated in red cloth and fresh flowers.

'Well, Dan, what's the latest gossip on the circuit? You know we don't have time to keep up with it all.'

'You know what I think?' said Dan, one of the most respected journalists in the sport. 'Delta is going to have trouble with their number one driver if he doesn't pull himself together.'

'How come?'

'It seems that Max Gregson's drinking far more than is good for him. Plus, he's too busy screwing to give interviews on the eve of the race. Now that's not going to do a lot for his driving, is it?'

'Tell me more.' Alex was more than keen to hear about any problems in his rival's camp.

'Fact one,' Dan leaned forward, not wanting to be overheard, 'Friday night at the sponsor's cocktail party he was drinking and I don't mean just one glass of champagne. He knocked back four, just in the twenty minutes I was there.'

'Are you keeping tabs on all the drivers when you go to these parties?' asked Alex half seriously.

'No, just Gregson. Someone not a million miles from his circle told me he was hitting the booze just lately, so I thought I would check it out for myself.'

'OK, so the guy has a couple of glasses of champagne. Max has the constitution of a horse. In fact, he probably drives better after a glass.'

'Last night I had arranged to interview him. A thousand bucks it was costing us. The guy never showed up. Mario came down instead. So what keeps a guy away from a thousand bucks for one half-hour of his time? I hung around in the bar having a drink with the Renault guys. It was late, around midnight, and who gets out of the lift with one real sexy bird?'

Alex laughed. 'Gregson? You mean Wonder Boy was at it the night before the race? Colin would throw a mega tantrum if he knew. I never did think Max was the type to be tucked up in his bed by eight o'clock with his book of bedtime stories, but phew, screwing is a bit heavy, especially here. You know as well as I do that this is one of the most demanding races of the season. The heat wears me out just getting up in the morning.'

'Then I guess your chaps will stand a good chance against him,' said Dan, finishing his drink. He stood up, noticing Terri was free. 'And now, do I have your permission to find out what your boys have been up to?'

'Nothing more than tucking into bowls of spaghetti, I can assure you,' said Alex with a loud chuckle.

Colin looked up at the grey threatening skies, his eyes twitching nervously. The tension on the grid where the cars were lined up before the start was unbearable. Colin busied himself, talking to the drivers in their cockpits, hoping desperately that nothing would go wrong at the last minute. The mechanics were now making the final adjustments to the cars. The blue and yellow outer shell, or monocoque, of Max's car was lowered ceremoniously over him, like some mystical ritual. It was then screwed into position. Max sat strapped in his seat, staring straight ahead while people busied themselves around him.

He cursed the uncomfortable humidity of the weather. At least the cloud had lowered the temperature by a few degrees. There were no scorching, penetrating rays of sun, just an airless stickiness everywhere. It was exhausting, oppressive. Max tried to ignore the dull heaviness of his body, instead concentrating on the two Ferraris ahead. They posed the greatest threat to him if he was to be on the podium after the long enduring race.

The cars revved up deafeningly. A hundred thousand Brazilians replied with a roar as loud as the cars themselves. The stands became a sea of yellow and green flags as they chanted their battle cry. The cry for Rodriguez went up. Mario was the undisputed hero of the race.

Mario could feel the sweat making his balaclava stick to his forehead. His engine behind screamed like a wild animal waiting to be let loose from captivity. The light turned to green.

The twenty-six cars accelerated off the grid, hurtling towards the first bend. Mario could see the blue and yellow flash of Max's car as they headed for the first corner side by side. The two drivers were closing in on the Ferraris. Max, on the inside of Mario and coming out of the corner faster, accelerated away. Behind Mario a swarm of cars was hard on his heels.

With his foot flat on the accelerator he glanced at the speedometer: 130 miles an hour. Then changing smoothly and swiftly from sixth to fifth, to fourth and third gear and with suicidal late braking, Mario went into the next bend and out again on to the long straight.

But as the race progressed Mario could see Max slipping away from him. Approaching the long straight on lap forty, the crowds gesticulated with typical Latin fervour. He had to do it for them . . .

Pressing his foot hard on the accelerator, hurtling the car round the corners, flashing through the gears at lightning speed, slamming on brakes at the last millisecond, he gave everything he could. He was hounding Max now and slowly, slowly catching him on every lap.

But the Ferraris remained in a strong lead and soon they were overlapping backmarkers. It was then that Max was held up by one of the Arrows he was trying to lap. The slower driver was making no effort to let him through. Mario was now right on Max's tail, with the Renault and Lotus bunching up behind.

At the next bend, Mario left braking a fraction of a second later than Max. Then he was alongside him and in a good inside position. But would Max close in on him, forcing him to brake dangerously hard? Mario saw Max's wheels inches away from his own. He was almost touching the kerb on the other side of him. He was committed, but Max stayed his course. Mario squeezed through and a swift glance in his wing mirrors showed that Max was securely behind him.

The crowds erupted deliriously. Mario felt their energy. It gave him a reassurance he had not experienced before. For the first time in his career he was part of a strong team and had the opportunity to drive one of the most competitive cars. And then there was Colin. He mustn't let him down. Mario held his position ahead of Max, but with fifteen laps to go still hadn't made an impression on the Ferraris.

His heart sank as he glimpsed the first drops of rain on his visor. It was only a slight drizzle, but enough to make the track slippery and extremely hazardous. Most of the cars had already completed a stop to change tyres at half distance, but Mario's had stayed good. Now with the wet conditions, the obvious move would be to pit stop for rain tyres with a heavy tread. Terri Dacco, the leader by some ten seconds, was already in. Outside the Delta pit wall a mechanic was holding up a sign, PIT STOP. They were wanting Mario to do the same.

Curse the rain, thought Mario. The track now had a soft, wet sheen and the driving was becoming difficult and slower. Ahead of him, the second-placed Ferrari spun off at a bend before crashing heavily into an armco barrier. The car disintegrated as it came to rest and smoke poured from the engine as the marshals rushed over to help the driver. Mario should have taken heed of his team's advice, but now he was in second position with ten laps to go. Max was closing in on him again. More experienced in wet conditions, Max was nurturing the car carefully but still at maximum pace. Mario was desperate to keep his second place. If he went in now he would surely lose it.

But the other cars on fresh tyres were also catching him.

Mario felt the car slide as he braked for a sharp bend. It fell away and only by instant correction of the wheel did the car respond and keep its course. Concentrate, concentrate. The words resounded in Mario's head. In his mirrors he could see Max only feet behind him. The World Champion was just waiting for him to make a mistake. Five laps to go. The Brazilians were screaming, 'RODRIGUEZ! RODRIGUEZ!'

On the long straight Mario's eyes flashed to the mirrors as Max edged out to overtake. Mario put his foot hard on the accelerator, willing every ounce of power from his engine. Once into the bend, Max tucked in behind him. Mario had held him off. Around each potentially treacherous bend, Mario nursed his car. Max was now falling back and was replaced by another in his mirror, and another close behind that. Mario's teeth gritted and ground in tension. Now only two laps to go but they seemed the longest of his lifetime. Then finally, the chequered flag came into view and he was through the line.

As he drove around the track waving to the rapturous crowd, Mario's tension gave way to euphoria. He had scored his first points in his Formula One career and finished an almost unbelievable second. As he climbed out of the car, security men formed a tight net as hundreds of fans surged towards him, anxious to catch a glimpse of their young hero. Up on the podium – along with Terri Dacco who had finished first and Jean Claude of Renault, third – Mario acknowledged the crowd. Cameras from all over the world captured the ecstatic smiles of this young man who had driven such an impressive race.

Max had finished sixth and had cruised the car slowly into the pits. He made no effort to get out as his head slumped to one side. Dick and the other mechanics rushed forward to help him. Taking off his helmet and balaclava, they saw an ashen-faced Max. The team kept his condition quiet, but the rumour was soon around the track that Max Gregson had collapsed with exhaustion.

# 20

Max could hear the phone ringing, but his body would not obey the signals to answer it. He drifted in and out of a light sleep aware of every muscle in his body aching. A deep pain reverberated through his skull. On the orders of the doctor, Max had gone to bed straight after the race. Exhaustion had been diagnosed and Max was in no condition to argue. Images kept coming before him. He was back in the race and driving recklessly, taking the bends far too fast. Suddenly, a hundred yards ahead of him, he saw a figure on the track. As he got closer he saw it was a man hunched up in a grey mac. An old man. Max tried to avoid him but the brakes were ineffectual. He pumped the brake pedal. Nothing. The car maintained its speed. He woke up in a cold sweat as he felt the impact of the car hitting the body. He was drenched in a clammy moisture. He lay awake for a while, afraid to close his eyes, but slowly he was engulfed by tiredness and succumbed to sleep.

Later that evening the phone rang again. He answered it drowsily. It was Sylvia, the Brazilian sex goddess, and it was his last night before flying home. Her voice was as inviting as her suggestion. Max would be revived after a soothing massage with body oil, she would relax him, restore his energy for an exciting evening ahead . . .

Max apologized for not seeing her. Even the thought of Sylvia's sensuous touch could not rouse him from the ineluctable despair and exhaustion that had him in its grip.

In the garages, Tom O'Leary and the Delta mechanics

were packing up the cars and the spares. Weary, yet pleased with the performance of the cars, their thoughts were focused ahead to a refreshing shower and a well-earned rest. Tom was off to replenish their cold drinks from the fridge in the motor home. It was then he noticed young Geoff Jones, the newest of the mechanics to join the Delta team. Geoff had been complaining of a stomach upset and was looking very white.

'Are you all right, Geoff?' Tom called over.

Geoff pushed a lank strand of hair away from his forehead, now streaked with grease and rivulets of sweat. 'Oh, yes thanks. It's just that I'm not used to all this foreign food and heat yet.'

'Well, take it easy. Go back to the hotel and have a rest. Don't forget, we have a long flight home tonight.' Tom was worried by the boy's pallor. If he was taken bad they would have to leave him here.

Geoff laughed nervously, as though to hide an edginess to his voice. 'Don't worry about me. A stiff brandy this evening will sort me out.'

Tom hoped that would be the case. Geoff was young and new to the job. Perhaps after a few more races he would settle down.

With meticulous care the mechanics set about packing the spares, making sure all were carefully accounted for. Everybody was so preoccupied with his own task that no-one noticed Geoff go to his holdall and slip out a brown paper package. Waiting until a quiet moment, Geoff slipped out to Mario's car, now waiting to be loaded on to a transporter. Deftly, he manipulated the package under one of the side pods. It took just a few seconds to wedge it there. In less than twenty-four hours the car and the package would be in London and hopefully would remain undisturbed until back at the factory.

Geoff felt enormous relief as he rejoined the others. Now there was only one more task left to do.

Jean Mercier's car dived in and out of the heavy traffic as he drove back to the hotel close to the Ipanema Beach. Colin, a nervous passenger at the best of times, hated every minute of it.

'These bloody dagos. Why can't they learn to drive? The mortuary must be fresh out of cold slabs the way these maniacs try and kill themselves.' He wiped away the sweat that was trickling under the rim of his sunglasses.

'You must be pleased with Mario's performance this afternoon,' said Jean, hoping that the change of subject might help relax his passenger.

'I'm very happy,' Colin enthused. 'But it's put Max's nose right out of joint.'

'And there were no specific problems with his car. It must have been an "off" day for him. Is he suffering from some sort of stomach bug he caught here?'

'There's nothing wrong with Max that a quiet life wouldn't put right. He made a few mistakes today. Something I've not seen him do for a long while. Something's troubling him. Maybe Dick can get to the bottom of it all. If not, I shall have it out with him and I won't be laying on the bedside manner either.'

For a six-million-dollar salary, Colin would not tolerate his drivers having 'off' days. He expected nothing short of perfection. Mario was on a fraction of the money, yet was already showing the dedication and talent of a more experienced driver. Colin relaxed a little at the thought that he would soon be with Mario again – in private and away from all the prying eyes.

He had consciously played down the jubilation and pride that had suffused him as he watched Mario's smiling face up on the rostrum. His joy had gone beyond that of master and protégé. Drivers could be hired and fired. Team owners could and often did change their drivers like commodities, replacing them if they thought they could do better elsewhere. There was no room for sentiment in this multi-million-dollar game of racing. Yet Colin still felt an overwhelming possessiveness for Mario. He had failed to control it in the restaurant on the previous night and now after the race, he was even more aware of its power. Colin had never felt like this about anybody before. It was a nagging but pleasurable, all-consuming torture. He determined to give Mario everything. Nothing would be sacrificed or overlooked in his quest to make Mario the new World Champion.

Mario lay on the bed, his slim bronzed body wrapped in a bath sheet. He was reliving the moment of stepping on to the rostrum in front of the thousands of adoring fans. It had been the realization of his dream. A discreet tapping at the door shook him out of his reverie. He guessed it must be Colin. He would waste no time in coming to see him.

'Come in,' he called, not bothering to move from the bed.

Colin, still dressed in the team uniform, looked drained after the long, hot day. The crowds, the noise, the tension had all taken their toll. But now alone at last with Mario, he could let his guard down. He sank down on the bed and reached out and touched Mario's chin with his finger.

'Well done, I knew you could do it,' he said gently.

Mario slapped him playfully on the arm. 'That was the best race of my life and you know something, Colin? I think we will have a brilliant season together.'

'The way you drove today . . . I don't dispute it. There's only one way for you now and that is up.'

'For sure. You know, maybe my lawyers will have to negotiate more money for this new star.' Mario chuckled, but shot a sly look at Colin. He wanted to test him, see how far he could push him. He had produced the results, so perhaps now was the time for Colin to recognize how much he was really worth. His true value must be far more than the pittance he had signed up for.

Colin stood up abruptly and turned his back on Mario, as if he had not heard his words. Then he turned and shot him a stony, dispassionate glance. 'Just remember one thing, this star is still rising, don't you forget that.'

'Hey, man, it was only a joke.'

Colin hoped it was. He hoped that Mario, against all odds, would be different from all the other drivers. Money became their obsession. He realized he paid Mario very little, but there were drivers who would have signed for less.

Sensing Colin's disquiet, Mario swung his legs over the bed. 'It's time we had something to drink to celebrate our day. Yes?' he asked lightly.

As he stepped towards the fridge, he let the bath towel drop to the floor. Colin stood, transfixed by his nakedness, catching the aroma of soap on his freshly showered body. Waves of excitement and lust engulfed him. Mario poured two glasses of champagne, taking his time while the bubbles slowly came to rest. He was aware of Colin's arousal, yet played distant with him. Mario turned and handed him his glass. 'Here's to the next time,' he said, taking a sip from his glass, his eyes never leaving Colin's. Placing his drink on the table, he made a move to the bathroom.

'Where are you going?' asked Colin in a tormented voice.

'To the bathroom, to get dressed.'

Colin felt his desire spilling over into anger and jealousy. Mario flaunted himself so casually. Why was he not filled with the same strong desires? 'Come here,' he commanded in a voice that quivered with emotion.

Two floors up in the same hotel, Alberto Scapini stretched out in his deep bath, a cigar in his mouth and a beer can at his elbow. The phone was balanced next to it. He tapped the ash of his cigar over the side and on to the carpet as he relished the feel of the cool water on his body. He wondered if there would be time before he left, for the dark Brazilian prostitute who had shared his bed the night before.

He was in particularly good spirits. First because the race weekend was over and in the next few hours he would be out of this stinking hot, noisy city and sitting in the first-class cabin of an aircraft on his way back to Italy. Second, his two drivers had finished a creditable eighth and ninth place, not at all bad, considering they had last year's engines. The new ones would not be ready until the start of the European season. Scapini had no illusions that his team could compete with the top few.

Ironically, a few years before he would have had sleepless nights worrying about the ways he could improve on the performance of his cars. He would push himself without respite to get the best from his team, the cars and the drivers. Now things were different. He hadn't lost his enthusiasm for racing, but he was taking life just a little easier. He had a good manager and a plentiful supply of funds to finance the team. Life was comfortable. Then there was his little project with Jones, the mechanic from the Delta team. His plot was working out nicely. The mechanic had taken the bait like a greedy fish to a fat maggot.

As the phone rang, his thin, pinched face screwed up into a grimace. 'Yes?'

'Mr Scapini. It's Geoff Jones here . . . ' The words were hesitant, disjointed.

'Well? Did you do it?'

'Yes, no problems as far as I can see.'

'Good. Call me when you get back to England and we can arrange the payment for you.' Scapini gave one of his rare smiles and contentment lapped around his body like the water in his bath.

'And then?'

'I shall have some more work for you, but I don't wish to discuss this over the phone. Goodbye for now, Mr Jones, and have a safe flight.'

Scapini replaced the receiver.

So, it was the first bite. He thought he might have had some difficulty persuading the mechanic to plant the drugs, but the guy was desperate for money. He had chosen the right man. So far it was plain sailing. His next job was to upset the smooth running of the Delta team. Jones might not be so amenable to that, in which case he would have to up the price, considerably if necessary.

His thoughts automatically turned to Colin Pritchard. He would soon have that smug little smile wiped off his face. His jaw tensed and he bit so hard on his cigar that the end dropped into the bath. He threw the sodden tobacco on to the carpet, remembering the time he had spent in jail. Two years was a long time out of his life and Pritchard was now about to pay dearly for those lost years.

Alberto Scapini was one of seven children and had been raised in a poor district of the city of Bologna, Italy. His father, Paulo, was wild and irascible and worked on the assembly line of a car factory. He had been caught leaving the factory with several car components and his small sideline of selling parts, and his job, had finished the same day.

Without any warning, Paulo disappeared, leaving his wife to bring up their five sons and two daughters. Three months later a short, poorly written letter had arrived from New York.

He had worked his passage on a cargo ship and found himself a job in the land of golden opportunity – America. He told his family of his empty dreams; that the job he'd found was good and that he had an apartment in a respectable part of town and soon he would be able to send for them. In reality, he worked as a kitchen hand in a large Italian restaurant in the Bronx and his living accommodation was in a squalid basement room in a run-down area. But he learnt fast that nobody was about to do him any favours in the inhospitable jungle of New York. His first week's wages had been stolen from him in a bar. He had stopped off for a drink to celebrate his first wage and had got chatting with two strangers, the first sign of friendliness he had encountered. When they left, he found the thirty dollars had gone from his pocket. He began to hate the ugly, violent city, but nothing would be as bad as the sickening life aboard the cargo ship. The stench was still in his nostrils. He decided he would stay put no matter how bad life was. But within a week Paulo had lost his job and was one of the hundreds living in shop doorways. Alberto Scapini never heard from his father again.

As soon as Alberto was old enough, he left school and, like his brothers, went straight to work to stave off the abject poverty that threatened the family. At twelve, he was delivering bread for a nearby baker. The few lire he earned was soon swallowed up in the massive debt his mother owed. Unexpectedly one day his boss doubled his wage. The greasy old man had suddenly developed a kinder attitude towards him, too. He smiled a lot – more of a leer, Scapini thought – but it was better than the evil expression he had met with before.

One afternoon, the young Alberto had finished work early. His boss had left an hour before, so Alberto went home to their flat. That day it had an unusual air of quiet about it. The small rooms were normally abuzz with the sounds of family life, but now it was deserted. Scapini was about to leave when a noise coming from the bedroom stopped him.

It was the noise of an animal, a low grunting. Scapini approached the door. A sudden cry made him open it. His sister was lying on the bed, her skirt around her waist, and on top of her was the body of a man with his face buried below her small stomach. She was naked except for her skirt and dusty grey ankle socks. Sophia was just thirteen. Fear and torment were etched on her young startled face when she saw her brother. Her wide eyes appealed to him helplessly.

The man had an air of familiarity about him; the greasy and unwashed grey hair, the fat crumpled body . . . With a loud cry, Alberto had dragged the old man off the bed with his trousers still around his ankles. He threw him against the wall, hitting and battering his skull, until he collapsed in a corner. A trickle of blood ran down from his mouth to his unshaven chin.

Along with his brothers, Scapini had dumped the unconscious body of the baker outside his shop. They had agreed that it was best for Alberto's own safety for him to leave the city for a while. So, carrying a small bag, he caught the first train heading south where now he would be isolated from his family and without a job. Whether it was fate or coincidence, he had followed in his father's footsteps.

In his early years away from home, he had worked in

night clubs and gambling dens and had made dubious but advantageous connections with the Mafia. But his curiosity and love of motor racing had got the better of him and at twenty he had gone to work for one of the small Italian Formula Three teams. Thirty years later, he was running a twenty-million-dollar racing team. Now his salary ran into hundreds of thousands of dollars a year and another fifty thousand was quietly disappearing into a Swiss bank account. Scapini was comfortably off, but more important, he had power. He was addicted to it, and many an innocent who had crossed him had learnt of its crushing might. There was not much happening in the motor-racing circle that he did not know about. With his huge backing of Mafia money, he was a force to be reckoned with.

He also knew he was irrevocably tied to the Mafia. If he did not obey their rules he could lose his position and perhaps his life. His tough upbringing, however, had made him shrewd in manipulating people and money. He had come up the hard way and had no intention of losing what he had fought so hard to achieve.

# 21

The day before the Delta team arrived back in England, Rachel Pritchard suggested to Vicky that they meet up for some lunch at her new health club. Rachel had just joined and was so impressed, she thought it might interest Vicky. They helped themselves to an ample buffet of salads and bowls of chopped goodness coated in a light dressing. Two glasses of wine were the only indulgence to an otherwise healthy lunch.

'You like the club?' asked Rachel, her beautiful auburn curls turning the other women envious.

'It's very impressive,' said Vicky, trying to sound enthusiastic. But she was not feeling much enthusiasm for anything at present. Her life seemed to be shrouded in dull misery since Phil had left. Remembering the fun they had had together only increased her gloom. The days were so empty without him. The fact that he had run out on her again had left her deeply hurt and angry. There had been no phone message, card or letter. Just a silence that became more difficult to bear each day. Time and time again, she wondered why he hadn't called. Did their lovemaking mean so little to him? And yet, on that last afternoon, he had seemed so happy to be with her. Or was it all a big pretence and she, a convenient pastime? Vicky concluded that Max must have frightened him off, otherwise why else would he have left so suddenly? Her already anguished mind grew more restless as she realized she had not the faintest idea where to start looking for him. If only she had taken the number of his brother in London, then at least she would have had some contact. Now, there was nothing . . .

'Any time you want to use it just let me know and you can come as my guest, unless, of course, you were thinking of joining yourself.'

'Sorry?' Vicky was startled from her thoughts.

'I was saying, any time you want to use the club . . . '

'Thanks,' said Vicky, wishing she could confide in Rachel about her plight. 'Now the racing season's started, I feel I'm a race widow again.'

'Me too,' agreed Rachel, languidly contemplating the three inches of curly endive at the end of her fork. 'It's back to all those lonely weekends . . . and nights. Colin comes back, sleeps the jet lag off for an hour or two, points me in the direction of his suitcase of dirty washing and he's off again. We barely get the chance to say hello, let alone anything else.' She gave a droll laugh. 'It's a jolly good thing I've got dear old Spender at the end of the phone.'

'Who's he?'

'You know Spender. You met him at the Christmas drinks do . . . the local landowner and lady killer of Upton Ashthorpe.'

'Aston Upthorpe,' corrected Vicky. 'I remember him now. Quite a charming character, I recall.'

'He grows on you. Do you know he comes on the pretext of delivering fresh eggs to the house at six o'clock every Saturday morning when Colin's away?'

'Really?'

'Mmm,' Rachel smiled whimsically, not wishing to divulge the details of her rampant sex life that usually commenced at two minutes past six on those mornings.

'Whatever happened to your young Italian driver?'

'Roberto? My dear, sometimes they are as bad as our husbands. Here today, racing tomorrow. There is too much of the, "I 'ave to test tomorrow, I 'ave to do my work-out this afternoon." Too many excuses and pit stops for my liking. I need a bit more stability to my life.'

'In the form of Doug Spender . . . ' Vicky couldn't help smiling, despite her sombre mood. She had known Rachel a long time now – they had been friends for more than eight years – and nothing she did surprised her. Rachel was not a woman to sit at home, pining away while her husband was off gadding about in far-flung places, nor was she the type to play second fiddle to a racing car. She was her own person and enjoyed her own set of friends and social life.

'And what about you, Vicky? You don't appear to be yourself at all. You're looking rather pale and drawn, if you don't mind me saying so.'

'I don't feel myself. I'm worn out since I . . . we lost the groom and Maria, the au pair.' She couldn't bring herself to mention Phil's name. 'I must say, I've been finding it difficult without the help.'

'You certainly can't look after three horses and that big house by yourself . . . you must get some help soon. Shall I ask Spender if he knows of anyone? By the way, why did what's his name leave anyway? Was Max getting jealous?' Rachel laughed innocently, then saw the expression on Vicky's face. 'Sorry, did I come pretty close to the truth? Well, Vicky, you know how Max is. He's fearfully protective of you. And anyway he . . . '

'Let's change the subject, shall we,' said Vicky, suddenly losing her appetite. She drew her knife and fork together as if to close the topic of conversation and dabbed at her mouth with her napkin more than necessary. 'How about a coffee or some dessert?'

But Rachel wasn't listening. Instead, she watched Vicky closely as if she had seen her for the first time that day. There she had been rambling on about her own distractions while Colin was away, but never ever wondering how Vicky was. She saw now that she was deeply unhappy about something. It was reflected in her eyes and her hollow smile. She had obviously touched a raw nerve when she mentioned the groom. She wondered if Vicky had really found a friend and lover in him and if Max had found out. She was not about to question Vicky further after her reaction. But she would find out sooner or later, when Vicky was ready to tell her. Rachel knew Vicky was a private person and she would never risk her friendship by prying further than she should.

Max returned home after the race to find an uneasy and unexpected peace with Vicky. He noticed how quiet and listless she appeared. They were not good company for each other. Max was still feeling tired and jet lagged even after three nights back in England.

They were driving Vicky's new XJS to a dinner with friends in Oxford. Vicky was wearing her latest red Chanel suit with bold brass buttons. Her hair was elegantly tied back with a large black velvet bow which showed off a pair of sparkling diamond earrings.

'You look very elegant tonight,' Max commented as he cast a glance towards her, despite reaching speeds of eighty miles an hour down the country roads.

'Thanks, Max,' Vicky caught his handsome profile as the dusk faded into darkness. He was tanned and Vicky could smell the rich piquancy of his aftershave. She was aware how attractive and strong he was. He had a physical presence that she had never known in anybody else. Nothing had ever beaten him and she had always admired his toughness of spirit. Unexpectedly, Max reached over and touched her hand. It was just a slight squeeze of pressure, but it was enough to tell Vicky that Max felt close to her tonight. They had made love after lunch and a few glasses of wine. Some of the old fire had been rekindled and Max had been very gentle and loving, almost as if forgiving her, Vicky thought.

Since he had returned home he had hardly left the house but had been happy to laze around with Sophie and the dogs. Neither had broached the subject of Phil's disappearance or of a replacement for him, but a new au pair was due to arrive tomorrow, a young Swedish girl. This time the choice had been left to Max. The previous one, Vicky's moody Italian, had done nothing to ingratiate herself to him.

The shock of discovering Vicky's unfaithfulness had affected Max deeply. Now back at home, his thoughts were far more preoccupied with their life together than with seeing Kelly again. Disappointment and fear that his marriage could be in jeopardy were jostling about in his mind. For the first time, he realized just how much his racing depended on having a secure home life. Divorce and racing were not compatible. He tried to imagine life without Vicky and Sophie. It was a cold, bitter feeling that ran through him like an icy wind. He chose not to dwell on it. Old insecurities came flooding back to him.

He remembered the nightmares that disturbed his sleep as a young boy: waking up and creeping to his parents' bedroom to find his mother's side cold and empty; having to accept the harsh fact that she was never coming home again after she had left with her younger man. Max had remained with his father, now lonely and distraught and made seemingly helpless by the departure of his strong, resourceful wife. Max had endured those difficult years without his mother. It had made him tough and resilient, but it had also left him deeply marked. He had witnessed how a woman could break a man's spirit. The one he had loved most had broken his heart and he would make sure that that would never happen again.

'I've been thinking,' said Max as they approached the brightly lit streets of the city. 'How would you like to come to California with me for the Grand Prix in two weeks' time?'

Vicky considered for a minute. Her mind raced back to all the good times they had spent in Los Angeles after the races at Long Beach. The warmer climate was appealing too.

'Yes, why not? Sophie will have settled in with the new au pair by then and Mrs Weeks can come in daily to see that she's all right.'

Mrs Weeks had been the district nurse who had helped Vicky after Sophie's birth. She was now an old friend of the family and especially popular with Sophie.

'Good. I'll ask Dick to fix up a ticket with the airline tomorrow. By the way, we're staying on the *Queen Mary* this year.'

Vicky smiled in approval. The majestic ship, now a hotel, would be a pleasant change from the normal run of hotels. It was almost a year since she had been to a race and it would give her the chance to meet up with old friends. She would have time to forget the disturbance in her home life and it would be a change from the horse rides in the forest which had become so routine of late.

Max was pleased too. It would do his image some good to be seen with his wife rather than give the journalists the ammunition they were looking for. A week of playing the dutiful husband would not only dispel any rumours about his marriage faltering, it would also appease Colin who was becoming irritated by his off-track activities.

## 22

The Californian weather was pleasant for the end of March. The sun had burnt through the haze along the coastline at Long Beach, adding a dazzling burst of colour to the scene. The palm trees were vibrantly green against an ultramarine sky, and as Vicky stood in the pits she was aware how strongly it contrasted with the anaemic colours of the English winter she had left behind. She looked cool and distinctive in her pink shirt and fuchsia coloured cotton trousers which complemented her pale blonde hair casually swept back in a pony tail. Her only accessories were the pit pass around her neck and a pair of Ray Ban sunglasses.

She watched as Max stepped into the car for the last practice session before the race on the following day. Even though she did not share the blinding obsession of the racing fraternity, she could still experience the thrill of anticipation and excitement as the drivers set off to try and improve on their times.

This, like the start of the race, was one of the moments of high tension, the time when the eyes of all the race engineers and team managers were glued anxiously to the monitors, hoping for an extra tenth of a second to be knocked off a lap time which might bring their drivers up with the front runners.

Not much had changed, she decided. Colin was still barking orders like a drill sergeant, dancing attendance on the cars and drivers, as nervous as an expectant father. Dick, the antithesis of Colin, was calm and reassuring as always, sorting out any problems in his cool, unflappable way. Hardly any of the faces had changed in the team and they all gave her a warm welcome. And yet there was something different. What was it about Colin?

It was when Mario Rodriguez appeared, handsome and fresh faced, that she had first noticed the glint in Colin's eye as they talked to each other. She had been introduced to Mario the day before and she had immediately been aware of his shyness with women as he shook her hand and fiddled nervously with his ear plugs. His bright alert eyes reminded her of a young deer. He seemed too young to be risking his life in those unforgiving machines.

Vicky wished him good luck as he pulled on his balaclava and helmet ready for practice. After his surprise second place in Rio, everybody was now watching him with great interest, and there were a few team owners who were kicking themselves that they had not had the foresight to recognize his talent and sign him on for the bargain price that Colin had negotiated.

After completing his last practice lap, during which he had clocked the third fastest time, Max sat on one of the large boxes in the garage reflecting on the race ahead tomorrow. He felt comfortably at home, surrounded by all the familiar accoutrements of the racing world: the stacks of tyres all carefully labelled; the array of tools; the smell of hot rubber, of fuel, grease and cooling engines; the staccato sound of the air pressure gun changing a tyre; the last whining gasp of an engine coming in from practice, followed by the sudden quiet. This was as much a part of Max's life as getting up in the morning and he belonged here. The garage was now filling up with team personnel and pass-holders coming to view the post-practice activity.

'Hi, Max.' The gentle voice of a female came from behind. Max spun round and instantly found himself staring into Kelly's eyes. She looked marvellous. The tightest pair of white trousers hugged her slim hips and this, along with a white T-shirt, showed off her tan. There was heavy gold jewellery on on her wrists and neck. She looked every inch a model, with her classic good looks and thick blonde hair falling about her shoulders.

'Kelly, what brings you here?' He stood and kissed her on both cheeks.

'I'm doing some work in Los Angeles for two weeks, so I thought I would give the race a look.'

It was six weeks since he had seen her, and they had spoken only a couple of times on the phone. Seeing her now made him realize how much he had missed her.

'How are things with you?' asked Max, thinking of a dozen questions he would like to ask but not knowing where to start.

'Fine, I have plenty of work right now.'

'And admirers, I shouldn't wonder,' said Max, seeing a tall bronzed Californian hovering awkwardly in the background. He exchanged a suspicious look with Max.

'That's Bill, a photographer here. Perhaps I can introduce you later?'

'Perhaps,' said Max unenthusiastically. 'Are you going to be around after the race tomorrow?'

Kelly nodded. 'I see your wife is here.'

'You've met?'

'Not as such. We were in the pits together this morning. Good luck for tomorrow,' she said brightly and left with her photographer in tow.

But although she appeared happy to see him, their separation had not yet healed the heartache she had suffered after his cold, detached behaviour following the miscarriage. She had known she would have to face him sooner or later, and why not here in Los Angeles, where she would be happy and relaxed amongst her group of old acquaintances? She had also met up with Julian and some friends of his.

As Kelly left, Max was left with the memory of the magic of their sexual chemistry. Seeing her again had opened up a temptation as tantalizing and as sweet as any before.

Max's thoughts were interrupted as he saw Colin approaching with a delegation of Arabs. A diminutive figure in the centre was surrounded by a forbidding group of security men. The Arab wore a suit of immaculate silk, gleaming brown loafers and an impressive display of gold on his wrists and fingers. A pair of dark glasses helped cover a beaked nose and strands of hair had been carefully arranged to cover his balding pate. He was flanked on either side by two younger Arabs also wearing silk suits and ostentatious jewellery.

'Well, what have we here?' Max murmured to one of the mechanics. 'The Arabian Knights or a henchman's convention?'

The mechanics looked on amused as they busied themselves with their tools, trying hard not to notice this distinctly out-of-place group. Colin seemed decidedly ill at ease as he introduced the Arab and his two sons to the team. Max had been forewarned that this was one of their latest sponsors, Sheikh Al Rabida, who was contributing two million dollars to the team. The Arab chatted in perfect English to Max.

'What are your chances of giving us something to celebrate tomorrow evening?' the Sheikh asked when the formal introductions were over.

'Pretty good, I would say,' replied Max. 'The car is set up well. We had a few problems, but we've sorted them out.' Max was sure the Arab would not want to hear the technical details of the gear-box linkage and alternator belt. Though he felt confident about the race and was pleased with his third place on the grid, he was aware of the hard, penetrating stare of the Arab behind his glasses.

'Well, good luck, Mr Gregson. Let us hope you repeat your performance of last year and win again.'

Vicky and Max were looking forward to having dinner in the magnificent wood-panelled dining room of the *Queen Mary*. Max poured Vicky and himself a drink in their luxury stateroom, then lay on the bed contemplating a long bath.

'Oh damn, just look at this mess,' said Vicky, holding up a pearl choker with its four strands tangled.

'Here, let me do it,' said Max gently.

Vicky knelt close to him as she watched his long fingers patiently unravel the pearls.

'Thanks, darling,' she said, kissing him lightly.

Max wrapped his arms around her. 'How about a cocktail in the Observation Bar before dinner?'

'You're being terribly considerate tonight,' Vicky remarked. Normally she would have to fit in with Max's hectic schedule at the races. There was often little time for quiet drinks together.

'Am I?' he asked, surprised, wondering if perhaps Kelly's presence was contributing to this. He would have to be ultra careful now that the unthinkable had happened and both of them were here at the race. He couldn't afford to give Vicky any cause for suspicion. He was about to pull her down on to the bed with him when the phone rang.

'Max? It's Colin. Sorry to disturb you, but I've got a favour to ask.' More meetings with sponsors, thought Max; more 'quick' guest appearances at some fancy party half way across town. Max had plans for a quiet dinner and an early night and intended to keep them.

'What is it?'

'Have you heard of the American singer, Christiana?' Christiana was the latest sex siren to grace the screens of America. She had also become a bit of a rock goddess by adding singing to her many talents. Her records were being played as far away as Japan.

'Yes, I have,' said Max guardedly.

'She's putting in an appearance tomorrow. The organizers would like you to drive her round the track in a Chevrolet before the race,' continued Colin.

'Oh, lord,' Max groaned.

'Yes, I know there's enough to think about already, but they do assure me it will take literally ten minutes. You get in the car, drive slowly round the track, and that's it. She'll be one of the big attractions at the race tomorrow.' And, Colin reminded himself, he wanted her as a big attraction for the Arabs, too. They had expressly asked to meet her. After Max had driven her round the circuit, there would be plenty of opportunities to introduce them to her. Above all, he wanted to keep his latest sponsors sweet. Next year they had mentioned doubling their two million dollars if things went well.

'If you can guarantee there will be no hanging around waiting for Miss Superstar to turn up or to fix her make-up, then I'll do it, but I've no intention of hanging around to do part-time chauffeuring jobs before the race.'

'Understood, Max. Why don't you come and meet her this evening? A quick introduction, that's all, and you can tell her yourself.'

'Where?' asked Max.

'Observation Bar. Seven thirty.'

'How come she'll be on the *Queen Mary* this evening?'

'Coincidence, I expect,' said Colin cheerfully and put the phone down.

Coincidence indeed, thought Max. As he stepped into his bath he called to Vicky who was lying on the bed, reading a potted history of the ship. 'Have you heard of this Christina woman?' he called.

'Yes, of course. Her name is Christiaa-na, by the way. She's coming to the *Queen Mary*?'

'Better get yourself ready to meet her in half an hour at the Observation Bar.'

Vicky was excited at the thought of meeting this sex goddess who was fast becoming a legend in her own lifetime. She remembered reading about her in the papers and magazines. She leaned against the side of the bathroom door watching Max deep in thought and bubble bath. 'Well, Max Gregson, it will be interesting to see your reaction to her.'

'How do you mean?'

'I've read that she's spent a fortune having her body "remodelled". She's quite something.'

'These women are always disappointing in the flesh.'

'Is that right? I hope you don't say that about your wife.'

'Don't be ridiculous, Vicky, and anyway, you don't need surgery.'

'Would you pay for it if I said I wanted to have something done?'

'Like what?'

'Oh, I don't know. Let's start with higher cheek bones, a slight shave off the nose, a tuck behind the ears . . . '

'Vicky, cut it out. You don't need any of that.'

'Good,' she replied. 'I just wanted to hear you say it.'

* * *

The meeting with Christiana was due to take place at a pretty exclusive cocktail party attended by a fair sprinkling of Hollywood folk. When she had not turned up by eight fifteen Max became decidedly restive. He had booked a table in the dining room for eight and was more than ready to enjoy an unhurried dinner and an early night. The eight-hour time change was still affecting his eating patterns and as he glanced at his watch he realized that it was already past four in the morning at home.

The hushed buzz of voices and heads turning signalled that the guest of honour had at last arrived. In true Hollywood fashion, Christiana entered the room followed by security flunkies and a flashing of camera bulbs. The guests parted like the waves of the Red Sea as she swept through the room to meet the VIPs of Long Beach.

At five foot eleven, she would have made an impressive entrance dressed in Levis and T-shirt, thought Vicky. She had a perfectly curved figure silhouetted in a full-length gold lamé dress with high Elizabethan collar that finished around her long, swan-like neck. Her ebony hair, teased into a million tiny curls, fanned about her delicately structured face and a pair of flamboyant jet and diamond earrings emphasized a symmetrical jaw line. Almost as dark as the jet were her eyes, wild and smouldering.

'Gross' was a word Vicky had often heard used in America and Vicky had to concede that Christiana was grossly beautiful. There was no other way to describe the vision that entered the room and arrested conversation as abruptly as if the British sovereign herself had appeared.

By now Max was involved with a group of race organizers from Australia, who were drawing up plans to hold a Grand Prix in Adelaide. Max had shown great enthusiasm for the idea and they were discussing the possibilities of the project, when Max glanced up to see Christiana being escorted in his direction. He felt the hairs on the back of his neck rise and hoped the sensual, tingling sensation he felt was not apparent to Vicky standing next to him. Introductions were brief and Colin, sensing Max's impatience to tie up the driving arrangements for the following day, ushered Max, Christiana and her publicity manager away from her group of admirers.

'So, this is the race champion who's gonna take me round the track,' Christiana said, studying Max. 'Champion or no champion, I don't intend risking my ass in some high-speed demonstration of his driving.'

Her comments were directed at Colin who stood next to her like a bewitched gnome. Max had never seen him look so uncomfortable. Miss Superstar had a mouth, it seemed, as large as the tits bursting out from underneath her chin.

'I can only reassure you that your publicity manager and I have already agreed that Max will drive at a steady pace to show you off to the crowds. He'll be saving the fast driving for later,' said Colin as firmly as his cracking voice would allow.

'Well, Max, no impressing the crowds, OK?' Christiana inclined her head, making her earrings swing like chandeliers in the wind.

'It won't be a problem,' Max assured her.

For the first time her face relaxed into a smile. 'It betta not be, honey. I eat men like you for breakfast.'

'Try me,' bristled Max.

Colin swallowed hard. If this Christiana was going to provoke Max any more he had visions of Max hurling her round the track at breakneck speed. He gave her an embarrassed smile and shot a pleading look towards her publicity manager.

'Well, remember, no fancy driving. We *cruise* over here. OK?'

'OK, Christina, until tomorrow,' said Max, deliberately pronouncing her name wrongly.

Leaving Colin with an apologetic smile on his face, Max walked casually away but quietly fuming. As he did so, he heard her growl, 'The man doesn't even know my name.'

He found Vicky standing with a group of Americans, and taking her by the arm, made a hurried exit from the party.

The next morning, shortly before noon, Christiana arrived at the track, late again for her appearance. She was nestled in a long black stretch limousine, like a rare exotic bird afraid to leave its gilded cage. Her four security guards had performed an inadequate job of shielding her from the hordes of fans that had pursued the car as it made its way to the paddock area.

'Get these goddamn people away from here,' she screeched as she felt the car being buffeted by excited autograph hunters. She withdrew further into the thick velour pile of the seat. She hadn't wanted to come to this goddamn race in the first place and she certainly hadn't envisaged being mobbed by a load of race-car fanatics.

Max, strolling along from the garage, smiled at the fracas around the car. Through the windows Christiana watched as the security men pushed the fans roughly away, and then through a sudden gap she spotted Max with a droll smile on his face.

She pounced on the button that operated the electric windows. 'If you wanna take me for a ride, you betta get me outta here,' she shouted.

The crowds parted as they saw the figure of the racing driver dressed conspicuously in cream racing overalls. The

American fans were not sure if he was the Englishman, Max Gregson, but he was a driver all the same and had to be treated with the respect he was due. Max put his head through the window of the limo. The security guards eyed him suspiciously. 'I don't know what all the fuss is about, but it seems you have more fans than I do,' Max teased.

Impatiently Christiana slid across to the door and climbed out, taking Max's arm. The crowds cheered. 'This is not exactly my idea of a fun day out,' she hissed beneath her breath.

'You mean you don't like motor racing?' asked Max, feigning surprise.

'I never watched a Grand Prix before and I doubt if I'll stay to watch this one.'

Max flinched as she pronounced the word 'grand', English style. 'Well, perhaps I can change your mind, Christina.'

'The name's Christiaa-na,' she snapped through a smile to the waiting fans.

'And the race, we pronounce the French way, "Gron Prix",' corrected Max politely.

They made their way up to a roped-off area through a barrage of photographers.

'Come on,' they shouted. 'Let's have a nice close-up of the two of you together.'

While the cameras clicked and films rolled, Christiana glanced sideways at this cool and self-assured man. His smooth, mellow voice inspired confidence in her. How different he was to all the wimpish, crawling escorts she had been out with. Maybe it wasn't going to be such a bad day after all.

The mayor of Long Beach and race organizers greeted their famous celebrity effusively and for once Max found himself taking a back seat. He watched as Christiana glided up the steps to the VIP suite in a pair of tight blue jeans that emphasized her firm little bottom. Max thought it irrelevant that it had come under the knife of a surgeon. It was still the neatest he'd ever seen. Her jet black hair bounced as softly as candy floss. Even in her casual jeans and burnt-orange suede jacket she still looked every inch a star.

After lunch, Max joined Christiana in the VIP suite. They looked on in horror as a bright pink Chevrolet drew up, bedecked with flowers, balloons and a large American flag. They shot each other a glance that said they both agreed on its distastefulness.

'Kerist, I've got to drive that?' Max said, pushing the hair back from his forehead in exasperation.

'It looks like somethin' out of a circus. What the hell's that gonna do for my image?' Christiana wailed.

'Leave it to me.'

'What d'ya mean, she refuses to drive in the car. What's wrong with it?' snapped one of the organizers that Max had collared in the VIP suite.

'Listen, buddy, we're not part of some circus act. Now get *your* act together and get us a decent car or I'm off to the motor home.'

'OK, OK. Let's get somethin' sorted quick. I guess we don't wanna delay this thing any more than we have to.'

'Right. I'll give you another five minutes, then I'm off.'

'OK, Mister Gregson, but what exactly is it you and the lady want?'

'Something with a bit of class. And try and get a convertible.'

'Will a Rolls-Royce do?'

'As long as it's not pink, yes.'

Max left the organizers chasing up sponsors and guests to find an owner of a Rolls-Royce convertible or something similar. He knew they wouldn't be able to find one in the short time that was left before the three o'clock start to the race. He decided to make his own arrangements and just hoped the others would agree to it.

Five minutes later he reappeared with the throaty roar of a Harley Davidson underneath him. 'It's this or nothing,' Max called up to the organizers who were fussing around Christiana in the VIP suite once more.

Christiana, now on her third glass of champagne, leant over the balcony in horror. 'I can't ride those things. I just *hate* bikes,' she protested to the cluster of red, embarrassed faces around her.

'Trust me, I'll take it easy,' shouted Max with a bemused smile.

Christiana swept down the steps to where Max was impatiently revving up the bike. The crowds were now cheering in anticipation of her appearance on the track.

'What are you waiting for?' Max teased. 'Get on the back.'

'Oh, hell,' she said, gritting her teeth as she swung one of her long legs over the seat. 'Two wheels are gonna scare the shit outta me. Max, I don't mind admittin' I'm as nervous as a kitten. If I hit the deck on this thing, I'm warning you, I'll sue you for every cent you've got.'

'I don't mind admittin', I'm as nervous as a kitten,' sang Max as he accelerated slowly off. 'You could make that your next song.'

Christiana leant forward and held on grimly to Max's waist. They glided gently on to the track and even the other Formula One drivers were leaning over the pit wall for a better view of the proceedings. Was Max going to scare the hell out of her? they wondered. The rumour had got around she had treated him pretty meanly at the party.

'Still nervous?' asked Max, as he hit the straight.

'I'm getting used to it,' she called above the noise of the bike and the crowds.

Once again Christiana felt the reassurance of being with this Englishman and, quite contrary to her expectations, she was beginning to relax. She even managed to wave at the packed grandstands.

'I think the bike is pretty neat. It's been a long time since I rode one.'

Christiana leaned forward, closer to his ear. And it's a long time since I held such a gorgeous hunk of man, she told herself. It was months since she had met a man she found so attractive.

'Mind if I open up the throttle?'

'You can open up my throttle any time, honey.'

Max accelerated to a gentle forty miles an hour. Christiana responded with a tighter squeeze of his waist. Max toyed with the idea of going faster and then thought better of it. After all, he was enjoying the ride as much as she was. Why bring it to a close too quickly?

After circling the track they swung into the pit lane to a loud cheering from all the pit crews and a breathless Christiana climbed off. She kissed him long and hard on the lips in front of the waiting cameras. Vicky turned away, pretending not to notice her husband apparently enjoying the attention. It was all part of the job, she reminded herself, but it still gave her a sharp pang of jealousy.

'I think I'll stay and watch you race, after all,' Christiana breathed in his ear.

'You don't know how close I was to giving it full throttle,' Max joked.

'Why, because I threatened to eat you for breakfast last night?' she asked, flashing her dark eyes.

'Something like that. It's just a pity you won't get the chance.'

'Well, next time you're in town, leave your wife at home. OK?' she said and lifting her head back she laughed, catching the disapproving eyes of Vicky upon her.

Max drove off, wondering what the consequences might have been had he been on his own. Certainly wild and definitely exciting were his last thoughts before he tuned his mind into the race ahead.

By now every seat in the grandstands was taken. Kelly and her friends made their way to their seats on Shoreline Drive, which would give them a view of the first hairpin bend after the start. Across from the palm-lined track, the Pacific Ocean sparkled in the brilliant sunshine. Small boats bobbed idly in the faint whisper of a breeze. The *Queen Mary*, a familiar silhouette against the skyline, lay sedately at berth, away from the maddening din of the circuit.

Max made his way to the pits in a quiet, confident mood. The television cameras caught him as he approached his car and Paul Newman was there to shake his hand and wish him luck. But Max was shutting off from all the buzz and hype around him now. His mind was totally concentrated on the work ahead. He had won here last year and he felt positive he could repeat the success. Rio had been a dismal race. He had succumbed to distractions and paid the price. But that was out of his mind now. The only problem that clouded his day was that Vicky had forgotten to pack his lucky red underpants.

Max made a good start. From his third position on the grid, he had kept close to the leading Ferrari of Terri

Dacco. It had all the makings of an exciting race. Then, on the thirteenth lap, the car had developed a bad vibration, too late for him to turn into the pits and have it checked. He swore to himself as he braked hard at the end of the long straight. With lightning speed he dived through the gear changes down to first but even as he did so, he knew the car was not going to follow the sharp curve of the bend. It veered off, as if with a mind of its own, and bounced heavily into the tyre barriers amidst a cloud of dust and flying metal. The nearside wing and aerofoil broke up and scattered like paper across the grass to the gasps of the crowds. Max felt as if he were being pushed through a threshing machine and thanked his maker when the car came to rest without serious injury to himself.

Up in the stands, Kelly stood up in horror as she watched the car fly off the track. Her face had turned ashen as the car hit the barriers with a heavy impact. Then, as Max climbed out of the car unhurt, an overwhelming relief swept over her.

Christiana, who had been viewing from a TV monitor in the VIP lounge, gave a terrified yelp, pressing her hand to her mouth, 'Oh shit,' she exclaimed loudly, as she saw the car spin off.

Vicky, standing in the pit lane, had been unaware of the event. She hid her emotion as the pit crew told her that Max's car had 'left the track'. But she gave a heavy sigh of relief when Colin told her that Max was all right. The stifling tightness in her chest and the pain that was gripping her insides receded. Fate had done no worse than finish Max's race prematurely. Vicky was thankful it was not his life.

# 23

The long sleek lines of Sheikh Al Rabida's yacht sat gleaming in the water of Newport's most impressive marina. Her eighty-foot hull of burnished gold and white looked majestic in the setting sun. The mooring lines running from stem to stern were perfectly tied. A permanent crew of ten made sure of that.

A helicopter circled overhead and landed neatly on the top deck, bringing the Sheikh and his two sons back from the race. Below deck, preparations for a party were well under way and by seven thirty the crew had laid out a sumptuous array of food in the main saloon, all exquisitely displayed on the finest gold plate. Two towering table lamps gave an intimate glow to the mahogany panelling around the walls and discreet spotlights were directed on to magnificent displays of pink orchids and other exotic blooms. Three steps led down to a smaller saloon and a rectangular seating area in peach satin and grey silk pile carpeting. The ceiling of gleaming black and gold mirrors gave the room an ostentatious air of luxury and reflected the taste of a man who indulged in good living.

Max and Vicky arrived at the marina with Julian and an American former girlfriend of his. As they stepped out of the car they stopped to admire the array of yachts.

'Well, you don't have to ask which one the party's on,' said Julian, giving a long low whistle at the sight of the yacht ablaze with lights from stem to stern. A uniformed officer stood waiting at the gangplank.

'I hope they're not going to put to sea,' commented Vicky. 'We could end up in Hawaii.'

'I think I could cope with that,' laughed Julian, 'as long as they don't run out of champagne.'

Max, who had not wanted to go to the party in the first place, was not sharing their enthusiasm. It was Colin who had insisted that he make an appearance and when Max had made excuses, Colin had hastily reminded him that it was part of his job to meet the sponsors, especially the Arab who had contributed such a large sum of money to Delta for very little in return.

It would be another evening of small talk and the usual barrage of questions. Why had he spun off during the race? Was it the car or a miscalculation of the bend? How did it feel to leave the track at ninety miles an hour and slam into a wall? Did he suffer any shock? And so on and so on . . .

Despite the fact that Max had escaped with only superficial cuts and bruises, he was still angry at not having finished the race. The start he had made to the new season did not bode well for the rest of the championship. Only one point for two out of the sixteen races was a bad start, especially in comparison to his team mate.

Mario had driven a superb race and finished fifth. The press and TV were full of praise for his 'courageous drive' and were hailing him as the young driver with the most promise, speculating that perhaps the race in Rio had not been a 'one off' for him, after all.

Once on board, in spite of his dark mood, even Max was taken aback by the luxury of the yacht.

'Apparently the Sheikh has every conceivable gadget on this thing *and* another one quite similar in Cannes,' remarked Julian.

'Not bad for someone who came out of the desert on a camel,' replied Max sardonically.

'Max,' reproached Vicky.

'It's true. His old man was a goat herdsman with a few acres of not so prime land in Saudi, until they discovered he was sitting on an oilfield.'

'He's certainly in the big time now. Even the waiters have enough gold braid on them to dress the Saudi navy,' replied Julian, as yet another glided up bearing more glasses of Dom Perignon. 'And he's got good taste in champagne.'

As if the Sheikh had heard the compliment, he came over to them smiling graciously. He appeared comfortably at ease in his surroundings and took obvious pleasure in having such distinguished guests aboard. 'Good evening, Mr and Mrs Gregson.'

Max introduced Julian and his companion.

'I must say, Mr Gregson, you have a most attractive wife,' commented the Sheikh, his eyes swimming over her in one fluid movement.

Vicky was indeed one of the most lovely women there. She looked cool and chic in a blouson shirt and trousers of emerald green silk and her hair was elegantly swept up into a chignon. In sharp contrast, the Arab's escort appeared at his side wearing a black sequin dress finishing in a beaded fringe which only just covered her bottom. A matching headband kept her wild black hair in place. At the centre of the headband was the most enormous midnight blue sapphire, as vivid as a peacock's eyes. 'May I introduce Veronica?' said the Sheikh as he watched Max scrutinizing her closely.

Veronica smiled back woodenly, but before she had a chance to speak their host had whisked her off to meet the other guests. As he admired the sexy walk of the feline Veronica, Max's attention was caught by a group of new arrivals. Taking a long sip from his glass he tried to conceal his surprise as he saw Kelly amongst them. It was then he heard the quiet hum of the turbo engines and a glance out of the window told him they were under way. Oh God, he thought, it was bad enough that his wife and mistress were at the same party. But to be on a yacht with no immediate means of escape was ten times worse. Vicky also seemed to be on edge. The night had the potential to end up in disaster. Furthermore, Max was in no mood to placate Vicky if she started getting suspicious.

'Who is the pretty girl over there?' she asked.

'Where?' he asked, as if suddenly myopic.

'The one in the yellow dress. You were talking to her yesterday in the garage.'

'That's Kelly O'Brien, an old girlfriend of Julian's,' Max replied evenly, relieved that Julian and his girl were now up on deck.

'It's odd he's never mentioned her before.'

'Well, you know what the old Romeo's like – breaking hearts all the time. He probably missed that one out.'

'That doesn't sound like him at all,' said Vicky with a questioning glance and in a tone that set alarm bells ringing in Max's head.

'No? Well, how about another glass of bubbly?' asked Max, desperate to change the subject and to avoid implicating his friend further. Thankfully, at that moment Vicky spotted an old acquaintance from Max's early racing days amongst a group of people nearby. A tall woman with broad shoulders and long straight hair gave Vicky a beaming smile.

'That's Georgina Stubbs. Do you remember, we met her in London at last year's Sports Personality awards?'

'So it is,' replied Max vaguely as Vicky went to greet her.

Max decided to go up on deck for some fresh air and hopefully to find Julian.

The yacht had now made good way into the harbour and the lights of the luxury waterfront houses on the other side twinkled in the darkness. Standing in the subdued lighting of the aft deck, Max found Julian and his companion admiring the view before them.

'How's the party going downstairs, Max?' asked Julian breezily. After a few glasses of champagne, he was feeling an extreme sense of well being.

'Kelly's here and not only that, Vicky's giving me the third degree on her. Why is it that women are so intuitive?' replied Max moodily.

'Nothing you can't handle, old boy. It's not like you to let a female ruffle your feathers.'

'I'm not in the mood to steer Vicky off the scent. She suspects something, so if she asks, Kelly is an ex of yours. OK?'

'I'm not as good as you at the old porky pies. But, come to think of it, I'd be very flattered. Kelly's the most stunning woman here tonight – apart from Vicky, of course.'

'Please don't let me down,' Max insisted and went in search of another drink. His progress was halted by one of the Arab's sons.

'Oh, Mister Gregson, I'm sorry about the accident this afternoon. How did it happen?' He hung on to Max's every word as his hero again went through the story he wished to forget.

When Max got back to the main saloon he was relieved to find that the Sheikh had taken Vicky on a tour of the yacht. He found the champagne slipping down easily now and as he listened to the noisy chatter of people around him he felt engulfed by lethargy. His eyes automatically scanned the room for Kelly. After a while he saw her slip away on her own. He followed her into a corridor with several doors. Curiosity made him open one. He was taken aback at the opulence of what he saw. In the subdued lighting he made out a vast circular bed covered in gold and cream silk. The walls were of flecked brown suede and above the bed was a smoked glass mirror that covered most of the ceiling. Large marble sculptures were the only other decoration in the room. Max took it all in fleetingly. Checking the next room, he found it was also dominated by a large bed and its ornate Egyptian designs of blue and ochre gave it an exotic ambience. Clothes lay scattered on the floor and a black sequinned dress hung from a headboard in the form of a sphinx. Coming from the bathroom, he could hear the sound of someone humming and the noise of a jacuzzi bubbling softly. He was on the point of making a discreet exit when he heard the silky purr of a female voice. 'Hey there, why don't you come and join me?'

In the dim light, Max could see the voluptuous naked form of Veronica standing in the jacuzzi like a Greek goddess with steam and bubbles rising below her. She was still wearing her headband with its glinting sapphire. The room reeked of hashish and she smiled dreamily at him. 'Come on in,' she coaxed.

'Er, not tonight, thanks.' Stones on the head and stoned in the head, Max thought, as he exited rapidly. It was then he almost fell into the arms of Kelly.

'Hey, what's up with you?' she said in surprise. 'Doing something you shouldn't?'

'No, but someone in there is trying to and I don't want to be the one caught doing it.' Kelly gave him a puzzled look. 'I'm glad I've found you. Can we go somewhere and talk?'

'Where do you suggest? A bar down the road?'

'Come on, Kelly. I feel we should clear a few things up.'

'No. This is not the time or the place,' Kelly said firmly. She had been determined that if Max was at the party she would have nothing to do with him. It was best that way while his wife was around. Yesterday had been the first time she had seen Vicky and she had been pleasantly surprised. She had a gentleness about her manner and she was far more attractive than she had imagined. For the first time, she had a sense of guilt about their affair.

Max took hold of her arms. 'I know. But I've missed you. And stop putting on that pouting expression of yours. It doesn't suit you. Let's talk for a minute at least.'

Max led her through a door and on to an open deck. They had the view of the harbour to themselves. Only the muted throb of the engines and the high-pitched laugh of someone below disturbed the stillness of the clear night. Max leaned over the rails, watching the ink-black water rippling past below.

'Kelly, I'm sorry about what happened. Truly I am.'

Kelly stood next to him, her back to the rails. 'So am I, but then the true colours of a person are often revealed in times of crises. I was able to see yours more than clearly.' Kelly had no recrimination in her voice, only disappointment. 'It's just a pity it had to finish this way.'

Max turned to her and searched her eyes. 'You don't mean that.'

Kelly gave an anguished laugh. 'Max, I should have realized a long time ago that the only thing that matters in your life is you. Other people are comfortable accessories there for the using.' She fidgeted restlessly and tried to control her anger. She had bottled it up for far too long. Seeing Max again was harder than she thought. She was fighting hard to remain objective. It was over between them. She had seen a different side of Max and even though she was desperately sorry for him after the death of the old man, it couldn't alter the way she felt. Her pregnancy had been an inconvenient hiccup in his life and no more.

'Can I call you when I get back to London?'

Kelly's heart was aching. As Max drew her closer she noticed a sadness in his eyes, a quiet desperation she had never seen before. The confident, successful Max was not himself. She detected a chink in his armour. She felt unsteady again, her fury dissipating. She was helpless against the power of his charisma. Just then, one of the doors on to the deck opened, making them jump apart. The large figure of Bill Kiley, the American photographer, was silhouetted against the light. 'Kelly, there you are. I've been looking all over for you. Are you coming down for another drink?'

'Sure,' answered Kelly. 'I'll be right with you.' She turned to follow him, then stopped.

'Goodbye Max. I'm sorry about the race today. Better luck next time, hey?' And she kissed him lightly on the cheek and was gone.

Max had no desire to rejoin the party. Armed with a glass of champagne, he made for the bridge which was dark and aglow with the lights of computers bleeping their facts and figures. It was an impressive as the flight deck of an aircraft. Max introduced himself to the young skipper whose eyes were fixed on a green buoy ahead. They discussed the instrumentation and Max became absorbed in the array of advanced technology before him.

'We're cruising pretty slow right now,' explained the skipper in a heavy West Coast accent. 'About five knots. Maximum speed, if the boss is in a hurry, is thirty-four knots.'

'And the acceleration?' asked Max.

'Not quite like the machinery you drive, Mr Gregson. But it's got a sensitive throttle.'

'Could I try?' Max was itching to get his hands on the yacht's power drive. He loved the sound and feel of the turbo engines.

'Sure, here's the throttle lever. Just take it nice 'n' slow.'

Max did as he was instructed and watched the dial move slowly forward to twelve knots. The skipper was focusing on the radar screen.

'OK. You see the green buoy ahead. We'll do a turn to port and head back into harbour.'

Max, on the spur of the moment, decided that the party was in need of livening up. The buoy was no more than three hundred yards away. He leaned on the throttle, the boat picked up speed and Max felt the same exhilaration as he did when driving.

'I think we're going a little too fast, Mr Gregson.' The skipper watched anxiously as his beloved boat continued to pick up speed.

'No problem, Captain. Let's see how she handles.' Max turned the wheel, giving the buoy a wide berth. The yacht responded perfectly, but not without listing at the sudden short turn.

The skipper was aghast, as if someone had just jumped all over his favourite toy. He coughed to hide his annoyance. The boss would not be amused.

Down in the main saloon, Julian had been chatting to Kelly. He was pleased to see her back to her old self again.

'You seem to be coping better than Max this evening, Kelly.'

'You mean being at the same party as his wife? It's not a big problem,' she said unconvincingly, carefully avoiding Julian's eye.

'Are you sure about that?' Julian sensed her unease.

'I've just told Max we're finished. Tonight seemed as good a time as any. I've had enough, Julian.'

'I'm sorry to hear it . . . but you've shown more forbearance and patience than most, my dear,' he said, squeezing her hand. 'Does that mean I can take you out to lunch tomorrow before I fly back to London?' he asked cautiously.

'Terrific idea.' Kelly's emerald eyes flashed conspiratorially.

Julian reproached himself for being unduly thrilled at her response. 'I know of a nice little place in Malibu . . . ' he began and then he saw Vicky coming over to join them. 'Oh, lord,' he muttered. 'It's introductions time, Kelly . . . '

At that moment, the boat listed sharply to one side and Julian had to catch Kelly to prevent her from falling. Glasses on the bar slid slowly on to the floor and opened bottles of champagne followed like falling skittles. The Sheikh, struggling to stay on his feet, looked in horrified amazement at the angle of the floor, helpless as his hand-woven silk carpet became a shambolic mess of broken glass, china, champagne and orange juice.

A woman's screech broke the silence, followed by 'God, we've hit something.' There followed a loud muttering. Some of the guests pretended nothing serious was amiss while others disappeared on deck to find out what had happened. The waiters looked on embarrassed, waiting for orders, unsure whether to make some attempt to rescue the sodden carpet or to attend to the women's designer outfits which had caught splashes of airborne alcohol.

Some minutes later the yacht had docked and the Sheikh had bidden his guests good night with effusive apologies. It was only when Max came downstairs that he realized the extent of the damage he had caused. The Sheikh accepted his admission of guilt benignly and they parted on friendly terms.

Once in the car, heading back to Long Beach, Julian gave a loud guffaw. 'Are you telling us that it was you at the helm, playing at slaloms with twenty million dollars worth of machinery? I just hope Colin doesn't get to hear of it. Pranging cars and nearly capsizing a mini-liner's not bad for one day.'

'And I hope he doesn't send us the bill for his carpets,' said Vicky soberly.

Max smiled to himself. He was seated in the back of the car next to Julian's ravishing sexpot of a companion, and felt her hand running slowly up his thigh. These American girls enjoyed a bit of excitement.

# 24

Before the team flew back to London, two things happened that could quite easily have passed unnoticed, but for Tom, Max's chief mechanic, and Stuart Ewings, a sharp-eyed reporter from one of the English newspapers.

After the debriefing of the Long Beach race, it had been concluded that Max's accident had been caused by error of judgement. Max had admitted he had taken the corner too fast and had missed a gear. However, there was some niggling doubt in the back of his mind that all was not right with the car. It had slammed violently into the wall, smashing most of the front and nearside chassis.

Tom, like any diligent mechanic, had spent hours going over every detail to find out what had caused the accident. He had sworn blind that Max, with his driving ability, was not the sort of guy to drive into a wall. He had checked and rechecked the tyres. Even though one of the front tyres had blown on impact, the wheel had not come away from the chassis. On further examination, Tom had discovered one of the wheel nuts dangerously loose. This would account for Max's difficulty in handling the car. But perhaps it had come loose when the car hit the wall? He would discuss it later with Colin.

That evening several of the reporters, having faxed their stories back to their respective editors, were holed up in a hotel bar. They were giving noisy vent to their opinions on the race. Most were pleased that Terri Dacco in the Ferrari had scored yet another victory. As to other drivers, there was plenty of good-natured banter back and forth on their various merits and weaknesses.

'Herrea? You really think he's got a chance this year? He's a Sunday afternoon driver as far as I'm concerned,' boomed Fred Stubbs, one of the sport's most outspoken writers. 'Now take that young Rodriguez. He's coming up in the field very well since he's been with Delta. Third in Rio and fifth here. He's got a good future ahead of him.'

'And with Colin, I shouldn't wonder.' It was Stuart Ewings who spoke. Stuart was thirty-two and gay. He covered many sports apart from motor racing, which he didn't have a great affinity with. It was too noisy, for one thing. He preferred the more easy-going coverage of cricket and cycling. His quiet aside did not go unnoticed by the Australian, Reg Watkins.

'And just what are you hinting at there, old Stu boy?'

'It's just a feeling I get between the two of them.'

'Like Colin is one of your lot, you mean?'

Stuart gave him a hurt, disapproving look and pursed his lips.

'Come on, old boy, don't get a sense of humour failure. It's only Uncle Reg having a go.'

Stuart knew him well enough. Reg didn't have an ounce of malice in him. Still, the way he had said 'your lot' rankled. 'Apologies accepted, but just cut the old boy touch, will you?'

'Are you serious about Colin and Mario, though?' Reg took another gulp of chilled Michelob.

'Mm . . . but this is just between you and me. I was in the same restaurant as the Delta team one evening in Rio. There was a young Brazilian girl who worked there and she comes up to Mario and starts fooling around with him. Mario joins in and starts singing and dancing. Everybody's enjoying themselves except Colin. You should have seen his face. It wasn't that Mario was drawing attention to himself. It was when he started messing around with the female. He was as jealous as hell. Couldn't stand it any longer and got up and walked out.'

'Yes, but it's well known that Colin throws moodies at everyone. He's cantankerous when he wants to be.'

Stuart was warming to his theory. 'Have we seen much of them around at Long Beach? No. And when we have seen Mario, Colin is always there . . . Believe me, those two have got the hots for each other.'

'Well, I'll be damned. There was a Spanish driver a few years back. Rumour had it he was gay. Mind you, a lot of people changed their minds when he ran off with another driver's wife. He had us all fooled.'

'OK, Reg, but take a look next time. It's all a great shame really.' Stuart sighed. 'A beautiful boy like that with Pritchard . . . '

And that's how rumours are started. In the motor-racing world they travel faster than the aircraft the race people travel on. By the time the 747 carrying most of the teams had landed at Heathrow, the rumour had gone round. Mario Rodriguez and Colin Pritchard were lovers.

On the same morning the Delta mechanics arrived back in London, Tom went straight to the factory, hoping to find Colin who had flown back the previous evening.

'Colin? May I have a word?' Tom's face peered round the door of his boss's office.

'Sure, Tom. It's a surprise to see you here. I thought you would be at home sleeping off the jet lag. What is it?' Colin got up out of his seat and closed the door behind Tom whose face was etched with concern.

'I'm on my way home but I wanted a word with you in

private. It's about something I found wrong with the car after the race. I'm afraid I don't bring good news.'

'Sit down.'

'Thanks. It's about Max's accident at Long Beach. I don't believe it was driver error. The front off-side wheel nut was loose and I believe it was like that when the car crashed. Max had mentioned he felt a vibration before it happened.'

'Who changed the wheel for the race?' enquired Colin, deep in thought.

'Geoff.'

'Geoff. Of course it was. We changed him over to replace Bernard who had split his thumb open.'

'I know he's still pretty inexperienced, but . . . '

'Yes, I get your drift. We can't let mistakes like that happen again. We'll have to keep a close eye on him. Otherwise he'll have to go.'

As Tom left, Colin was deciding whether to tell Max about Tom's theory. No, he thought, I won't pursue it further. Let Max think it was driver error. It might sharpen up his senses some more. In the meantime, he would keep Geoff away from any more wheel changing. That was a mistake Colin couldn't afford to let happen again.

# 25

Max sat on the paddock fence watching Sophie and Vicky on their mounts. The sun shone brightly and a warm breeze sent lazy ripples across the long grass in the fields nearby. Soft cumulus clouds cast fleeting shadows over the rolling countryside. Vicky, blessed with the patience of a Mother Theresa, was teaching Sophie how to jump. Sophie, looking every inch the professional horsewoman, sat erect and engrossed in her mother's advice. Vicky led the pony around and jumped it over a small obstacle. Then Sophie tried it on her own and with intense concentration jumped her pony clear. Vicky and Max applauded Sophie's first successful effort.

It was a rare day of relaxation for Max. Casually dressed in jeans and T-shirt, he was enjoying this time with his family. He needed the quiet ambience of his home more and more these days. Being World Champion was taking up a lot more of his time. Every day his secretary dealt with invitations of one sort or another: opening stores, charity functions and sports dinners. Then there were interviews and film crews at his home for news coverage and magazine stories. Sometimes he and Vicky felt their lives were under a magnifying glass.

As Max watched Vicky handling her horse so competently, he heard the approach of a helicopter. It dropped lower and lower and circled overhead. Max recognized Julian waving from one of the windows and waved back. The helicopter passed overhead and disappeared over the front of the house, where it would land on the wide expanse of lawns.

'Who's that?' asked Vicky who had jumped off to steady the alarmed horses.

'Julian. He's come to pick me up for our helicopter lesson.'

Julian appeared, his tall straight figure and smiling, affable face making him every inch the eligible bachelor that he was, thought Vicky. He was wearing an open-neck shirt and off-white trousers, and still had his Californian suntan. 'Sorry, hope I didn't startle the horses. The pilot brought us in a bit low.'

'That's all right, Julian,' said Vicky, responding to his warm hug.

'Hello, Uncle Julian,' called Sophie, who was leading the two horses round the field. Julian returned her greeting and vaulted over the rails of the paddock to admire the two magnificent animals.

'You didn't tell me you had a helicopter lesson today,' remarked Vicky to Max.

'Sure I did, but I didn't expect to get picked up in one.'

After Vicky had tethered the horses and proudly shown Julian her lively new colt, they strolled round to the front of the house. Five minutes later, the rotor blades whirred into action and Sophie watched spellbound as the machine lifted noisily but smoothly off and up into the sky, taking her father with it. Vicky's attention, however, was on her immaculate flower beds of purple and red tulips whose feathery petals were now being scattered across the lawn like giant confetti.

The pilot handled the controls with relaxed confidence, while Max and Julian enjoyed the panoramic view at the same time as keenly watching the pilot's flying technique.

They had gained their correct height when a red flashing light on the instrument panel caught their attention. The pilot checked the oil gauge and pressed some switches. 'It looks like we're losing oil,' he said calmly. The gauge needle flickered and vibrated backwards and forwards.

'Is it serious?' asked Max.

'It will be if it doesn't correct itself in a few minutes.'

'What if it doesn't?' Julian enquired, his face showing increasing concern.

'We land in the nearest field,' answered the pilot confidently.

A few minutes later the pilot was searching for a convenient stretch of pasture in which to land. When he had located a suitable field he brought the ailing machine carefully down. The field was a few miles from the nearest village, and the pilot volunteered to walk to a nearby house to phone for assistance.

'And check out the nearest pub, if you can. I could murder a beer after all this,' suggested Max.

Max and Julian sat on the grass enjoying the sunshine. It was unusually warm for the time of year. Max had been looking forward to his lesson. It was only his third but already he was mastering the complicated technique of getting the machine off the ground and landing it.

Julian had spoken only briefly to Max since he returned from California. He thought better of telling him about the pleasant lunch and afternoon he had spent with Kelly up at Malibu. He was secretly hoping that Max was no longer seeing her. Instead, he recounted the tales of jacuzzi parties that had gone on until dawn and the horse-riding weekend he had spent in the mountains outside Los Angeles. 'California is a beautiful place,' he said fondly, his mind focusing sharply on an afternoon stroll he had taken with Kelly along the beach.

'It's OK for a time but I wouldn't want to live there. Would you?'

'I'm not so sure about that. It has a great climate, beaches, and mountains for skiing,' enthused Julian.

'It also has smog, earthquakes and a lot of crime in the cities. For my money I'd rather stay here.' It was hard for Max to imagine living permanently away from England, especially on such a spring day. The first of the brilliant green foliage was colouring in the bare silhouettes of the trees all around them. 'Maybe a few years ago when I was single and bumming around, the surfing and ski life would have appealed to me. Now there's too much emphasis on the greenback.'

'Money certainly talks in Beverly Hills . . . and there's an awful lot of it around. Take that Sheikh, for instance . . . he doesn't know what to spend his money on next. His sons have got this huge pad in Bel Air . . . '

'I can tell you where he's *not* going to be putting his money any more. The Delta team.'

Julian was astonished. 'You're joking.'

'I wish I were. He's just pulled out to the tune of one million dollars.'

'You mean he's stopped the sponsorship already for this season?' Julian paused. 'It wasn't anything to do with the night of the party?'

'Unfortunately, it was. And Colin was not very amused, to put it mildly.'

'What happened?'

'Briefly, the Sheikh decided to pull out his money, contract or no contract. It was my fault. It seems I upset him. Colin found out and I was hauled over the coals. In fact, if Colin had another driver at his disposal, I think he might even have fired me.'

'He couldn't fire the World Champion,' said Julian in disbelief.

'I think he realized that in the end. It wouldn't do the team any good. But I'm not so sure he will offer me a contract for next season.'

'You don't seem too upset about it.'

'I was thinking maybe a change of team might do me some good. I suspect that Colin would like Mario as his number one driver for next year anyway.'

'Ever thought of retiring?' asked Julian thoughtfully.

Max hesitated. 'Three months ago I would have said no, definitely not. But now . . . Once you've won the World Championship, you haven't got a lot to prove except that you can win it again. The motivation is still there, but not the hunger you need to win all the time. The edge has gone off it a little. And that worries me.'

'You wait until you've had your first win this season. It will come back, I'm sure.'

'You're probably right. I haven't had a lot of luck so far . . . ' Max was thinking of his personal life as much as his racing. 'But then I've probably brought a lot of it on myself.'

The last time Julian had seen Max so serious was the night he had come to the flat after the car accident. It was a rare thing for Max to get reflective about life. Maybe the events of the last two months had changed him. 'Max, remember you have achieved things that most men can only dream about.'

'Mm. Five years in Formula One . . . ' Max paused ' . . . and no big accident yet. Maybe I shouldn't push my luck . . . what's left of it.'

'Let's keep it in perspective. You had a sixth in Rio and a "no finish" in Long Beach. That doesn't exactly sound like a catalogue of disasters to me.'

'Yes, you're right, but it's since I had that accident with the pensioner . . . things are going against me.'

'Max, I'm an old mate of yours and I hope you won't take this the wrong way. But I think you would do yourself a favour if you snapped out of this depression and started to think more positively.'

'Depression?' Max sounded surprised.

'I know you've had a lot of problems at home. It creates pressure and that's one thing you don't need in your life. And the booze doesn't help either.'

Max sat up abruptly. 'Hey, cut out the lecture, Julian. I get enough of those at home. Next you'll be suggesting I give up women.'

'That wouldn't be such a bad idea either,' said Julian with a chuckle. Particularly if it's Kelly, he thought.

A few minutes later, the flustered pilot appeared at the gate in the field. 'There's nothing we can do about the chopper right now,' he explained, throwing a frustrated glance at his beloved machine. 'The company is sending someone over, but it will take some time. I've told them I'll wait until they arrive. In the meantime, I got you guys a cab from the village to get you back home.'

'Thanks,' said Max, impressed that the pilot had organized things so quickly. 'What about the lesson? Shall we leave it for another day?'

'Not if you can make it for this afternoon. I should be out of here one way or another in a couple of hours. How about we arrange it for four o'clock? Give me a ring first to check I'm back.'

'Great,' replied Julian. 'That means we've got time for a spot of lunch at that little country restaurant near you, Max.'

'The one with the gorgeous barmaid with the large . . . '

'That's the one,' grinned Julian. 'Right, we'll be off then. Thanks for getting us a lift back.'

'Er, there's one thing, fellas, before you go – it's about the taxi . . . '

'Don't worry, we'll pay for that,' Max assured him.

Max and Julian walked across the fields to their waiting 'taxi'. They stopped in amazement when they saw the old rust-eaten Morris Oxford with the bumper hanging off. An old, shrunken farm labourer sat at the wheel. It took them an hour to do the thirty miles back to the farmhouse.

Vicky roared with laughter when she saw two pathetic figures climb out of the car, Julian nursing a sore back from the lack of suspension. 'Well that's a bit of a change in style from the way you left,' she remarked, stifling a giggle.

Both Max and Julian looked at her as if she had done them a grave injustice, then ambled off to fire up the Ferrari.

# 26

Kelly's sitting room was filled with a haphazard collection of mementoes from her trips around the world. A large bust of an African woman stood in one corner. Underneath a sprawling palm were Indian stone carvings from Mexico. Bokhara rugs covered a polished wood floor and on a low coffee table, two brass lamps from the Far East dwarfed a small forest of pot plants.

Max had always felt comfortable in the casual disarray of Kelly's flat. He even warmed to the cats that sat about blinking contentedly. How different it was from home, he thought, as he moved a pile of magazines and a dozing cat to sit back on an over-stuffed sofa.

Kelly appeared from the kitchen with two glasses of wine. She had received his phone call with mixed feelings. Their meeting in Long Beach had reopened old wounds and she had left the party that night more confused than ever. She had wanted to discuss it with Julian over lunch in Malibu, but somehow the opportunity never presented itself.

Despite putting Max off a couple of times, she had relented and agreed to see him again. She had often wondered how Max would have reacted if she had had the baby. It was likely that he would have cut her out of his life completely. But then fate had interceded. Perhaps it had chosen right for her in the end. She would never know.

Max sat across from Kelly, unsure of her reaction to his visit. He liked the unpredictability of her moods. She was distant with him, as if meeting up was a formality, nothing more. She had refused dinner, so he had arrived with an armful of flowers and wine. And now as he looked at her, sitting on one of the large floor cushions, he was aware once again of her beauty and of an inner strength that she seemed to have acquired during their separation, which gave her a new allure.

He had asked himself why he had wanted to see her; what it was that drew him back. Was it that he needed to be forgiven for the accident, and his lack of concern over her pregnancy, or was it a bond that had grown between them because of her miscarriage? Maybe it was just that he needed a warm and caring lover – she'd certainly been that for him in the past, before all this.

'I came to say sorry, Kelly – about the baby. Can we drink to the future and forget the past?'

Kelly noticed his eyes had the same expression of despair she had seen on the yacht. She thought of the irony of it all, that Max should have fame and wealth at his feet . . . and yet happiness was eluding him. 'We don't have a future together, do we, Max?'

'No, I suppose we don't. But does that matter if we still feel something for each other?'

'I want more than just a physical relationship . . . now. I realized that when I became pregnant. It's changed things for me.'

'I understand, but I'm married and I can't offer you anything more.'

'Then what do you want from me that you can't get from all the other women that follow you around?'

'Your love, your caring.' Max stared hard at the rug in front of him, as if the answer to his happiness lay there. Then, he lifted his head and slowly turned to Kelly, his eyes fixing her with a plea for help that set her heart thumping wildly and her pulse beating rapidly. He was a part of her in some inextricable way. There was no escape. Not yet.

'Damn you, Max Gregson. How can I fight against you when you look at me like that?' she said fiercely. Then her face broke into a smile and she went to him and threw her arms around his neck, any resolve to finish with him abandoned.

They made love in her bedroom, slowly and passionately in the glow of the many candles that were arranged around the cosy room. Max had carried her there and they had undressed each other slowly and with great deliberation, all the time kissing gently. They aroused each other with a new-found intensity. Kelly gave herself with a desperation, knowing that she was going to lose Max . . . She knew now that he would never be hers.

Max was more tender than he'd ever been, perhaps searching for something he had lost in his childhood and hoping that he might find it in Kelly. Or perhaps it was that he sensed her vulnerability. Whatever the reason, his tongue now stroked and caressed every part of her body, as if he were discovering it for the first time. It lightly feathered the soft skin around her neck, breasts and stomach, giving her a feeling of such acute pleasure that, when at last she felt him reach between her legs, she was already wet and ready to take him into her. As she climaxed for the first of many times in what was to be a long night of slow and passionate lovemaking, she wept and cried out in joy and anguish: 'Damn you, Max. Damn you. I just wish I didn't love you so.'

# 27

In a tree-lined street behind Knightsbridge the first cherry blossom buds were showing in a faint tinge of pink against the bare, black branches. Spring was late this year.

Mario stretched in his bed and relished the thought. He had not enjoyed his first winter in England. It had been wet and dull. The first few days of April had not been much better. He had missed his country, his family and his friends. But in a few days he would be off again. His hectic timetable would not allow much opportunity to brood on the English climate. The constant travelling had also prevented him from making friends in London. There had been a few dinner parties given by acquaintances and entertaining by sponsors but very little else in the way of a social life.

Tonight, however, he had been invited to dinner by Colin's wife, Rachel. She had been concerned that the young Argentinian driver might be lonely, so she had badgered Colin to invite him over. Colin had finally relented. Mario lay in bed for a while contemplating an easy day ahead – the first in many weeks. Apart from a two-hour workout in the gym, his time was his own. Throwing on a dressing gown, he went into the small but immaculate kitchen of his bachelor flat to brew some coffee.

The phone rang. Answering it he heard a dull crackle and recognized the call as a long-distance one. 'Hello?' He half expected to hear his father's voice.

'Mario?'

'Yes, who is it?' he asked, hearing a South American accent.

'Mario, it's Chico. You have forgotten your friend already?'

Chico Gazzara. A friend of his sister's. They had met at a party after the race in Rio. Chico was gay, although nobody would have guessed, least of all his sister who had brought him along.

Mario and Chico had hit it off straight away. In a foolish moment, Mario had agreed to see him the following day. Still on a wave of euphoria after the race, he had acted carelessly and they had made love in Chico's flat. It had been a fun experience for him. Nothing more. He was still coming to terms with his bisexuality. Chico was not so ready to forget. He had persuaded Mario's sister to give him his telephone number in London.

'Chico, how are you?' Mario's voice was flat.

'I'm well . . . how are things with you?'

'Fine, thank you.'

'I was thinking of coming to London next week. Will you be there?'

The line crackled and Mario caught the echo . . . Chico, coming to London? His heart sank. He didn't want any distractions in his life right now. All his energies were directed towards racing. He still had a lot to prove. 'I'll be testing in France for most of next week. Then I'll be busy getting ready for the Italian Grand Prix.'

'But Mario, you don't understand . . . I want to see you,' Chico implored.

'I don't think it's a good idea,' Mario replied firmly. 'I'm very busy.'

'I realize that. But what would your family think if they hear their beloved son prefers men to women? And what about all your fans here? Don't make me do it.'

Chico's voice betrayed no hint of the threat that the words carried.

There was a long silence. Mario was weighing up the situation rapidly. Should he call Chico's bluff? How well did he know this man? He was a headstrong Argentinian, wealthy and no doubt used to getting his own way. It was emotional blackmail. Well, let him come over. When he was here he would find a way of silencing him.

'OK. I cannot stop you from coming, but it is not possible for you to stay here. I can book you into a hotel not far away.'

'I can't wait. I shall arrive on Sunday.'

Two days' time. Mario put the phone down. His carefree mood had disappeared as quickly as the clouds scudding across the April sky.

Rachel loved entertaining, filling the big draughty manor house with friends. It came alive with the sound of voices and people. She was looking forward to the dinner party that evening. For once Colin had arrived home early and was fussing over the table layout. Rachel found him in the long oak-panelled dining room. The oblong table was beautifully laid with two large candelabra and an exquisite flower arrangement decorating its centre. It was set for eight people.

'What *is* all the fuss about tonight, Colin? I don't think I've ever known you show such interest in a dinner party. Are you feeling all right?'

'Of course I am. I just wanted to check the place names.'

'I thought naturally as the hostess I would sit next to Mario. I've seated you between Beverly and Bridgette with Stef on the other side of Mario. Dick and Anthony are there,' she said, pointing to the two remaining settings.

Colin scowled and his right eye twitched. 'Stef who? Do I know her?'

'Of course you do. She's been here several times. She's my tennis partner at the club. Forty, divorced, with an outrageous sense of humour.' Stef was also one of her few friends who knew a little about motor racing. It would be a good cross-section of people.

As soon as Rachel had left the room, Colin changed the place names around. Mario could sit next to Bridgette who was thirty-five, fat and bossy. The last thing he wanted was for his wife to make a play for his lover.

Rachel looked ravishing in a Bruce Oldfield dress of deep turquoise and a cluster of diamonds around her neck. The necklace had been a present from Colin after winning the Championship.

'My dear Mario,' Rachel said effusively when he arrived. 'It's so lovely to meet you after all this time.' And in a quieter voice, 'Your photographs in no way do you justice.'

Mario fiddled with his tie nervously. He was feeling uncomfortable in her presence. He was cheating her, yet at the same time he knew he could never compete with such beauty.

Colin blinked rapidly, giving only half an ear to the ebullient Stef who was enthusing endlessly about how lovely the house looked. He knew that Rachel would find Mario attractive and watched her jealously as she conversed eagerly with him.

Over dinner Dick and Colin discussed the events of the last race with their mutual friends, Anthony and Beverly. Mario had been entertaining Bridgette and Stef and much to Rachel's surprise showed a great interest in matters other than motor racing. He was not like many of the other drivers she had met who seemed to be totally wrapped up in their careers.

They had all complimented Rachel on the succulent Beef Wellington and excellent French claret. Once or twice during the meal Mario had caught Colin staring at him. It was a curious irony that he found himself relaxing and enjoying Rachel's company. She was warm, friendly and caring. He wondered if she had any idea of her husband's sexual inclinations. Colin had never discussed it with him. They had managed to keep their relationship separate from any external factors, so far. Mario would never in a million years wish to be the cause of a breakup of Colin's marriage. He was quite happy to be part of a triangle. He was a free spirit and could never imagine himself possessive of Colin. It was curious the way their relationship worked so well. Colin had given Mario a sexual fulfilment he had never known before. With Chico it had been fun, but with Colin . . . he had been the first. He had opened a door that had been locked for so long and Mario was grateful for that.

'Mario, would you like to help me with the coffee?' asked Rachel gently. Rachel's eyes were lit up with a sensuality that made Mario restless. She was one of the sexiest women he had ever met. He couldn't fathom why she should be married to a man like Colin.

He followed Rachel into the kitchen. It was large and spacious with the aroma of fresh coffee emanating from a pot on the cooker.

'This is a beautiful house you have here,' said Mario, admiring the high beamed ceiling decorated with bunches of dried flowers and a variety of copper and brass pans. 'Have you been here long?'

'We bought the house when the children were very

young. Now they are away at boarding school, it's over-large for the two of us.'

'Don't you get lonely here?' It was an innocent question, but suddenly Mario was aware of an implication in it that he hadn't intended.

Rachel was aware too. 'Yes, of course. Colin is away so much and when he does come back to England he is always at the factory. Life can get a little dull.'

She finished arranging the tray of cups and saucers and placed it on the worktop close to Mario. 'It's a long time since I had fun . . . just pure, simple fun . . . Colin is so serious. How about you, Mario, are you terribly serious?' After a few glasses of wine Rachel was feeling flirtatious. She was taken with the naivety of the young man. He had paid her several compliments during the evening, but in a simple and innocent way.

'No, I guess not . . . not all the time,' Mario answered diffidently, sweeping his dark hair from his forehead.

Rachel was standing just inches away from him now. She had a playful smile on her lips. 'Life is so short. In your job you must be very aware of that. We have to enjoy life every minute, don't you think?' She reached up and touched him gently on the cheek.

Mario was rooted to the spot, totally under Rachel's spell. It struck him that in her way she was as persuasive as Colin. In their own way both were strong and charismatic. Mario held Rachel's stare, looking directly into her honey-coloured eyes. Then loud hissing from the cooker gave him the excuse to turn away.

'Your coffee?' he murmured, indicating the dark liquid bubbling over on to the hob and trying, unsuccessfully, to hide his embarrassment.

Rachel went to the hob and switched off the flame

underneath the pot. 'Why Mario, I do believe you're shy? Do I frighten you?' She was back close to him again, enjoying her teasing with the handsome young Latin.

'Rachel, forgive me for being so direct, but I did not think English ladies so . . . ' He paused to think of a suitable word.

'Forward?' A river of excitement flowed through Rachel's body. One more look like that from him and she was sure it would burst its banks.

'You are a very attractive lady. In fact . . . ' Mario was saying as the kitchen door burst open. It was Colin. He stopped in the doorway seeing Mario and Rachel standing close together, almost touching. Jealousy and pain exploded in his head, the veins in his neck bulging.

*'Leave him alone!'* he screamed and leapt forward in rage. He had to separate them with his own hands . . . he had to destroy the terrible image of the two of them so close together. He knew only too well how successful Rachel was at seducing young men. He would make sure she never did that to Mario. He grabbed her roughly by the arm. 'Don't you *ever* touch him again! Do you hear me?'

Rachel was dumbstruck. She had never seen Colin so angry before. She had never known him to be so possessive about her . . . or perhaps it wasn't about her at all? Perhaps it was the young driver who had made Colin so unusually protective?

When Rachel finally took the tray of coffee into the drawing room, she was met by embarrassed looks on the faces of her guests. They must have heard Colin's outburst. Only Stef was looking faintly amused. She couldn't wait until tomorrow's game of tennis with Rachel to find out what Colin's fit of temper had been about.

After everyone had gone, Rachel lay awake until the early hours of the morning. Sleep had eluded her as she recalled the events of the evening. She blamed herself for flirting with Mario. It had been harmless enough. Colin knew her of old, but why had he reacted so strongly this time? They always had an unspoken agreement that she could find her sexual gratification elsewhere, as long as she stayed with Colin.

But tonight was different. Poor Mario was so distressed he had left immediately. The other guests had diplomatically drunk their coffee and departed soon after. What was it that Dick had mentioned in an aside to her as he left? It was almost a word of warning. He had said something about a special relationship between Mario and Colin. Colin, he thought, had this fanatical determination to make Mario the World Champion and nothing was going to stand in his way.

Rachel finally fell asleep. Her last and lingering thought was that somehow, unawares, she had not only stirred up a hornet's nest, she had walked right into it as well.

# 28

The North London pub was grey and dingy on the outside with a nineteen fifties' decor inside. The nicotine-stained wallpaper was as uninspiring as the worn plastic seats of the chairs. Alberto Scapini was not used to such squalid surroundings, but it was appropriate for the brief meeting he had planned, since there was a million to one chance that he would bump into anyone he knew in a place such as this.

Scapini's face was as cold and hostile as the north face of the Eiger. It had a sallow tinge of unhealthiness about it that came from an excess of smoking and caffeine and a lack of exercise. Deep lines either side of his thin mouth accentuated his pinched face. It bore little sign of compassion in a man who had fought every inch of the way to become a team owner in the world of Formula One.

Geoff Jones had already been seated in a corner anxiously sipping a half-pint of bitter when he had arrived. Scapini had bought himself a Scotch and sat down next to him.

'So, how is it going at Delta?' asked Scapini, lighting up a cigarette.

'No problem so far. I think I've settled in well. Tom O'Leary gives me plenty of encouragement.'

'And Pritchard?'

'He's pretty much wrapped up with the drivers and sponsors, thankfully. I keep clear of him if I can.'

'Just don't get on the wrong side of him,' said Scapini, thinking that maybe Colin's character bore a faint resemblance to his own.

'They don't connect me with the accident in Long Beach, not yet anyway. Colin is adamant it was driver error. Max Gregson's not his favourite driver at the moment.'

'Bearing in mind he took that corner at high speed with one wheel about to fall off, I think he did remarkably well. But don't think it's all over. Gregson would have known there was something wrong. They may well get to the bottom of it yet.'

'Well, they'll have to put it down to my inexperience, won't they?' said Geoff, and then asked impatiently, 'What about the money?'

Scapini reached into the inside pocket of his jacket. Discreetly he pulled out a bulky envelope and pushed it across the table. 'You've earned yourself quite a lot in the last two months and there's more to come.'

'How much is here?' asked Geoff, tucking his payment into his pocket.

'Four thousand for the drugs out of Rio and two thousand for the other job,' Scapini said under his smoky breath.

Geoff smiled and nodded. The left side of Scapini's mouth lifted imperceptibly. He had seen it all before. These greedy young guys were like putty in his hands.

Sitting in his flat, Mario was distinctly uneasy. Opposite him, and reclining in an oversize leather sofa, was Chico. The young man was smiling and exquisitely dressed in tailored trousers, a brown mohair jacket and fashionably tasselled Gucci shoes. How different he was from Colin, who rarely wore anything but casual, unstylish clothes. Chico's chocolate-brown hair framed a face of fine features. Prominent eyebrows dipped to an aquiline nose and a wide mouth. A deceptively honest-looking face, thought Mario.

'Well, Chico, what are your plans while you are here?'

Chico leaned forward in his chair, sliding his manicured hands up and down the tall glass of whisky Mario had poured for him. 'I have a cousin here I would like to see, but apart from that, I was hoping to persuade you to continue with our relationship. It was good between us, yes?'

Mario swallowed hard and spoke slowly and deliberately. 'You have to understand that it's all over. It was one night, for God's sake.'

'And what a night, eh Mario?'

Yes, there had been a good chemistry between them. Mario hadn't forgotten that. But on his return to England, he had closed his mind to it. There was the next race to concentrate on and his relationship with Colin. 'I must ask you to promise me not to breathe a word of this to anyone. I have thousands of fans back home. It would not be easy for me if these things leaked out.'

Chico smiled, long and slow. 'Don't look so worried. It's not a problem.'

'No?' Mario was surprised and relieved.

'No, not if we stay lovers.'

Mario felt a cold shiver run down his back as he remembered Colin's fury on the night of the dinner party. 'That is not possible.'

'I am very attracted to you. Is that so bad?' asked Chico with a dreamy smile on his lips.

'You must understand I don't have lovers. What happened between us in Rio was a moment of madness for me.' If Mario had not been so frightened by this whole affair he would have been the first to admit that Chico was an incredibly handsome and desirable young man. He paused, unable to avoid the question that was troubling him. 'Is it money you want?'

Chico rose to his full six feet and walked across to Mario. He bent over so that his face was inches away from Mario's.

'Mario, I beg of you . . . '

Mario was suddenly afraid that he would give in to him. He was confused, frantically so. He had to break the spell that was suffocating him.

Chico was pleading again. 'Come on, Mario, you know it was the best experience of your life. I am a wonderful lover . . . I don't have to tell you that . . . '

Mario's self control snapped. He had heard enough. Brushing Chico aside, he stood up. 'You must get out of my life. Go back to your other men, go back to Rio, but *leave me* alone! I beg of you,' he entreated in a raised voice.

'I like it when you get angry,' Chico teased, giving him a lascivious smile.

'Get out!' Mario screamed.

Chico grabbed him by the arm. 'Not so fast. You want me as much as I want you. Look at you, you're as hard as a stallion. What is it, you feel guilty? You have another lover? So what? Come on, Mario, you want *me* . . . ' Chico's words hit Mario's conscience as painfully as hailstones on his face.

'*No!*' Mario grabbed his leather jacket and the keys to his car. More than anything, he had to be alone, away from the strong lure of sex.

'You'll change your mind, you'll see,' called Chico, but Mario was already through the door.

He climbed into his black Porsche and with wheels spinning, screamed off into the London traffic. He dodged in and out of the cars as he headed towards the M4. It was a relief just to be behind the wheel of a car, listening to its throaty revs and feeling the power of the engine. Unlike his emotions, this was a situation over which he had perfect control. Driving was the way to restore his calm. As he reached speeds of a hundred miles an hour, he realized what a turmoil his life was in. He was being pulled in too many directions . . . by Colin . . . by Chico. Above all, he wanted his life off the race track to be free of any pressure.

For some inexplicable reason he turned off the motorway towards Oxford and was soon on the country roads, heading in the direction of Colin's house. It had not been a conscious decision. Why? he asked himself. Was it to see Colin or Rachel? Did he want to prove to himself that he could still enjoy a woman?

He began driving with increased *brio*, taking the bends at high speed. Driving was his true passion and nobody, not even Chico, would deny him the thrill of it. Coming up quickly behind a truck, he could see a bend in the road ahead. There was enough room for him to pass. He did a lightning gear change down to third, accelerated and was almost past the truck when he caught sight of a car coming towards him. Had he been a few feet further on, Mario could have swerved in front of the truck and just made it. Instead he had only one choice to avoid a head-on collision. He swerved off the road, hoping against all odds that he would not hit the trees that were now in his vision. He veered off on to the verge and hit the brakes. At the same time the oncoming car clipped his near side with such force that the Porsche overbalanced. Mario tried to correct it but it was too late. Slowly, it seemed to him very slowly, the car rolled and Mario felt the impact of a shuddering crack, as the car hit one of the trees. His last memory was of staring at the caved-in roof of the Porsche and wondering how much damage he had done to his beautiful car.

# 29

Twenty-four hours later Colin was on his way in the company jet to the Paul Ricard circuit in the south of France. Max was with him for a three-day test session. Colin had been in a blind rage over Mario's disappearance, and despite numerous phone calls, had been unable to trace him. His anger had mellowed to concern as the hours passed. He was beginning to wonder if Mario's disappearance was in any way connected with his own outburst at the dinner party.

An hour after Colin's jet had left Heathrow, the Delta factory received a phone call from the police informing them that Mario Rodriguez was in the John Radcliffe Hospital in Oxford in a stable condition following a road accident. He had regained consciousness and was miraculously unhurt except for bruising and a couple of cracked ribs. Colin's secretary rang Rachel to tell her the news.

Rachel drove to the hospital straight away. She sat on the edge of the hard plastic chair next to Mario's bed. Bottles with drips and a heart-monitor machine, now superfluous, stood close by. Rachel studied the pale, sleeping face of Mario. He would wake soon, the nurse had told her. He had been sleeping a lot since he had regained consciousness, and was still suffering from concussion. He looked so young and peaceful, it was hard to believe that he risked his life so often on the race track.

It was half an hour before Mario stirred. As he opened his eyes Rachel reached out and touched his smooth tanned hand. 'Mario?' she whispered.

A hint of a smile crossed his face as he saw hers clouded in a veil of concern. 'Hi, it's good to see you,' he said.

'How are you feeling?'

'Fine, no problem, except that I have this big pain inside my head.' Mario tried to sit up but winced in pain.

'Careful, Mario. You have two fractured ribs somewhere down there.'

'Ouch, I guess so. Do you have a cigarette?'

Rachel reached into her bag and pulled out a packet. 'I didn't know you smoked.'

Mario smiled. 'I gave it up when I was twenty.' He drew shakily on the cigarette that Rachel had lit. 'Does Colin know I'm here?'

'He will by now, I'm sure. You know he went to Paul Ricard yesterday – the police only contacted the factory this morning.'

'My orders . . . I did not want to see Colin . . . '

'Why ever not?'

Mario shrugged and turned away to the green-painted windows and the forlorn grey sky beyond.

'Who knows? I thought if he saw me here like this, he might start looking for a replacement driver.'

'He's been worried out of his mind – you know how much he thinks of you – he wouldn't let you go that easily. Dick told me your car was in a terrible mess.'

'Yes, he came to see me this morning.'

'Do you remember anything about the accident?'

'Yes,' Mario sighed deeply. 'I remember I was driving a little crazy . . . '

'Well, thank God you weren't seriously injured, Mario. Were you on your way over to see us? You were pretty close to our home.'

Mario stared down at the annoying piece of plastic with

his name tag strapped to his wrist. With one sharp yank he tore it off. 'This damn thing irritates me. It makes me feel I'm labelled for the mortuary.' Mario didn't want to explain his reasons for being so close to their village. 'No,' he said finally. 'I was on my way somewhere else.' Mario took one more pull on his cigarette and looked round for an ashtray. Rachel passed him one and he stubbed it out.

'Rachel, thank you for coming to see me. Will you do me one more favour?'

'What is it?' As she spoke Rachel threw her long gleaming copper hair over her shoulder. Mario couldn't help but admire her. She must be five years older than him and yet she had a natural warmth and youth about her that was infectious.

'I want to get out of here. The next race is in a few days.'

'Forget the race. You're staying here until the doctors clear you. You've got concussion, Mario.'

'If I stay here I will go mad, for sure. My body will seize up. I need some fresh air and exercise.'

'OK. I've a suggestion to make. If, and only if, I get the all clear from the doctors, why don't you come and convalesce with us? There's plenty of fresh air and I can make sure you have lots of rest and good food.'

Mario's expression darkened. 'Thank you, but I don't think it is a good idea.'

Rachel was reading his thoughts. 'If it's about what happened the other evening, don't worry, I'm not going to seduce you.' She hoped Mario would share her joke but he remained serious. She went on, 'Colin feels very bad about the way he behaved. He'll be fine, you'll see.'

'I'm not so sure.' Mario could not imagine being under the same roof as Colin and his wife. It seemed bizarre. He wanted no more complications in his life.

'Leave it to me,' Rachel assured him and, kissing him on the cheek, went off to find the doctor in charge.

Colin sat in his office in a rare moment of contemplation. The test sessions at Paul Ricard had not gone well. Max had crashed heavily on the first day and written off a car. Luckily he had escaped with only bruising. Then two engines had blown on the second day – £70,000 worth of machinery in one morning was expensive, even for one of the highest financed teams. Then there was Mario. Staring at the pictures on the wall, he wondered where Mario had been going the afternoon of the accident. Was it just coincidence that he had been a few miles from their house? Had he been on his way to visit Rachel?

Now Colin was without a driver for the next race at Imola in Italy. Good drivers were hard to find at such short notice. He had called up an old friend of his, Don Soxon, who had retired from Formula One a year ago. Don was driving saloon cars at Donington that weekend. The only other possibility was a young Italian driver, Hugo Amarti, who had showed great promise as a test driver with one of the other teams.

When Hugo received a phone call from Colin, he jumped at the chance to drive for the Delta team. With the replacement driver found, Colin then issued a statement to the press. He played down the seriousness of the accident and stated that Mario was suffering from bruising and slight concussion and would be fit to drive after the San Marino Grand Prix. However, there were still questions that Colin alone needed answers to and he intended to find them soon.

Mario was sitting in the conservatory finishing a light breakfast when Colin joined him. It was the first chance they had had to be alone since the accident. Mario was reading a small article in the *Daily Telegraph* about his accident and his replacement for the next race. His eyes stung with disappointment.

Colin sat down in one of the white cane chairs and poured himself a cup of lukewarm coffee. The room had a pleasant ambience with its terracotta tiled floor and abundance of greenery. Colin had often complained that Rachel's love of gardening had gone too far. The conservatory bore too great a resemblance to Kew Gardens for his liking. 'Are you going to tell me about it?' Colin asked bluntly. The mood between them was subdued.

Colin had been furious with Rachel when she had installed Mario in the house without consulting him. Mario was a part of his life which he liked to keep separate and for the two to merge was unthinkable. It was a threatening intrusion.

'About the accident you mean?'

'You were only five miles from here. Were you coming to see Rachel?'

Colin studied the tense young face. He wanted to be gentle with him, but Mario was hiding something. He couldn't relax until he knew the answers.

'Where is Rachel?' asked Mario. He didn't enjoy being here with Colin alone. Rachel might appear at any moment.

'She's gone into Wallingford to do some shopping. Well?'

'For God's sake, Colin, I was out for a drive.'

'How did you lose the car on that bend? It's not a tight corner – I've driven it a hundred times myself.'

'I just did,' said Mario sulkily and suddenly weary.

'Mario, I am your employer, remember? I deserve an explanation.'

'OK. I was overtaking just before the bend. I was half

way past a truck when this other car came very fast the other way. I had no choice but to leave the road.'

'And nearly kill yourself, you bloody fool.' Colin's fists clenched tightly. The accident had only further proved to him how strong his feelings were for Mario.

'You mean it's OK for me to risk death on the race track but not on the road? Because I'm not getting paid for that. Is that what you are saying?' Mario choked back his anger. Colin was treating him like a wilful child again. He hated it.

'No, that's not what I mean. It's just that sometimes I get scared about what might happen to you.'

Mario gave a mocking laugh and stood up. 'Then perhaps it would suit you better if I quit my job tomorrow,' he replied fiercely and left the room, still limping badly.

Colin gave a deep sigh of exasperation. That Mario was his lover and also a driver who risked death at every race were two thoughts that did not co-exist easily in his mind.

Mario had become reclusive in the house while Colin was there. When Colin left for the Grand Prix in Italy, he was even more depressed. The days seemed to stretch on interminably. Rachel did her best to mother him and distract his thoughts from the race. It was a hard battle.

The weather was warm and fine for early April. Mario sat in a sheltered corner by the house dozing in the afternoon sunshine, listening to a bee making an early foray from its hibernation. His thoughts were never far from the Grand Prix and his frustration at having to miss a race with his new team.

Rachel popped her head round the conservatory door. 'Mario, there's a friend of yours on the phone. Do you want to speak with him?'

'What is his name?' asked Mario indifferently.

'Chico something. Sounds like he's from your part of the world.'

'No, tell him I'll call back,' said Mario, suddenly agitated. He wondered how his tormentor had found his whereabouts and phone number.

Rachel returned and sat down in a chair next to him. 'Is Chico a close friend of yours?'

'No, not really.'

'He sounded pretty upset that you wouldn't come to the phone. He wanted to come and see you, but I thought I would ask you first. Anyway, I've left his number by the phone.'

'You have been very understanding with me over the last few days. I want to thank you, Rachel.'

'I've enjoyed it. It's been marvellous to have some company. I do get bored here on my own when Colin is away.'

Mario smiled. 'I know. I remember you telling me the night of the dinner party. You nearly caused an international incident.'

Rachel sat back in the chair, luxuriating in the feel of warm sun on her face. Mario studied her smooth complexion, her sparkling eyes, the handsome line of her profile. She had been so caring and giving of her time with him. He was indebted to her. She had also handled Colin very well when he had become petulant as she had fussed over their guest. Rachel felt Mario's eyes upon her. 'You don't approve of me, do you?' she asked, mildly amused.

'I think you are a wonderful woman,' replied Mario sincerely.

'But that first night we met . . . disapproval was written all over your face.'

'I work for your husband, Rachel – I have to be extremely careful.'

'Do you know something? Sometimes I feel Colin thinks more of you than he does of me. In a funny sort of way, I'm almost jealous of you . . . And you have this wonderful bond with the racing.' She sat up and gave him one of her quizzical looks. 'But it doesn't stop me fancying you terribly.'

'You certainly are a very direct lady,' said Mario, dying with embarrassment inside. 'I also think you like playing games with people. Maybe you would like me as your plaything, but I'm not like that.'

'More's the pity,' Rachel laughed. 'Do you have many girlfriends?'

'Yes, a few back home, but there is nobody important in my life.'

'Well, I guess you're no different from any of the other drivers. I believe they all have a lot of women followers.'

'Some do. Others are more interested in their cars.'

'And Max?' Rachel asked casually. 'Does he have anyone?'

Mario gave a wry laugh. 'Max? He is the worst. He is crazy with women.' Then suddenly aware that it might get back to Max's wife, he stopped. It was best to stay quiet on these things.

Rachel thought of Vicky at home and wondered if she knew he played around. If she were married to someone like Max she would make damn sure she wore him out long before he got near a race track.

# 30

Nowhere is the magnetic attraction of Formula One more apparent than at the San Marino Grand Prix. In reality the San Marino is another Italian Grand Prix. The tiny self-governing principality with its inadequate road systems does not lend itself easily to a grand prix, so the race takes place fifty miles from San Marino at Imola on a track named after the late father and son, Enzo e Dino Ferrari.

The fans, or *tifosi* as they are known, eat, sleep and breathe the sport. They learn from a very early age that the Ferrari team is accorded a status that comes second only to that of the Pope. The fans flock to experience first hand the rapture of the sport and to worship their drivers. They scan the pit lane from the distance of the grandstands, hoping to spot their favourite driver. They wait by the entrance to the paddock for hours, hoping to get an autograph from their heroes.

Max stood in the pit lane enjoying the warm spring sunshine, his overalls tied around his waist and his red T-shirt still showing the patches of damp sweat from a hard morning's practice. He had been glad to get out of the car. It was one of those days when he never seemed to find the break to make a fast lap. He consoled himself that there was the afternoon session yet to come. His thoughts were interrupted by a balding Italian journalist who spoke little English and reeked of garlic. He was firing rapid questions at Max who was losing interest just as quickly. His eyes strayed to a young Italian girl in amongst the pit lane bustle. She was talking to one of the mechanics. Her hair, gleaming and black as a raven's, fell to within an inch of her waist. Her body was lithe and trim.

Max excused himself from the journalist and made his way to the motor home, followed by a trail of fans.

'Could you give me your autograph?' asked a voice as he was about to shut the door. He was pleasantly surprised to see the coquettish smile of the young Italian girl. Her face, although ordinary, radiated an innocent happiness.

'Sure. What's your name?'

'Michelle,' she answered, her eyes alight with excitement.

'You are French?' Max asked, scribbling on her programme.

'My mother – she is French, my father Italian.'

Max's entry into the motor home coincided with the departure of the chief designer of Scapini's team. They exchanged a nod and a smile. 'What did he want?' enquired Max of Colin, who was busy writing at the table.

'It's what I want from him,' replied Colin succinctly.

'He'll be giving no secrets away,' said Max, helping himself to an orange juice from the fridge.

'I want him to come and join us on the design team, next year.'

'What about Jean?'

'We keep him working on next year's design. I want Raphael for a brand new car two years hence.'

Max raised his eyebrows in surprise. 'Two designers in one team. Isn't that a rather expensive luxury?'

'Jean is good and I don't want to lose him, but Raphael, he's the best there is. He could be a valuable asset to the team.'

Max sat down at the table opposite Colin. 'Does Scapini know anything about this?'

'No, and it would be in Raphael's best interests if it is kept secret. Scapini won no prizes at the Italian Charm School and he will probably be after my hide if Raphael does agree to work for us.'

'Didn't you have some altercation with Scapini in the past?'

Colin shot Max a penetrating glance. 'Yes. He's a nasty piece of work and I for one wouldn't have any compunction about poaching one of his team.'

Max wondered if Colin knew what he was up against. It was one thing to head-hunt a designer from another team, but to take on Scapini with his rumoured Mafia connections? It left Max just a little apprehensive about the consequences.

Later that evening Max was sitting at the hotel bar enjoying a beer with Jean and Dick. Dick raised his glass. 'Well done, Max. You certainly put it all together this afternoon. Let's hope tomorrow will be the same.'

A broad grin spread across Max's face. He had driven like a man possessed and he had set the fastest time. If he could repeat it tomorrow for final practice, he would earn his first pole position of the season and hopefully win his first points.

A group of noisy Italians entered the bar – among them Hugo Amarti, Mario's replacement. Max had decided he was cocky and too full of himself, even though he had surprised everyone by his creditable fourth in qualifying. The race on his home territory had turned him into a national hero overnight and he was already behaving like one.

To Max's chagrin he also noticed the girl from the pits standing next to Hugo. Max's reaction did not go unnoticed by Dick. 'You've got disappointment written all over your face,' he said wryly. 'That's Hugo's sister. Better not meddle there. Our Italian friend is known for his fiery temper.'

Max gave a mock sigh. 'Thanks, Dick,' and he turned his back on the group. *Domani*, there was always *domani*.

The Italian crowd were screaming and hysterically waving their prancing-horse flags. The atmosphere was charged with an excitement that only the Italian fans can generate. They waited breathlessly for the hammerhead nose of the Ferrari to appear round the final bend.

The qualifying times were now crucial. A thousandth of a second separated Max from the Ferrari driver, Terri Dacco. In the few remaining minutes of practice, Terri snatched pole position and the crowd reacted as boisterously as if he had won the race.

For once, Colin was not unduly disappointed that Max had lost pole position. He knew it would give Max the extra challenge to get past the Italian driver and he had no doubt that if his reactions to the green light were a split second faster than his rival's, he would manage this on the first bend. Hugo had also done well, keeping a cool head despite an earlier spin, and had scraped sixth place. For only his second Grand Prix it was an impressive achievement. Colin hoped he wouldn't lose his nerve in the race. It was often the failing of new drivers.

At six thirty the following morning, Geoff Jones was awakened by the sound of the phone ringing shrilly a few feet from his ear. It seemed like only five minutes ago he had put his head on the pillow. It had been a late nightshift for all the mechanics. 'Hello,' he answered wearily.

Scapini did not introduce himself. He came directly to the point. Geoff was to loosen an electrical connection in Max's car some time before the race.

'That might not be so easy . . . ' Geoff began.

Scapini sensed his reluctance. 'Just do it,' he barked. 'You're getting paid enough. Electrical failure is common enough. They won't suspect a thing.'

When Geoff put the phone down, he was slowly beginning to realize the stupidity of what he had got himself into. Having just worked like a slave to get the car perfect, he now had to undo all the hard work he and the rest of the mechanics had done. He tossed and turned for a few minutes, feeling like the worm in the apple. Then the prospect of the handsome reward allayed his anxiety. He told himself that it was more compensation for what had happened to his father. Like Scapini he wanted revenge on Colin.

Back in the early days of Delta his father had worked in the factory on the machine tools. A faulty machine had caused his father's hand to be mangled around a high-speed lathe in a bloody spectacle of dismembered fingers and crushed bone. His father was left with a stump where his hand had been. Colin had denied negligence and blamed the accident on his father's lapse in concentration. His father hadn't had the courage to fight back.

Now Geoff was old enough, he set about seeking revenge. Pritchard was ruthless. Yes, it was time the tables turned for him. He had enjoyed success. Now it was his turn to experience disappointment and disillusionment, just like Geoff's father. It was lucky for Geoff that his boss had made no connection with his surname. But then Jones was a common enough name.

* * *

Max skipped breakfast in the main dining room of the hotel and drove early with Dick to the track, carefully avoiding the press and other team personnel.

'Well, what happened to you last night?' asked Dick as he drove through the already snarled-up traffic.

Max put his hand up to his eye which was still sore and puffy and turning an inky shade of blue.

'Looks like you had a problem?'

Max grinned sheepishly. 'You could say that. You were right about that Hugo. He's got a really mean streak.'

Dick burst out laughing and had to swerve to avoid some crazy Italian trying to overtake him. 'Tell me more.'

'I was having a very pleasant evening with his sister, Michelle, in my room. We were enjoying a meal together when there was a knock at the door and a voice calls "Room Service". When I opened it, there was bloody Hugo jumping up and down like some incensed toad. He wops me one round the eye, drags his sister out of the room and leaves me with a fortune in Beef Wellington and champagne.'

'Wopped by a wop!' chortled Dick. 'How are you going to explain that one away to Colin?'

'The bruise? I shall tell him I walked into the bathroom door in the night.'

'I think he'd be more likely to believe you if you said you tripped over your zimmer frame.'

Max had never known such enthusiasm from the Italian crowds. The grandstands across from the pits were a sea of banners and Italian flags, and rang with a chanting of the Italian drivers' names. *'Hugo! Hugo! Terri! Terri!'*

There was the usual buzz of activity on the grid as the twenty-six cars took their positions for the race. Max sat in the car, switching off from all the uproar and excitement around him and trying to ignore the throbbing above his eye. Ahead of him was one car and he had to beat it. Terri would have the crowd of a hundred thousand behind him and that always accounted for an extra second a lap for the favoured driver.

Geoff Jones had been sent back to the transporter that acted as their spares workshop, to find a part for the car. The countdown to the start was on. Geoff came running back to the grid. Colin was waiting impatiently for his return, his right eye twitching frantically. He had never got used to these last-minute emergencies and wiped his brow for the third time in as many minutes.

Geoff, on the other hand, had only one thought pounding in his brain as he rushed back to the grid. Would he have time to sabotage Max's car?

An hour or so into the race, Terri Dacco was maintaining a lead of two seconds ahead over Max. The crowds were deafening in their approval. For Max the two seconds – the time it took to breathe in and out – were crucial. He would need every last ounce of concentration to get past Terri. There were now only eighteen laps to go. The front runners were lapping the slower cars and although young Hugo was still hanging on to eighth position he was a lap behind Max.

Terri came up behind a bunch of the slower cars. He overtook them before the sharp Rivazza bend. Max, hard on his heels, attempted to do the same but his two-second disadvantage meant that he could pass only two of the cars. One still lay ahead before the bend and Max recognized the familiar colours of his team mate, Hugo.

Max was now level with him and Hugo kept to the inside line as they accelerated out of the corner. To the spectators in the grandstands witnessing this exciting moment it was hard to grasp exactly what happened. Had Hugo gone wide or had Max cut in?

As Max accelerated past him their wheels clipped. Metal touched metal and Max could feel the vibration and bump as Hugo's front spoiler separated from the car. The young inexperienced driver left the track and spun off, hitting the armco barrier, once then twice, before coming to rest in a cloud of dust.

Now only ten laps remained. Max desperately needed to win this race to prove to himself that his luck had returned. There had been so many disappointments lately, he was beginning to believe that something or somebody was against him.

He could see the brake lights of the Ferrari getting closer. Slowly he was reeling him in. Then he was right on him. It just needed a second for Max to pounce and he would be through.

Then suddenly it was if someone had cut the invisible cord between the two cars. Max felt a sickening sensation in his stomach as the car lost power. The engine had cut out and he was cruising to a halt. His head swirled with the unreality of it all and then anger tore through him, flooding his veins in short, hot blasts as he realized his chance for victory was over.

At a press gathering after the race, Hugo vehemently blamed Max for his accident. There was a replay of the incident on the TV and there remained little doubt that Max had not left Hugo sufficient room. Back in the motor home, Max had changed and was ready to leave. He had had enough for one day and was in no mood to face the irate Italian and more of his rantings. Before he could leave, however, Colin cornered him. 'What the hell happened, Max? Taking off your team mate is pretty bloody stupid in my book.'

'Hugo took a wide line. There was little I could do,' said Max defensively.

'Bullshit, Max, and you know it. If you think he was in the wrong you better go and look at the replay.'

It was then that Hugo's white, drawn face appeared through the door. His eyes looked accusingly at Max. 'So you take your vendettas on to the race track,' he wanted to scream at him, but he held back. It had been sweet revenge for him that Max had also not finished the race.

'Sorry about the shunt,' Max apologized. But Colin could detect a far too casual ring to Max's voice. There was more to this than either driver was letting on. He could feel the animosity raging between them. Colin would choose his time to have it out with Max. In the meantime there were other problems.

'Now about this electrical failure?' he said, addressing the two race engineers who had arrived for the debriefing. 'Any ideas why it didn't show up in practice?'

Max joined the traffic leaving the circuit and was soon in the slow procession that led to the autostrada. Instinctively he weaved his way through the lines of cars back to the hotel. It had been another bad race for him and he wondered when his luck was going to change. It was the same for many drivers. Once they got a run of bad luck, they grew nervous and that seemed to compound the problem. He found himself thinking the ridiculous. Had he changed an item of his clothing? Was he wearing something different to what he normally wore? He dismissed his superstitious thoughts as quickly as they sprang to mind.

But as he drove into the hotel car park he was seriously

considering that perhaps his red underpants were not lucky for him after all.

By seven o'clock he had showered, changed and opened his first cold beer of the day. He sipped it slowly, shutting the accident with Hugo out of his mind. It had been unfortunate that their cars had touched and Max was still unsure in his own mind if it had been an error on his part or Hugo driving wide.

At that moment Michelle came out of the bathroom. She, too, had showered and her hair fell in heavy cascades on to the short silk dressing gown that Max had bought her in the exclusive shopping arcade of the hotel. He could see the outline of her tall, slim body and in the parting at the front, her small brown bush peeped through provocatively. Max was more than ready to continue where they had so abruptly left off the night before.

# 31

By the time Colin had returned from Italy, Mario had moved back to his flat and received the all clear from the specialists to drive again. He had been in the flat only a few hours when he received the call he had been dreading. It was Chico, anxious to see him. Mario could see little point in postponing their meeting.

Chico arrived at the flat full of exuberance, but he could see straight away that his mood was not reciprocated.

'How long do you intend to stay?' asked Mario, pouring him a straight Scotch.

'Who knows? This is my first visit to London and I'm enjoying it very much. I think I will stay for a while, especially now you are well again.' Chico took a sip from his glass. 'Hey, I've found this club in Chelsea – lots of Italians and great English guys. How about we go one night?'

'Let's get one thing straight. I am not interested in you or your clubs. If you want to stay in London, that is up to you, but I don't want you ever to contact me again. Is that understood?'

Mario had braced himself against any further pleading from Chico. He was no longer a threat. The enforced rest had left him stronger, more in charge of his life. The affair with Chico had taught him a salutary lesson; that he could indulge only in relationships with people he could really trust. Otherwise . . .

'If we cannot be lovers, then at least let us be friends,' said Chico affably.

'Friends? Since when do friends threaten to blackmail?'

Mario paused. 'Is there anything you need before you leave?' he asked in a quieter voice.

Mario waited for the bottom line. He was sure that Chico would demand a pay-off for his silence. Chico shrugged as if the thought had not occurred to him. 'Well, living here is very expensive. I have run up a lot of bills.'

Mario walked over to his leather-topped writing desk and took a large envelope from underneath a pile of letters. It was bulky and sealed. 'Here, take this. It will see you through your stay. To save you asking, there are three thousand pounds in there.'

Chico studied the envelope, then Mario. 'I don't want this . . . ' he protested lightly and feigned an expression of indignation.

'Take it. Now, if you will excuse me, I have an appointment in ten minutes.'

'Sure, I understand. But can I see you before I leave?'

'No more calls, no more contact,' said Mario sharply.

'OK, OK.' Chico stood up hastily and put on his coat. '*Caio*, Mario. Stay cool.'

He smiled as he left and was still wearing the same smile as he hurried down the stairs. It was the easiest three thousand pounds he had ever made. He could hit the clubs tonight without giving money a second thought. And, he reminded himself smugly, there was plenty more where that came from.

Colin arrived early to see Mario. As he climbed the stairs he almost bumped into Chico. Colin gave him a wary look. Had he just come from Mario's flat? Colin suppressed the jealousy welling up inside him. He steeled himself as he rang the doorbell. But Mario seemed genuinely pleased to see him and was full of questions about the race.

Colin was quick to take in everything around him. The

room was expensively but simply furnished. On the oval, marble coffee table was a neat pile of magazines, a vase of carnations left by the cleaning lady, and a large bowl of carefully arranged fruit. Colin also noticed a half-finished glass of Scotch. 'You're not hitting the hard stuff, are you?' he asked disapprovingly.

'No,' said Mario, taken aback. 'I just had a friend call.'

'I passed him on the stairs,' said Colin with a hint of suspicion in his voice. 'Is he Argentinian?'

'For sure. He's over here visiting. He called to bring news of my family.'

'Have you known him very long?'

'A month or so. Colin, what is this? Questions, questions. Don't you trust me?'

Colin gave him a penetrating glance. He was not sure of him yet. He was not sure of himself with Mario either. He had berated himself for being so possessive. It wasn't easy. He must relax and enjoy his friendship.

As if he had been reading his thoughts, Mario's face broke into a smile. 'Relax. Come, sit down and have a drink.'

'Mario, just one thing.' Colin and Mario were lying in bed watching the dusk darken the room and the street lamp cast a warm glow. 'You wouldn't lie to me, would you?'

Mario turned and looked at Colin. 'No, what made you ask that?' he said carefully.

Colin couldn't answer; he didn't have an answer. All he knew was that he had an overpowering infatuation for this beautiful young man and that Mario would always call the shots as far as their relationship was concerned. He was uncomfortable with the vulnerability of it all. Nobody had ever held that power over him.

*   *   *

Vicky was hanging new curtains in the large bay window of the hall, the warm colours of red and gold contrasting brightly against the dark oak sill and beams in the high vaulted ceiling. The phone rang a few feet away from her. She stepped down from the stepladder and her heels clicked on the polished wood floor as she went to answer it.

She heard Rachel's breezy voice on the other end. 'Hi, Vicky, how are you?'

'Rachel. I'm well and how are you?' answered Vicky, delighted to hear from her.

'I'm surviving – just! The house seems awfully empty without Mario.'

'Is he better now?' Vicky remembered the young Argentinian she had met at Long Beach.

'He's tons better. I think he enjoyed his convalescence with us. He's very shy, mind you.' Being shy in Rachel's terms probably meant he didn't try and seduce her. 'Anyway, I was ringing to find out if you are free for lunch next week?'

'That sounds like a good idea. Seems ages since I saw you.'

'It is. That's why I thought we should meet for a news update. How about Wednesday?'

'Fine. Shall we make it in London? I need to buy a few things up there.'

'Yes, why not. Usual place, midday?'

'I'll look forward to it. 'Bye.'

At twelve thirty San Lorenzo's in Beauchamp Place was already buzzing with customers. It had a friendly informality about it and Vicky loved the pampered ambience. She arrived wearing a tailored suit in beige linen with a bronze taffeta blouse. Her hair was tied back, revealing a pair of large pearl drop earrings. Her slim figure and chic appearance made many a head turn as she sat down at the table.

Rachel had left home as usual in a blazing hurry, having lost all track of time because of the string of phone calls she had received that morning. She had thrown on a black wool dress, a long jacket of mauve wool and a string of pearls the size of small eggs. Despite her mad dash she still appeared elegant. Her auburn hair fell softly about her shoulders and she looked so pretty that as she took her seat at the table, Vicky could not help admiring her flawless complexion and clear wide eyes.

'The traffic out there is horrendous. I need a drink,' Rachel said breathlessly, her expressive mouth showing a touch of tan lipstick. 'Vicky, you look lovely as usual. Did you manage to do all your shopping? Ah, there's the waiter. Vicky, what shall we have, a bottle of the Mersault?'

'Slow down, Rachel, and get your breath back. I've already ordered two glasses of Kir.'

They chatted animatedly over a lunch of pasta, salad and a bottle of wine, catching up with each other's domestic news. It was only later that they mentioned the racing scene, the other half of their lives.

'I was thinking of going to the race at Monaco in a couple of weeks' time,' said Vicky.

'That's after the race in Belgium, isn't it? It's not like you to socialize with all those *nouveaux riches* and *poseurs*,' returned Rachel with a wicked grin.

'I know. But I fancy a hedonistic weekend. Some friends of Julian's have a yacht in the harbour, so we will be able to relax there. Besides, I was hoping to persuade Max to take a few days off after the race and drive to Provence. It's so lovely at this time of the year.'

'Sounds terrific. Trying to entice Colin into having a holiday is like trying to persuade the Pope to take a wife. I guess we'll have to wait until the winter now.' Rachel sighed.

Vicky sensed a lurking discontent in Rachel and noticed she was drinking far more than usual. When her friend called the waiter over and ordered another bottle of wine she showed her surprise. 'Rachel? Are you sure you ought to? What about driving home?'

But Rachel was unabashed. 'Don't be a spoilsport. You can drive me to the nearest train station or I can catch a cab. It's no problem.'

'If I wasn't meeting Max later, I could drive you home,' said Vicky apologetically.

'Dear Vicky, always so caring and responsible. Don't you ever want to do anything a little crazy yourself?'

'Like what?' asked Vicky cautiously.

'Get wildly drunk, or have an affair? We all need some sort of release from this pressured world.'

Vicky felt herself blushing. In the old days she would have told Rachel about any affair she was having. They would have laughed and chatted about it. Now it was different. She couldn't share her secret. The affair with Phil had hurt her deeply and she had put it behind her. Those fleeting moments of happiness had left her with guilt and remorse. Not much else had been gained by it.

'You've gone very serious, Vicky,' said Rachel. 'You're not thinking of having an affair, are you?' She stifled a small giggle.

'No, I'm not. I know Max is no angel, but I still love him, and whatever happens he always comes home to me . . . '

'So does Colin at the end of the day, but there's little love lost between us.' Rachel let the waiter refill her glass and took a sip. 'There is this big empty void in my life . . . '

'What became of Doug Spender?'

'Hum . . . he decided to try and put all his eggs in one basket and they cracked.' Rachel gave a shrill laugh.

'How do you mean?'

'He got very jealous of Mario being in the house. Well, it did put paid to our early morning romps. But he suddenly decided that he wanted me to leave Colin and go and live with him. I mean, can you imagine it? A harmless flirtation like that and he goes over the top. I soon put a stop to that . . . and his damned eggs.'

'I thought you liked his eggs,' said Vicky meekly.

'Well, you can have too much of a good thing. Besides, I prefer free range . . . and to range free.' She giggled at her own joke.

'Is it really worth it in the end?' asked Vicky thoughtfully.

'Getting drunk? No. I always pay a high price with the hangover. Having an affair? The pleasure of that lasts a hell of a lot longer and I never seem to suffer any after effects.'

'You're very lucky then.'

'Vicky, you're hiding something from me. I know it, but don't tell me if you don't want to.'

'I'd rather not.'

Rachel touched her hand and looked at her with concern for a moment. 'Well, I promised Colin I'd buy something for the divine Mario's birthday present. Any ideas?'

'Nothing that springs to mind. Have you heard the latest? I hear he's not exactly interested in women.'

'What do you mean?'

'Well, I heard from a reliable source, he's gay.'

'Gay?' shrieked Rachel across the restaurant.

'Sorry to tell you the bad news,' said Vicky, watching the shock spread across Rachel's face. 'You didn't fancy him that much, did you?' she whispered.

Rachel couldn't believe what she had just heard. Her mind was full of confused signals. A peculiar and frightening sensation was running through her. A vague thought that had been lurking in the back of her mind suddenly began to crystallize into something terrible. The conversation she'd had with Mario in the garden came back to her. What was it she had said to him? '*. . . I sometimes feel that Colin thinks more of you than he does of me in a funny sort of way.*' In a funny sort of way . . . what way?

Rachel, with a growing revulsion, fought off the idea that was now invading her mind. She shuddered and suddenly felt horribly sick.

# 32

The study was a room of ordered and methodical tidiness. Next to a silent computer and fax machine sat a couple of reference books. Under the window looking out on to a small stretch of lawn and rambling walled garden was a large oak writing desk. Carefully arranged on its polished top were a pile of papers, a small brass clock, a blue telephone and a large leather-bound desk diary. An enamelled lacquer tray held a neat arrangement of pencils and fountain pens. The only non-functional pieces were two photographs in silver frames, one of Sophie and Vicky running along a beach and another of a proud-looking schoolboy standing next to an old Austin Seven. The car had given Max his first experience of driving and he still remembered it vividly. He had been taught to drive by his indulgent father and had spent his happiest childhood days driving around the circular drive and out on to the farm track behind the house.

One wall of the study was covered with shelves holding a variety of books, old and new. The other walls were given over to memorabilia. A tall oak cupboard with clear glass doors displayed a selection of cups of all sizes. The three largest of gleaming gold and silver were placed on top, too big for the inside of the cabinet, their sheer size dominating the room. On the walls next to these was a careful arrangement of photographs of Max's victories. Above a white marble fireplace was a painting of the car in which he had won the World Championship.

Max sat in his chair staring absently out of the window.

A helicopter manual lay unopened on his lap and his briefcase was on the floor beside him. He had a dozen bills to sort out and appointments to confirm. He was unaware of Vicky standing at the door watching him.

'Hi, I'm back. Everything OK?' She had been to the village post office to post some letters.

'Fine. Did Sophie get to school all right?'

'She was a bit reluctant at first, but then she saw a couple of her friends and she was off like a shot. No doubt we'll hear all about "my first day" later tonight. Fancy some coffee?'

'Yes, please.'

Five minutes later Vicky came back with a tray of coffee. She placed it on the desk.

'Thanks. How was Rachel yesterday? You didn't mention your lunch when you got back last night.'

'By the time I'd got round to it you were fast asleep.'

'Too many late nights recently . . . ' Max yawned.

'It was just past nine,' Vicky admonished. 'Anyway, we had a pleasant lunch together but she wasn't too well afterwards.'

Max sat back in his chair and sipped his coffee. 'Why was that?'

'Well, she drank an awful lot and then reacted very strongly to something I said. I happened to mention that Mario was a bit the other way.'

'Gay, you mean? Who told you that?' Max asked, surprised.

'Maggie Spencer – the wife of the Arrow team manager. Apparently it's all round the circuit.'

Max chuckled. 'Is it now? Well, well, I did wonder about him. You sense these things sometimes. So why was Rachel upset? Don't tell me she fancies him like crazy?'

'Yes – no. She was very taken aback; no, more than that . . . shocked. Then she stared at me and said, "My God, I should have guessed it all along" and ran to the Ladies. She was still there ten minutes later. She had been throwing up. I didn't know what to make of it.'

Max poured himself another cup of coffee. 'Perhaps *she* has been having an affair with Mario. She's had plenty of opportunity, let's face it. Or just maybe . . . '

'What Max, what are you thinking?'

'No, it doesn't matter. It was just a vague thought.'

A vague thought yes, but a possible one, Max pondered. Was Colin a homosexual too? It was not inconceivable that they were having an affair.

Rachel had driven straight home after lunch with Vicky. She had sobered up rapidly after being ill. She had one thing on her mind – to be alone to think.

Mechanically, she parked the Mercedes in the garage. In the kitchen she set about making coffee, her mind a turmoil of confused thoughts. She tried to dismiss the idea that Colin was homosexual and having an affair with Mario. She kept telling herself that there was no proof that Mario was gay, just malicious gossip. But she had known there was something different about Mario right from the start. He had always been on the defensive as if he had something to hide . . . and then she remembered the night of the dinner party and Colin's violent reaction at catching them together.

It was Mario his jealousy had been directed at, not Rachel. She had threatened to come between them and that was what had upset Colin so much. Yet all the time Mario was under their roof she never had an inkling that anything was going on. Colin had remained aloof, often staying out late and leaving home early, long before

Mario was up. She shuddered to think what might have gone on when she was not there.

And yet, she thought, staring at her untouched coffee, if I can accept that's how Colin is . . . if I can accept . . . She couldn't. She had been viciously betrayed and humiliated. Tears rolled down her face and she broke into loud sobs.

She poured herself a large brandy and wondered how she would ever face Colin. But she must. She must confront him. How would he react? She wondered if he would deny it and blame her wild imagination. She drank large mouthfuls of the fiery liquid which sent a warm glowing sensation to the pit of her stomach. She shivered in spite of it. She needed advice from someone who knew Colin well. She couldn't tackle this one on her own. But who could she turn to?

Max received Rachel's call the next afternoon. Vicky had gone to collect Sophie from school and Max was changing for a game of tennis with an old friend. He rang to cancel the tennis and drove the twelve miles to Rachel's house.

Rachel was cool and composed when she answered the door, although Max could see she had done well to conceal her puffy and bloodshot eyes. After she had poured a beer for Max, they sat on the rattan sofa in the conservatory. There was a warmth and understanding between them. She had always known about Max's wandering eye and, she fancied, he knew that she was given to the odd affair outside her marriage. 'Max, thanks for coming,' she started to say.

'Being with an attractive lady on such a nice afternoon beats a game of tennis any day.'

'This may sound crazy to you, but . . . '

'Try me,' said Max.

'It's about Colin.' Rachel fought back the tears from

her hollow eyes. 'Max, I'm pretty sure that there's something going on between him and . . . Mario.' She gave Max a swift glance to judge his reaction. 'Vicky told me about Mario being gay.' She related to Max about the dinner party scene and how Colin had flown into a jealous rage. She went on, 'Then as Dick left he said something almost like a warning, about a special relationship between Colin and Mario.'

'If you've no proof it's very difficult. It's not the sort of thing you want to accuse your husband of and then find you've got it all wrong. But . . . '

'Yes? I think you know I'm right, don't you, Max?'

Now that she had put the question so directly, he couldn't deny it. 'If I felt it was a lunatic idea, I would say so.'

'Thanks, Max. That's what I wanted to know.'

Max wore a pensive expression. 'You have to come to terms with the possibility that he is gay. You can't fight it – if you do, you'll never win. Do you think you could accept it and stay together?'

'No. If he was having an affair with another woman, I could come to terms with that. But to imagine him with another man . . . I couldn't possibly share him under those conditions.' The tears flowed down Rachel's face and Max wiped them away with his handkerchief.

Max felt deeply sorry for her. It was an ugly situation for her and the children, especially as the rest of the motor-racing world had discovered the truth before her. He had never become involved with gossip about other people's affairs, but he had a strong loyalty to Rachel. If he had been honest with himself, he would have identified in her a like-minded soul. They both grabbed life with both hands, often heedless of the consequences.

He drove home in melancholic mood and his mind

turned to his own circumstances. He winced at the thought of Vicky's affair. For the first time in his life he had become possessive of her.

But what of himself and his own affairs? Fidelity was a virtue that eluded him. Vicky knew of his weakness and luckily for him she had turned a blind eye to it in the past. But would that always be the case? He walked a fine line and he knew it. He was strangely old fashioned in that divorce scared the hell out of him. To be separated from Sophie and Vicky on a permanent basis was inconceivable and yet . . . he had to admit he was playing a dangerous game.

'Max, you're incorrigible,' Kelly laughed in a moment of pure enjoyment.

'And you are the sexiest woman I've ever met.'

Max lifted his head up from the water, blowing bath bubbles. He had submerged himself below the deep foam to kiss Kelly's thighs. The feel of the warm water and of Kelly's silky smooth skin had excited him further. Whitney Houston was singing a slow melody in the background and after a bottle of Bollinger, Max had temporarily forgotten the pressures of his work and of his family life.

He wiped the water away from his face with his hands, brushing away his hair to reveal a warm sexy smile. Kelly's heart leapt. She wished in that one moment that their life could always be like this, together and having fun. Time and people ceased to exist for her when she was with Max.

It was two days before Max was due to fly to Belgium, the venue for the fourth Grand Prix of the season. Max had arranged for Kelly and himself to dine with some racing friends that evening, but when Max had arrived early at Kelly's flat and caught her in only her camisole and panties, their plans had changed. Spontaneously they had reached for each other and made love on the sofa in the sitting room. Afterwards, Max had hurriedly cancelled the dinner arrangements and then opened a bottle of champagne. After that the evening had run its own course.

They sat on the floor wrapped in bathrobes eating smoked salmon sandwiches and finishing off a second bottle.

'Max, when is the Monaco Grand Prix?' Kelly asked. Max had promised her that one day he would invite her to the race. She hoped it might be this year.

'Sixteenth of May. Two weeks' time. Why, do you want to come?'

'I'd love to,' said Kelly, surprised at this unexpected invitation. 'But what about Vicky? Doesn't she normally go to that race?'

'She's been a couple of times. She was coming to this one, but yesterday she mentioned something about Sophie being desperate to go to some riding event on that Saturday, so it looks as if she may be staying at home.'

'In that case, I'd love to come. Where are you staying?'

'On a very large yacht owned by a friend of Julian's. I shall arrange some accommodation for you.'

'Is Julian going as well?'

'Yes, of course. He's not missing out on a freebie invitation like that.'

'Good.'

'Why do you say "good" like that?' asked Max curiously.

'Oh, I don't know. He's good fun to have around, that's all,' said Kelly quickly.

'Meaning your old friend Max is boring company at the races?'

'Don't be silly, Gregson. It's just that I know how busy

you are. It will be pleasant to have some company to pass the day.'

'That's fine by me,' said Max, kissing her.

And that was the last thought Max gave to his invitation. The events of the week ahead were to preoccupy his mind more than anything that he had previously arranged in his social life.

# 33

Mario pulled the collar of his anorak tightly around his neck. A chill wind blew the fine rain straight into his face. 'This bloody Belgian weather,' he muttered as he broke into a short run to the shelter of the garage behind the pits. The two Delta cars sat proud and sleek, like pedigree greyhounds cossetted by their owners.

'Hi,' Mario greeted the mechanics. 'How does my car look for this morning?'

'Hello, Mario,' said Tom. 'Nice to see you back again. The car's all in one piece. How's yourself?'

'OK. I'm in one piece, too, thankfully. Just fed up with this terrible weather. Don't you have a summer in Europe?'

They both cast an eye towards the heavy leaden skies. 'Every once in a while, but these are familiar skies in Belgium.'

'Well, I just hope it clears up for this afternoon's practice. Until then, I guess we have to go with it,' said Mario unenthusiastically.

The rest of the teams were preparing their cars for the first day of practice in one of the prettiest locations of the Grand Prix circuit, Spa Francorchamps. The track was set deep in the Ardennes countryside, amidst thick, verdant forests and rolling farmland. On a sunny day nothing could match the unspoilt beauty and freshness of the clear, invigorating air. Today it was shrouded in a dismal, grey mist. Mario stood under a wide umbrella watching the blanket of rain turn to a steady downpour. A few of the cars were revving up in anticipation that the rain would soon stop.

'I can't think of a nicer way to earn a living today. What say you?' The voice had a touch of sarcasm. Mario turned to see Max behind him grinning broadly.

'For sure, look at those clouds. They are pissing on us,' said Mario forlornly.

'Let's go and piss all over the opposition,' said Max and strode towards his mechanics waiting with the car.

But Max's enthusiasm was a mask covering an alien sensation that was suffusing his whole being. For the first time ever in his career he felt utterly demotivated. The enthusiasm and relentless striving that had driven him all these years had vanished like the Belgian sun under the heavy threatening sky.

Most of the other teams waited for the appalling conditions to subside. Then there came a break in the clouds, followed by a sudden flurry of activity and twenty-six cars and drivers made a hurried exit to start the serious business of practice. But it was short lived as the heavy downpour returned with a vengeance.

Only Max stayed out on the wet track, leaving a trail of flying spray behind him. Normally he loved the challenge of driving in rain and he wanted to recapture the old feeling. But as he approached the sharp right hander, the rear of the car began to slide. He corrected it instantly and the car stayed on course. But the niggling doubt in his mind remained. It grew uncontrollably, so that by the time he had driven to the pits, he was stricken with self doubt. Had he taken the corner too fast? Too tight? Suddenly, Max Gregson, World Champion, veteran of Formula One, was unsure of himself. His driving no longer made any sense. What the hell was he doing risking his life in treacherous conditions at a hundred and forty miles an hour? He didn't need to do it. He had won the World Championship. He had nothing more to prove. Why tempt fate in this dangerous game any longer? There had been too many signals lately that his luck had run out or was about to. It had all started with the death of the old man. Was it time to make reparation?

A guy could have only so much luck. It didn't last for ever. It needed only one mistake. The merest suggestion of his vulnerability now attached itself firmly in his mind like a cancer. It tormented him like the nightmares of his youth and even with an unassailable, strong character such as his, there remained a sickening fear and worry.

Race day brought another bleak, grey dawn and more rain. It dripped monotonously from the trees, leaving large puddles reflecting the darkness of the sky. Then, as if an artist had lifted his brush, the sky became streaked with lemon and warm pink. The morning sun broke through to dry up the oppressive dampness. For those on the periphery of racing, it was a morning to revel in the glorious views of the countryside, the forest and the fields shimmering in their new spring green. The air was as pure and fresh as nature intended, and as at every race, tinged with expectancy and excitement.

The drivers and team managers were directing their gaze skywards, but not for aesthetic reasons. By twelve o'clock their anxious faces noted that the small cumulus clouds had turned back into threatening masses, blotting out the sun at more regular intervals. As the first few drops of rain fell, they had to choose between wet or dry tyres. As the track was now covered in a wet sheen, Delta decided to race on 'wets'. But it was a gamble with the elements. Apprehensively the teams assembled on the grid for the start.

As the rain slid down the gleaming body of his car, Max could see no let-up in the gathering clouds. During yesterday's practice, he had put in some good laps and qualified in third place. It had drained him of energy and this morning he had woken up with all his old fears uppermost in his mind. Furthermore, he felt isolated. There was no-one he could share his angst with. He wondered if any of the other drivers ever faced this problem.

As the light turned to green, the cars hit a crescendo of noise and accelerated away to the first bend – a sharp hairpin. In the few seconds it took them to reach it, they were like a swarm of bees funnelling into the long stem of a bottle.

Then the first two cars that came into the corner touched wheels. One was launched sharply into the air and the scene became one of mayhem. Pieces of car were torn off; a rear wing spun across the track and took off as it hit an oncoming car. Bodywork disintegrated and wheels catapulted through the air.

Max braked hard and veered violently on to the grass to avoid the carnage. He came to rest heavily against one of the barriers. Cars behind him were braking and those not fast enough or not having the room to manoeuvre careered into the stationary machines. Mario, who had been in sixth position, was shunted from behind and spun sideways off the track. In split seconds, millions of dollars of superb technology took on the appearance of a breaker's yard. Marshals nearest to the scene jumped over the barriers with fire extinguishers to release the drivers. Mechanics ran to help with the rescue.

For a second, it was as if the whole commotion was frozen to a standstill and a hush fell over the track. The race had been halted with such abruptness it had left the crowds gasping. Then, as if the cameras had started to roll again on a film set, the drivers struggled to release their harnesses. The first two cars were the most badly damaged. Marshals rushed to assist Terri Dacco and Jean Claude trapped inside their machines, aware of the urgency to get them out. The fire risk was high. The cars still had full tanks of fuel.

Flashing lights signalled the arrival of the medical team. Twenty minutes later, Terri was carefully lifted on to a stretcher and put in an ambulance, his left foot sticking out at an odd angle to the rest of his leg. The other drivers, including Jean Claude with a badly bruised thigh, miraculously had escaped any serious injury.

Max walked back to the pits alone, drenched in a cold sweat. The accident had further confirmed his dilemma. God, what was the point of it all? he asked himself as he saw a tight-lipped Colin coming towards him, his face grim with worry and frustration.

An hour later, after frantic work by the mechanics, the cars – many of them spare ones – lined up for a second start. Only second place remained empty where Terri's car had been. He had been whisked off to hospital by helicopter with fractures to both feet. The cars got away without incident and it was an uneventful race, for Max at least. He finished a disappointing eighth.

Dick and Colin were waiting for Max when he arrived back at the pits. The atmosphere was heavy and humorless.

'Christ, I made a pig's ear of the race,' Max growled.

Dick shook his head. 'It wasn't that bad. Come to the motor home as soon as you can. We've hit a problem.'

Max's immediate reaction was that Mario had been disqualified from his impressive third place for some infringement, judging by the serious faces around.

In the motor home, Colin instructed Kathy, the woman who was looking after them, that there were to be no interruptions on any account.

'What's this all about?' asked Max as soon as Mario had joined them after his press conference.

'We've had a problem with Geoff, the new mechanic. He's been messing around with the electrics of the car,' Colin announced grimly.

Max swallowed hard. A shiver ran up the back of his spine as the implication of the words sank in. His face drained of colour. He noticed Mario's face do the same. Their lives depended on those mechanics. Driving at such high speeds an accident could be fatal. Trust and confidence in their abilities played a vital part in their relationship.

'What's he been up to? And on whose car?' demanded Max.

Colin looked at him gravely. 'Yours.'

'Holy shit,' said Max. 'But why?' He had heard of friendly rivalry and disagreements among mechanics, but never an actual sabotage of a car.

A silence hung heavy. Then Tom spoke. 'We don't know why. It happened just before the start. Reg, whose job it normally is to monitor the electrics, told me that Geoff had insisted he do it. When Reg examined what he'd done he found the wiring was wrong. There's no way that car would have finished the race.'

'Where is he now? Why isn't he here?' Max exploded angrily.

'He's gone,' said Colin.

'Gone, gone where?' Max's adrenalin, even after the race, was still pumping rapidly through his system.

Jean, Colin and Tom, along with the race engineers,

could only sympathize as they recognized the enormity of the problem.

'After I questioned him, he disappeared,' said Tom. 'I had a word with Colin. Then I went to find him. He'd vanished, taking his briefcase and passport with him.'

'Basically, we can assume by his disappearance he was up to no good,' said Colin. 'We'll catch up with him, though.'

'What about informing the police?' suggested Jean.

'No, I want this kept as quiet as possible. There are a few questions I want answered first.'

'Like why the hell he was doing it,' Max's angry outburst spoke for them all.

Colin gave Max an anxious glance. 'It's not the first time we've had cause to doubt his work.'

Max remembered the last two races; two disappointing retirements. 'You mean he fucked up the electrics at Imola?' Max was incredulous.

'And we have a suspicion now that he tampered with the car at Long Beach,' said Tom quietly.

'There was a problem with the wheel, you said,' Max was having difficulty still registering the awful facts that one of his mechanics had deliberately sabotaged his car. His face registered disbelief.

'Yes,' agreed Tom, 'but then after the race I found one of the wheel nuts loose. Geoff had been responsible for putting on the tyre. It was too much of a coincidence now looking back on it.'

'Then why the hell didn't you tell me about this, for God's sake?' Max's vitriol was directed at Colin. 'You kept me in the dark when you had suspicions. You were prepared to let me go out there and risk my life when you thought there was a chance that one of the mechanics was playing around with the car?'

The assembled group looked uneasily at Colin. Max was right. He should have been informed earlier.

Colin was calm. 'There was no proof. This afternoon was the first time we could point the finger of suspicion at Geoff. The wheel nut could have quite easily been an error on his part. He was new to the job. The electrics at Monza – we had no proof then that he had tampered with them. It is only his sudden disappearance that makes us sure he was up to no good. Max, we still can't prove anything. If we had had conclusive evidence before this, then of course I would have told you *and* sacked him. But it was only supposition.'

Colin was adamant he wanted everyone to remain calm and underplay what had been brought to light. There was too much at stake for everybody to lose their confidence now.

Later that evening, Max, Mario, Jean and Dick flew back with Colin to London in the company jet. Mario's creditable third place had been overshadowed by the shattering news. Both Max and Mario were still visibly shaken. Colin stared blankly out of the aircraft window. It had been one hell of a day. He couldn't remember one like it.

First there had been the massive shunt at the start of the race and the chaos that followed in the rush to get the spare car ready for Max and to repair Mario's car which was less damaged. Then the incident with Geoff. It was beyond his comprehension that someone would ever feel strongly enough to put a driver's life at risk. Geoff had been out to kill Max or ruin Delta, possibly both. He had to find the bastard, to find the reason behind it all. Suddenly he felt an uncontrollable anger and as a cold, blind fury swept over him, he slammed his fist into the window.

The others glanced at him but, aware of his volatile character, they left him to give vent to his feelings.

That same evening Alberto Scapini flew back to Italy. It was eight the next morning when he received a phone call from a panic-stricken Geoff. Scapini listened carefully to his story. Geoff had been so scared at being found out he had run off. At least he had not tried to make contact with him at the track, thought Scapini.

'So what do I do now?' pleaded Geoff.

'Well, you rather spoilt everything by taking off like that. It only serves to confirm your guilt,' answered Scapini coolly. 'I should give it a couple of days and go back to your Mr Pritchard and tell him you misunderstood instructions or something like that. Over the phone, of course. Then tell him you're quitting. Whatever you do, don't go back to the factory. If I were you, I'd take a holiday for a while . . . somewhere in the country.'

'What about the money?'

Scapini had expected this to be the next question. 'I shall send you some . . . not to your home, but to your private box number. I think another three thousand should cover your inconvenience.'

'Three thousand? But I've lost my job.'

'Only because you ran off so stupidly. I think I'm being very generous in the circumstances.'

'But I'm finished in the business now . . . ' Geoff started to say.

Scapini was at a loss to understand how short term these young men thought when it came to making some fast money. 'Geoff, I think you were aware of the risks before you agreed to work for me. It's unfortunate that you were caught. I have another call waiting for me. I have to go.'

'And what if I go back to Delta and tell Pritchard about your schemes?'

Scapini laughed acidly. 'Do you think I haven't covered myself for just that situation? The truth is, the drug plant was merely an insurance against your silence. You were filmed planting the drugs in the car. I have only to send that to the police with a covering letter. What is the term of imprisonment for drug smuggling in England? Fifteen years?'

Scapini hung up leaving Geoff, speechless and stunned, still holding the phone.

The following day at the factory, the long inquisition began. Colin called all the mechanics into his office to find out as much as possible about Geoff: his whereabouts, which pubs he hung out in, his friends, girlfriends, family. Had he been talking to any outsiders at the races? He wanted to know every detail about him.

The mechanics and engineers stood listening to Colin like the twelve just men. They themselves, a close-knit bunch, would never have believed that the likeable Geoff was capable of anything so criminal.

Later that morning, one of the younger mechanics knocked at Colin's door.

'What is it, Martin?' asked Colin.

The mechanic answered reticently. 'I didn't like to mention it in front of the others – it didn't seem important at the time, but on the flight over to Belgium, I sat next to Geoff. As we were getting ready to disembark, his briefcase fell open and I bent down to help him pick up the papers. We were laughing and fooling around – we'd had a couple of beers. I picked up a card with Scapini's name on it. It surprised me – Scapini isn't the sort of guy we mechanics would want to know.'

'Did you say anything to Geoff?'

'Yes, I laughed and said, "You're not going to work for that miserable Mafia bastard are you?" and he went dead quiet and never said a word to me. Anyway, I thought I'd mention it 'cos we all know what sort of man Scapini is . . .'

'Yes, Martin, thank you very much. You've told me exactly what I wanted to know,' replied Colin, already deep in thought.

# 34

There were only a few days left before the team was due to fly out to Monaco and there remained a lot of rebuilding work to be done on the cars following the pile-up in Belgium. Colin spent long hours at the office working late every night. Except one. He had succumbed to a hankering to see Mario and had spent an evening with him at his London flat. When he arrived back home later that night, it was after midnight and he was surprised to find the lights still on. Rachel was in the drawing room standing in the half light of the fire. Or was it she? It was a woman of her height and build, but there was something drastically different about her.

'Good God, Rachel, you gave me a shock. I thought it was somebody else for a moment. What have you done? You look like a hedgehog.'

Rachel had been pleased with the job her hairdresser had so painstakingly done. Her long wavy tresses had been chopped and her hair was now an inch long all over, giving even more emphasis to her fine features and delicate bone structure. She was wearing a severe black suit, cut into the waist, a pair of silver earrings and a chunky necklace.

'Don't you like the change?' she asked lightly.

Colin poured himself a brandy from the decanter on the drinks table and scrutinized her. 'Hmm, it'll take some getting used to. What made you have it cut so short?'

'I wanted to give myself a new look and get away from the soft feminine image.'

'I liked the way you were,' Colin said absently, sitting down on the deep russet sofa that matched the lavish pelmets and curtains. He glanced down at *The Times* that was beside him and stretched out his legs.

'Did you really like my hair the way it was?' Rachel asked sarcastically. 'I should have thought you would have preferred something a little more . . . masculine?'

Colin noticed a glass of brandy next to Rachel on the mantelpiece and realized that it was not her first drink of the evening. Colin was suddenly aware, too, that this was no ordinary polite end-of-the-day chat. Alarm bells rang in his head.

'What are you talking about?' he asked abruptly.

'Let's stop playing games, Colin. Why don't we be honest with each other?'

Colin was beginning to realize he had unwittingly walked into some kind of trap. He braced himself for what was to come.

'Rachel, I've had a very long day. Can we make this brief?'

Rachel sat down in one of the large armchairs opposite him and took a deep breath. She had postponed the confrontation time and time again. Then she had woken up that morning with the inspiration to have her hair cut, drastically so. It was a defiant gesture, a statement on how she felt about herself. Her femininity had been cut to the quick. Now she lived in a nightmare situation of knowing that perhaps Colin had always slept with other men and that the odd occasion they had made love had been a perfunctory chore in their marriage.

'It's about you and Mario . . . '

'What about us?' Colin finished his brandy in one swallow, his right eye twitching nervously. He wanted to leave the room before any more was said.

But Rachel had him firmly ensnared.

'I believe you're pretty much involved with Mario,' Rachel said carefully, her shaking hands clasped tightly together.

Had Colin not been at his lowest ebb, he would have put on a strong and convincing argument. He would have fiercely denied anything and everything and put Rachel's accusations down to her own wild imaginings. But he couldn't fight back. He had neither the energy nor the will. He leaned forward and studied his clenched hands. When he looked up, Rachel saw a tired defeated man. His eyes had glazed over and there was heavy emotion in his voice.

'How long have you known?'

'You kept your secret well – from me at least. I only guessed a few days ago. It's true then?'

'Yes.' Colin sighed deeply. The atmosphere was charged with emotion. Only Colin could retrieve the situation now. 'Listen carefully, Rachel. I've dreaded the day when you might find out about . . . the other side of my life.' His voice was quivering. 'Believe me, I never wanted to hurt you. I love you and the children, but there is a part of me that I can't control.'

Rachel had no room for anger now as she sat watching the pitiful figure before her. 'How long has it been going on?'

'With Mario? About four months.'

'And before? There were others?'

'No, well, at least not for a long time. Rachel, don't make this any worse for both of us . . . don't ask.' The tears welled up in Colin's eyes as he realized his worst nightmare had come true.

Rachel had hoped for a single moment that he would deny the accusation and they would be able to hold on to their fragile marriage. But as the impact of his admission struck home she was left numbed and shocked. In a situation like this there were no winners, only losers.

She stood up slowly. 'There's little point in us continuing this farce. I'm leaving you . . . and I shall want a divorce.' Even as she said it, she could hardly believe the harshness of her words.

Colin clasped his head in his hands and his whole body shook as he tried to control his sobs. He didn't see or hear Rachel leave the room.

# 35

A gloriously fresh May morning burst forth from the dawn mist spreading an incandescent light over the yachts that lay sleeping in the harbour. Surrounded by a natural amphitheatre of rock, now thrown into shadows of blue and ochre, the harbour boasted some of the biggest and the most expensive floating palaces in Europe. Ensigns fluttered lazily in the first stirrings of a breeze.

Above, in the winding streets of Monte Carlo, brown and green shutters opened on to a cerulean clear sky. The smell of freshly baked bread spilled out from every prettily painted boulangerie. Yacht crews were already up and about buying fresh baguettes, croissants and copies of *Nice Matin* and returning to their yachts in preparation for another busy day of entertaining. The magnetism of Monte Carlo was never greater than at Grand Prix time.

Colin glanced at his Ebel watch. It was seven thirty. Time for breakfast before the rest of the hotel guests descended on the restaurant. After his shower, he dressed in the Delta team uniform of pale yellow shirt and blue trousers. He brushed his hair briskly, paying special attention to the small thinning patch on the top of his head. He wondered what Mario would be doing now. Was he up? Would he fancy an early breakfast? Colin decided not to call him.

He had stayed up with Mario late last night and in his depressed state had succumbed to three or four brandies. It was enough to make him feel bleary eyed this morning.

He picked up his pass for the pits and slipped on his loafers. Neither Mario nor the brandy had helped ease his melancholy. They had sat on the balcony of Mario's room at the Loews Hotel overlooking the Mediterranean, which was shimmering delicately under a full moon. Mario was the only person he could confide in. He had listened patiently and he had not been unduly surprised at Rachel's discovery. He always had given her more credit for her astuteness than Colin ever had. Nevertheless, he was shocked to learn that she planned to leave Colin and take the children with her.

'It is a bad scene for her,' Mario had reflected. 'She is a good woman.'

'I know,' said Colin. 'That makes it even harder for me. It's not easy to live with such guilt.'

Mario had put his hand on his shoulder as a gesture of sympathy.

'And the children?' Colin went on. 'Supposing they were to find out? I don't know what to do.'

'Maybe you should try to convince Rachel that you will give up the other side of your life – if you can.'

'You know the answer to that. I damn well can't.'

In exasperation, Colin had poured himself another brandy. His life was falling apart around him. As if the sabotage problems with Delta were not enough, now his family life was disintegrating. His only hope was Mario. He was the shining star in his life. Colin held the firm conviction that Mario at least would not let him down. He had even made plans to have Mario as Delta's number one driver next year and he had proposed the idea to Mario that evening.

Mario had been overjoyed at the prospect. His career was gaining momentum far quicker than he had expected. 'I won't let you down,' Mario had promised. 'I know after the last two races that I can win,' and his eyes had shone with optimism and a new confidence.

Colin took the lift down to the lobby of the luxurious hotel heading for the dining room and breakfast. As he made his way across the lobby, he almost collided with a couple of journalists who bounced along breathing heavily after an hour's exertion on the tennis court. As they brushed past him, they nudged each other. It was as the lift doors were closing that Colin overheard one say to the other, in a voice he made no effort to hush, 'I wonder where his boyfriend is this morning?'

Colin's blood ran cold. His right eye began to twitch rapidly and suddenly he didn't feel hungry any more.

As Max made his way off the yacht which was his base for the weekend, his mind was anywhere but on the arrangements he had made with Kelly. Having invited her to Monaco, he had completely forgotten to confirm any arrangements with her. Now, as he sauntered past the yachts, his thoughts were concentrated on the day ahead.

The yacht on which he was staying was owned by a French banker, Philippe de Cours, and was one of the largest in the old port. Three levels high and eighty foot long with a crew of six, it looked impressive and menacing with its long pointed bow and dark tinted windows. Philippe de Cours, whom Max had met in the company of Julian several times before, had done everything to make Max's stay as comfortable as possible. He had installed him in a stateroom complete with its own office. With five other luxury staterooms and a spacious saloon, there was plenty of room for Max and the other guests to relax.

In just under an hour Max would be starting practice. He glanced at the street that curved round the port, up the hill into a long tunnel, and decided he was not looking forward to the frustrating drive. It was his least favourite circuit, an opinion shared by most of the other drivers. The race invariably ended as a procession, there being few opportunities for overtaking. And it was dangerous. Twenty-six cars all jostling for space at ninety to a hundred and thirty miles an hour on such a tortuous circuit made little sense to any of them. Least of all to Max that morning. Having a multi-million-dollar salary did little to sharpen his enthusiasm. His indifference to the whole scenario stuck to him like burrs to a sheep's coat. He was unaware of the beauty of the morning around him as he strode to the garage area. But he knew that once dressed in his overalls and amongst the noise of the cars, he would have no option but to shake off his lethargy. He would have to eradicate the doubts from his mind and concentrate . . . concentrate, just as he used to so effortlessly before.

In the garage area, tucked away from the harbour by large canopies, Jean and Colin were locked in discussion.

'Nice day for it,' Tom called to Max.

'It's OK if you're lying on the beach on the Côte d'Azur. And I know where I'd rather be,' replied Max.

Just then, one of the mechanics started up Max's car and the quiet of the day was shattered. The engine revs whined louder and louder.

For the rest of the team it was another race weekend, another opportunity to perfect the cars and try to beat the opposition. It was a time of exhausting work, little sleep and high adrenalin. But for Max there was the recognition that his heart was not in racing any more. The incident with Geoff and the sabotage of his car only brought home to him the craziness of his job. It was an unnerving and solitary experience.

* * *

At the end of the afternoon practice, Max returned to the yacht and after a shower went up on to the aft deck now bathed in evening sunlight.

'Good evening, Max. Come and join us.' Philippe de Cours was relaxing with his other two guests. He sat in a large cane chair drinking a glass of chilled Muscadet. 'Come and meet Claudia and Bertrand Dupont.'

Max smiled as the little Bertrand, also in banking, jumped up and shook hands with him. Bertrand was wearing what appeared to be the standard uniform for Monaco: Lacoste T-shirt, designer trousers, Gucci loafers and Rolex watch. Max, in trainers and jeans, was happy that he did not have to worry about such incidentals. Claudia, Bertrand's wife, was also chicly dressed in matching mustard trousers and linen shirt. A gold turban emphasized a classic facial bone structure and brown eyes.

'And how did practice go for you today?' enquired Philippe.

'All right,' said Max, hoping that the conversation of the evening would not revolve around the Grand Prix. 'We hit the right set-up for the car on this circuit straight away. If the weather stays fine for the next practice session, we should be qualifying pretty close to the front row.'

'And who are your main competitors?' asked Philippe, whose knowledge of Formula One was limited to the French teams and drivers.

'Ferrari are running well. Their engines are suited to this type of circuit where you need short bursts of power.'

A stewardess dressed in pink silk shorts and T-shirt, matching the colour of the massive gladioli arrangement, brought him a glass of beer. His host had good taste in women, Max thought to himself as he glanced at her attractive face. Her hair, the colour of bleached sand, complemented her striking ice-blue eyes.

'Hi, everybody,' called an enthusiastic voice slightly out of breath. It was Julian. He shook hands with his French host and the other guests, then collapsed into a chair, grumbling about the crowds he had just been forced to carve a passage through to reach the sanctuary of the yacht.

Max sat back in his chair enjoying the company and conversation, which had thankfully changed from racing to the Cannes Film Festival. Above all, he wanted to switch off from the pressures of the race ahead. He watched the early evening sun slip behind the steep hills of the town, throwing the apartments, stacked like building blocks, into deep shadow. On the summit, the palace stood aloof, embracing its tiny principality in a way that served to remind Max that this was a fairy-tale world that belonged to princes and princesses of untold wealth.

Shortly before six thirty, Philippe, Bertrand and Claudia left to change for the evening. Max and Julian were alone discussing the exotic display of cars lined up on the harbour front when they spotted journalist Reg Watkins weaving his way amongst the crowds of casual onlookers. One of the crew put a hand up to him as he approached the gangplank.

'Don't worry, that scruffy fellow is with us,' Julian called over from the guard rail and laughed at the crew's stern appraisal of their visitor.

'So this is where the rich Poms hang out?' bellowed Reg, wiping his forehead after the exertion of his walk. 'Do I need some sort of pass to get on this mini liner?'

'You certainly do,' replied Max. 'Didn't you see the sign at the bottom of the gangplank? "Strictly no journalists." '

'On this occasion I've left my notebook behind,' Reg retorted affably, and took one of the vacated seats.

'Can we get you a drink?' Julian asked.

'Thank you. A cold beer would go down very well.' He mopped his brow again. 'I think I'm becoming allergic to fast cars, pretty girls and multi-millionaires, all of which seem to be here in overabundance. Have you seen anything like it before?'

Max and Julian grinned in sympathy as the pretty Swedish stewardess came to refill the ice bucket which held two bottles of wine.

Reg observed the pert little bottom peeping out from under the girl's pink shorts. 'There you are,' he whispered. 'I'm feeling my allergy coming on again. It does my constitution no good at all.'

They all laughed at Reg's mournful gaze.

'Too many distractions, that's your problem, Reg.'

'I know,' Reg sighed, taking a long draught of beer from his glass.

'And you should see the rest of the crew,' said Max. 'There's another dozen down below. The masseuse is the best so far, wouldn't you say, Julian?'

Julian grinned. 'The face of an angel, the muscles of Atlas.'

Reg grunted. 'Well, if you wouldn't mind letting me know when it's her day off, she can come to my bijou broom cupboard, which I'm being ripped off for – extortionately, I might add – and maybe she can brighten my day.'

'Shame on you, Reg. What can we do for you, besides the masseuse?'

'Nothing specific – I just thought I'd have a chat about the car. I know how much you love this circuit . . . '

'The car is bloody quick,' said Max. 'It's the tyres we've got to sort out. They're going to be our biggest problem.'

The constant braking and accelerating on the twisting circuit meant that the tyres would be subjected to immense wear. Throwing the car into corners at ninety miles an hour between strips of armco barrier meant that it was essential to make the right choice of tyre.

'Well, I have to say Colin's certainly not looking as if all is well. What's his problem?' Reg was moving on to the real purpose of his visit.

'If I were to tell you, you wouldn't believe me anyway,' said Max seriously.

'You mean he hasn't read the latest Fleet Street missive?' It was Reg's turn to hide the apprehension in his voice.

'He hasn't mentioned anything. What are the latest rumours? What have they managed to manufacture this time?' questioned Max.

'Dick Saunders has been pretty scathing . . . ' Reg began.

'Dick Saunders should have kept to his comic cuts,' Max interrupted. 'He's a tight-assed little runt.'

'Seems he doesn't like you either, my old friend.' Reg bent down and produced the newspapers from his brief-case. He turned to the sports column. Max took the paper and scanned through the article on the Monaco race. He stopped when he caught sight of Mario's name.

'The surprise amongst this year's drivers has to be Mario Rodriguez. His dedication to the sport is obvious, both on and off the track, and his driving is showing an improved maturity now that he is under team owner, Colin Pritchard. His zeal and determination make him a disciple out of the Pritchard mould and his team mate, Max Gregson, would do well to watch this young Argentinian. Delta's number one driver could find himself relegated to a second division team if he continues to produce such poor results. Pritchard must undoubtedly be asking himself if this is just a temporary hiccup in the career of one of Britain's most brilliant drivers.'

*Auto Review* was no better in its scathing comments:

'After Max Gregson's successful championship year it would appear that he is not carrying the momentum through to this season. Now that he has won this coveted prize, has Gregson not also left his will to win sitting on the mantelshelf alongside the trophy? This is even further highlighted by the spectacular results of his team mate, Rodriguez . . . '

'Holy shit . . . ' Max's face registered the shock of seeing his own private thoughts there in print before him. 'They're not exactly giving me a character reference.'

'There's only one thing for it, Max. You've got to go out there and show them they're wrong. Daft as an aborigine's toothbrush, those two journalists, anyway,' said Reg, trying to make light of it but watching the anxiety cloud Max's normally calm face. He wondered what problems Max was wrestling with. Reg knew him well enough to notice an imperceptible change in his character.

Max shrugged his shoulders. 'We've had our problems,' said Max quietly. 'But I feel better in my mind now.'

Max hoped he sounded credible but he knew the press hounds were right. He *had* lost his motivation. He was adrift in the wilderness of his own fears and unable to control his destiny any more. He felt a frightening vulnerability and suspicion . . . suspicion that wouldn't leave him; that the credit stakes on the card of fate were overdrawn. Sooner rather than later, he was going to have to pay for his success.

Darkness brought a new enchantment to the fairy-tale town. Lights shimmered in the harbour, reflecting the opulence of the floating palaces. Around the port, cafés and restaurants took on an intimate appearance, but with the majestic silhouettes of the Café de Paris and the Casino dominating the scene, there lingered a sense of romance and opulence. The town had a carnival atmosphere. People promenaded in their finery, and open-topped Bentleys and Rolls-Royces cruised the narrow streets.

Max walked up to the Tip Top Bar, the traditional haunt of the drivers during the race weekend, to join Julian, Claudia and Bertrand for an early evening drink. The bar was crowded as drinkers jostled to be seen near the drivers.

Dinner on the yacht came as a welcome relief after the bustle outside. It was as relaxed and informal as it could be considering the palatial surroundings. Classical guitar music played in the background. In the intimately lit saloon, a large mahogany table, lined with a dozen Hepplewhite chairs, had been laid with Belgian lace, the finest Wedgwood china and crystal glasses which gleamed in the glow of the table lamps. A centrepiece of blue and yellow flowers matched the colour of the stewardesses' outfits. A nice touch, thought Max, that Philippe had chosen Delta's team colours for the occasion.

Bertrand and Claudia, Philippe and Julian were in good form and Max tried hard to join in with the jovial repartee. Despite the general good humour, he was restless. Tomorrow, Friday, was by tradition a day off for the drivers. Final practice was on Saturday, followed by the race on Sunday. Already Max was feeling claustrophobic. Three days amongst the crowded glitterati was exhausting enough without the prospect of the race ahead.

Max's eyes wandered inevitably to the pretty Swedish stewardess who kept topping up the glasses with a fine Chateau Pavie.

After coffee, Bertrand jumped up energetically. 'Would anyone like to join us at the Casino?' he asked.

Philippe, a recognized figure amongst the Black Jack tables of Monte Carlo, thought it an excellent idea, as did Julian. Max, however, was not so keen.

'How about we meet up later in the Café de Paris for a nightcap?' he suggested with a smile. 'I have a couple of things to catch up with.'

Julian had seen that smile before and knew that Max's 'things' did not include work. He gave him a wink and surreptitiously tapped the side of his nose. 'Keep out of mischief, if you can,' he said, as he disappeared out of the double doors of the saloon and into the night.

It was after midnight when Julian found Max in the lobby of the Café de Paris. Philippe had suffered heavy losses at Black Jack and had stayed to try and recoup some of his money. Claudià and Bertrand had gone in search of more night life in the still buzzing town.

Languishing in a Louis XV1 sofa with his arms around two companions, Max was oblivious to the comings and goings around him in the sumptuous marbled lobby. Large tumblers of brandy sat on the heavily gilded table in front of them and one look at Max's eyes told Julian his friend had had far too much to drink.

'Let me introduce you to the two most beaootiful girls in Monte Carlo.' Max uttered each word emphatically, in an effort to maintain coherency. 'Thish is Inga and thish is Astrid.'

'Hi, girls. We've already met, Max, remember?' said Julian breezily. He wondered which was the most discreet way of getting Max out of the place before he attracted any more attention. It was difficult not to notice his two blonde Swedish companions from the yacht. Inga, with her almost white, blonde hair swept up into a French plait, looked stunningly chic in a black linen dress. Astrid, too, was attractive, but in a different way. Her hair fell in soft curls about her face and she wore little make-up. In her jeans and casual shirt she looked much younger than her friend.

Max caught the attention of a passing waiter. 'Julian, what are you having as a nightcap? Before you answer, I've reserved Inga,' and he leant forward and gave her a warm hug.

'How about we go back to the yacht and have one there?' Julian gave the girls a look that pleaded for their assistance.

'A good idea,' Inga agreed, standing up. 'I have had too much to drink and so have you, Mr Gregson.'

'We can always continue the party back at the boat . . . that's if the crew don't mind staying up a little longer. These girls,' Max said warmly, 'these girls saved me from a night of bloody introspection and from falling into an abscess of depression.'

'Abyss,' corrected Julian. 'Come on, let's get you home before the whole of Monte Carlo finds something to talk about.'

The girls exchanged knowing looks. Max, in his drunken state, would be harmless as a mouse and would no doubt fall asleep as soon as they reached the yacht. They helped him stand up, while Julian quickly settled the bill, but not without raising an eyebrow at the amount. It was just as well he had won a few hundred pounds at the tables. They left the hotel, past the noncommittal stares of the doormen, Julian praying quietly that no-one would recognize the current World Champion in such a state.

* * *

Max awoke the following morning and turned over to look for Inga, before remembering she had left his bed at six to prepare breakfast for the crew.

It was just as well there was no practice today, he thought, as he lay back on the pillow. A thumping hangover had taken up residence in the top half of his head as he recalled the events of the previous night. He had feigned collapse in the arms of the caring Inga, who had then taken him to his room. She had got no further than removing his shoes when in a matter of minutes the roles were reversed and it was Max who was undressing her.

She had kissed him playfully on the neck and face and sat astride his hard erection, moving tantalizingly across his body. Wild with desire, Max had thrown himself on top of her and slipped quickly inside her. There was nothing demure or delicate about the athletic way they had made love and it was in a comatose state of exhaustion they had fallen asleep.

Max got up slowly. Glancing through the cabin window, he was pleased to see the sun reflecting brightly on the water. Philippe had suggested taking the yacht further up the coast for lunch. Before leaving, Max strolled up to the Loews Hotel to keep his appointment with Colin and Dick. The atmosphere was strained as they discussed the bad press reports over coffee.

Meanwhile, there was the prospect of a relaxing day ahead away from swelling crowds and traffic in the congested town. There was also Inga and he felt his appetite for her returning as his hangover receded. As he approached the yacht, her name, *L'Esprit de Vie*, emblazoned on the stern, the crew were making preparations to leave. Up on the rear deck, Max spotted Inga moving a huge arrangement of flowers into the saloon. It was then he caught the back view of someone who was all too familiar. Max stopped in his tracks as he saw the unmistakable profile.

'Oh, lord, it's Kelly,' he muttered fiercely as he strode up the gangplank. He had forgotten all about his invitation for her to join him.

# 36

Rachel twisted her wedding ring nervously on her finger. She watched as Sophie scampered down the sweeping lawns and under the bowing willow trees that lined the fast-flowing stream.

Vicky poured another cup of tea and passed it to Rachel. She had been amazed at the change in her friend. Her short severe haircut had given her face a gaunt appearance and her eyes were transparent in their sadness. Vicky felt desperately sorry for her.

'If you feel you want to get away for a while, there's always our house in France,' she suggested.

'Thanks, but I feel I should sort out my life here first. There's the children to think of. They finish school in two months' time.'

'Have you made any plans for the holidays?'

'We usually go to Cornwall for the first three weeks in August. Colin is always away then, so they won't be any the wiser. Then we're staying with my sister for the rest of the summer. They have a farmhouse in Wales . . . It all seems so crazy.' Rachel sighed. 'It's only now when I talk of making plans with the children that I feel so damned scared about moving out of the house.'

'What if Colin were to go instead? Surely that would be the best thing for the children?'

'I've thought of that, but the house is far too big. I'd like a smaller place.' She lit another cigarette. Vicky noticed she had been smoking heavily since she arrived before lunch.

Rachel crossed her legs and leaned back in the comfortable reclining chair. The sun showed itself from behind a cloud and the flower beds that bordered the lawns came alive with a blaze of bright colour. A warm breeze rustled the leaves on the large oaks and dipped the willows' wispy branches into the water.

Just then Sophie came into view, carrying an armful of buttercups she had picked in the field. Rachel watched her sunny, carefree face and felt wretched at the turmoil of her own circumstances.

'These are for you, Aunty Rachel,' she said, laying the flowers on Rachel's lap and reaching up to kiss her. Even Sophie had noticed that Aunty Rachel was in need of cheering up.

Vicky was about to suggest they go and look at the horses when Ella, the new au pair, appeared.

'There's someone to see you, Mrs Gregson. He's in the kitchen.'

'In the kitchen? Why didn't you show him into the drawing room, Ella?'

'He just walked in.'

'Well, who is it? What's his name?' asked Vicky, irritated at the intrusion.

Before Ella could reply, she saw Phil striding out towards them, his leather jacket slung over a shoulder and his brown leather boots showing the usual signs of neglect. Vicky got up hurriedly, hoping that Rachel would not notice her deep flush of excitement.

'Phil, what a surprise,' she said briskly. 'This is Rachel Pritchard. I don't believe you've met.'

Phil smiled, giving Rachel an appreciative glance as he sat down.

'Phil used to work here, last winter . . .' Vicky began, but she could see neither Rachel nor Phil was listening.

Rachel was studiously watching this tall, handsome man dressed in faded jeans and scruffy boots.

'Mind if I have one of your cigarettes?' he asked confidently.

Rachel reached into in her handbag and brought out a packet. Vicky could read Rachel like a book. She had thrown off her melancholy and her face had become alive again.

'Would you like a drink?' Vicky asked.

'Thanks,' Phil said, flashing her a winsome smile. 'A beer would be fine.'

'Ella, could you bring a beer for Mr Adams. Rachel, would you like something stronger?'

Rachel shook her head. She was busy admiring Phil as he lit up his cigarette. He was terribly attractive, she decided. She was also aware of an animal sexuality that seemed to exude from him. Phil shot her a glance that sent a shiver down her back.

Ella, who had been standing motionless watching the scene, snapped out of her reverie as she heard her name and disappeared in the direction of the house, wondering what it was about this stranger that had unsettled the two women so.

'What brings you back here?' Vicky enquired when she realized that Phil was not about to elucidate on the reason for his call.

'I've started a job not far from here – in Watlington, so I thought as I was passing I'd call in and say hello.'

'We live on the edge of Watlington,' said Rachel. 'Where are you working?'

'A stud farm on the Wallingford road.'

'It's owned by Colonel Stuart, isn't it?'

'Yes,' said Phil, surprised. 'You know him?'

'We've met him several times. Our daughters are at

the same school. What is the Colonel like to work for?' asked Rachel, returning his stare.

'He's OK. A bit of a tight bastard, and I don't have the same perks as I used to get here, Vicky.' He gave her a slow wicked smile as he blew out the smoke from his cigarette slowly. Vicky was growing more and more uncomfortable.

'Have you seen Sophie – she's over there . . .' she remarked.

Phil turned to see Sophie's head bobbing up and down in the long grass on the opposite side of the stream.

'Sophie,' Phil called to her, but she was out of earshot. He got up and with long strides walked across the lawn towards her.

'Well, you dark horse. You kept him very quiet,' whispered Rachel as soon as he was out of earshot. 'What's between you two? Seems like he upset you a little.'

'He left very suddenly, that's all. I told you about him, remember.' Vicky hoped her voice sounded casual.

Sophie gave a great whoop of delight as she caught sight of Phil. He picked her up and held her high above his head. As far as she was concerned, he was the most wonderful man with horses she had ever met. She had been inconsolable when he had left unexpectedly.

Vicky, too, had had her share of worry and heartache after he had gone. She had never again dared broach the subject of his disappearance with Max. Now that Phil had unexpectedly returned, he had stirred up her emotions once more.

'Seems a bit of a wild character, your groom. I'm surprised at Max employing him,' said Rachel smugly.

'Why?' asked Vicky. 'He seemed perfectly all right when he started working for us.'

'No, I meant having a guy like that around when Max is away so much.'

'A guy like what?'

Rachel shot her a bemused glance and laughed abruptly. 'Come on, Vicky. The man oozes sensuality and don't give me your naive "well it never occurred to me" look. I know you too well.'

Vicky opened her mouth to protest, but closed it again. Now was not the time to argue the point. 'You must bring the children over when they break up from school and play some tennis,' she said, changing the subject.

'They would like that. Thanks, Vicky. But now I must be making a move.' Rachel stood up, smoothing her yellow linen skirt. 'Thanks for a lovely lunch – and for being such a good listener.' She kissed her warmly on the cheek.

'You know where I am. Call me any time.'

'Thanks again. It's times like this your friends count for an awful lot. I must say goodbye to Sophie before I go,' she said, picking up her bunch of wilting buttercups.

Vicky watched as Rachel bent down and kissed Sophie. Words were exchanged between her and Phil and there were warm smiles all round as they made their way back to Vicky.

'Don't bother coming back to the house, Vicky. I'm sure you want to catch up on all the news with Phil.'

As Rachel disappeared into the house Vicky gave Phil an awkward glance. Should she invite him to sit down again? She was still hesitating when Ella returned with his beer.

'Do you mind if I stay for a short while?' he asked. 'I don't think your husband is expected home for a couple of days.' Vicky looked surprised as Phil smiled knowingly at her. 'It's not difficult to figure out. I do follow motor racing myself.'

'Of course, but what made you . . .'

'Come back and see you after all this time? I wanted to explain why I left in such a hurry . . . and to tell you what a bastard of a husband you've got.'

'Phil!' exclaimed Vicky, relieved that Sophie was out of earshot. 'What did Max have to do with it?'

'Quite a lot. Your husband has a pretty nasty way of dealing with people.'

'What exactly happened, Phil?' Vicky could tell by the angry tone of his voice that the answer was not to be pleasant.

'He must have found out about our affair. To warn me off, he put a snake in the cottage. I found the loathsome thing curled up in the kitchen early one morning. It was ready to have a go at me, I can tell you. And that was your husband's polite way of telling me I was no longer wanted around here.'

'How can you be sure that it was him?' asked Vicky aghast.

'He left a note.'

Vicky sat back in her chair, too stunned to speak. She sighed heavily and shook her head. She could not believe it of Max. He would never do anything like that. She could not imagine him plotting revenge. He was a man driven by relentless ambition and determination. Nothing, it seemed, would ever get in his way. And yet, aggressive as he was on the track, in private he was usually quite the opposite. Vicky's heart went out to Phil. The affair had, after all, been as much her doing as his.

'Phil, I just can't believe Max would do such a thing.'

'You have a very possessive husband. Are you aware of that? He wanted to ensure that I wouldn't be back again in a hurry to mess with his wife.'

'Possessive. I'd never considered him to be that.'

'Perhaps it was just as well we finished. After all, you might have overcome your guilt and fallen in love with me,' Phil teased.

'Don't be so boorish,' retorted Vicky.

Yet, she had realized when Phil had left, how dependent she had become on him and now the same feeling of loneliness returned.

Phil caught her reflective gaze as he finished his beer. 'Cheer up, Vicky. It's not the end of the world.' He stood up and walked to the back of her chair, resting his hands lightly on her shoulders.

'Phil, I can only say I'm sorry about what happened. And if it means anything to you, I did miss you terribly.' Vicky's voice was a whisper as she touched his rough hands.

'I missed you, too. Time and time again, I wanted to come and see you. It wasn't easy. But I guessed it was best to leave things as they were.' He paused. 'Goodbye Vicky.'

Before Vicky had time to reply, Phil had slipped his hands from her shoulders and, without looking back, was walking steadily away.

Max found Kelly on the upper deck. Philippe and Julian excused themselves to go to the bridge, as the yacht was about to leave harbour.

'Kelly, what a pleasant surprise,' he said weakly. 'How did you get here?'

'You invited me, remember?' she said, kissing him fondly on the cheek. Max returned her embrace and was relieved to notice that Inga was no longer around. 'Max, don't tell me you'd forgotten. Didn't you get the phone message I left with your secretary?' Kelly had called his secretary and given her name. So as not to arouse suspicion, she had told her she was a journalist and would be arriving Friday morning for an interview. Kelly was sure that Max would have received and understood the message. Instead, she had the feeling that she had interrupted some intimate little party.

'No . . . I didn't. But life has been so chaotic recently and I clean forgot to arrange some accommodation for you.'

'Don't worry. I'm fixed up right here.'

'You mean you're staying on the yacht?' Max was still incredulous at this sudden turn of events. His freedom and the prospect of kissing Inga's thighs again were suddenly evaporating.

'Yes, darling . . . you don't look too thrilled about the idea. Julian explained the problem to your charming host and he has insisted I stay here,' said Kelly.

'Well, that solves one problem. It would have been impossible to put you up anywhere in the town.'

Kelly refused to show her annoyance at Max's cool reception. He was obviously not over the moon at her unannounced arrival. Well, that was tough on him, she decided. It never failed to amaze her how vacillating Max could be. Since the night of their reconciliation, Max had played the devoted lover. Now, suddenly, it was not convenient to have her around.

Max's face still bore the expression of an offended small boy when one of the stewardesses came to show Kelly to her cabin. As she left, the crew released the bow and stern lines and, with a surge of power, the magnificent yacht began to leave the harbour, watched by an envious crowd.

The day was hot and breezy and as the yacht got under way, Max, Julian and Kelly sat with Philippe on the top deck enjoying a cool Pimms served by the other stewardess, Astrid. Max could tell by the way Astrid eyed Julian that she was attracted to him, but he remained unusually distanced. He had other things on his mind.

Philippe was entertaining the group with a story of the party he had attended on a neighbouring yacht after recouping his losses at the Casino. For a man in his early fifties it was obvious that he had taken good care of himself. His firm, toned body was tall and upright, and his twinkling grey eyes gave the impression of someone much younger. He laughed heartily like a man who had found true contentment in life. 'It was crazy,' he said. 'There was this actress from New York with a husband old enough to be her grandfather. He behaved like one, too. He tells her to stop drinking. Well, OK, she had had lots to drink, as we all had, but she gets so mad with him and shouts "Stop treating me like a child or I will behave like one." Of course, everybody thinks she is acting, but it is for real. Then she starts flirting with one of the younger men – I think he is a racing driver – and the next thing is she strips off and throws herself into the water. So, the young man, thinking she has fallen overboard, dives in after her. She is making some terrible noises like a cat having its neck wrung. He pulls her out and cannot understand why she is naked. I tell you it was a wild night. The host is laughing so much he chokes on his cigar and the crew thinks he is having a heart attack and they rush to help him . . .'

By this time everybody was laughing with Philippe. 'I tell you it was better than the movies . . .'

After he had stopped chuckling he turned to Julian and Max. 'And how was your night? I hope you had fun, too.'

'It was quiet by comparison,' replied Julian, 'but I came out ahead on the roulette.'

'And how about you, Max? Were you lucky, too?' Max detected a glint in his eye and couldn't suppress a smile as he thought, The old bugger, he knows.

As the yacht made its way along the coast, the clear Mediterranean water sparkled like aquamarine. It was a rare day of idle relaxation for Max and he was enjoying it immensely. Even the untimely arrival of Kelly did not detract from the pleasure of being in good company in an idyllic setting.

Once the yacht was moored quietly in a small bay, the party settled down to some sunbathing before lunch. Julian and Max stripped off and stretched out in the sun. Kelly went off to change, while Bertrand and Claudia, quickly tiring of lying in the midday heat, dived into the sea to cool off.

Julian covered himself with suntan oil and lay on his back in a pair of bold orange and green striped swimming shorts.

'Are you still suffering from last night's hangover or have you fallen so in love with Astrid that you're dumbstruck?' enquired Max.

Julian rolled over on to his stomach. 'Max, if you don't mind me saying, you really are being a bit hard on Kelly.'

Max squinted at Julian through his sunglasses. Julian sounded unusually rankled. 'How do you mean?' he asked.

'You've made it perfectly clear that she's upset your plans for the next two days. Remember, she's had to put up with a hell of a lot recently. You owe her.' Julian thought back to the awful night he had visited her in hospital. He had never seen her so shattered. She had been through a rough time and yet Max in his selfishness seemed so oblivious of it all.

'I guess it was my fault – forgetting that I'd invited her in the first place,' he murmured.

'Well don't be too sure that she's interested in you any more.'

'How do you mean?'

'Philippe has had the discretion to put Kelly in a separate cabin and I might add not too far from his own. It's pretty obvious he's got the hots for her and Kelly's pretty vulnerable at present too.'

Julian lay back on his sunbed hoping he had given Max some food for thought. He didn't like seeing Kelly being messed around. She was far too special for that.

Everyone was in a fine relaxed mood over lunch. Champagne corks popped and the crew laid out a table heaving with seafood and salad. Inga carried on with her duties as normal, even though she was aware of Max watching her every move. Kelly had ignored these little games and become engrossed in Philippe's anecdotes of his polo-playing days.

After lunch everyone stretched out to sleep off the wine and food. Max, however, decided to take something for his headache. The hangover from last night had returned with a vengeance after a spell in the midday sun and more wine. On his way to his cabin he bumped into Kelly. She gave him an icy look. Her eyes were as green and as sharp as the silk sarong she was wearing.

'Kelly,' Max tried unsuccessfully to hide his unease.

'I believe these assignations on yachts are something you make a habit of,' she snapped. 'Remember Newport? The circumstances were slightly different then. You weren't ignoring me.'

'Please don't think I'm ignoring you, Kelly.'

'Then what the hell do you think you're doing?' Kelly could feel the anger rising inside her. 'Why do you have to make it so damn obvious that you're playing around with someone else?'

Max sensed the makings of an argument. He didn't want the other guests or Inga being party to a scene. 'Everything's fine,' he lied, 'and I'm not avoiding you, OK?'

He went to kiss her on the lips but she pulled away.

'Save that for your Swedish liaisons,' she hissed, and stormed off up the stairs to the upper deck.

An hour after tea had been served, Max could hear the electronic winches winding up the two anchors. Slowly the yacht made a stately return to the old port of Monaco and Max's thoughts raced to the two days ahead. He tensed up as he studied the race track of winding streets. Subconsciously he went through the gear changes, one every second. Tomorrow it would be work as usual once more.

Philippe had booked a table for dinner at Rampoldi's, the fashionable and elegant eating place for the race fraternity. At six o'clock Max left on his own for the drivers' cocktail party. He had thought better of taking Kelly with him. Besides, it seemed she now had Philippe de Cours' entire attention. Later on he joined the others at the restaurant. Julian had brought along a couple of friends from Formula Three. Claudia and Bertrand seemed to be wrapped up in each other. Kelly sat quietly with Julian, who sensed her discomfort and was trying very hard to make her feel at ease. She was grateful for his company. He was always so sensitive to her needs. Why on earth hadn't he met some adoring woman by now and settled down? Kelly wanted to ask him. But it was not the time for intimate talk.

Dinner was subdued after the boisterous lunch they had enjoyed, and Max was pleased to slip away after coffee. He had the perfect excuse for an early night and the others were impressed at his self discipline to retire at such an hour. Only Julian and Kelly knew that it was not sleep he was returning to the yacht for.

There was little time for words when Max and Inga reached the cabin. They kissed passionately and Max realized how frustrated he had been all day at not being able to get close to her. They lay down on the bed and Max removed her clothes, kissing her warm brown stomach and burying his face in her full breasts. Her nipples were as hard as acorns. Soon they were both naked and Max stroked and teased every inch of her beautiful body until she reached a blissful climax. Then he slowly entered her, a little at a time, until she was desperate for all of him. With every exquisite thrust, Inga came again and again, each orgasm more intense than the last. Max, swept along on the tide of carnal pleasure and unable to bear the sweet torment a moment longer, gave himself in a blinding and frenzied rapture.

For Max it was a sweet fulfilment and only the guilt of knowing that Kelly was not far away distracted him from an otherwise pure moment of tenderness. As they lay back, wet with perspiration, Inga asked Max about Kelly.

'Is she your girlfriend?'

'We've had a long-standing affair,' explained Max. Long by his standards, at any rate.

'And your wife, does she know?'

'Hopefully not.'

It all seemed normal to Inga. In her home country, it was accepted to have affairs outside marriage. 'Are you a jealous person?'

'Why do you ask?'

'It's just that I noticed something a little strange in Monsieur de Cours' cabin.'

'What would be in his cabin that could affect me?' he asked, running his hands over Inga's smooth shoulders.

'Your girlfriend's clothes.'

'What? All of them?' Max was stunned.

'No, just the ones she was wearing this afternoon.' Inga gave Max an impish questioning look.

Max lay back on the pillow. He tried not to let Inga see his crushed expression. He felt a ripple of jealousy and disappointment run through him. His male pride was hurt. But then he reasoned, Kelly, after all, was a free agent. Nonetheless, it was only Inga's fine and delicate touch that restored his spirits again.

By one o'clock the following afternoon, the grandstands around the harbour were packed and all eyes were focused on the track, waiting for the cars to come round on the final timed practice session.

Both Mario and Max were tense. They desperately needed to make a fast lap as here, more than anywhere, grid positions were important. Colin was expecting results and a change in the team's luck now that they had found the cause of their misfortune. He would be damned if Scapini was going to spoil his chances of a good race for his team. But he still had the look of a haunted man. He regarded every stranger who came to view the cars with suspicion and it was only the innocent and foolhardy who attempted to make friendly conversation with him. Even the journalists were wary.

When the flag signalled the end of the hour's practice, Colin was relieved. He pulled off his headphones and checked the times on the computer. Max and Mario had qualified third and fourth respectively. Jean Claude had made it to pole position, just ahead of Ferrari's number two driver, Angelino Moratini.

Julian and Kelly made their way back to *L'Esprit de Vie*.

'So, is one allowed to ask what is going on between you and Max?' Julian enquired, tucking into a late lunch of pâté and French bread in the main saloon.

Kelly leaned back in her chair, pushing her sunglasses back on to her thick mane of hair. The yacht seemed curiously silent after all the din of the Formula One cars. It was a rare moment of quiet reflection during the hectic weekend.

She watched Julian eating with relish and felt a surge of warmth for him. She was touched at the way he sometimes appeared to be so like her younger brother, who had always been her guardian and confidant. She loved their close rapport and there was this same feeling with Julian. His thick hair, she noticed, was flecked with ginger in the sunshine that streamed through the open cabin door, outlining his handsome profile. 'Your guess is as good as mine. It's obvious he has an infatuation with this Swedish girl, but this time . . .' she shook her head '. . . he's gone too far. Max is a man who puts himself and his pleasures first and to hell with anyone else.'

Julian chuckled and sipped his wine. 'I was like that myself once.'

'Don't be crazy, Julian. You could never have been like that. Max is all . . .'

'Cock?' suggested Julian.

'Well almost,' said Kelly, not responding to Julian's attempt to make her laugh.

'Come on, Kelly, you must eat. Try some of the pâté. It's delicious.'

Instead, Kelly picked up a peach from the mountainous fruit bowl and absently began to peel it.

'Max and I are definitely finished this time,' she said. 'I've had enough of being hurt.'

Julian gave her a knowing wink. 'I've heard that before. You two seem to gravitate towards each other like the tide to a beach.'

'Not this time. His naughty boy act won't work with me any more. Besides, I think our Monsieur de Cours is rather charming.'

Julian looked up from his plate. Suddenly, for no reason, his lunch had lost its appeal. 'He seems to have made an impression on you. But for God's sake don't do anything you'll regret later,' he said firmly. Julian was of course unaware that she had gone to Philippe's cabin the previous day. Unable to get her shower to work, she had asked one of the crew if there was another bathroom available. Philippe had overheard her and insisted she use his bathroom. She had deliberately left her sarong behind, knowing that Max's Swedish princess would inform him of the developing friendship with Philippe. That would give Max something to think about.

# 37

Monaco was a feast of colour. The splendid beauty of spring flowers adorning the gardens in front of the Hotel de Paris temporarily paled into insignificance as the spectacle of people and advertising slogans swamped the pretty principality. Large adverts in foot-high letters for Gitanes Blondes competed with the familiar red Marlboro logos. The banners for Fosters' beer draped above the streets matched the vivid blue paintwork of the grandstands around the harbour, now filled to capacity with eager spectators. The marshals in their orange overalls and yellow helmets were positioned like soldiers on sentry duty every few yards along the track, ready to assist a broken-down car or wave their well-rehearsed flag signals.

An hour before the race there had been a light-hearted atmosphere at the drivers' briefing. All drivers assembled like first formers about to set off on their first away day cricket match, all anxious to get on with the real business of the day, but happy to accept the briefing as a necessary prelude to the race. A moustachioed boffin, the Clerk of the Course, with the brass buttons of his blazer twinkling as brightly as his squinting eyes, droned on about the hazards and changes to the circuit.

Max leaned back and yawned, his legs stretched out in front of him, giving only half an ear to what was to most of the drivers just a formality. Mario sat upright and alert next to him. 'So, you think our luck will change now?' asked Mario as the briefing came to an end.

'If it doesn't, then I'm bloody well ready to pack the whole thing in,' said Max despondently.

Mario shot him a look of incredulity. 'That's not such a good thing to say just before the start of a race,' Mario whispered to him, afraid that the others might have overheard Max's blunt delivery. 'You don't mean it.'

'Like hell I don't,' said Max. He clenched his hands together in suppressed frustration. 'I've got to finish this race, otherwise it will finish me.'

Mario saw the tension in Max's face and suddenly concern swept over him. He had never seen Max so demoralized before a race. *He* was normally the one to suffer pre-race nerves, not the World Champion.

At least the weather forecast did not predict rain which made it easier on everybody, not least for the girls strutting in their flimsy designer shorts and bikini tops. Prince Rainier and his two daughters, Caroline and Stephanie, stood behind closed windows watching the activity on the grid and in the pits below them.

Max sat in the pits shaded by an umbrella pine tree and feeling as restless as a caged animal.

'What's going on?' Julian called across to him from behind a roped-off area where only the Delta cars, drivers and personnel were allowed. With a nod of consent from Max, the gendarme on guard let Julian through.

'The ropes are Colin's way of ensuring maximum security for the team. He's anxious to avoid any more sabotage attempts, and grenade-throwing Italian fans.'

The Italian fans still hadn't forgiven Max for his ousting their young hero, Hugo Amarti, at Imola.

'I thought it was to keep the female pit groupies away,' Julian laughed.

At that moment Inga appeared and slid her neat figure

under the ropes, smiling bashfully at the gendarme. Even the photographers and journalists had been banned from entering the Delta area, which only served to fuel the rumours that either the team was getting paranoid about its privacy or it had some new modification for the race. Colin refused to be drawn into conversation on the subject and went about his business mutely.

Once on the grid, the drivers stepped out of their cars chatting to team managers, press and TV crews. It was a mêlée of work, glamour and posing. Wives and girlfriends strolled self-consciously down the grid, cameras pointed in their direction. Mechanics bustled around the cars that were still in various stages of assembly and disassembly. Colin, with eyes like a hawk's, watched any and everyone who approached his cars too closely.

'Relax,' Dick urged him as he caught him swallowing a tranquillizer. 'The mechanics are not letting anyone get within six feet of them.'

Colin, looking tired and strained, watched as one of the mechanics pushed a photographer roughly away from Max's car. A heated exchange followed. 'I don't care who you are a fucking photographer for . . . *Get away from that car!*'

The photographer only just managed to save his camera equipment from being yanked from his neck and backed off rapidly, but not before he had given the mechanics an earful which was captured live on British television. The camera zoomed in on a close-up of Colin looking as twitchy as General Custer about to shake hands with Sitting Bull.

A dazzling raven-haired beauty in tight jeans and beautifully tailored navy jacket approached Max, notebook in hand. A pair of immaculately painted red lips parted as she stretched out a hand. 'Max Gregson? Hello. My name is

Helen Butts from *Mirage* magazine. Could I have a minute of your time?'

Her sleepy, pale green eyes with incredible lashes that curled and swept upwards were enough to make Max wish he had an hour to spare. 'How can I help?' he asked now, directing his whole attention to this girl who was turning heads and cameras like royalty.

'A few questions about the job.' Her soft mouth curved upwards. 'What do you like most about the Monaco Grand Prix?'

'The plane trip home on Monday,' Max replied, smiling.

'You don't like this circuit?'

'No, nor the whole razzmatazz that goes with it,' he said, glancing around at the overcrowded yacht harbour and pit lane.

'How do you feel about the race this afternoon?'

Max paused. How did he feel? He would never admit to anyone how glad he would be when the whole thing was over, not just this race, but the whole season. He knew now that he had had enough of racing; the whole sickening mess of it all. The clamour for fame and fortune was over. He had achieved that, but now he was left with a nasty taste in his mouth. Somewhere, sometime he would have to pay for the life he had accidentally taken. Every time he stepped into the car he wondered if that time had come. The price for risking his life was too high now.

Helen Butts watched Max's eyes intently as they seemed to freeze and cut off from everything around him. Dark brown, as tender and as doleful as a labrador's. She felt a pang of compassion as she realized that for the next two hours he would be risking his life to win, to try and achieve the form he had had last year. 'Do you think you stand a good chance of winning?' she asked.

'Sure. Once the procession is over and the unreliable cars have dropped out. Who knows?'

'You feel lucky today?' She tilted her head and her eyes never left his.

'Something like that. You have to feel positive. Otherwise there's no point in racing. Twenty-five other meanies will walk right over you.'

'Does racing still give you a buzz?' she asked, detecting a hint of false optimism in his voice.

'Almost as much as making love to a woman,' he said with a broad sexy smile.

'I've heard that Concorde pilots find the aircraft so exciting that some of them have been known to ejaculate on take-off. Do these cars give you as much excitement?'

'I save my ejaculations for the bedroom.' Max grinned.

A serious little Frenchman walked past the cars carrying a large 'THREE MINUTES' board close to his chest. As Max put on his helmet, he glanced across to the pit wall to see Inga blowing him a kiss and giving him a cheeky grin. Then came an explosion of sound as the cars revved into life, halting conversation and leaving the unprepared rapidly covering their ears.

As the red light turned to green, the cars screamed off, shattering the stillness of the Sunday afternoon. Siestas had been cast aside as the inhabitants leaned over every apartment balcony and out of every office window to get a better glimpse of the cars.

Mario saw it all as a blur: the packed grandstands, the waving banners of the group of Argentinian fans that had congregated. He changed through the gears; bang, bang, bang, bang, and then braked into Casino Square.

The gear box would have to withstand a toll of at least two and a half thousand gear changes before the race had finished.

Mario followed the rear of Max's car as if he were attached to it by a line. He knew overtaking would be difficult, but his reflexes had never been so sharp. As a cat stalks a bird, so Mario remained poised. It was only a matter of time before Max would lose a second of concentration and then he would pass him.

Kelly, Julian and Philippe de Cours watched the race from the top deck of the yacht. They could see the cars emerging flat out from the tunnel, following the circuit parallel to the harbour, past the swimming pool, to brake sharply for the La Rascasse corner that took them back into the town.

Julian was unusually quiet as he sipped on his first glass of champagne of the day. Kelly turned to him, temporarily taking her eyes off the track, where she had been following Max's every move.

'Are you OK?' she asked. Julian's face was showing the same dismay as she felt inside. Her pride and her heart were in tatters after Max's cold shouldering all weekend.

'Sure,' Julian replied. 'Lost a couple of grand at the Casino last night and overdrowned my sorrows, that's all.'

He grinned and Kelly was relieved to see him his old self again. Julian's natural insouciant charm was something she always took for granted. She relaxed as she sensed his good humour return.

Kelly was unaware of Julian's real concern. Ever since Kelly had confided in him about her pregnancy, he had felt a growing protectiveness towards her. Of course, he had been flattered that he was the first person she had turned to, but there was something else that unsettled him. More and more he was reacting to Max's off-hand treatment of her. First the miscarriage, then the on-off way he had dropped her and picked her up again when it suited him. He really felt he must have it out with Kelly once and for all. She was far too gentle a person to be subjected to Max's selfish behaviour.

Even though Max was one of his closest friends, he couldn't approve of the way he handled his women. He wondered if it was time he found himself a long-term relationship. Maybe he had grown out of his roistering ways, maybe his days of playing 'homme fatal' were over. Perhaps, unlike Max, he was weary of his playboy image.

His attention now fully back to the race, he watched the leading Ferrari coast to a halt outside of the tunnel. Only the fifth lap and already the race had claimed its first victim. He could imagine the driver's disappointment.

'Do you believe in bad luck?' screamed the French journalist.

'You are going to know what bad luck is all about if you don't leave me alone,' Max bellowed at the man. Their voices were drowned out by the scream of the cars passing alarmingly close to them. Only the guard rail separated them as Max walked back to the pits, helmet and gloves in hand. Right now he didn't want to talk to anyone, least of all a journalist. Max had left his car parked in a wall at the Loews hairpin bend. It was not a pretty sight. Most of the bodywork was in a crumpled heap. Max had seen the accident coming and was bitter that he hadn't been able to avoid it. Mario had been breathing down his neck from the start and had made every attempt to pass. After thirty laps Max had got irritated by the constant view of Mario in his mirrors. He had committed the unforgivable sin and allowed himself to get harassed, and clipped the wall. His car had bounced off and ended up on the opposite guard rail. Mario only narrowly missed him and Max was lucky to escape serious injury. If Mario had touched his car, there would have been the makings of an horrific accident.

It was a long walk back to the pits and Max was feeling shaken as he sat down.

'Fetch him a doctor,' called Colin, as he saw one of the mechanics hand him a bottle of water. Max looked the picture of dejection.

Colin left the pit wall and came over to him. 'What happened? Was there a breakage on the car?'

'No breakages this time, only my bloody driving.'

Colin scowled resentfully at Max before disappearing back to the pit wall. He would have a long frank talk to Max after the race. In the meantime, Mario had overtaken the second car and was hot on the heels of Jean Claude. It was turning into a thrilling race. Mario was driving as if he were a man possessed and Colin couldn't bear to miss any of it.

Max lay on his bed staring at the large compass design on the ceiling. He was enjoying the coolness of the air conditioning. He wondered if Mario had managed to win the race, but decided he didn't much care. Inga knocked gently at the door and came in with a large cup of coffee and a brandy. Max knocked back the brandy.

'Max, your leg!' Inga stared in horror at the purple swelling the size of a grapefruit on Max's thigh. 'How did you walk with that?'

'You don't hit a wall at ninety miles an hour and come out with nothing. There's another one here.' Max rolled up the sleeve of his silk dressing gown and Inga gasped as she saw the angry bruises covering most of his arm.

'Let me get something for those. I have a liniment that takes out the bruising.' And before Max could reply she had left the room. Max lay back on the bed, the shock of the accident beginning to hit him more forcefully now. He felt utter despair. Last year he had been so confident, so supremely confident that not only would he win races, but win the Championship. Now this season, already five of the sixteen races had been run, and he had scored only a single point.

Inga came silently back into the room. 'Sorry I took so long,' she said, and began massaging the cream into his leg. Neither heard the gentle knock at the door.

'There's a couple of people outside who would like a word with you, Mr Gregson,' called one of the crew.

Max dressed and went out to see who it was. Colin and Dick were sitting in the saloon and a group of pressmen gathering by the gangplank. He limped stiffly to a chair and sat down.

'What's up?' he asked, seeing both Colin and Dick with downcast expressions.

'I'm afraid we've bad news for you, Max,' said Colin. 'Sophie has had a fall from her horse.'

Max felt the blood drain from his face. 'How is she? Is she . .?'

'She's on her way to hospital. She's lost consciousness. Vicky phoned the news through just after the race.'

'We're sorry to hear the bad news,' said Dick.

Max covered his face with his hands and then reminded himself he must keep a cool, clear head. 'Mind if I use the company jet to get home?' he asked.

Colin nodded. 'I was about to suggest that. The pilots are ready when you are.'

Max stood up, wincing with pain as he did so. Dick noticed how old he suddenly appeared. His face was pale, almost grey, and there was a listlessness about him. The vital energy that was so much a part of him had gone.

He collected his things together rapidly, helped by Inga. When he had packed his bag he pulled her close.

'Max, please don't say goodbye for good . . . please don't let us end like this.' Inga was trying hard not to cry, but the tears ran down her soft cheeks.

'I can't think straight right now. I have a sick daughter at home who needs me. I can't promise anything.' He kissed her gently on the lips. 'Goodbye,' he whispered.

'Don't forget me,' sighed Inga, looking into his deep sad eyes.

Ten minutes later he was airborne with the two pilots in a helicopter that shuttled between Monaco and Nice airport. His goodbyes to Philippe de Cours, Julian and Kelly had been brief. Max had already arranged for a case of Dom Perignon to be delivered to the yacht that evening, which was just as well, he thought, on reflection. There would be plenty of celebrating to do. As he left the circuit, he heard that Mario had won the race. Nobody, not even Colin, had dared mention it to him.

# 38

Kelly wrestled with her emotions as she watched Max's hurried departure. She was utterly miserable. For three days she had fought with the realization that this time Max's attentions had wandered elsewhere for good. The sexual chemistry between them had gone. She was aware of it in the cold way he looked at her. She had hoped to get him on his own for a few moments to talk with him, but the chance was lost. Maybe he would call her, but her intuition told her he had walked out of her life for ever.

She had been upset by the news of Sophie's accident. She knew how much his little daughter meant to him, and she wished she were with him now. She had noticed a vulnerability about him in the last few days – a remoteness that seemed to have taken a hold of him. As she dined out with Philippe and Julian that night, Kelly fought back tears of despair. Even worse was the thought that they were wasted on him. He would never change his ways. Julian was right.

Mario was ecstatic. He kissed the large gleaming trophy and threw his arms around Tom, the chief mechanic. He laughed and joked with everyone who came to congratulate him. The motor home was crammed with people and there was a merry jostling crowd outside trying to catch a glimpse of the winner. The sponsors, all heavyweight captains of industry, were equally thrilled and a champagne party was soon in full swing in the hospitality marquee.

Only Colin was missing from the celebrations. After he

left the yacht he made his way to Scapini's motor home. It appeared deserted from the outside and the heavily tinted windows gave no sign of life inside. How quiet it was compared to his own, Colin thought. It served as a stark reminder to him of the difference between a winning team and a losing one. The door was opened by a frail-looking Italian girl, plain and nondescript. There was none of the heavy mob that normally stood guard. The girl left Colin at the door. He could hear hushed voices coming from inside. Then she reappeared and beckoned him in. The motor home smelt strongly of the cigarettes that Scapini smoked. Several of the blinds were drawn. In harsh contrast to the bright sunlight outside, the scene that greeted Colin was shadowy.

'Sit down, Pritchard,' commanded a voice from the couch. Colin recognized Scapini sitting with two of his Mafiosi. They were dressed in slick grey suits, and wore oversized watches and a gaudy display of gold chain. Colin sat down.

'So, you've persuaded Raphael Gabbiani to remain with your team? What else are you holding over his head, besides money?' asked Colin, coming straight to the point.

Raphael, Scapini's designer, had at the last minute refused to sign a contract with Delta. Colin was bitterly disappointed. Raphael had a wealth of talent and Colin had already envisaged him as a key member of his design team. He had spoken with him several times and his answer was always the same. Scapini would not release him from the contract. Both knew that contracts were only pieces of paper. There was more to it than that. Colin was positive he had been threatened, but Raphael would not be drawn on the subject.

Scapini shrugged. 'He doesn't want to leave the team.

That's the way it is. There was no threat involved, if that is what you are accusing me of. You forget that everybody has a price.' He smiled thinly and lit a cigarette. The frail Italian girl brought him a clean ashtray.

'Raphael was excited at the idea of joining Delta. So what happened?'

'He changed his mind.'

'Like hell he did. You may put the fear of God into the rest of F1 but you and your sidekicks don't scare me off so easily.' Colin gave the men either side of Scapini a look of disdain.

Scapini smiled mockingly. 'It's all straightforward business, nothing more.'

'You call sabotaging cars a part of the business?' Colin watched Scapini closely. Scapini lowered his eyes and the thug sitting beside him fiddled nervously with the gold links on his bracelet.

'Sabotage. That's strong language, Mr Pritchard. I think you better arm yourself with some evidence before you start accusing me of such things.'

'I will, don't worry. When Geoff and I have a chat. I think there will be plenty to bring out into the open.'

Scapini's eyes flickered with interest, then focused on the smoke escaping from the cigarette he had just stubbed out. 'Who is Geoff? One of your mechanics? I heard one of your men had disappeared rather suddenly. Any word from him yet?'

'Yes,' Colin lied. 'We're meeting next week. He's rather anxious to speak with me. You obviously didn't pay him well enough.'

Scapini smiled again. He had an evil aura about him.

'Just one more thing,' Colin said. 'You try and lay a hand on one of my cars or team members again and I'll blow your little operation sky high.'

Scapini laid a restraining hand on one of his scowling minders who was about to show Colin the door. 'A word of warning, Pritchard. The small bird does not try to fight with a colony of eagles. You would do well to remember your strength.' Scapini's voice was menacing.

'Damn you, you won't get away with this. You and your Mafia bunch don't control this set-up, and I for one am not afraid to fight you.'

Colin stormed out of the motor home in a fury. He knew as well as anyone that you did not cross the Mafia with impunity, but he would make damn sure that Scapini would never get near his team again.

The jet taxied to the Field's Executive Centre at Heathrow and shortly after Max was at the wheel of his Ferrari and heading towards the M4. The brief message Vicky had left him at the airport wasn't good. Sophie was to have a brain scan and an operation might be necessary.

Max dodged in and out of the traffic, oblivious of the high speeds at which he was driving. He had to get to the hospital as soon as possible. His daughter's life was in danger and he had to be there.

He found Vicky in a waiting room, still wearing her jodhpurs and boots. Her face was the colour of grey marble. Instant relief swept over her as she saw Max. 'Thank God you're here,' she cried.

'How is she?' he asked urgently.

'In theatre . . . they're operating.'

'How serious is it?' he asked, swallowing hard.

'She has a haemorrhage on the brain.'

Max paled at the thought. An onslaught of possible repercussions came into his mind: brain damage, paralysis. A picture of Sophie mentally handicapped flashed across his brain. No, it couldn't happen. Max took hold of

Vicky and held her as tightly as the fear that gripped his insides. 'What the hell happened?'

Vicky burst into tears. Then she choked back her sobs and blew her nose. 'She had a fall from her pony. She was practising over the jumps. Apparently the pony refused and Sophie fell heavily . . . ' her voice tailed off.

'You mean, you weren't there?' Max looked at her incredulously.

Vicky shook her head and sobbed again. 'No, I wasn't. I had gone to the house to take a phone call and left her there with the au pair. I was gone only a few minutes . . . when I came out she was lying on the grass . . . Before you ask, yes she was wearing a riding hat. It fell off before she hit the ground.'

'She hadn't done it up?'

'No, I suppose not. We took her inside . . . her arm was in a lot of pain. We lay her down on the sofa . . . she complained of being dizzy. Then she was sick. I knew there was something wrong. Before I could get her to the hospital she lost consciousness. I was afraid to move her . . . an ambulance came for her.'

'And the brain scan?'

'They did one straight away . . . found the haemorrhage and decided to operate . . . she couldn't be in better hands, Max. They've got one of the top surgeons. I met him very briefly. He's doing something called a Burr Hole to release the pressure of the haemorrhage on the brain. Once they've done that, recovery can be pretty quick.'

'And what if . . . '

'I don't know.' Vicky covered her face with her hands to stop a new flood of tears.

'How long till we know?' Max's voice sounded flat and weary.

'About half an hour. The sister said she would be in theatre about an hour. She's been in almost half an hour now.'

The half hour passed slowly. Max paced up and down the empty waiting room, his eyes never far from the clock ticking on the wall. He felt helpless. What if the worst did happen to Sophie, their only child. She was far too young to relinquish her life . . .

Max thought back over his own life. He risked it every time he stepped into a racing car. He taunted death, played with it. But now it was his child's life that was in the balance, a life which was beyond price. He prayed that it be spared, wishing that it were him on the operating table instead of her. He remembered the pensioner he had knocked down . . . was this his retribution? A life for a life . . . His thoughts flashed back to that day.

Caught up inextricably in the euphoria of his own success, he had lived with the wild misconception that he was infallible. He had agonized over that accident a hundred times. If Kelly hadn't told him about her pregnancy, he wouldn't have drunk so much. There would have been no arguments. He would have driven steadily. The old man would still be alive today and enjoying his life. In his weakened state, he considered telling Vicky about it, then decided not to. What good would it do?

Vicky was also feeling guilt and remorse. Guilt because she had allowed Sophie to ride without her hat being secured properly and remorse for leaving her to go and answer the phone. Her carelessness could cost Sophie her life or . . .

Max guessed her thoughts. He put his hand gently on hers. 'Don't blame yourself for any of this, it could have happened whether you were there or not and I know you've told Sophie a hundred times about doing up her chin strap.'

Vicky laid her head on Max's shoulder. 'She's all we've got, Max. Our only child. She is so precious . . .' She wept again. Max tried to think of something encouraging to say. It wasn't easy.

The minutes ticked by. An hour passed. She should be out by now, thought Vicky. Why are they taking so long? She was about to suggest to Max they go and find someone, when the door opened abruptly and the surgeon came in.

He had changed out of his operating gown into a navy suit. Max jumped up immediately. He searched his face for a sign that would tell him that Sophie had made it through the operation.

The surgeon shook Max's hand. 'Nice to meet you, Mr Gregson. I'm glad to tell you that your daughter's going to be all right.' He smiled at Vicky and saw the relief on her face. 'Sophie's responding well. We gave her a light anaesthetic and she came to almost immediately – as soon as the pressure on the brain was relieved. That is what we would expect – but she will have to stay in for a week, so that we can keep an eye on her. Then she can go home . . . as long as she takes it easy for a while.'

Max felt as if a great weight had been lifted from his shoulders. He shook the surgeon by the hand once more and thanked him. Vicky did the same.

'May we see Sophie?' Her voice had a new lightness.

'Yes, for a few minutes. I'd better warn you . . . she's had half her head shaved. She may not appreciate that too much. It might be an idea to find her a good hairdresser when she comes out.' The surgeon winked at Vicky and she returned his warm smile. The hair would not be so much of a problem, she thought. Trying to keep her off a horse might be.

As Max drove home he told Vicky about the race. 'A bizarre thing happened on the way back to the pits. This young French journalist – couldn't have been more than twenty-five and still wet behind the ears – asked me if I believed in bad luck. I almost stuffed him into the pit wall.'

'Well, do you?'

'What?'

'Believe in bad luck?'

'Believe in it! Look at me. Right now I'm buried under a landslide of it.'

'Max, please don't think like that. Life was never meant to run smoothly all the time. And we have a hell of a lot to be thankful for. Sophie is going to recover, that's the most important thing. And,' she added carefully, 'it's situations like this that bring people closer together.'

She put her head on Max's shoulder as he drove unhurriedly home and wondered if this accident might have that effect on them. Over the past few months she had discovered a new side to her husband. Possessiveness, jealousy, the desire for revenge . . . Characteristics she would never have considered him to possess. She hoped that some good would come from their misfortune. Maybe Max would see sense now and be more devoted to his family. The accident had certainly brought home to Vicky her priorities – to have a close, united family – and she was determined to work at it to keep it that way.

A month later, Sophie was back to her old self. Vicky had taken her away to Dorset for a week, and they had returned tanned and healthy. Sophie's hair had grown an inch all over and she had come to terms with her boyish appearance.

Max had returned from America and another Grand

Prix in Detroit. There had been a heated exchange of words with Colin before he left to come home. Colin's patience had been growing thin and Max's poor driving – he had finished tenth – only exacerbated it. (Mario had driven superbly again and finished a close second to Jean Claude.)

For Max there were more bad press reports. One American magazine, not known for its journalistic subtleties, had attributed Max's poor performance to a drink problem. Not content with that, they embellished the story with the suggestion that Max was having treatment for his problem and also that his marriage was shaky and his Swedish mistress pregnant.

For Colin, this meant big trouble with the sponsors. They would desert him faster than they could tear up a contract if they thought one of the drivers was being sidetracked by outside influences. They wanted results and value for money. Max at present was providing neither. Colin made no attempt to deny the rumour that he would replace Max at the end of the season. Max had stated openly that he wouldn't consider staying with the team, anyway, which left him in a difficult position for the following year. There were plenty of teams who would snap him up, but they could not match the money or the competitiveness that Delta offered. Max flew back to London wondering where his future lay, and with what team.

Three days later he was off to the South of France for four days of testing. On his return to England, he drove to the Delta factory and met up with Dick. He, like all the team personnel, was anxious to hear of Sophie's progress. They had sent her get well cards, flowers and a huge teddy bear. Dick called Max to one side. 'Fancy a coffee in the office?'

Over cups of freshly brewed coffee they discussed the new car design Jean was working on for next season. 'It would appear I won't be in the driving seat of that one next year,' Max commented sardonically when he saw the drawings on the desk.

'How long have we known each other, Max?' Dick asked, leaning forward in his chair.

'You tell me . . . five . . . six years?'

'Six and a half, to be exact. So I hope you will take this from a friend, Max, nothing to do with Delta management. There are a lot of people around at the moment who, like myself, are bloody worried about you. What's going on?'

'Nothing that a run of good luck wouldn't sort out.'

Dick laughed. 'Come on, don't give me that bullshit. I'm being serious. I know we had problems with Scapini – that would scare the hell out of anyone – but it's over now. There's nothing at all to stop you winning races – except the will to win.'

'And I've lost that, right?'

'It would seem that way. What is it? Have you lost your nerve? Or has the large bank balance made you soft?'

'What's this all about?'

'I'll tell you what this is all about and don't get mad with me. I hate to see great talent wasted. You're one of the best drivers this country has produced in a long while. You've got years of brilliant driving ahead of you. You've tasted success – you've got the World Championship and now you're throwing it all away. Why?' Dick hesitated. He could see he had touched a raw nerve with Max, who now seemed withdrawn. 'You don't have to tell me . . . all I want you to do is to get the answers clear for yourself. Find out what is destroying you.'

'Destroying me?' Max looked nettled. 'It's just not happening for me this year, that's all.'

'And the longer you believe that, the worse your performance will get. Don't you see, all this drinking and womanizing is affecting you? You've lost your form. Unless you're one hundred per cent serious in this job, you're finished or you end up dead. What's it to be, Max?'

'Since when did a few drinks and the odd diversion ruin a driver? When I get in that car my mind is one hundred per cent on the job . . . '

'Maybe, but you've got to keep yourself in top shape. Driving after binges isn't exactly great for the reflexes.'

'I hear what you're saying, Dick . . . The old adage is true – it's hard enough to win . . . but to stay at the top is the hardest of all.' Max stood up and smiled languidly. 'Maybe I should retire from the game now that the hunger is gone.'

'Don't disappoint me . . . you know that's bullshit. You haven't lost your hunger. You've lost yourself for a while. And all the boozing and women in the world is not going to help you find what it is you're after. Whatever's happened, Max, don't let it ruin your life a moment longer. If you can get results for the rest of the season, Colin won't let you go.'

Max raised an eyebrow. 'And who says I want to stay here next year?'

'Better the devil you know . . . '

'Dick, you're one of the few people in this mad circus I can listen to. Thanks for the chat. I'll bear in mind what you've said.'

Dick got up from his chair and laid his hand on Max's shoulder. 'Don't blow it, Max, for Vicky and Sophie's sake.'

'You're only as good as your last race. I'm beginning to see the truth in that,' said Max thoughtfully.

Max was still reflecting on Dick's words as he drove home in the Ferrari, letting it have full power on the straight dual carriageway and flirting with it round the corners. Dick was right, of course. He would be a fool if he didn't acknowledge what was happening. There was a new attitude to his racing that had superseded his will to win. Something in the back of his mind was telling him that he couldn't do it any more.

He drove through the sun-dappled country lanes listening to Eric Clapton on the stereo. He stopped the car where his land bordered the road, climbed a grassy bank and walked into the field. The tall grass bowed before a strong breeze and the racing clouds sent fleeting shadows across the expanse of green pasture in front of him. He sat down. Moments like this were few and far between in his hectic schedule of dashing around the world.

How different things were now. Before, he had never allowed himself time to reflect. He was always thinking forward to the next race; the next challenge. The last few years had been exceptionally successful but fraught with pressure. Each time he raced he had got closer to his ultimate goal, and the rewards of success had finally been his. Now he had reached the top, he had to get used to the idea that sooner or later he was going to fall.

After Sophie's accident and the relief of her recovery, Max found himself treasuring every minute he spent with her. Which made him reconsider the possibility of retirement. Did he need to go out and risk his life now that he had won the World Championship? Perhaps he should move in another direction – there were plenty of business offers coming his way.

He wondered about his playboy image, too, and the

almost compelling need to have affairs with women. Like his racing, sex was pretty addictive. Perhaps now he should try and reconcile himself to being faithful to Vicky, for the sake of their marriage and all it meant to her. Unable to find an answer to his problems, he walked back to his car and drove up to the large welcoming farmhouse.

# 39

Despite the warmth and brilliance of the summer's day, Rachel felt depressed as she drove to Wallingford. She was leading a solitary existence in the manor house. Colin had returned only once to pack a suitcase, before setting off on his travels again, and she had decided to stay on until the children began their holidays. Besides, she wanted to be near Vicky after Sophie's accident and it would also give her more time to find a suitable house in the area.

She parked the car and absently bought a few things in the supermarket. Now that Mrs Brooks, the housekeeper, was on holiday, Rachel was left to run the house, a job she did not relish. On her way back to the car, she called at a newsagent to buy some magazines. There was a queue at the counter and among the group she recognized someone familiar – a tall distinctive man with brown, curly hair and a brown leather jacket and faded jeans. For the first time that day her mood lifted. 'Hi, Phil, how are you?'

Phil spun round and for a moment did not recognize the woman with the large, brown eyes and sensuous smile.

'I'm Rachel, remember?' she prompted. 'We met at Vicky's.'

'How could I forget you?' Phil gave her one of his huge grins. 'How are you?'

'I'm fine. How about you?'

'I'm all right. I wish the horses were as well as I was. One of our best yearlings developed breathing problems yesterday evening. I've been up with the vet for most of the night. The Colonel was in a right panic.' Phil spoke quickly, obviously concerned for the animal.

'How is he now?'

'The horse or the Colonel?' said Phil smiling.

'The horse,' laughed Rachel.

'The horse is much better. The Colonel, not so. He is recovering from a surfeit of brandy he drank to keep his spirits up.' Phil placed his hand lightly on Rachel's shoulder as they left the shop. They reached his mud-splattered Land Rover and Rachel spotted two black Labradors inside. They were eyeing her enthusiastically.

'And is life keeping you busy?' Phil turned to face her.

'Yes, far too much,' she lied.

'A pity. I was hoping you might be free for lunch next week.' Phil had the same keen look as his dogs.

'I think I could make that.'

'Good. How about Wednesday? One o'clock at the Beagle. Do you know it?'

'Yes.' Rachel hoped her reply was not too transparently eager.

'See you then.' Phil jumped into the Land Rover to a chorus of barking dogs, drowning out the spluttering engine. With a puff of black smoke, he rolled out of the parking space and was off down the road.

Rachel remained where she was for a few moments. Slightly disorientated by the chance meeting with Phil, she had to stop and think what day it was. She caught sight of herself in a shop window. Baggy cotton trousers and shirt, spiky hair and no make-up. It was time she started taking care of herself again.

Colin pored over a folder of documents en route to Milan. In a hectic day's schedule he was meeting a sponsor for lunch and then driving on to a factory some sixty miles outside the city to discuss engines with a leading motor manufacturer. He anticipated arriving back in London late that night. The Learjet was comfortable and quiet and the only other passenger was Jean, also immersed in drawings of the new car design and possible engine configurations.

One of the pilots emerged from the cockpit and handed Colin a note. It had come through from the factory marked urgent. It was brief, but the words hit Colin like a thunderbolt.

'Jesus, I don't believe it.'

Jean looked up. Colin's face was ashen.

'Not bad news?'

Colin handed Jean the piece of paper. It read, GEOFF FOUND DEAD BESIDE CANAL BANK. POLICE SUSPECT SUICIDE.'

'How can this be so?' Jean asked in disbelief.

'Scapini – the ruthless bastard. I warned him I was going to talk to Geoff. He must have got scared and bumped him off.'

'He would kill to keep him quiet?' Jean whispered.

'I would lay my life on it. Scapini is far more dangerous than we would believe.' Colin swallowed hard. He felt partly to blame for Geoff's untimely death. If Scapini were trying to lower the morale of the Delta team, he was succeeding. The mechanics were becoming edgy, always on the alert for trouble. Max had his mind on his problems at home and even Colin had to admit he was feeling the strain. The worry uppermost in his mind was that Scapini would try and sabotage Mario's car. It was a nightmare he lived with. The risks involved in racing were high enough without Scapini trying to 'fix' their cars.

Mario, on the other hand, was the one who was keeping a cool head about the whole business. He was unaffected by all the suspicions and nervousness in the team. It had only served to strengthen his resolve to win.

Mario sat in the sauna, the sweat oozing from his pores after an hour's punishing workout in the gym. These days he was totally preoccupied with racing. His ambition to be the best driver in the world had become an obsession. Life was a strict regime of healthy eating, exercise, early nights and no alcohol.

In fact, he had cleared all distractions from his life except one. Colin Pritchard. Mario wondered how long their relationship would last. Although he had tried hard to push the problem from his mind, it gnawed away at him like toothache. Colin was inextricably linked to his career. As long as he stayed at Delta he was committed to Colin, who was becoming more possessive and volatile. He had experienced the unwelcome pressures of a relationship with Chico. With Colin it was a hundred times more complicated. He watched the sand in the timer on the wall run its last minute and wondered where his career was heading. Should he stay at Delta or leave, to break free of Colin?

Mario took in deep breaths. The heat was getting to him now. A few moments longer and he would jump under a welcoming cold shower. He threw his head back, enjoying the heavy tiredness that the combination of the heat and exercise had brought on.

The door opened and a tall lean figure climbed on to the boards. In the semi darkness Mario could make out an attractive face and a head of thick wavy blond hair. The man lay back on one arm, allowing the towel to drop from his waist. 'Excuse me asking,' he said after a moment, 'but you're Mario Rodriguez, aren't you?'

'Yes,' replied Mario, sitting up and pulling a towel around his waist. The heat was overpowering now.

The handsome stranger smiled. 'You probably don't know me. My name is Peter Morgan. I work in F1 – I do PR for some of the teams.' Mario detected a slight accent.

'Hi, nice to meet you,' said Mario, shaking his hand briefly. 'Will you excuse me? If I stay in here any longer I think I shall melt.'

'Sure thing. See you around.'

Mario braced himself to take the full force of the ice-cold shower. After the initial shock, every nerve became invigorated and his body tingled with pleasure. Having dressed, he made his way to the bar. It was then he glimpsed the man he had met in the sauna under the shower. From the back view, Mario admired his firm apple-shaped bottom, his long thighs and well-developed calf muscles. His body was in superb condition. Peter Morgan switched off the shower and turned to reach for his towel. He recognized Mario again and smiled.

'Would you join me for a drink in the bar?' asked Mario.

'Thanks,' came the reply. 'A mineral water will do fine.'

Sitting at the bar fully dressed, Peter was an even more striking figure, Mario decided. They shared a large bottle of mineral water.

'Are you a member here? I haven't seen you here before,' Peter remarked.

'I only joined a week ago. I was a member in Kensington, but I prefer this club. So which teams do you work for?' asked Mario, more at home on the subject of motor racing.

'Renault and Scapini.'

Mario stiffened at the mention of Scapini's name. 'Have you been doing the job long?'

'Three years. Before that I was with Indycars in America.'

'I thought I detected an American accent,' said Mario, warming to this personable man.

'Nearly right. Canadian. I'm from Toronto actually, but spent most of my working life in the States.' Mario guessed he must be about thirty, although it was difficult to tell. 'How about you? How long have you been living over here?'

'Three years. This is my second year in Formula One.'

'Well, I know all about your F1 career. I'm a great fan of yours.' Peter grinned.

'You are?'

'Sure, I've been following you very closely this season – your driving has been pretty phenomenal.'

'Thanks. It has improved a lot, thanks to the team I'm with.'

'I'll give Pritchard one thing – he's certainly brought Delta together. How do you get on with him? I hear he can be difficult to work for?'

Mario searched Peter's face, wondering if the question was as innocent as it sounded.

'Sometimes yes, he can get a little anxious, but he's OK.'

'Do you think you'll be staying with the team?'

'Are you sure you're not a journalist?' Mario asked quickly.

'Sorry. That was a bit of a loaded question – I must sound like one.'

'I have to be careful. Sometimes a casual conversation can end up in print, especially when team changes are involved.'

'I can appreciate that. So no more personal questions.' They both laughed and shook hands on it. They finished another glass of Perrier and said goodbye, but not before Mario had invited Peter to the team's motor home at the next race.

When Colin returned to the factory after his trip to Italy, he immediately called a meeting. By eight thirty, Tom, Jean and Dick and the two race engineers were assembled in his office.

Colin went straight to the point. 'You've obviously heard about Geoff's death and the suspicion of suicide. I have my own ideas on how Geoff died, but it's up to the police to draw their own conclusions. I don't want a police investigation going on here. We've enough to do to get these cars ready without any further diversions.'

'You mean, you're not going to tell them about Geoff sabotaging the cars?' enquired Dick.

'No, I want to let the matter rest. Understood?'

The others nodded. It could lead to a lot of unnecessary publicity and messy business. Geoff was dead and nothing would change that, they agreed.

Then Colin's expression changed. Unable to hold back a moment longer, he gave one of his rare economical smiles. 'We've landed the engine deal for next season,' he announced calmly.

The response was infectious. The group was as joyful as if they had just won another World Championship. 'Well done,' congratulated Dick. 'That's fantastic. But how did you do it?'

'A lot of talk and persuasion. It also helped that I could speak Italian.'

'But wasn't it on the cards that Scapini's mob were to sign the deal?'

'Very much so,' replied Colin, rubbing his hands together. 'But nothing had been agreed definitely. In fact,

I'm sure Scapini still thinks he's getting the contract.'

'What made them change their minds? After all, an Italian engine for an Italian team was the obvious choice.' Dick crossed his legs, wondering where the catch lay.

'Absolutely. But one of the directors told me in confidence that they didn't think the team was going to produce the results. Too much laundering of sponsors' money.'

'They actually said that?' It was Jean's turn to stare in disbelief.

'Not in as many words. The truth of the matter is they don't want to be seen doing business with what is generally considered to be a team with Mafia links. They have their own image to think about . . . so Scapini's little mob are going to disappear down a big hole, hopefully. Unless they find another manufacturer.' Colin's eyes shone with satisfaction.

'At last we've done him,' said Dick gleefully.

'Yes, and you can bet the team personnel will abandon him like rats off a sinking ship. It could be an easy matter now to persuade Raphael to join us. Another piece of good news is that the manufacturers are developing a new prototype engine that in conjunction with a new type of fuel will give extra horsepower.'

Dick gave a low whistle. 'Sounds like Christmas a hundred times over. But what's the bottom line, Colin?'

'In return for the engines? That's simple.' Colin paused. 'We give them a World Champion.'

'We do?' exclaimed Tom and the race engineers in unison.

'Basically they're prepared to sign a two-year contract which will be extended for another two years if we win the Championship. If not they have the option to go elsewhere.'

'That should give Max something to think about,' Dick mused.

'I happen to think it's Mario who's going to do it for us this time,' Colin said firmly. 'If, and I say if, Max stays with us, they will have equal standing. But it's Mario who's our best chance, don't you think?'

Dick could not help but notice that Colin's voice had softened, as though he were talking about a favourite son. The others were more surprised by his open denouncement of Max.

# 40

July in southern France and the beaches are predictably crowded. Nine miles inland, north of Toulon, is a race track, the Paul Ricard, and this year it was home to the French Grand Prix. The teams and press corps had flown down there several days before and its more bibulous members were now enjoying the cheap, plentiful wine before the hectic lead up to the Grand Prix.

In complete contrast, however, the mood in the Delta camp was as icy and gloomy as a winter's day. Colin had been offhand with everyone, snapping at the mechanics, journalists and photographers alike. But it was his public disagreement with Mario on the second day of practice that had most surprised everybody. Mario had driven into the pits after a disappointing session and was immediately approached by Colin, who had handled the situation as diplomatically as a bellowing bull.

'How was the set-up?' he demanded.

'Fine,' replied Mario smoothly.

'Tyres?'

'Perfect.'

'So, what the hell was the problem? We've spent the last two days getting the race set up perfect and your lap times were more than a second slower than yesterday's.'

'The traffic was bad. You could see for yourself I couldn't get a fast lap,' Mario said defensively.

'Don't give me excuses, Mario. It's up to you to find

a time when there's no traffic to get a fast lap.' Colin's voice which had now reached fever pitch could be heard throughout the garage and was attracting the attention of the journalists who were listening in surprise to the open disagreement between the two.

'Hey, cool it, Colin,' Mario said, surprised at Colin's sudden outburst. 'Let's sort this out at debrief.'

Colin shot him one of his withering looks and walked away. Addressing Dick in a voice he knew Mario and the onlookers would hear he said, 'The guy's driving like an imbecile. I could put one of the ice cream sellers in the car and he would go faster.'

Mario's pride was stung, painfully. He spun round, 'I hear what you say. Don't push me, OK?' His normally easy-going temper snapped and his expression was as vitriolic as Colin's.

The mechanics pretended not to hear, busying themselves with removing the monocoque from the car. Peter, Mario's Canadian friend, joined him and together they left, leaving Colin clearly upset and staring blankly at a computer screen discharging its facts on to sheets of paper.

'You know what's behind all this? I wouldn't mind betting he's as jealous as hell about that Peter Morgan. It's getting him all twisted up,' remarked Max later to Dick Chance over a beer by the hotel swimming pool.

'Peter?' Dick sounded surprised. 'Why should he be jealous of him?'

'Because they're having an affair. It appears the whole paddock knows about it. They're even calling Mario, Maria.'

Dick looked incredulous. 'An affair?'

'C'mon, Dick, I know it might seem far fetched, but it's true. And it explains a helluva lot.'

'Yes?' asked Dick, still unable to digest that driver and team owner would be conducting anything more than a professional relationship. It seemed totally incongruous.

'Why Colin signed up Mario. OK, he might have believed he had talent and he's been proved right, but what else influenced his decision? He fancied his ass, that's my guess.'

Dick shook his head and was about to suggest that it was all a malicious rumour. But Max was right. There had been something about the two men that Dick had been unable to put his finger on all along.

Later that afternoon, Mario bumped into Max at the hotel and invited him to join himself and Peter Morgan for dinner. Max readily accepted and suggested a table at a restaurant along the coast renowned for its exquisite cuisine. Max was looking forward to the evening, not only because the restaurant had the reputation of being one of the best in southern France, but also because he now had something in common with Mario – the wrath of their boss.

The owner of the restaurant greeted Max and his two companions with effusive bonhomie. The other diners glanced discreetly in their direction as the distinguished clients sat down at a table by the window.

The restaurant was a beautiful nineteenth-century house overlooking the water and decorated in lavish style. Heavy brocade drapes hung at the vast windows, which afforded a panoramic view of the coastline. Pristine white linen napkins and tablecloths and gleaming silverware decorated the tables, along with sprays of fresh orchids. A grand piano played quietly in the background.

As they finished a first course of the finest *foie gras*, the topic of conversation inevitably drifted away from the lavish praise of the food to motor racing and the Championship prospects. Jean Claude of Renault was already in an impressive lead with thirty-one points. He had won in Detroit, as well as Belgium, and with three seconds and a third he was well placed ahead of Terri Dacco of Ferrari. Before his accident Terri had started the season impressively with victories in Rio, Long Beach and Italy. But since the accident in Belgium he had been out of action for the last three races. Now restored to health for the French race, he desperately needed to make up for lost time and points. It was Mario who, at present, was closest to Jean Claude in the points for the Championship. Despite missing the race in Italy he still had managed to gain eighteen points with consistent finishing in the first six places.

'It could be anybody's year,' commented Max, but my own, he thought to himself.

'We still have ten races left,' Mario agreed.

'If you keep up this consistent driving, who knows, you could win the Championship this year?' said Max amiably.

Mario smiled at the thought. 'I bet you never thought you would be saying those words at the beginning of the season.'

'Too damn right,' replied Max and with a slow smile drained his glass of vintage Chateau Lafitte.

Max found Peter Morgan relaxed in their company. Unlike Mario, he took life very unseriously. For him motor racing was a pretty unsavoury business run by a bunch of money-hungry sharks. There was too much wielding of power and unscrupulous manipulation of people. He was even more cynical about it after having witnessed Colin's outburst to Mario that day, and when Max asked Mario if he had any plans for the following season, Peter waited with interest for Mario to reply.

Mario shrugged as he cast a glance at the dark orange sun disappearing behind a magenta-coloured sea. 'I don't know if I can say . . . Colin is great in many ways, but . . . '

'He's bloody difficult to work for and that's an understatement,' Max interrupted.

'For sure, he gets a little crazy sometimes,' Mario agreed quietly. Off the track he could handle Colin's outbursts, but his outright criticism of his driving in public was something else. Mario hadn't forgiven Colin for that and it would be a long time before he did. It had given him a smug satisfaction to see Colin's disappointment when he had declined to have dinner with him that evening.

'The decision is whether to stay . . . ' Mario was thinking aloud. 'I trust you, Max, and value your opinion. What would you do? Would you stay or leave?'

Max reflected for a moment. 'If you want to win the World Championship, assuming you don't do it this year, then I advise you to stay with the team for another year. If anyone will make you Champion, Colin will. He has the best to offer and, as you know, next year is going to be even better.'

'You know I want the Championship more than anything. I feel so positive about it,' Mario insisted.

'And so you should – you've come a long way this season. I don't doubt your ability for one moment.'

Max envied Mario just then. Mario was still climbing the ladder of success. He had that inherent hunger for it. He had yet to prove to the world that he could be the world's best driver. There was everything to work for. And that was just what Max had lost – the need to prove to himself he was the best.

The following day, Sunday, the sun blazed down on a capacity crowd at Paul Ricard. It made a bright spectacle as the tanned spectators sported multi-coloured sunhats and T-shirts. The heat sizzled off the race track soon to be echoing to the sounds of the cars lapping at average speeds of a hundred and twenty-five miles an hour. The high speeds combined with the length of race, a hundred and ninety miles, made it a taxing one on fuel. With the banning of refuelling during the races, it meant that the engines' fuel efficiency would be severely tested.

Max sat in his car waiting for the grid to clear. Ahead of him were five cars. He thought of Mario in eighth place. Mario would be sitting in the car, his mind totally concentrated on the race ahead. As the track cleared, the mechanics fired up Max's engine and his mind emptied of thoughts like birds scattering after gunshot. He revved up the engine and drove round on the parade lap before taking his sixth place.

Max got off to a flying start and overtook the car in front before he reached the first bend. The adrenalin was surging through his body as he flew down the Mistral straight at two hundred miles an hour. After twenty laps, Max couldn't resist a smile as he saw the blue and white helmet of Mario in his wing mirror. It was Monaco all over again, only this time Max was not going to let himself be harassed.

Mario hounded him like a bitch on heat. At every corner, on every straight, he waited to pounce, but Max would not give him the chance. The crowds were at fever pitch, willing the two men on in their own private battle.

Now there was only one car ahead of Max – Terri Dacco in the Ferrari.

Three laps to go. Max had his foot flat on the floor as he turned into the Mistral straight. Once again Mario pulled alongside him. Then Max felt his car lose power. It coasted gently to a halt. In a blind fury he flung off his straps and threw his gloves to the ground. He walked back to the pits in an ugly mood. By the time he got back, Mario was passing the chequered flag. He had finished second.

Ignoring the shouts of consolation from the crowd, Max made his way through to the busy Delta garage and made for Colin. Before he had time to protest Max grabbed him by the shirt collar. 'You know what's wrong with your fucking car this time?' he hissed.

Colin looked sheepish. 'Max, cool it . . . '

'Cool it? I'll tell you why I didn't finish that goddamn race. I ran out of fuel. That's what happened. I ran out of fucking juice. And how come Mario didn't? That's what I want to know.'

Colin put up his hand in a gesture of resignation. Max let go of him. Colin's eyes darted around the gathering crowd of goggle-eyed press men.

'*No!* Let everybody know what you're up to! You want Mario to be number one, don't you? The whole thing stinks.' Max threw down his helmet and stormed off to the motor home.

'That's torn it,' muttered Tom to one of the other mechanics.

Later, at a press conference, Max would not be drawn to comment further on the reason for his car running out of fuel.

Mario came over and shook his hand. 'It was a great pity,' he said sincerely. 'We were having a good race.'

'Too damn right,' Max laughed. There was no point in showing his anger to Mario.

The next day the newspapers gave good coverage to Max's outburst. Julian, who had stayed at home in London to watch the race, was in hysterics as he studied the photograph of an alarmed Colin staring at a glowering Max, who had virtually levered him off the ground by his shirt collar.

# 41

'You know, I shouldn't be doing this,' said Julian.

Julian and Kelly were sitting at the bar in Dominique's in Kensington drinking Kir Royal. It was a typical London wine bar – polished wood floors and tables, a scattering of palms and jungle plants and background music. A couple of men were giving Kelly appreciative looks. Dressed in a pale cream linen jacket and exquisitely cut brick-red trousers, she looked every inch the elegant model.

'We just bumped into each other and you're buying me a drink. What's wrong with that?' Kelly smiled to hide her nervousness.

She had persuaded Julian over the phone to tell her where he was meeting Max that evening. She was desperate to see him again. She knew that if she called his home there was every chance Vicky would answer the phone. If she did manage to talk to Max, he might not want to see her anyway. To bump into him 'accidentally' seemed the only way, even if it was a pretty transparent ruse. Julian was of the same opinion. 'Max won't fall for it, for one thing,' he said. He also hoped that Max was not going to be acrimonious towards her.

Kelly sipped her drink. 'I can never get hold of him these days. I don't think he's purposely avoiding me. It's just that he's never at his flat and I don't want to call him at home.'

Julian sighed. It was obvious that Kelly was blind to the fact that Max had finished with her. In spite of his rebuff at Monaco, she was still hanging on in some hope he would change his mind. But Julian knew Max's character of old. Once he had made up his mind there was no going back. Julian wondered if he should warn Kelly. Then he told himself firmly he wasn't going to get involved in their on-off relationship any more. If this was the way Kelly wanted to find out, then so be it.

'Well, well, what a surprise, Kelly! What brings you here?'

Kelly's heart missed a beat. She turned to see Max's familiar face. 'Hi,' she said, feigning surprise. 'I just bumped into . . . '

'Sure you did, Kelly,' said Max, unconcerned. He kissed her on the cheek. 'Now let's get a bottle of wine. I'm parched. Or would you prefer the same again?'

Julian shook his head. 'Let me get it. How about a Sancerre?'

'Fine. Let's find a seat.'

Max led Kelly over to a small table. 'Who organized the conspiracy . . . or was it a carefully planned accident?' asked Max, amused.

Kelly couldn't work out if he was pleased to see her or just carefully hiding his irritation. Whichever, he was acting very cool about it.

'Max, I wanted to see you . . . ' Kelly's normally sparkling green eyes had a dullness about them, Max noticed, but her complexion still gleamed and shone like the smooth gloss of her hair.

'Well, here I am,' he said, but Kelly could detect a chill beneath his smile.

Julian placed the bottle of wine and three glasses on the table.

'Will you excuse me for a minute? I've a couple of calls to make from the car.'

'Don't be long, I've got some news for you,' said Max, pouring two glasses of wine. Kelly was silent as Max handed her a glass. A Whitney Houston ballad, 'You're Still My Man', filled the room. It was the same haunting song that had been playing the last time they had made love in the flat. The words echoed Kelly's mood.

Max raised his glass and smiled. It was a controlled smile, one he reserved for the press photographs. Kelly swallowed hard, trying to suppress the tears welling up inside. Why had she come here? Then, with the lyrics of the Whitney Houston song echoing in her ears, words began to tumble out of her mouth. 'Look, I know I'm making a complete fool of myself and I know I shouldn't have come, but . . . Max, I need to talk to you. I can't let our relationship just hang in the air. I want you to tell me if . . . '

'Kelly, you must have realized in Monaco that it was over between us.' The words, the realization, struck Kelly with a force that left her breathless. She had clung on to the hope it might be different. She knew that this time Max meant what he said. There would be no going back. Like the first raindrops on a spring morning, tears spilt over Kelly's eyelashes.

Max took her hand and held it tightly. 'I never promised you anything, Kelly,' he said quietly, 'and I don't want to hurt you. I'm sorry . . . I really am. But where would it end between us? I'm married . . . '

'That's debatable . . . ' Kelly bit her lip. She remembered the times in her flat when he would stay with her, the warm touches, the phone calls at midnight, the happy evenings and wild dinners with Julian.

Julian. Where was Julian? She needed his warm smile, his comforting arm to dispel the blackness . . .

'Kelly, we've had great times together, but so many things in my life have changed. I never did learn how to stay faithful to one woman. You knew that.'

'And it's time you moved on, is that it? Time to get some other woman to fall in love with you. It's easier that way, isn't it, Max? Always cutting off, just before you get involved.'

'I can't help the way I am. That's how it is.'

Kelly took a deep breath. 'It's a lie . . . you're lying to yourself and one day you will find that out.' Her voice grew louder. 'One day you'll stop running away from whatever it is that stops you loving a woman.'

Max poured himself another glass of wine and glanced around the room. Kelly was attracting stares from the group of men at the bar. There were a few hushed whispers and Max could see they had recognized him. The men turned their backs as if to feign disinterest.

Max turned back to Kelly. 'I don't think this is a good place to discuss our problems. How about we go and have dinner with Julian, just for old times' sake?'

'For old times' sake? Max, how could you say that? You think I can walk out of this relationship as if it never happened?' Kelly knew the alcohol was taking charge of her emotions now. The calmness was dissipating, the heartbreak giving way to anger.

How could Max sit there so calmly when she was hurting so deeply inside? She wanted to scream and shout at him. Her love was dissolving into hate. How could she have loved this man who treated women so badly? How had she had the tenacity to put up with him for all this time? The words were unspoken, but her silence conveyed her bitterness. She stood up abruptly. She must leave before she made more of a fool of herself. Resolutely she made a decision. She didn't need Max

Gregson any more. From this moment he was out of her life.

'Goodbye Max,' she whispered through her tears.

Kelly ran out into the street, relieved to be in the fresh air again, and almost fell into Julian's arms.

'Hi, I was just coming in.' Then Julian noticed Kelly's tear-stained face.

She wrapped her arms around him and sobbed uncontrollably.

'Where are we going?' she sniffed later as Julian's Range Rover pulled up at some traffic lights.

'My place,' said Julian angrily. 'And we're going to get horribly drunk.'

It was gone midnight and the encounter with Max now seemed like a bad dream. Kelly lay outstretched on the large feather-filled sofa, her jacket and shoes strewn on the floor.

Two bottles of wine stood empty on the glass coffee table. Kelly sighed as she thought of Julian preparing coffee and cheese on toast in his small bachelor kitchen. Tall, gallant Julian. Warmth and kindness exuded from him. He had rescued her from a disastrous evening and here in his flat she felt safe and protected.

'Fancy a brandy with your coffee?' Julian called to her.

'Why not? You know, Julian, you are the most adorable friend I have. The lady who captures your heart will be very lucky indeed.' Kelly threw her head back and sighed.

When Julian came back into the room, she had an irrepressible smile on her face. By now she was quite drunk. Julian lowered the carefully stacked tray on to the table.

The empty coffee cups on top of one another tottered and fell on to the sizzling toasted cheese. Hastily, Julian moved them and, catching the milk jug with his shirt sleeve, sent the jug and its contents flying on to the other plate.

'Ruined! One carefully prepared supper,' he wailed.

They giggled, slowly at first like two children, then almost hysterically as they retrieved the remains of their supper, feeding each other with the soggy toast, Kelly scooping up the melting strands of cheese from Julian's chin.

Then Julian stopped eating and held her hand tightly. His eyes were fixed on hers. 'Kelly,' he said seriously. 'I want you to forget Max.' Then lowering his voice, 'Will you let me help you?'

Kelly was aware as much as he of the poignancy of the moment. Her heart thumped wildly. Whilst she was with Max she had thought of Julian as a good companion and trustworthy friend. But now Max wasn't there any more. A strong and indelible bond had grown between them and they both knew it. 'How?' asked Kelly helplessly.

Julian stood up and wandered over to the large balcony windows. The curtains remained undrawn and he stared into the quiet street below. 'Come to France with me next week. I have to go and visit this dotty old aunt of mine.'

Kelly remembered he had told her about his aunt living in the family chateau overlooking the Dordogne. She had seen a photograph of it; a magnificent three-storey building with gables and corner turrets in a woodland setting.

He turned to face her. 'Well?' he asked apprehensively.

She hesitated. 'Julian, do you think it wise?' Do you think we might get involved? was what she really wanted to say. This was no casual spur of the moment invitation. Kelly had understood that much. Her mind was racing in a turmoil of confusion.

Julian came and sat close to her. His eyes bored into hers with an intensity she had never seen before. 'You have to forget Max.' He paused. The alcohol released his thoughts from their long imprisonment. He had to tell her. 'I care a lot for you. You must know that.'

Kelly was silent.

He continued in a whisper. 'You want me to spell it out for you? I happen to be in love with you.' The words fell on Kelly like blossom falling on to the warm summer earth. The stillness was tangible. 'You never were very good at seeing what is right for you.'

'Julian, I . . . don't know what to say,' Kelly stammered.

Julian held her hand and kissed it gently.

'We've got plenty of time,' he whispered, as he watched the colour return to Kelly's pale cheeks.

# 42

Rachel hummed tunefully as she drove along the country lanes that led to Vicky's house. She smiled as she recalled the turn of events in the last fortnight. A casual lunch with Phil had turned into a blossoming relationship and since then they had seen each other as often as possible. His relaxed approach to life made her feel at ease with him. He wasn't in the millionaire bracket along with the rest of her friends, but so what? He had an enviable attitude to life. He took it as it came with no thought for tomorrow. Mortgages, career moves, stress were not a part of his thought processes. His life revolved around horses and the outdoor life. He appeared to have no problems and was more than ready to listen to Rachel's.

She pulled up outside the farmhouse and slammed the car door behind her. Seeing the front door ajar, she went on in, through the spacious hallway and into the large farmhouse kitchen from which an appetizing smell of pasta was coming. 'Vicky?' she called, sniffing hungrily.

'Aunty Rachel?' said a small voice behind her. Rachel swivelled and bent down to kiss Sophie, whose elfin face was now framed with short blonde hair. Rachel gave her the parcel of books she had brought as a present.

'Rachel, just in time.' Vicky appeared at the back door, fresh faced, holding a lettuce from the garden. She noticed Rachel's glowing complexion through the lightest of make-up. 'What have you been up to? You look positively blooming . . . found a new man?'

'Vicky . . . my life doesn't always have to revolve around a man,' she protested lightly.

'No, but it certainly shows when there is one.' Vicky laughed gaily as she held the lettuce under a gushing tap. 'Would you like a sherry? You can pour one for me if you like.'

Over lunch they discussed Sophie's return to school for the last two weeks of term. After dessert Sophie disappeared to have a rest, eager to study her new books in private.

'Well,' said Vicky. 'It's marvellous to see you looking so much better than the last time I saw you. Are you managing all right?'

Rachel bit her lower lip. She still hadn't decided whether to tell Vicky about Phil. She leaned back in her chair and sipped her coffee slowly. 'I'm absolutely fine. I feel I've shed an old skin now that Colin has finally been open with me. He won't contest the divorce. Let's face it, he couldn't really. It's so strange to realize after all these years that we were just good friends all along. The sexual side of our marriage was always forced, it never happened naturally. I only hope that now we can remain good friends.'

'I hope so, too. It's always best for the children in the long run. I'm really glad you're getting over it.' Vicky smiled compassionately and they exchanged understanding looks.

'The worst thing is how to tell the children. I've been putting it off until they finish school. I went over to see them last weekend, but they were so excited to see me that I couldn't bring myself to break the news. Colin has agreed we should do it together when they are back at home. Then they have the holidays to help take their minds off it . . . ' She lowered her voice. 'How is Sophie? She seems much better . . . '

'She's going in for a final check up next week. She's improving day by day and by the time she goes back to school her hair will be a reasonable length. She was so self-conscious at first.'

'Until she saw mine, I bet,' Rachel laughed.

'It suits you the way it is . . . it's very becoming.'

'Phil likes . . . ' Rachel stopped, realizing she had let his name slip.

'Phil Adams? You've seen him recently?' asked Vicky cautiously.

What the hell, thought Rachel. After all, Vicky is an old friend and there's nothing to hide. 'Yes, several times in fact.'

'I thought you two would get it together somehow,' said Vicky, but it was obvious that she did not share Rachel's elation.

'What is it, Vicky? Don't you like him?'

Vicky fiddled with the napkin she had been folding. 'Let's say I think he spells trouble.'

'How do you mean?'

'He's unreliable. He idles his time away with horses with no real end in sight.'

Rachel stifled a nervous giggle. 'I do believe you're jealous, Vicky.'

'Rubbish. Of course I'm not,' said Vicky crossly.

She stood up quickly and started to clear the table. An uneasy silence followed.

Rachel had been so happy about her new relationship. Now her bubble had been burst. 'I've only seen him a couple of times for a drink. It's no big deal,' she said.

Vicky turned to her. 'You've been through a bad time with Colin. Now give yourself a break . . . find someone who is good for you . . . not some crazy stable boy.'

Crazy stable boy! Rachel was amazed at Vicky's open dislike of him. Then she remembered Vicky's fluster when Phil had turned up uninvited at her house. She had sensed a friction between them. Now Vicky was over-reacting to her news. It served only to confirm her earlier suspicions. Something had been going on between them both and she was determined to find out about it.

Later that evening Max arrived home feeling tetchy. This was not helped by Vicky's apparently sullen mood. Rankled at having to pour his own drink, he disappeared into the drawing room and browsed through the newspaper. Later on, over dinner, there were heavy silences. Then Max dropped his bombshell.

'I don't think I heard you right.' Vicky put down her knife and fork and stared disbelievingly at him.

'I said I'm going to retire at the end of the season.'

'Just like that?'

Max nodded. 'Aren't you pleased? I would have thought this is the news you've been waiting for.'

'But this is the first time you've mentioned it. It would have been nice if we had talked about it first.'

'OK. Let's start again. I'm thinking of retiring at the end of the year. How do you feel about it?'

'I'm shocked,' Vicky said fiercely. 'Racing is your life, Max. It always has been. Why the sudden change of heart?'

'I've had enough, that's all. I should have retired on a high at the end of last season, not now when things are going badly for me. However, that's the way it is.'

Vicky fought back her exasperation. 'Max, I'm your wife, in case you've forgotten. You decide to change your career overnight without even discussing it with me. We used to communicate.'

'Communicate?' Max stood up, throwing down his napkin. 'Do you know exactly how difficult a proposition that is with you? Do you ever ask, do you ever bother to find out what's going on inside here?' He tapped his forehead. 'No, because you're so caught up with your damn horses and country life you know nothing of what is happening in the motor-racing world. I doubt if you even bother to read the papers any more.'

Vicky exploded. 'The last time I read anything of you, it was about you and some young thing in the South of France. Yes, I am wrapped up with my damn horses and country life, as you call it, because I'm afraid of what is going on out there in that world of yours. I know about your women, your one-night stands. Do you think I can cope with all that without shutting myself off?'

'You seemed to cope when the groom was around,' said Max caustically.

Vicky glared at him. 'And while we're on the subject of the groom, I never realized you were such a bastard – putting a snake in the man's cottage was a pretty vile thing to do.'

Max was taken aback. How had Vicky heard about that? 'So you're still seeing him?' he said accusingly.

'No, I'm not and I never want to see him again either.' Vicky was ready to burst into tears. She couldn't handle these arguments and recriminations. She wanted to forget the past. 'Max, we can't go on like this,' she pleaded. 'We're drifting apart. For God's sake, can't you see that? Either we get back to how we used to be or let's just forget the whole thing.'

'You mean divorce, separate? Is that what you really want?' Max yelled.

Vicky had never seen him so angry.

Just then the door opened to reveal a white-faced Sophie standing like a frightened ghost in her long nightdress. 'Mummy, Daddy, why are you fighting?' she asked in a small voice.

Max and Vicky exchanged guilty looks.

'Darling, I'm so sorry.' Vicky scooped her up in her arms and Sophie nestled her head into Vicky's hair sleepily.

It tore Max apart to see the two of them together so vulnerable and defenceless. He imagined Sophie growing up without him, another statistic, another child from a broken home, just as he had been. He would never wish that upon his beloved daughter. Furthermore, Vicky was right. Their marriage was drifting apart. He had betrayed her more times than he cared to remember through his waywardness and selfishness. He didn't blame her for her affair. He had pushed her into it. He had taken his family far too much for granted in the last year. Sophie's close brush with death had given him a sharp awakening. He could cope with his career turnaround, but not losing his family. The price was too high. He went to Sophie and Vicky and opened his arms to them both. 'No more fighting, Sophie, I promise you,' he said gently.

After Vicky had put Sophie to bed, Max found her in their bedroom. She had been crying. 'Vicky. We must talk.' Max held her as he sat next to her on the bed.

Vicky nodded and stifled a sob. 'Max, I don't want anything to happen to us, but I'm not prepared to let our marriage drift on with your affairs and . . . '

'I realize that now. Too many things have pulled us in different directions. I remember sitting in the hospital, waiting for news of Sophie . . . I considered how much I had to lose . . . the both of you. Don't even think of divorce or separation. There's too much at stake.'

'But, Max, when are you going to learn a marriage is not about playing around, drifting from one affair to the next? It's built on trust and caring. If I could take back everything that happened this year, I would, even . . . my affair,' she said quietly. 'But what's happened can't be reversed. And when I stepped out of line I knew it was wrong, but it brought home to me how desperately lonely I was to do such a thing. Promise me, Max, you mean it this time. There will be no more playing around.'

'On my heart, I promise you.' Max sighed and held Vicky tightly. Despite his despair, he felt closer to Vicky than he had in a very long time. 'I love you, Vicky. Never forget that.'

# 43

*'Go for it, Gregson!'* shouted a small group of fans in the stands opposite the pits. The crowds were ebullient, expectant and waving their banners wildly. For them, the noise of the cars held the same adrenalin charge as a rock concert. The first roar of 700hp engines gave them the same tingle of excitement as the first chords of a song from their favourite pop group.

Silverstone, on that warm July Saturday, was an orderly encampment of cars, caravans and tents set in the flat, verdant Northamptonshire countryside. The quiet hamlets around had braced themselves for this three-day invasion of people, traffic and helicopter noise. This was the mecca for British race fans and they had come to cheer on their hero, Max Gregson.

Max ground his teeth. There were ten minutes remaining of the final practice session. Two thousandths of a second separated the first two cars, then a full tenth of a second between third and fourth car. A second behind them, in fifth position, was Max.

His eyes scanned the TV monitor positioned in the front of him on the monocoque of the car. The times of the other drivers were flashing up on the screen.

'Shit,' Max swore to himself. 'The car is about as responsive as a tractor and there's still too much understeer on the corners.' Each time Max braked at a corner, the car felt heavy and out of balance. The mechanics still hadn't managed to sort out the problem. Max was not happy. It was a foregone conclusion that he was going to disappoint the home crowd.

Colin was behaving so irascibly that Max had taken to answering him in monosyllables or through one of the engineers. Max wondered if Colin was going to fire him at the end of the season. Well, he would save him the trouble. He had decided to announce his retirement at the next race, in Germany.

Max winced as he saw Mario's name above his own on the screen. He looked up to see Mario cruising back into the pits, having just completed a brilliant lap which would no doubt assure him of third place on the grid. He was unconvinced that he could make up that one-second gap. But he'd give it all he'd got.

The pressure on him now was as great as it ever was at the start of the race. If he didn't make good his position or pull up some places he would have to start in the middle of the pack and that would make for a difficult race.

Max signalled to the mechanics by raising his right hand. As if by magic, the TV monitor disappeared, tyre covers were whisked off and the air pressure starter fired the engine into life. There were only a few cars left on the track now and a few precious remaining minutes. He might just have a chance to make a fast lap . . .

He drove like a demon, but missed a gear out of Stowe corner. Coming into Brooklands, he was forced to brake by one of the slower cars. As he swung into the pits, his tyres flatspotted by the sudden braking, he was forced to accept the fact that he would now be in eighth position on the grid tomorrow. It had been a miserable session.

'How'd it go, Max?' asked Reg Watkins. The journalist's concern for his friend deepened more every day.

'I blew it.' Max placed his helmet on the car and combed his hands through his hair.

'Car no good?'

'Same as yesterday, still too much understeer on the corners.'

Max's body language showed all the signs of a man weighed down by weariness. As he talked about the set-up of the car, shoulders hunched and arms folded, Reg was aware how much Max seemed to have aged. The heavy lines around the mouth and eyes and greying temples were more obvious now and the dull timbre of his voice hinted at a man who was facing defeat and knew it. Reg had seen it happen to many drivers before. He remembered the words of Juan Fangio, the great Argentinian driver. He had once said that racing is beautiful when you are full of enthusiasm, but when it becomes work you should quit. Reg wondered about Max. Boredom and frustration were not easy partners in a job like this. They could lead you to the grave.

From the helicopter, Max watched the unbroken snake of traffic at a standstill around the circuit. Every road in the area was jammed and had been so since seven in the morning. Silverstone had a fairground appearance as the flags fluttered in the breeze and the clean white marquees gleamed in the sunshine. From above, the cars and caravans, arranged in neat rows, appeared like sheets of coruscating metal as the sun reflected off their roofs. Faraway into the clear distance stretched fields dappled by the shadows of small cumulus clouds.

Vicky sat next to Max, taking in the view below her. Max studied the track as the helicopter made its descent. The track turned and twisted like a giant metal exhaust pipe. Max was back in the driving seat on the race track, driving past the start line, into Copse corner, then Maggotts, Becketts, Chapel, down the long Hanger straight (flat out at a hundred and eighty-five miles an hour) into the right hander at Stowe, then diving downhill into Vale. A sharp left into Club corner, through to Abbey, flat out again, then a fast sharp right hander into Bridge corner and back past the pits. It was a circuit he loved. He had fond memories of last year when he had won the race. The crowds had spilled out on to the track and taken it over in a Mardi Gras atmosphere. It had been an unforgettable day . . .

'Look at those hot air balloons down there. Aren't they a most beautiful colour? Sophie would have loved to have seen them.' Vicky brought Max back to the present. He thought of Sophie and the disappointment on her face when they had decided she should stay at home. It would have been a long tiring day for her. Instead she had agreed to watch the action on the television.

Vicky caught hold of Max's hand. He seemed lost in his thoughts. 'Max? Are you OK?'

'Sure I am. It's nice to have you along,' he said, smiling. As he said it, he was surprised to find that he meant it. It was only the second time this season Vicky had joined him and, for some unknown reason, he was glad to have her by his side.

Vicky felt reassured. Life at home had been strained after the evening of their argument. Max had been quiet and withdrawn. She had promised herself she would try to participate more in his racing life. Like all his friends, she was aware that something deep and disturbing was going on inside him. She was desperately worried that his state of distraction would carry over into his driving. It was with trepidation and foreboding that she arrived at the circuit. She tried to push the thoughts from her, but they lingered like hoar frost on a freezing morning.

Despite the warmth of the sunshine, Vicky shivered as she entered the paddock and watched the near delirium of activity. It made her wish she hadn't come. Even the gargantuan transporters had a sinister air, lined up menacingly behind the pits. Her fears were not allayed when she entered the motor home and received a perfunctory greeting from Colin.

At least Dick hadn't changed. 'Vicky. Nice to see you again,' he said, hugging her warmly.

Vicky sat down on the sofa, feeling lost amidst all the comings and goings, strange faces at the doors, looking around and disappearing again. Dick introduced her to some of the journalists and personnel who called by. She noticed the fleeting look of casual interest on their faces, their minds preoccupied with other things. It struck her there was an indisputable difference between now and her last visit to Long Beach. Being wife of Max Gregson no longer gave her automatic status.

After lunch, Vicky stood by the pit wall watching the cars assemble on the grid. Prince Michael of Kent walked leisurely between the cars talking to the drivers. Vicky was totally removed from all the razzmatazz. It turned her stomach to see the cheering crowds. Were they there hoping to witness some major accident? Would it make their day if they could go home and say they had seen some driver crash? Didn't they realize those drivers were out there putting their lives on the line, that if a mechanic hadn't tightened a screw properly, one of them could end up a messy corpse? Suddenly the odds seemed too high.

She whispered good luck to Max before he climbed in the car. He said nothing as he put on his helmet. Instead, he squeezed her hand tightly.

Mario was in bright spirits and the centre of press attention. He had completed the fastest lap in the warm-up.

Many, including Colin, were pretty sure he could win the race.

At two o'clock exactly, the red light turned to green and the twenty-six cars flew past to begin the fifty-nine laps of the race. Vicky tried hard to swallow her fear. She had never believed in premonitions, but today she knew something was going to happen. She had been too far removed from Max's life. The old protective love for him surged back to her. She had always wanted him to win. But in today's race, just to come back safely was enough. She watched, rigid, as his car jockeyed for position at the end of the straight. The sparks flew from behind his car. He was pushing himself and the car to the limit.

The commentator's voice gabbled away in a high-pitched crescendo as the race gained momentum. Then Vicky heard Max's name mentioned.

'Max Gregson overtook the young Italian driver, Bertorelli, on the last lap, but he's struggling for pace now. He's having a dreadful year – a complete switch from his successful championship year – and now the young Bertorelli in the Minardi is trying to overtake. It looks like a tussle down at Copse. Is Max going to give him room on the corner?' The question was never answered. As Max went into Copse corner, the car flew off, hitting the barrier in an explosion of dust and orbiting wing parts. Vicky could see everything from where she was. The wall of tyres took the impact of the car. A wheel flew off and the crowd in the grandstand gasped and then fell silent. It seemed an age before the marshals reached the scene. Vicky's heart stopped. She felt a comforting arm wrap around her shaking body.

It was Dick. 'They'll get him out in no time, don't worry.'

Vicky strained to see a sign of movement from the car.

'Thank God,' she cried, as she saw Max emerge from the wreckage. Assisted by two of the marshals, he was limping heavily.

The faces in the Delta pit showed quiet concern for Vicky. It was only Colin who showed no reaction. He was staring impassively at the Longines timing device on the pit wall. His concern was for his number two driver who was battling it out for second position.

'How is he?' asked Vicky, her eyes anxious with worry.

Dick held her hand tightly. 'He's OK. He's with Professor Watkins now, being treated for burns and bruising to his thigh.'

'Burns?'

'Yes, unfortunately the water pipe burst on impact and spilled hot water over him.'

They were sitting quietly in the motor home. The roar of the cars, although deafeningly close, belonged to another world. Vicky stared at the few remaining copies of Max's biography. They were all that were left after a signing session that morning. 'I know this sounds crazy, Dick, but I knew something was going to happen today. I just knew it. I thank God it wasn't anything worse. Something's happened to Max . . . I don't have to tell you that . . . '

Dick took a deep breath, his face clouded in a heavy frown. 'He's had a run of bad luck. It happens to all the drivers at some stage or other. They go with the good times, then when the world turns sour for them, they have to hang on until it comes right again. Max just didn't hang in there long enough and in the meantime he lost his confidence and the will to win . . . '

'Did you know we were having problems at home?'

'What sort of problems?'

Vicky looked embarrassed. 'We grew apart. We both went our own ways for a while. I. . . '

'Don't tell me if you don't want to.'

Vicky shook her head. 'No, I want to. I feel as if I've been living with a stranger for the past two years. Oh, I know he plays around, but I shut my mind off from it. The trouble is I shut myself off from Max as well. I lost touch with him. I'm just beginning to realize how much. I'm very afraid for him, Dick. I fear he will kill himself. God knows, he drinks far too much.'

'Yes, it hasn't gone unnoticed. But he's a survivor of the toughest sort. He may have lost himself for a while, but he'll come through it all . . . you'll see. Come on, Vicky. It's all over now. OK, he's taken a bit of a bashing, but I bet you a pound to a dollar, he'll be up and driving tomorrow. But it would do him some good if he listened to you about the drinking. Will you talk to him about that?' Vicky nodded. 'Good. Now shall we go and see him? I'm sure he'll want some tea and sympathy.'

Max winced as he sat down in a large cane chair in the garden. The scalding water from the burst pipe had taken several layers of skin off his thigh, leaving an angry red burn the size of a teaplate.

Sophie kissed her father's tired face and sat down next to him. She loved him being at home and to have the opportunity to fuss over him. 'Why do you have such a dangerous job, Daddy? My friend Natalie told me you could have been killed in the accident and that it was a stupid sort of job you have. Is that true? Could you have been killed?' Sophie's eyes, wide and innocent, held a gravity Max had never seen before.

'No, darling. Sometimes my job is dangerous. But soon I'm going to give it up and have a job like Natalie's father. So no more worries, please, my little Sophie?'

'I don't mind you doing your job, Daddy. It's far more exciting than being a stockbroker. It's just that I don't want you to get killed.'

Max kissed Sophie tenderly. 'No fear of that, I promise you.'

In the last few days, Max had taken time to re-examine his life. Alcohol, he reasoned, offered no solution to his problems. It was a short cut to death. Then there was his womanizing. Oddly enough he found he didn't have the energy for an affair. His sex drive seemed to have buried itself. Kelly came into his thoughts less and less now. They had enjoyed good times together but after her miscarriage their relationship had changed and Max had admitted to himself that his own selfishness had come between them. All he could think about was getting right for the next race. He still had something to prove before he retired. There were still eight races to go. They had reached only the half way point in the season. There was still time to get some good results, he told himself. Otherwise, he would retire into a humiliating oblivion.

He glanced up to see voluminous clouds billowing forth across a perfect blue sky. A delicate perfume of flowers pervaded the air – roses, sweet peas, delphiniums, lavender – all vying with one another in a mosaic of colour. It was the first time he had sat in the garden this summer. He wondered why he hadn't made time to do it before.

'Can I get you a drink?' Vicky was standing behind him. She slipped her hand into his. 'Don't get too hot out here. It won't do your leg any good.'

'Stop fussing, Vicky. I'm in the shade. I'd love a beer.'

'There is a phone call for you, Mr Gregson,' called the Swedish au pair from the kitchen window.

'Who is it?'

'A man from *Road Sport* magazine.'

'Tell him I'm getting drunk under an apple tree,' replied Max.

'Don't tell them anything of the sort,' said Vicky sharply. 'The next thing is it will be in print. Tell him he's with the doctor.'

'Right-tee-ho,' came the reply.

'Max, you really must be more careful what you say to the press. They're dying to . . . '

'To what? Blacken my name even further? I'm surprised they even bother to print anything about an old has-been like me.'

That evening after dinner they sat outside admiring a full moon that shone so brightly, the fields beyond were bathed in an eerie light. A nightjar could be heard churring in the oak trees.

'Are you still sure about retiring?' asked Vicky quietly.

'Do you want me to?'

'I would like you to get out of the game in one piece. Before it's too late. The accident made me realize how truly afraid I am for you. I hadn't faced up to it before.'

Max sat silently watching the moonlight play on the shivering leaves of a poplar tree.

Vicky went on. 'There's something else I hadn't realized either.'

'What is that?'

'How much I still love you.'

Max pulled her close and kissed her cheek. She sat on the arm of his chair stroking his hair. 'It hasn't been an easy year for us, has it?' Max reflected. 'I'm mostly to blame, I know that. But it's brought home a few things to me too; that you and Sophie are very, very precious to me for one.' Vicky squeezed his arm, waiting for him to go on. 'I've felt very vulnerable. That fate was out to get me. Well, it nearly did. This may sound foolhardy, but I think I've come through that. Maybe I can get lucky again.' They sat in silence for a while.

'And what about us, Max?'

'I feel lucky about us, too.' He turned and drew Vicky's face close to his own. 'I've had some growing up to do, I admit that, but I'm through with playing around.'

'You really mean it this time?'

'I do, Vicky.' Max knew now that all the chasing of women to satisfy his sex drive had been a challenge, a rather empty one, he reflected. Ironically, he thought of Kelly's words. What was it she had said? He was running away from the something that stopped him loving a woman? Well, he had stopped running. Max was more committed to Vicky now than ever.

Vicky was left wondering about Max. She had never known him so open and frank about his feelings, or so serious either. She held dearly to the belief that this time he had changed. Her intuition told her that this time she could be right. The only nagging doubt in her mind was how convinced Max was about his retirement.

# 44

The small Learjet taxied on to the runway in the last of the evening light. 'We're cleared for take-off, Mr Pritchard.'

Colin fastened his seatbelt, as did Max and Mario. As the aircraft gathered speed, the runway lights chased past the window.

Colin had seen little of Rachel since the night of their confrontation. It had been the worst night of Colin's life. The part of him that he had kept hidden all those years had finally been dragged out into the open. And yet he realized he could not have lived a lie with Rachel for much longer. She was too good for that.

Then there was Mario. He was a son, lover, friend and confidant. He was everything to Colin. Colin studied him as he sat reading a newspaper alongside Max, wondering how to come to terms with his passion for the boy. And his possessiveness that so often spilled over into jealousy. Mario got up from his seat and joined Colin. The steward brought them coffee.

'We shall be landing at Frankfurt in one hour, Mr Pritchard,' the young man said, placing the cups on the small table in front of them.

Mario sat back contentedly, his tanned arms contrasting with his white short-sleeved shirt. Colin noticed the delicate gold chain and Ebel watch. Both had been gifts from him after winning Monaco. 'You're looking pretty pleased with yourself, Mario. Any particular reason?' Colin asked.

'No, not really,' replied Mario with a warm smile. 'It feels good to be going away to another race, that's all.'

Colin wondered where he had been the night before. He had wanted to see him, but Mario had declined, saying he had made other arrangements. Colin wondered if they had included Peter Morgan. 'If you finish ahead of Terri Dacco you will be level on points and only five behind Jean Claude. You could become a real challenger for the Championship.'

'I know, and I have a good feeling about Hockenheim. I always like the German Grand Prix. The track is fast and if the weather holds . . . '

'The forecast is for rain tomorrow and Thursday, clearing up by the weekend. Let's hope it does.'

The Hockenheim track always presented difficulties for the race engineers. The long straights, the chicanes and fast curves made it notoriously hard on engines and fuel. It was a long, dangerous circuit through gloomy pine forests. It had claimed the lives of Jim Clark in 1968 and Patrick Depailler in 1980 and it was where Didier Pironi had suffered a horrific accident when his Ferrari had mounted Alain Prost's Renault in blinding rain. But Mario was filled with a boyish expectancy that Colin could so easily identify with.

'Has your Argentinian TV company confirmed they're coming over to film the documentary on you?' asked Colin.

'For sure.' Mario felt it a great honour that he should be the subject of a TV film. He would be even more of a celebrity in his home country.

'We mustn't let them interfere too much. If they want any long interviews, arrange them for the evenings. We don't want them getting under our feet during practice and debrief.'

Max, who had been browsing through a helicopter manual, looked up. He had just a few more lessons before he qualified for his licence. 'Is your mate Pete Morgan coming over for the race?' he asked Mario.

'I believe so. Why do you ask?'

'It's just that he has some contacts for some consultancy work I have in mind to do.'

Colin fell silent. His affable mood disappeared. He went back to reading his newspaper and stayed silent for the rest of the flight.

Somewhere between his arrival in Germany and checking into the luxury hotel several miles away from the track at Hockenheim, Mario had lost his exuberance. After a restless night he went down to breakfast feeling jaded and out of sorts. Oompah music, incongruous and too loud for such an early hour, played in the coffee shop. Mario picked at a plate of fruit, anaemic slices of cheese and pumpernickel.

'Mind if I join you?' asked Dick cheerfully.

'Please,' said Mario, pointing to a chair.

The waitress briskly refilled Mario's coffee cup and was about to pour the same for Dick. 'I'll have tea, please.' The waitress gave him a sullen look and walked off.

'How did you sleep?' Dick enquired, aware that Mario seemed downcast and distracted.

'The rooms are far too hot. I dislike the air conditioning and I sleep badly if I can't open a window. So I went for a run at six this morning. I feel a little better.'

The waitress returned with a cup of hot water and a floating tea bag. Dick regarded it dismally. 'It's times like this I wish I was back home,' he remarked.

A loud guffaw broke the sound of the music, the unmistakable laugh of Reg Watkins. Dick smiled across to the table of journalists. He also noticed Scapini at another table.

Mario glanced at his watch. 'Is it OK with you if we leave for the track at nine?'

'Sure, I won't be long getting to grips with this breakfast.' Dick got up and made his way over to the large buffet table in the centre of the room, stopping to chat to the journalists on the way.

Mario, anxious to get back to his room, swallowed his coffee hurrriedly. He felt a hand touch the back of his chair. He turned to see the weasel-like face of Scapini. There was a suggestion of a smile on his lips. His manner was impeccably polite. 'Mario, it's good to see you. I have a favour to ask of you. Would you call by the motor home some time after practice this morning? I think we might have something to discuss.' Scapini's eyes darted across to Dick at the buffet table. 'And, of course, use your discretion. We don't want any of your team to know of the visit. Not yet.'

Mario gave him an imperceptible nod. Scapini's presence made him feel uncomfortable. A few months ago he would never have envisaged talking to him, let alone discussing business with him. But events in his life had altered that.

He went up to his room and glanced at the letter he had written to his mother at five o'clock that morning. He was a bad correspondent at the best of times. He much preferred to pick up the phone and hear the warm tones of her voice. His letter, written in a large untidy scrawl, told of his success and new-found contentment at living in England. He still missed home desperately, he confided in her, but had made new friends. He was thinking of Peter, with whom he was beginning to build a close and trusting relationship.

'It won't be long before I am home,' he concluded. 'The constant travelling and racing takes its toll. Sometimes I feel I could opt out and come home for a quieter life. Then the racing gets a hold of me again. It gives me a high I could never experience from anything else. It is hard to imagine the perfect sense of aloneness I feel when I am driving. Do you remember when I was very small we used to take long walks into the mountains (they seemed so long then, but I'm sure they weren't)? I used to be in awe of their size and grandeur and yet I was at one with them. That is how I am when I am in my race car.

'I know you don't approve of my chosen career, but I won't let you down. I always knew that one day I would succeed and now my dream is coming true. I am almost there. You will be so proud of me when I win the World Championship, as I know I will . . . '

Mario slid the sheets of paper into his briefcase and taking it with him, closed the door on his room.

Dick drove along the crowded autobahns that led to the race track. The surrounding countryside was a sea of dense pine forest. On such a dull day it appeared gloomy and forbidding. Earlier, storm clouds had appeared from nowhere and a cloudburst had threatened to blot out a perfect summer's morning.

But Mario was optimistic about his prospects. Despite his poor night's sleep, the adrenalin was beginning to flow. I shall fly like an angel, he thought. For the first time in his career he felt confident he could make it to pole position.

As Dick and Mario reached the circuit, raindrops fell ominously on the windscreen. They dashed for cover to the motor home and found the atmosphere as oppressive as the weather outside. There was an uneasy silence. Mario wondered if he had been spotted talking to Scapini.

Colin grimaced at Dick. 'You're cutting it a bit fine, aren't you?'

Dick glanced at his watch. There was still half an hour before practice. 'We left the hotel in plenty of time but there was heavy traffic outside the circuit. Someone had fallen off his bike.'

Max yawned. 'Are you sure it wasn't someone falling out of his pram a bit closer to here,' he said, referring to Colin's tetchiness. Colin glowered at Max and then went over to Mario who was changing into his race overalls.

'They're fixing a modification to the suspension on your car. It should be ready by now.'

His eyes seemed to devour Mario. It was several days since they had spent time together. Colin was desperate to be alone with him, away from all these prying eyes. He averted his gaze, unsure of the transparency of his thoughts. Tonight, Colin had promised himself they would have dinner together. He would arrange it after the practice at lunchtime. Drawing on his jacket, Colin went out into the rain and walked briskly towards the best aphrodisiac he had ever known; the sound of a Formula One engine surging into life.

'What was the frosty reception all about?' asked Dick, sitting down next to Max. Kate appeared from the kitchen, bringing a jug of freshly brewed coffee and plate of croissants.

'Colin doesn't approve of the timing of the announcement of my retirement.'

'Retirement? Max, you can't be serious. You're going to retire?'

Max nodded.

'What did Colin say?'

'He accepted it. I think he was half expecting it – hoping for it, more like. It saves him the problem of finding a way out of my contract for next year.'

'Give it some more time, Max . . . wait a while.'

'My mind is made up, Dick. I'm as sure now as I ever will be.' He didn't want any more time . . . time in which he could change his mind.

Mario, who had heard the exchange, remained silent. Max watched him pull on his yellow race jacket.

'You haven't given me your verdict yet, Mario. What's your opinion?'

'I'm sad to hear your news,' Mario said thoughtfully. 'If you go, we lose one of the best drivers the sport has. It won't be the same.'

The rain was now sweeping across the track in heavy sheets, bouncing off the smooth surface, streaming off umbrellas and canopies. The mechanics let the engines die. There was no point in risking their precious expensive machinery in the downpour. Mario sprinted to the shelter of the garage, trailed by a cursing bedraggled camera crew.

Practice had been delayed for half an hour to allow the storm to pass. Mario sat on one of the work-benches ready to start his interview with the TV crew. A diminutive man clambered over the lighting cables with a clapperboard and snapped it shut self-importantly. The interviewer began his chat in front of the rolling cameras. The sound engineers fussed about avoiding the tools, tyres and other pieces of equipment. Only Mario, the focus of it all, remained still and undisturbed in the glare of the lights. He seemed removed from all the chaos.

Underneath his casual veneer, Mario was feeling restless and frustrated. His eyes kept darting to the outside, waiting for the rain to cease. When it did, there was a sudden hush, broken only by the sound of water running from a broken drainpipe.

Fifteen minutes later, the sun had broken through and

the track dried quickly in the humid conditions. By now the grandstand opposite the pits was becoming a sea of faces as the umbrellas were folded away. An engine whined into life.

Peter Morgan was busy photographing Mario. He found his changeable face a fascinating study; one minute pensively watching the clouds, the next absorbed in conversation with Colin, then bursting into a bashful smile to share a joke with Max. Peter used plenty of film that morning.

Mario climbed into the car, charged with energy. He tore out of the pits and after two laps spun the car. He flicked the wheel to retrieve the balance, but it was too late. The car ploughed into the catch fencing. Angry with himself, he walked back to the pits. Luckily the car had escaped with very little damage, but the mishap was enough to calm Mario down.

During the morning word had already leaked out about Max's retirement. The paddock was abuzz with rumour. Max called a press conference at lunchtime and soon the rumour became fact. It was met with surprise and shock. The journalists scribbled furiously and hotfooted it to the press room to fax the news back to their headquarters. It had stirred a whole mixture of reactions.

Dick was waiting for Colin at the motor home. They were alone except for Kate, who was busy in the kitchen. 'You're not going to accept Max's resignation just like that, surely? Is everybody going crazy round here?' For once, even Dick had lost his patience.

Colin glanced up from the press announcement he was checking over. He was about to announce his new engine deal. It held far more priority than the resignation of one of his drivers. 'Max has made up his mind and as far as I am concerned that closes the matter,' Colin said indifferently.

'Max was right. You are glad to see him go.'

Colin looked up in amazement. It was the first time Dick had ever criticized him to his face. 'What do you want me to do? Counsel him on his career moves. I'm not the bloody Career Officer round here,' Colin shouted.

'No, as far as you're concerned, Max is just a hired hand. You're treating him like he's already superfluous to the team. He won the World Championship for you. Remember?'

'I happen to think he's doing the right thing,' Colin said, regaining his composure.

'Well, I don't, and I also think you've treated him pretty shabbily,' Dick said vehemently. 'You can't show favouritism in this sport.'

'What the hell do you mean?' asked Colin angrily. His eye was twitching rapidly.

'It's pretty obvious, and has been all season, that Mario counts for far more in your books. Do you take us all for idiots? If I were Max Gregson now, I'd be feeling pretty sore about the way I'd been treated.'

'But you're not,' Colin countered. 'He's a grown man. He can look after himself.'

Dick shot him a scornful glance. 'Let's hope your new number one doesn't let you down,' and he slammed the door in rage as he left Colin to contemplate the future of his team.

# 45

The afternoon weather was as temperamental as the morning's had been. The storm clouds hovered threateningly over the forests, adding to the sultry atmosphere. Mario mingled with the mechanics, inspecting the repairs to the car. Peter joined him.

'Hi,' Mario greeted him warmly.

'How's the car?' Peter asked, as they both admired the sleek gleaming bodywork.

'It's all back together again. Fortunately I only crunched the front wing.'

'Well, I hope the weather stays fine. Doesn't look so good.'

Mario shrugged, smiled resignedly and reached for his helmet. As he put in his ear plugs his eyes screwed up under a deep frown and he swore quietly.

'Anything wrong?'

'No. It's just that I arranged to see Scapini at lunchtime. The accident threw it completely from my mind.'

'Can it wait or shall I give him a message?'

'No, it can wait,' Mario said calmly, although his face betrayed an anxiety. Peter wondered what the two men had to talk about.

Mario had been right in his predictions that morning. During the afternoon session, the first timed practice of the weekend, the car positively flew. With each lap, he perfected the cornering; finding a half second here, half a second there. He stormed into the pits for fresh qualifying tyres. His eyes were glazed over. The pit crew found him difficult to communicate with. His mind was concentrated totally on the next lap. It was going to be his best one . . . ever. His times were up amongst the front runners. Only two thousandths of a second separated him from the Ferrari of Terri Dacco. Max was half a second behind him. The circuit led down into the forest, disappearing into a tunnel of trees. Mario accelerated out of the chicane, blasting through the gears. He felt euphoric. His heart beat wildly. He had no fear as he floored the accelerator, the G force thrusting his head back sharply. He had no premonition as he left braking to the last second approaching the bend.

Then the rain began to fall again. One more lap, Mario told himself. He wanted to experience the feel of the car in the rain. He wanted to push it to its very limits. After all, the tyres were still good.

The crew were expecting him in the pits. He glimpsed their surprised faces as he ignored the red flag that signalled the halt to the practice session. Amongst the huddle of bodies standing under umbrellas by the pit wall, he could see Colin, a concerned and irritated expression on his face.

As the car was swallowed up in the dense spray, Colin shivered. An irrepressible sense of foreboding surged through him. At that moment he would have done anything to bring his Mario back to the safety of the pits.

Out in the forest, the tall sentries of trees bowed in the strong breeze. Mario's was the only car left on the rain-sodden track. He was driving as if in a vacuum.

At the end of the straight he was reaching speeds of a hundred and ten miles an hour, leaving a spray twenty yards behind. The rain battered his helmet. He stamped on the brakes for the sharp Ost Kurve. Suddenly, the car gave a jolt and slowly, very slowly it seemed to Mario, lifted off. He was a passenger in his projectile now. The car performed a perfect somersault. How would he explain to Colin about this one? It seemed an eternity before the car landed. Mario saw trees, spray and pieces of debris flying past his helmet. The car was being torn apart around him.

*'This is going to be a big one'* were his last thoughts as his bones snapped like dry sticks in the disintegrating, gleaming bodywork that his mechanics had so painstakingly laboured over a few hours before.

Somewhere in the crowd of fifty thousand spectators, a small boy held on to a large blue balloon which the force of the wind tugged relentlessly. Suddenly the balloon snapped free from his hand and soared away with the boy's sad eyes following its path into the sky . . .

As Mario's car crashed against the barriers, it broke up like a huge wave unleashing its power into a myriad of pieces against the rocks. The noise was sickening, deathly.

It took fifteen seconds for a safety marshal to reach the wreckage. He struggled in vain to move the upturned car. He was joined by another marshal, then another, all desperate to save the young driver's life. The body remained motionless.

Mario was still conscious. He could feel no pain, only surprise at the difficulty in moving his legs, which were buried in the tangle of wreckage. Then he saw a large ugly splinter of bone staring out at him from his right thigh. The blood stained his cream overalls a bright strawberry pink. His neck was numb, broken in two places, and the right side of his ribcage was smashed to a honeycomb.

He could hear the cries of panic from the marshals, their harsh guttural tones betraying their urgency.

'Don't hurry,' Mario whispered. 'There's no hurry.'

He heard the dull wailing of an ambulance approaching the scene. A stretcher was laid beside the car. Medics in white uniforms rushed towards him. Professor Watkins, the Senior Medical Officer, felt his pulse. It was weak, very weak. There might still be a chance.

The balloon floated higher and higher, its pale blue shape standing out against the dark.

The doctors lifted Mario on to the stretcher, but his life was ebbing away . . . his spirit preparing to leave his body, to follow the balloon into the emptiness of the stratosphere.

The rain stopped as abruptly as it had started. A stillness settled over the car.

Colin knew something had happened a few seconds after Mario should have come through on his next lap. Later, he recalled how he had heard the sudden silence after the cut of the engine. It had sent shivers running through him. The track had been empty save for Mario's car.

Why had he stayed out there? Was he crazy?

Colin heard the news calmly. The car had broken up in the catch fencing at the end of the Ost Kurve. Yes, it was a mess, a bloody mess. An ambulance was on its way. Colin heard the dull forbidding siren, the sound every participant in Formula One dreads. The crowds were silent, save for a few mutterings. How bad was the crash? Where had it happened? Speculation was rife in the paddock. It was not good. Rodriguez was trapped in the car . . .

It took twenty agonizing minutes for Mario's body to be released and carried to the ambulance, Professor Watkins trying desperately to stabilize the driver's condition.

Everywhere was hushed. The trees unburdened their tears on to the track. The raindrops slid over Mario's name written on the blue and white helmet the medical team had abandoned by the car. As the ambulance left the scene, there was only the whisper of water hissing on to hot pipes. Mario was helicoptered to a hospital a few miles away. It was announced the accident was serious . . . not fatal. There was still a glimmer of hope that the Professor could perform a miracle.

Tom O'Leary shook his head. 'Some are lucky, some aren't. The fortunate get out without a scratch. The not so lucky have their legs held together with pieces of metal. Then, every once in a while, there's some poor bugger like Mario . . . ' He couldn't bring himself to finish his words and turned away to hide his tears. The mechanics carried on packing up the tools, tyres and spare parts in the garage, trying to restore some normality to their day that had ended in such a horrendous nightmare.

It was six o'clock before the message came through that Mario was dead. Dick arrived a while later, having left Colin and Jean at the hospital. The paddock had a deathly spiritless air about it. Everyone was in shock. Friends and colleagues came by the garage with messages of sympathy. The ghoulish stood by, hoping to see pieces of the wrecked car. Max stayed with the mechanics, believing that their strong bond, which was made even more real at times like this, would offer some consolation. By being there amongst the tools of his trade, he hoped to find a way to accept Mario's death.

The tragedy would leave a gaping hole in the motor-racing world. A life had been lost. It was a curious irony, Max thought, that it was Mario who had been killed and not himself. *He* was the one who had been so sure that his luck was running out.

Max broke the heavy silence. 'Has anybody figured out why he stayed out on the track? He must have seen the red flag along with everyone else?'

'That was Colin's very same question. He kept repeating it over and over on the way to the hospital,' said Dick.

'How is Colin taking it?' someone asked.

Dick's voice faltered. 'He's going through the motions . . . talking to the doctors . . . making all the necessary arrangements. They say when he saw Mario's body he stared at it, then closed his eyes as if he were praying. Then he collapsed.'

'I've never seen him get so close to any of his drivers,' remarked Tom.

'That's true,' said another mechanic. 'They had a special relationship.'

Dick thought back to the argument with Colin earlier. He wanted to obliterate the awful thing he had said: 'I hope your new number one doesn't let you down.' By some quirk of fate, Mario was no longer around to let him down.

# 46

Rachel giggled as she watched Phil running round the room with one boot on, the other in the snappy jaws of a lively black labrador puppy.

'George, here boy,' he commanded. Then in exasperation he bellowed, 'George, give me back my bloody boot.' The puppy wagged its tail mischievously, hanging on stubbornly to its prize.

Rachel sat on the sofa, feeling at home in the untidy disarray of Phil's flat. The hearth of the large open brick fireplace was cluttered with a collection of horse magazines, two flourishing pot plants and a pair of stout walking boots. The walls held a fine collection of horse prints and photographs of race horses. Old newspapers and empty cigarette packets lay on the oak coffee table. Underneath the table was a half-chewed dog bone.

'OK. Plan A is back on schedule. Are you quite happy to go on a picnic?'

'Sounds a good idea,' replied Rachel.

'The forecast is for showers. In fact, heavy rain.'

'Not such a good idea, after all. Any alternative to Plan A?'

'Plenty.'

'For instance?'

Phil leaned over her and kissed her cheek. Casually dressed in jeans and white shirt, Rachel was a far cry from the woman he had first met in her designer clothes and carefully applied make-up. She had the body of a twenty year old and a spontaneous, youthful spirit that bemused him. 'We could stay home,' he whispered in her ear.

Rachel suppressed a shiver of unequivocal lust, passion and happiness. Apart from their obvious sexual compatibility, there was also an empathy between them that made for an easy-going relationship. They had both slipped into an affair without any forethought or premeditation of its consequences. Rachel was experiencing a rare contentment with Phil and she was determined to enjoy it for however long it lasted. She gave him a searching look with her large, clear eyes, sending frissons of desire through Phil's strong muscular body.

'We could eat out at a restaurant or we could take a trip to the supermarket, buy something for lunch, open a bottle of wine . . . and have a lazy afternoon at home . . . ' Phil raised his eyebrows and gave her a wicked smile.

'Couldn't we combine the two? Eat out and have a lazy afternoon,' Rachel said. They had made love hectically only a few hours before, revelling again in each other's bodies, yet Rachel still felt a strong arousal.

'That's fine by me. Fancy some coffee before we go?'

'I'd love some.'

Phil disappeared into the tiny kitchen and as Rachel listened to the rattle of cups, she wondered if anybody could be as blissfully happy as she was. Her thoughts turned back to the time she had found out about Colin. Her world had collapsed in a humiliating mess and she faced black despair. Then, unexpectedly, Phil had walked into her life.

'What are you looking so smug about?' asked Phil, seeing Rachel's satisfied grin. He sat down next to her.

'I was just thinking how life can turn around . . . Just when you think your life has fallen apart, something good comes along.'

'Has it?' asked Phil, amused.

'Yes, and he's sitting right next to me,' said Rachel, playing with the thick curls around Phil's shirt collar.

Phil placed the coffee mugs on the table and took hold of her hand. 'I'll go along with that theory, but whether I'm good for you is another question.'

Rachel laughed as Phil gave her a saucy wink. 'Unquestionably, I would say that you are extremely good for me,' she murmured.

They kissed slowly, gently, enjoying the sensuous touch and pleasure they gave each other. For Rachel it was like stepping on to a merry-go-round that was going faster and faster. There was no stopping until the final union of their bodies.

They made love in the bedroom unhurriedly. As Phil undressed, Rachel admired the well-built hardness of his body. Every inch of it was taut muscle. Every touch from him was electrifying. His fingers sent flutterings of joy along every nerve-ending of her body.

As he laid her on the bed, Rachel wanted him more than she could have ever thought possible. Then Phil was inside her, mounting her with an urgency that was matched only by her own lascivious appetite. He clasped her body firmly. She gripped the rock-hard muscles of his arms and shoulders, clawing her nails into his skin. She bit hard with her teeth, her passion inextricably linked with the desire to make him feel the pain of wanting her.

Phil was revelling in the sheer ecstasy of her body. The clawing of her finger nails, the biting of his shoulders was turning him on even more. Thrusting harder and harder he took her with an intensity he had never known before. Rachel was an equal match for his strength. She writhed and struggled with him, wanting him desperately, but making him fight for her every inch of the way.

Exhausted, they lay back on the sheets, their hunger

for each other temporarily sated. They lay silently for several minutes, allowing their breath to return gently to their panting bodies. Then Phil turned to her and whispered, 'My God, woman. You're going to get a lot more of that before the weekend is out.'

Rachel laughed and pushed her hair back from her face in a sensual movement that flowed down her body to her hips. 'OK, but you'll have to feed me first.'

He kissed her. 'How about lunch at the restaurant by the river? That way you can get some fresh air . . . before we come back to make t-o-r-r-i-d- love again.'

Over lunch there were long silences that lovers are comfortable with. Loving looks were exchanged, instead of words, as they sipped their wine together and ate quietly. The outside world ceased to exist. Then Rachel broke the spell. 'I saw Vicky a short while ago.'

'What did she have to say?'

'She didn't seem very happy to hear that we are seeing each other. Was there ever anything between you two?' asked Rachel.

Phil stopped drinking and placed his wine glass on the table. He played with its long stem, then looked at Rachel, wondering how she would react to the truth. 'We did have a short-lived affair. I can't deny it,' he explained.

Rachel gave him a bemused smile, trying to ignore the stab of jealousy that tore through her body. 'You and Vicky? I would never have believed it,' she said, watching Phil from over the top of her glass of wine.

Phil looked deflated. 'I didn't want to tell you just in case you thought I was the local stud round here,' he confessed.

Rachel burst out laughing. 'I can think of a lot worse things people could say.' Then she turned serious again. 'And is that all it was?'

'Absolutely. I can assure you.'

Rachel wondered about Vicky. For whatever had happened between them, it obviously hadn't ended happily for her.

Contrary to the forecast, the August weather stayed fine all afternoon and the sun was still hot as Phil and Rachel walked with the dogs by the river. Rachel couldn't remember such a happy, carefree day. As they drove back to Watlington, Phil switched on the crackly radio of the Land Rover. Rachel dived for the volume switch as she heard a sports bulletin.

The Formula One world was in mourning for the tragic loss of one of their bright, new stars. Rodriguez had been killed during practice for the German Grand Prix.

Rachel's body froze rigid as the news was announced and tears sprang to her eyes. The cheerful young face of Mario flashed before her. 'My God,' she cried. 'Not Mario . . . not Mario . . . '

Rachel rang Colin's secretary and was told his plane was landing at nine thirty and that Dick was driving him home. As she waited nervously for the car headlights to appear up the drive, Rachel reflected on the tragic waste of Mario's life. A few minutes later, she heard the car pull up on the gravel driveway. Hurriedly, she answered the door. A hunched, shadowy figure stood before her. Colin's eyes, even in the half light of the hall, appeared dead. He looked at her blankly and, without a word, walked past her and up to his room.

# 47

The Delta team had withdrawn from the German Grand Prix as a mark of respect for Mario. It had been won by Terri Dacco in the Ferrari, but the celebrations were muted. Mario's death was in everyone's minds. At the Delta factory an immediate enquiry began into the cause of Mario's accident and it was a gruesome task sifting through all the wreckage, piece by piece. Every nut and bolt was checked and rechecked. The mechanics could find no technical fault to explain the accident. The joint opinion of Jean, Tom and the race engineers was that Mario had misjudged the corner and left braking too late, not inconceivable given the terrible weather conditions.

They held a meeting at the factory. Colin, Tom and Jean were in attendance. There was positive relief at the findings of the investigation. If there had been any question of a fault with the car, it would have been traumatic for the team. Colin sat deep in thought. It was Jean who spoke for everyone at the factory. 'Colin, at least there wasn't any sabotage involved.'

Colin shook his head. 'It could have been Scapini's final *tour de force*. He knew Mario was the one way to get back at me. He knew how much I thought of him.' His voice cracked as he spoke. 'If we can find anything to prove that this was not driver error . . . *anything* – then Scapini will pay for it and I make no secret of the fact.'

'Let's not be too hasty,' said Tom. 'Why should he kill a driver he wanted for his own team anyway?'

The words hit Colin like an avalanche. They gouged and tore another path into the sensibilities of his already battered mind. 'Scapini wanted Mario?' He sounded confused. 'How do you know?'

Tom regretted the thoughtlessness of his words. 'It's only something we surmised,' he said quickly. 'Mario was talking to Peter Morgan on the morning of the accident.' Colin's eye twitched. He did not want reminding of the growing friendship between Peter and Mario. 'Mario mentioned that Scapini had asked him over to the motor home. It's only a guess that Scapini was going to offer him a drive.'

'Did the meeting take place?'

'No, Mario forgot to go . . . or that's what he told Peter.'

Colin's thoughts skimmed back to the flight to Frankfurt. Mario had been looking pleased with himself. Had Scapini already spoken with him? Had he offered him a better drive, a huge retainer to persuade him to leave Delta? Mario knew that Scapini had lost the engine deal, but had he something else up his sleeve? Had Colin trusted Mario's loyalty too blindly?

There was only one person who knew the answers and that was Scapini. Colin would choose his time to confront him. It was too soon after the accident. Colin needed more time to get over the shock.

The funeral was a quiet family affair. Colin flew with the body to Argentina, and was taken to Mario's birthplace, a small village at the base of the mountains. Dick and Max also flew out for the sad occasion and were moved by the deep mourning of the local people. Argentina had lost one of its national heroes and the sense of loss was everywhere and on everybody's lips.

Mario was laid to rest in a small local cemetery, where the only sound to disturb the quiet was the occasional passing of a car and the wind in the tall pampas grasses. In the distance was the backdrop of the mountains.

Mario was back home now, back to his roots, a far cry from the world of fast cars and machinery that had so dominated his life. The garland he had received on the podium at Monaco was laid on his imposing marble headstone, a fitting memory to a talent that had never fulfilled its true potential.

Colin stayed on for a few days, spending time with Mario's family and getting to know them. Their hospitality was boundless and as Colin prepared to leave he felt an overwhelming sense of sorrow. He had found a peace amongst these people and their surroundings that he had never felt before. On his last day, Colin took a walk up into the mountains near to Mario's home. He breathed in the rich, clean air and absorbed the tangible silence. He thought about his hectic world back home and the long, high-pressured days of the racing and testing.

Racing was like war, he decided. He and the other team owners were the generals in charge of manoeuvres. The track was the bloody battlefield and sometimes, as in Mario's case, there were casualties. It was not always a clean war. There was corruption and greed. But there would be no end to this war. There would always be people like himself who were prepared to risk everything to triumph over their opponents. In Colin's case the risks had been too high. He had lost the person who meant more to him than anybody else. Mario was dead and would never win again in the war of speed.

Dick picked up the phone that seemed to have rung endlessly since the return of the team from Hockenheim.

'Max Gregson on the phone for you,' trilled his secretary.

'Hi, Max. How are you?'

'I'm fine. Any news from Colin yet?'

'Yes. He's coming in tomorrow. I think I better warn you, he's still pretty cut up. I spoke with Rachel yesterday and she reckons he's in a world of his own.'

'Mario meant more to him than a lot of us realized,' said Max.

Dick knew what Max was referring to. He sighed. 'It couldn't have been worse if he had lost his son.'

There was a pause on the end of the phone, then Max asked, 'Who is the replacement driver?'

'There isn't going to be one. He doesn't want us to hire anybody yet.'

Max wondered cynically if Colin would have replaced *him* if he had been the one to go. He had no doubt in his mind that the young Swedish driver Colin had been talking to at Monaco would have been warming his butt in the cockpit of his car by now. 'So, we go to Hungary with one car?'

'It looks that way.'

'It won't be an easy time for any of us, that's for sure,' said Max, thinking ahead.

He had seen how the death of a driver could affect the closely knit world of Formula One. A cloud of gloom would settle over the community for a couple of races after. Then it was back to business as usual and another driver would replace the one that had gone. There were always a hundred more eager fools to step into the shoes of the departed. Max wondered about the team and if Colin had the determination to pick up where he had left off.

Three days later the Formula One circus flew to Hungary. Despite the brilliance of the never-ending sunshine that toasted the vast hordes of Hungarian spectators to a brown crisp, the atmosphere amongst the teams was subdued. The normally buzzing vibrancy in the paddock was missing.

Hungary had become a firm favourite on the motor-racing calendar. With the splendours of the city of Budapest not far away, the track was set in a natural amphitheatre of the surrounding hillsides. The teams enjoyed the excellent organization provided by the authorities and the Hungarians themselves were cheerful, friendly hosts. Everyone liked the newly built track which proved to have a good balance of fast and slow corners.

Although the teams invariably looked forward to the next race with recharged enthusiasm, there was always the memory of the last one. Even more so in Hungary. Mario's absence was all the more poignant because Delta was running only one car. Half the mechanics had stayed behind in England. The cheery banter and whistling in the garage was something of the past.

The face of the Argentinian remained in the minds of everybody. Colin received the many condolences calmly. Apart from necessary business, he maintained a low profile. Both Jean and Dick had approached him on urgent matters, only to find that his detachment was matched by his vagueness.

Jean sat with Dick and Max in the motor home discussing the team's future. 'The team's going to fall apart unless Colin pulls himself together,' Jean said worriedly. 'Of course, people out there are sympathetic, but there's a limit to how long it will last – the sponsors still want results and something for their money.'

'Colin's walking round like an automaton. He's a million miles away,' Max agreed.

Dick was optimistic. 'Well, let's get through the race

tomorrow and by the time we get to Austria, who knows, he might be back to his old self?'

It was an unnerving thought that the team could lose direction. Although they were aware of Colin's many faults, Delta had flourished under his businesslike approach and meticulous attention to detail. Now, after the accident, they were facing the possibility that they could sink into obscurity. It was not a prospect they wanted to think about too deeply.

Max, however, did not disappoint the team. He drove superbly, showing his old flair. In the last minutes of timed practice on the Saturday afternoon he secured pole position for the race on Sunday. On a clear, cloudless afternoon, he led the line-up of cars around the smooth track to the start line. Waving in the breeze across from him in the grandstand was the Argentinian flag. Next to it was a banner. The simple message struck home. 'MAX – DO THIS ONE FOR MARIO.'

Max did. He drove faultlessly and finished a comfortable first.

The next race in Austria in mid-August also held good fortune for him. Max again took pole position and his lead was never once threatened. The chequered flag was his and he became the centre of attention for the press and media.

An English satellite TV station interviewed him straight after the race. 'Max, you drove a superb race today. Can you explain the sudden turn round in your driving in the last few weeks?'

Max wiped his forehead, still damp with perspiration from the exertion of the race. 'Not really,' he replied honestly. 'The car is going well and I seem to have found my touch again.'

'You had very bad luck at the beginning of the season

and if you don't mind me saying so, a lot of people thought you had lost your edge. Did you lose your motivation?'

'I certainly lost something. It was a nightmare. I had convinced myself I had run out of luck . . . and talent. It happens in every driver's career at some time or another. I guess mine was due.'

'There were rumours that you were throwing away your great talent, perhaps by living life a little too much in the fast lane . . .?' The interviewer gave a sheepish smile. Max Gregson was not the sort of character to provoke on live television.

So the guy was digging a little, Max thought. Well, he may as well be honest. He felt he had come through it all. He could look at the past few months objectively now. 'I won't deny that the pressures of the job got to me.' Max smiled lazily. 'And the press found plenty to write about.'

'And now?'

'Who knows what will happen? I've found my motivation again and I have one of the best cars in Formula One. But the Championship is a long way off for me, this year at any rate.'

'Now that you've found your old form, what are the chances of you reconsidering your decision to retire?'

Max had been ready for that one. 'I haven't reconsidered as yet,' he replied resolutely. The crucial question had gnawed away at him all weekend. Did he still want to hurtle himself round a race track tempting fate? Was he ready to give it all up? Mario's death had been a stark reminder of the high stakes that were at risk.

The paddock was alive with rumour about whether Max would renounce his decision to retire or not. Many were anxious to try to persuade him to change his mind, believing the sport would lose one of its great drivers.

He was still a winner. He had just proved that. Several team owners approached him with offers of a drive the following season. Max was in demand from everybody, it seemed.

Except Colin, that is.

On their return from Austria, Colin called Jean and Dick to his office. He had lost a lot of weight in the last few days. His eyes had sunk into his cheekbones, giving him an even more gaunt appearance. They could guess the news was not good. Colin sat hunched in his chair, his eyes glacial and remote. 'I'm giving serious consideration to selling Delta and going to America,' Colin announced. 'Under the present circumstances, I don't feel I can continue in Formula One . . . ' His voice tailed off.

Jean and Dick were under no illusion that this was a passing whim. Jean's nimble mind was already working at double quick time. Who would the buyers be? Who was available to buy the team? His heart sank at the first name that came to mind.

Scapini with his Mafia connections could easily find the multi-million-dollar sum to buy the whole shooting match. Jean could envisage the smile of satisfaction on Scapini's face at the prospect of negotiating such a deal. He was power-mad enough to grab the high-profile team with both hands.

Jean tried shock tactics on Colin. He had nothing to lose. 'You mean, you would let Scapini walk in here and take over?'

Colin bristled. 'Never. You know I would never hand over the team to him – at any price.'

'He would find a way of getting it – you know that as well as anybody,' Jean said.

'You can't sell out! The team is your life.' Dick stood up in exasperation.

'You're wrong, Dick. Mario was my life. It was my dream to make Mario the World Champion. Now that he's gone, I don't see any reason to continue.'

Dick and Jean felt the shock waves running through them. What was Colin saying? The man seemed to be even more obsessed with Mario now that he was dead.

Jean stood up. He had heard enough. 'OK, OK – if that is what you want. But for our sakes, don't rush into this. We've been with you for many years . . . through the bad times and good. Don't throw it all away. Give yourself time to get over Mario's death and then reconsider.' But even as he spoke he realized that his sympathies had run their full course with this introspective, brooding Englishman. He, for one, would waste no time in offering his services to another team.

As Dick closed the door of the office, he left Colin absorbed in the large blown-up photograph of Mario on his wall. It had been taken on the morning of his death by Peter Morgan. It was a curious study of concentration and searching as he looked up at the sky, as if questioning what the gods had in store for him that day. The normally large eyes were squinting, his handsome profile caught against the background of one of those billowing rain clouds that helped contribute to his death. Colin would always remember the intensity of his love for him that day.

# 48

As Colin opened the door to Mario's flat, he caught a breath of stale trapped air. He had dreaded this moment. Despite the mildness of the evening a numbing chill ran through him. His eyes cast around at the leather sofa and chairs, the cream marble-topped coffee table, the Regency-style desk and, there, in pride of place on the bookcase, was the magnificent gleaming trophy he had won at Monaco. The joyous memory of the victory they had shared came flooding back.

It brought Mario alive once more. Colin walked to the window and studied the quiet street scene outside, rows of parked cars, a cat dozing on the wall . . . the parking space where Mario's car usually stood. Colin sat down, skimming aimlessly through the magazines piled on the table, remembering Mario's boyish smile, the richly accented timbre of his voice.

He still could not accept that Mario was not coming back to him. Had he come to the flat hoping that he could turn back the hands of time? That in some way he could rediscover his closeness to the man who had left him with a fragment of his own sanity? Was there any way he could come to terms with this tragedy that was on the point of destroying him?

Colin walked through the rooms, hoping to find some solace from his affliction. He noted the neat tidy bedroom. Mario's habits had been like his mind: systematic and orderly. Then why had he stayed out on the track? Why had he been so foolish and suddenly behaved so out of character? Mario had died needlessly and there was nothing that could bring him back.

There was, however, one person who might be able to answer a few of the questions that tormented him. It was time to see Scapini.

Colin rang Scapini in Italy the following morning. His secretary brusquely informed him that Scapini was in London and, after a few minutes of wrangling, finally gave him his whereabouts. Colin left a message at his hotel and Scapini got back to him a few hours later. 'How can I help you?' His voice was coldly civil.

'I would like to talk to you about Mario,' said Colin evenly.

'OK. I'm leaving for the airport in one hour. I'll meet you at one of the hotels nearby.'

Colin was surprised to find his adversary so cooperative. 'Let's make it the Post House – the bar just off the lobby, at five?' suggested Colin.

'Make it five thirty.'

Without wasting time on pleasantries both men hung up.

It was the first time that Colin had seen Scapini without his usual retinue of flunkeys. He appeared smaller, almost emaciated, and for a man in his mid forties he looked much older than his years.

Colin sat down at one of the polished tables. At such an early hour they had the bar to themselves. The only distraction was the monotonous drone of aircraft overhead.

Scapini came straight to the point. 'What is it you want from me?' he asked, lighting one of his strong cigarettes. His eyes met Colin's briefly.

'I want to know if you can throw some light on Mario's death?'

Scapini grunted. 'You must be crazy. You think I would have wanted to harm Mario?'

Colin swallowed a mouthful of whisky, hoping to find some relief from the overpowering sense of disquiet he felt with this man. 'You are a vindictive man, Scapini. You will not forget the past.'

Scapini's mouth tightened and the lines on either side of it etched deeper into his cheeks. It was a humourless face, one that sought little amusement out of life, Colin decided. 'You expect me to forget that I spent two years in jail – and because of you?'

'I didn't put you away. The jury found you guilty.'

'But it was your testimony that did it.' Scapini's eyes narrowed. He was still bitter over the past.

Colin recalled how different Scapini had been in those days. The bright young Italian he had appointed as team manager to his Formula Three team had been a willing and enthusiastic partner. They were out of the same mould, eager and unscrupulous. Above all, was their desire to get the team established and, with a healthy injection of cash, to ride it through its first year.

In an extraordinary turn of luck, Colin had secured sponsorship from one of the large electronics companies. He had managed to convince the board of directors to support the struggling racing team. With twenty thousand pounds, a fortune to Colin in those days, they had acquired two reliable cars and a skeleton staff. The team had operated successfully and their two young drivers had shown promise amongst the well-established teams. More sponsorship had come their way.

Then large amounts of money had started to go missing from the funds. Colin had taken Scapini's word that it was all accounted for in the operating costs. After all, the two were partners and Colin had every reason to trust him. Or so Colin had assumed.

It was only after Scapini had disappeared and Colin had examined the accounts more thoroughly, that he had found they had been cleared of every penny. It had been a humiliating blow and left Colin's career in tatters. The team he had striven to develop so conscientiously had been put up for sale and bought by a Swiss entrepreneur for a pittance. The man was later found to be in league with Scapini.

Colin had sworn that he would catch up with his fraudulent partner. Scapini had destroyed his credibility in the motor-racing world. After a year of bickering with the Italian authorities, Scapini had been extradited and charged with embezzlement of the company funds. It had been a messy business. The proceedings had brought to light the fact that this was not Scapini's first offence for 'borrowing' money. He had been found guilty and sentenced to four years in jail. He had been released on remission after two. Meanwhile, Colin had had to start from scratch again and overcome a badly blemished reputation. Sponsors and banks had been unwilling to conduct business with him and it had not been until Rachel had come along with her generous investment that he was solvent once more.

But why had Scapini taken so long to exact his vengeance? Colin wondered.

'So you wanted to pay me back for putting you in jail? You thought the jury would believe you when you swore that you had only borrowed the money.'

'It was true, and two years is a long time to be holed up in jail.' Scapini's resentment showed in every word. 'But as angry as I was, I never set out to hurt Mario.'

'And Geoffrey and his clumsy little ways of leaving wheel nuts off and the like?'

Scapini shrugged. His silence was an affirmation of his guilt.

'Why did it take you so long?' asked Colin.

Scapini's eyes shot him a piercing glance. 'I despised your success. Now it seems fate has changed that. Is it true you are selling the team?'

Colin declined to answer. It was none of his damn business anyway. 'So what was your connection with Mario?' he asked tersely.

'Mario? I offered him a drive for next year.'

'But he turned you down.'

'On the contrary. Your young driver was on the point of signing a contract.' His lips lifted faintly at the corners, the only intimation of the smugness he was enjoying.

Colin moved uncomfortably in his chair and the tell-tale twitch in his eye revealed his uneasiness. 'You're lying,' he retorted. 'There was never any question of him leaving – especially to work for a team that had obviously sabotaged his own. Do you think he was crazy?'

'But you're wrong there.' Scapini's voice was almost a whisper, but Colin heard every nauseating word of it. It stabbed at the pit of Colin's stomach like a hammer blow. 'Mario needed money. A million dollars, to be exact. We agreed if he signed, I would give him the money in two instalments; one up front. His terms were a little out of the ordinary but I went along with them.'

Colin finished his whisky and left. His mind was deluged by the loathsome realization that Mario had betrayed him. He had negotiated with another team; worse still, with his arch enemy from the past. But why? Either Scapini was lying or Mario had been in some kind of trouble. Still reeling with the shock Colin drove to Mario's flat.

Any day, Mario's sister had been due to collect Mario's belongings and arrange the sale of the property. Colin was relieved to find nothing had been touched. He went straight to the writing desk. There was no time for sentiment now.

Stealthily he flicked through the neatly filed documents and letters, his fingers as nimble as a bank clerk's counting notes. Next, he searched the bedroom. His trip seemingly had been fruitless. There were no papers or documents anywhere to suggest that Mario had any debts at all. Colin wiped his forehead and slumped on to the bed. It was claustrophobic in the small airless flat. He almost regretted that he had met up with Scapini.

Then the heel of his shoe made contact with something under the bed. Lifting the valance, he picked up a paperback novel. Casting it aside, he saw lying next to it a slim leather briefcase. He hurried to the kitchen and finding a knife forced open the locks. A large foolscap envelope fell out. His curiosity was now tinged with dread. His hands trembled at the premonition that he was about to discover another side of Mario's life.

His heart raced as he studied the two large photographs in black and white. He felt a billowing wave of nausea flood over him and he swallowed hard to fight back the bile at the back of his throat. Yes. He knew the other man's face. He had passed him coming away from Mario's flat. At the time he had sensed that the man was a friend of Mario's. And here was the photograph of them both . . .

Colin was mesmerized by the two male figures entwined together, naked. There was also a note typewritten in Spanish with the name of the bank: Banco de la Provincia de Buenos Aires, and the account number for the sum of half a million dollars to be placed there. It was blackmail. Hurriedly, Colin snapped shut the briefcase and slammed the door of the small flat for the last time.

As he drove home he turned on the car heater to relieve the icy chill that suffused his body. Colin was relieved to find no sign of life about the house when he got back. Rachel must have gone away for the weekend.

It was gone midnight by the time Colin finished the bottle of whisky. His limbs felt like granite, but his tormented mind had thankfully been dulled. Mario's memory was beginning to wash over him like a warm sea, the bitterness ebbing away on a tide of sadness. Mario had, after all, never been his to possess. Colin had bought his services as a driver through a contract, but had he been foolish enough to believe he could also buy his affection? Had he in his crazy infatuation really convinced himself that Mario was his and his alone?

No, Mario had died like he had lived; a free spirit. Colin understood now why he had never approached him for the money to pay off his blackmailer. Mario would rather face Scapini than Colin's obsessive jealousy. The more Colin thought about it, the more lucid he became. The realization that he had alienated Mario by his possessiveness engulfed him in a shroud of pity.

Rubbing the weariness from his eyes, he summoned the strength to get up and make his way to bed. Then he remembered the photographs. Even in his dazed state he knew they had to be destroyed. He removed the firescreen from the large open hearth and slowly and deliberately tore the envelope and its contents into small pieces and threw them into the grate. The loathsome face of the Argentinian who had seduced Mario would burn, together with the damning evidence. He put a match to the papers and watched as the licking flames curled over their edges.

To make the fire burn more strongly he threw in the first thing that came to hand, an arrangement of dried flowers. They crackled and hissed as the flames devoured them. The grate became a glowing mound of charred paper and black ash. Now there were only two people who had known of Mario's indiscretion and the other was somewhere in Argentina.

The alcohol and tiredness had made Colin shivery. He threw kindling wood into the grate, and then some logs as the fire caught again. The comforting warmth reminded him of happier days when the family was at home; of bright Christmases; of winter nights when Rachel had a welcoming fire and supper prepared for him. As the flames held his attention, he thought of the irony of it all. Not only had he lost his wife and family, he had lost the person he had sacrificed them for. He had nothing left.

He opened another bottle of whisky, poured himself a large measure and faced the realization that at that moment he didn't really care whether he lived or died. As the sparks hissed and spat venomously towards him, Colin lay on the rug and drifted into a deep, alcoholic sleep.

# 49

The following evening, Max and Vicky had been hosting a dinner party for a small group of friends when Ella, the au pair, interrupted to say there was an urgent phone call from Dick Chance.

Max heard the news silently and went back to join the group. He sat down amidst the lively conversation and appeared lost in thought.

'Max, you look as if you've heard bad news. What is it?' enquired Vicky.

'Sorry. It is bad news, I'm afraid. Colin is in hospital. He's been injured in a fire at his home.' There were gasps of shock around the table. 'Rachel and Dick are with him now. I've told Dick to get Rachel to ring us as soon as she can.'

'Of course. She must come and stay here,' said Vicky, shocked.

'Yes, I've already offered, but she's fixed herself up to stay with friends near the hospital.'

The other guests who were acquainted with Colin were as devastated as Vicky. They wanted to know more details. How seriously injured was Colin? How had the fire started? Had Colin been alone? Then Max could sense a question that was buzzing through all their heads. It was well known that Colin had been totally destroyed by Mario's death. Had the fire had anything to do with it? Nobody mentioned a suicide attempt, but it was in everybody's minds. Max had imparted only the briefest details and the dinner party continued in a subdued atmosphere. It was only later when Max was alone with Vicky that he related the whole story.

Rachel had been staying away for the weekend, but on impulse had returned to the house late at night. As she had turned in the drive she had seen in the car headlights smoke leaking out of a downstairs window. She had dashed into the house and as she opened the door to the drawing room, the furnishings had ignited. In the choking, acrid smoke Rachel had spotted Colin's body on the hearth rug. In a monumental effort, she had dragged his unconscious burning body out into the drive and had smothered the flames with her coat and rugs from the car. Minutes later the fire engines had arrived, alerted by some neighbours who had spotted the flames licking out of the downstairs window.

The ambulance had arrived and Colin was taken to Casualty. Rachel had remained calm and in control the whole time, Dick had said, even with the ghastly sight of Colin's facial burns. Without question, her quick thinking and presence of mind had saved her husband's life.

For a week, Colin's life had been in serious danger. He had suffered second degree burns to his face and body, and his lungs had been badly damaged by smoke inhalation. During all that time, Rachel had kept vigil by his bedside and received the flowers and messages with courage and gratitude.

A month later, the motor-racing magazines were still giving full coverage to the plight of the Delta team. Dick and Jean had been placed in charge of its running. But the question in everybody's mind was whether Colin would sell the team. It seemed inevitable now.

The only visitors Colin had permitted were Rachel and Dick. It was after one such visit that Dick arrived at Max's house.

Max had been on a long walk with Sophie. The afternoon

was bitterly cold and they were making hot chocolate together in the kitchen. Sophie was emptying her pockets of fir cones when Dick peered round the door.

Max greeted Dick warmly. 'Come and join us,' he said. 'Fancy some hot chocolate . . . with brandy?'

'I'd love some,' replied Dick. 'Sorry to call in like this, but I've just come from seeing Colin at the hospital.'

'How is he?' asked Max, leaving Sophie to prepare the mugs of chocolate.

Dick and Max sat down at the kitchen table. Dick looked serious. 'Colin will have to have another operation on his face to replace the scar tissue. It's going to be a long job and some of the scarring will be permanent. But he's in good spirits.'

'Well, that's something. He must be going through hell.'

'Yes, apparently, he's still in considerable pain.'

'Poor bugger. What is the news of the team?' asked Max, thinking that Dick had brought news that Colin had decided to sell after all.

'That's what I've come about. Do you think we could have a few moments in private?'

'Of course. Sophie, can you find Ella and ask her to throw some more logs on the fire? We'll come through to the drawing room in a few minutes.'

'All right,' replied Sophie, 'but what about my hot chocolate?'

'Here, the kettle's boiled. I can make it right away.' Max got up and poured the boiling water into the three mugs and sat down with Dick at the table. Sophie, trailed by two dogs sniffing at her mug, disappeared out of the door, only to reappear a moment later with the brandy bottle in her hand. 'Here you are, Daddy. You forgot your special ingredient.' Max gave her a smile and a warm hug and watched her as she trotted off again.

'Is Vicky not here?' enquired Dick.

'No, she's out at the hairdresser's. Does this involve Vicky as well?'

'No, in fact it's better that she's not here . . . It will give a minute's breathing space to think about . . . '

'What?' asked Max, smiling curiously. 'You want me to put up some cash to buy the team. Is that it?'

'No, it's not that. Colin hasn't made any plans to sell the team. We have to wait and see how he recovers. He has asked me to see you, to persuade you . . . '

Max laughed. 'What, Dick? To come out of retirement?'

'Yes,' said Dick quietly. 'He wants you to drive for the team again, Max. We all do. *You* know Delta won't be the same without you. He wants your answer soon – in a few days' time. How about it, Max?'

Max sat deep in thought. The proposition had left him confused. Initially, the idea didn't hold any appeal, but then he still hadn't come to terms with his retirement. He hadn't reconciled himself completely to being out of Formula One. It was as if he were enjoying a long break.

The previous season had been a wasted one in many respects. Having lost that intrinsic edge that had always driven him to win, he had become a victim of his own self doubt. It was as if winning the World Championship had exposed a weaker side of him and he was blinded by the belief that there was nothing left to prove. Then all the distractions that had plagued him had gone. Whether Mario's death had contributed to this change in attitude, it mattered little. What was important was that he had resurrected his desire to win and the old flame, even now, still burnt as brightly as ever.

Over the past months, Max had done a lot of heart searching as to whether he had made the right decision to retire. The last races of the season in Italy, Portugal,

Mexico, Japan and Australia had added further proof that perhaps his career was not yet over. He was back on form and had lost the Championship by only two points to his French rival, Jean Claude.

'A new maturity' was how the press had described the dramatic turnaround in his driving. Off track, too, the fast player image was no longer in evidence, as Max settled down to a quieter existence. The scribes of Fleet Street suddenly found themselves without the usual ammunition. They had attributed this change to Mario's death and suggested that Max had realized that he could no longer afford to gamble with his life so irresponsibly on the race track.

Now he was being offered the opportunity to return to racing. But whatever the ultimate decision, this time he would be sure that he and Vicky talked it over together. He would allow them plenty of time to reconsider his retirement.

# 50

Kelly and Julian spent Christmas and New Year together skiing at Verbier in Switzerland. There were parties by log fires, torch-lit sleigh rides at midnight and long, invigorating days on the slopes.

New Year's Eve had started boisterously with a dinner for fourteen in the large villa nestled at the base of the mountains. There was fresh lobster, roast venison and buckets of champagne. Just as the dessert arrived, they were invaded by another group of inebriated friends. It was a wild and merry evening. But, before midnight, the two of them slipped away into the village, which was now covered with a fresh blanket of snow. Tomorrow they would leave together on the plane for Paris but now they sat in one of the crowded bars drinking glüwein by a roaring log fire.

Julian's eyes never left Kelly's for a moment. 'It's been quite a year, hasn't it?'

'Mmm, but the last few months have been the most exciting.' Kelly was thinking back to the start of their relationship. 'Who would have guessed what lay ahead for us?'

'I'm just glad it worked out right for both of us.'

They kissed tenderly as the singing and roistering gained strength as midnight grew closer. Kelly was remembering another time just before last Christmas when she had met Julian at the Grosvenor House Hotel and confided in him about her pregnancy. She recalled his strength and protectiveness, his warmth and understanding. His parting words had stayed with her, 'If it had been our baby, Kelly, we'd have been celebrating with champagne . . . ' But she had been obsessed with Max then. Now everything had changed. She no longer even missed him . . .

Looking back she often compared his moodiness with Julian's cheerfulness, the hours of waiting for him to arrive, the excuses and broken dates when domestic plans took priority; the unpredictability of never knowing when she was going to see him and for how long. She was just one piece in the busy jigsaw of his life.

Of course it had given a heightened tension to their relationship; an excitement and a hunger for each other in the snatched times they shared. But looking across at Julian, his dark, magnetic eyes glinting in the firelight, his warm smile, she knew he was the right man for her. Their relationship grew closer by the day, as they discovered new things about each other. Already Julian was talking about getting married and having babies.

'Sometimes I wonder how we could have been just friends for so long, and yet . . . '

'Without us knowing there was something deeper between us,' said Kelly.

'Yes, and now I can't bear to be without you.'

'Is that why you're coming to Paris with me?'

'Of course. I promised to take you there a long time ago.'

'But it won't be the same, Julian. I shall be working.'

'Not all the time. We can go to Maxim's for dinner, stroll through Montmartre . . . '

'I'm afraid not. The day's modelling is exhausting. Then I have to be up so early every morning . . . '

Julian wrinkled his brow playfully. 'Would you rather I stayed in Verbier?'

Kelly ran her hands through his thick curly hair. 'After

being with you for so long, how could I possibly enjoy waking up on my own?'

'Great. Then, I shall organize only one night out. The rest of the time you can stay in and look at a lettuce leaf from room service.'

Kelly felt a warm flood of delight flow through her. Julian was irrepressible and enthusiastic and she was drawn along by his positive, open approach.

'Have you heard from Max?' Julian asked, suddenly serious.

'He called a few weeks ago.' Kelly averted her eyes from Julian's and stared into the fire. 'He was pretty pleased with himself . . . '

'I must say he's done extraordinarily well to come back on the F1 scene like that, especially after Mario's death. Only two points separated him in the end from Jean Claude . . . To have such a disastrous start to the season and then . . . for everything to come right for him. That game is so unpredictable . . . winning in Italy, Portugal, Mexico, Japan and Australia like that . . . it was pretty incredible stuff.'

For a moment Kelly felt a pang of sadness. She no longer shared that, or any other part of Max's life now; his triumphs, his failures . . . they belonged to someone else.

'I'd rather not discuss Max,' she said wistfully. 'I thought we made a promise on that.'

'You're right, darling. It was tactless of me to bring up the subject, but he is still a close mate of mine, remember.'

'I know . . . it's just that I want to forget him right now.'

Julian studied Kelly, silently absorbed for a moment in her own thoughts.

'Well, what did he want?' he asked.

'When?'

'When he called?'

'Julian, you're not the teeniest bit possessive, are you?'

'Yes, a lot in fact, and I want to know what he said.'

Kelly grinned. 'Actually he rang to say how pleased he was to hear about *us*.'

'He also told me I was a very lucky man . . . So there are no hard feelings, right?' Julian kissed Kelly on the tip of her nose, then looked at his watch. 'Hey – it's two minutes to midnight. Time to crack open the champagne . . .'

As the corks popped, Julian and Kelly joined in the singing and the celebrations. 'Happy New Year, Happy New Year,' everyone called.

As the church bells rang out across the valley, the snow began to fall. Kelly and Julian trudged back to the villa in the early hours, crunching on the virgin snow. They were two solitary figures wrapped up in their own world. They laughed, threw snowballs and broke off the long icicles hanging from the low roofs of the houses. Kelly was sure she had never felt happier in her life.

# 51

A fresh breeze swept across the wintry fields carrying in its wake the sound of a car, the distinctive whine of a high-powered engine winding up out of Woodcote corner and on to the straight.

The Northamptonshire circuit at Silverstone looked bleak and grey. It was a far cry from the colourful spectacle of spectators and cars that had filled it to capacity for the Grand Prix in July. Today it had the forlorn atmosphere of a theatre after the players had gone, except for a small huddle of men in the large empty expanse of the pit lane. Here the Delta team were intent and absorbed in their work as on any race day. After a few laps, the car came in for a tyre change and the eager mechanics swarmed around her.

'How is she running?' asked Jean expectantly.

'She's superb,' said Max, lifting the visor on his helmet and grinning. 'Bloody fantastic, in fact.'

The Delta team had every reason to be pleased. The new season was only weeks away and amidst tight security Delta were giving the car its first test with the new engines. They had just beaten the previous Silverstone lap record. It was going to be one hell of a threat to the rest of the Formula One cars, Max assured them.

Later on, Max and Jean trooped off to the tea bar in the paddock. They were joined by Dick and together they discussed the day's lap times, drinking scalding hot tea to offset the chill of the day.

'No regrets then?' asked Dick, watching Max's alert and eager expression as he chatted enthusiastically.

'About coming back? No. I would have been a fool to pass this one up. The performance of the car has given us all a good shot in the arm.' The others nodded in agreement.

When Max had finally announced his re-signing with Delta, the public and press alike had welcomed the reversal of his decision. The prospect of Max quitting racing had been akin to laying a coat of grey paint over a colourful picture. He was one of the last of the great 'characters' in the sport and his departure would have left an unfillable gap in the field.

Max had no doubts about his decision. After a lot of discussion with Vicky, she had given him her full support to return. The prospect of a restless husband at home having second thoughts about his retirement was not a welcoming one.

For the last two races Max had been joined by the young Swiss driver, Hans Dürer, who had come to the team with talent and enthusiasm in abundance. Colin had given the go-ahead to sign him up for the coming season and everybody agreed that he and Max would make great team mates.

Then there were the cars. With the new design and engines, Delta were in an enviable position. Several of the top drivers, including Jean Claude the new World Champion, would have leapt at the chance of signing with the team if Max had stuck to his decision to retire.

Max had escaped a serious accident while testing the day before. Once more it had reinforced his awareness of his own vulnerability. Maybe, one day, like Mario, he would be carried away on a stretcher, but until that time, Max knew the only drug he needed in life was his driving. Behind the wheel of the car, Max Gregson was a complete human being.

* * *

There was a buzz of laughter and relaxed banter as the mechanics settled down at the table, hungry and thirsty after a long day's work. The small café was a welcome haven from the cold and soon the smell of frying sausages and chips emanated from the kitchen, misting the windows and sharpening appetites. In the jet-setting world of the sport, it was rare to recapture their early days, when eating in greasy-spoon cafés had been the norm.

Max was relaxed, sure in the knowledge that this was where he wanted to be. He was among good friends – friends who had supported him through a season of mixed fortunes.

With the noisy chatter and eager appetites of the group tucking into their first hot meal of the day, it was not surprising that nobody noticed the door to the café open. The warmly wrapped figure who had made such a quiet entrance stood by the door, his hands buried in his pockets, the collar of his coat turned up.

It was the buxom lady behind the counter who spoke to him first. 'Can I getcha somethin'?' she asked perfunctorily.

Max glanced up and found himself staring at a stranger. Except that there was something familiar about the man's eyes. Max flinched as he saw the scars that twisted and stretched the skin. Then a short, uncertain smile crossed the man's face.

Knives and forks were halted in their vigorous assault on the full plates and the noisy chatter stopped as each in turn recognized the man at the door. The lady behind the bar was about to repeat her question when she too became aware of the strange response he had evoked. Then she, too, saw the hideous scars. It was Dick who broke the silence. 'Colin, nice to see you.' He got up and shook Colin's hand and pulled out a chair for him. He called to the woman to bring another tea over. Stiffly, Colin sat down next to Max and Tom. 'How was it today?' he asked, as if it were just another test day for them all.

'Not bad, not bad at all,' said Max, grinning broadly. Colin's eyes flickered and the concern that had clouded his face lifted.

'It was better than we thought,' enthused Jean. 'The other teams will be in for a bit of a shock when they hear we broke the lap record by two seconds.'

The scarred parchment-like skin stretched into a smile. The group remained silent as they took in Colin's hideous disfigurement. It was the first time any of them other than Dick had seen Colin since the accident. 'I hear you had a bit of an accident at Woodcote yesterday, Max?' Colin enquired diffidently.

'Let's put it this way, we know the chassis is strong. It took one hell of an impact, and considering I climbed out with only a bruised knee, I don't think I came off too badly.'

'He's indestructible,' laughed Tom, 'which is more than can be said of the front wings and tyres.'

Colin drank his tea slowly. A pair of leather gloves hid the scars on his hands. Along with his face, they too had suffered horrendous burns from the fire.

The cause of the fire had been attributed to a smouldering log falling on to the carpet, although Colin had never volunteered a reason for lighting a fire on that mild August evening. Rachel couldn't explain what it was that had made her leave Phil to come home late that night either. Phil had accepted that Rachel was given to unpredictable whims and that she had decided to leave his warm bed to drive the few miles home had been one of them. Whatever her reason, it had undoubtedly saved Colin's life and prevented the complete destruction of the house.

Now with Colin sitting in their midst, the question returned to everybody's mind. His face gave nothing away. None of them could guess the stimulation he felt to be back among them all again. The old energy returned and his pride in the loyalty and dedication of his men glowed from within.

It had taken months of painful adjustment to accept the physical scars to his body. They had, he reflected, been an equal match to the emotional scars that still remained with him. He realized how lucky he was not to have died in the flames. He had buried his self pity and emerged as a gentler, more tolerant man. The days of Mario were gone and his only consolation was that Mario would never see him in this disfigured state.

Colin was aware of the questioning eyes focused on him. He coughed to clear his throat and winced at the pain to his damaged lungs. He was still a sick man. All the team knew that, but it was Colin's determination to overcome such difficulties that was foremost in their minds. Was he going to give it all up?

'Well, I'm not here on a social call. I'll come straight to the point,' he explained calmly. 'I've come to thank you all for your tremendous hard work on the development of this season's car. It's obvious from the test that we have another winner on our hands.' His voice had a new strength to it, coupled with a humility his men had never known before.

'I've given considerable thought to selling the team over the last few months. After the accident I believed I would not have the strength or will to run it, but now I would like to put an end to any speculation. Delta is definitely not for sale.'

A cheer went up round the table and Colin's face glowed with pride and pleasure at the response. There were a hundred questions to ask about the performance of the car. He wanted to know every detail.

They stayed chatting for much longer than the lady behind the bar would have liked, but she could only observe in amazement the charisma of this man in their midst. She had heard a great deal about the closeness of the motor-racing fraternity. Today she had seen proof of it. She wished them good night as she prepared to lock up and watched them disappear into the gathering dusk. She paused to glimpse the disfigured man climb slowly into his chauffeur-driven car and wondered how he had come by his injuries.

Max threw his padded jacket over his racing overalls and walked to the car park with Hans and Dick. They shook hands on parting and all agreed it had been a successful day. They would meet in a few days' time to discuss the testing programme with Colin.

With Colin in charge of the team once more, Hans had experienced first hand the respect they all had for him. He knew he would have a lot to live up to after Mario and Max's record of success, but he felt comfortably at home with them all.

Dick and Max stood together as the young Swiss drove away.

'You did a good job today,' commented Dick. 'That was one hell of a fast lap you put in there at the end.'

'Thanks,' replied Max. He hadn't told the team that he had spotted Colin's Jaguar parked at the side of the track for the last half hour of the test. 'It was good to see Colin again.' He voiced his thoughts aloud. 'You know, I think he needs the team more than ever now.'

'And he made it perfectly clear that he wasn't going to let you go in a hurry.'

'Well, I guess it's all a matter of better the devil you know . . . ' laughed Max.

'I go along with that,' said Dick, getting into his car.

As Max fired up his Ferrari, he realized that for the first time in a long while he felt a tremendous sense of well-being. He paused for a minute to watch the last golden glow of a luteous sun slip behind a sheet of grey cloud on the horizon and smiled to himself.

* * *

Vicky reclined in the grey leather seat and forced her gaze away from the small window and the views of green England down below. The Concorde had taken off like a rocket, with breath-taking acceleration, and now several miles up they were about to reach supersonic speed of Mach One. She smiled across at Max who was reading a copy of *Autosport*.

When he had suggested that they go away for a weekend she had no idea what was in store. Besides, Max never took time off in the race season. She was even more surprised when he had told her they were off to the romantic Cipriani Hotel in Venice and that it would be her first and long-awaited trip on Concorde.

Max put his magazine away as the stewardess handed them each a glass of champagne. 'Well, here's to us,' Max said, taking hold of Vicky's hand.

'Here's to us,' she echoed. 'And here's to the race season ahead, my darling,' she added, relishing Max's warm familiar smile.

THE END